Italian

BACHELORS

STEAMY
SEDUCTIONS

ITALIAN BACHELORS
COLLECTION

July 2017 August 2017 September 2017

October 2017 November 2017 December 2017

Italian BACHELORS

LYNNE GRAHAM
CATHERINE GEORGE
MICHELLE CELMER

HarperCollins
PUBLISHERS
Since 1817

Published in Great Britain 2017
By Mills & Boon, an imprint of HarperCollins*Publishers*
1 London Bridge Street, London, SE1 9GF

ITALIAN BACHELORS: STEAMY SEDUCTIONS © 2017 Harlequin Books S.A.

Challenging Dante © 2013 Lynne Graham
Dante's Unexpected Legacy © 2014 Catherine George
Caroselli's Baby Chase © 2013 Michelle Celmer

ISBN: 978-0-263-93135-8

09-1117

CHALLENGING
DANTE

LYNNE GRAHAM

Lynne Graham was born in Northern Ireland and has been a keen romance reader since her teens. She is very happily married, with an understanding husband who has learned to cook since she started to write! Her five children keep her on her toes. She has a very large dog, which knocks everything over, a very small terrier, which barks a lot, and two cats. When time allows, Lynne is a keen gardener.

CHAPTER ONE

DANTE LEONETTI, INTERNATIONAL BANKER, renowned philanthropist and the Conte di Martino to those whom
such archaic titles mattered, frowned at the news that
his childhood friend, Marco Savonelli, was outside his
office waiting to see him. Something *had* to be seriously
wrong to drag Marco from his village doctor's surgery
all the way to the fast-moving financial centre of Milan.

Lean, darkly handsome features composed in a
frown, Dante pushed long brown fingers through his
luxuriant black hair in a gesture of concern rare for
a man with his tough, self-disciplined temperament.
Surely Marco's visit could only be related to the fund?
Between them the two men were engaged in raising
money by a variety of means to finance pioneering
medical treatment in the USA for a village child stricken
with leukaemia. From the outset, Dante had offered
to cover the entire cost of the venture but Marco had
persuaded him that it would be much more diplomatic
to allow the village community as a whole to assume
responsibility and volunteer their services to raise the
thousands of euros required. Various public events had
accordingly been organised and a fancy-dress ball at
Dante's family home, the Castello Leonetti in Tuscany,

was the next big date and indeed the grand finale on the calendar, Dante recalled grimly, for he would have preferred to make a huge donation rather than be forced to dress up in comical clothes like a child at play. He had no patience for such nonsense.

His phone pinged and although he sighed he was conditioned by years as a banker to always be on the alert. But the message was not from one of his aides warning him of some potential crisis. It was from his mistress, the beautiful Della, and he frowned down at the picture of her superb breasts, his handsome mouth curling with irritation as he deleted the shot with an impatient stab. He didn't want dirty pictures on his mobile; he was *not* a teenage boy, he reflected grimly. Clearly it was time to give Della the proverbial golden handshake and make a smooth exit. Unhappily the prospect of pastures new to explore held no attraction for him yet he knew he was bored with Della and even more bored with her colossal vanity and her avarice.

Yet, genuine warmth filled Dante's uncommon green eyes when he crossed his big office to greet Marco Savonelli, a stockily built male in his early thirties, and the exact opposite of Dante in temperament for cheerful Marco was rarely seen without a smile on his face. Well, just this once his friend wasn't smiling, Dante noted. Indeed Marco's expressive face was unusually tense and troubled.

'I'm really sorry to disturb you like this,' Marco began awkwardly, very much a fish out of water as he took in the opulence of his surroundings. 'I didn't want to bother you—'

'Relax, Marco. Take a seat and we'll have coffee,'

Dante advised, urging his old friend in the direction of the luxurious seating area.

'I had no idea how fancy your place of work would be,' the other man confided ruefully. 'To think that I thought I'd reached the height of sophistication when the practice manager installed my computer...'

The coffee arrived at lightning speed. 'It's not like you to take time out from your patients,' Dante remarked, eager for Marco to tell him exactly what was wrong. 'Has someone embezzled money from the fund, something of that nature?'

Marco, evidently very much more innocent than Dante had ever been, shot him a look of horror. 'Of course not! It's nothing to do with the fund and...er... actually, I was coming to Milan anyway to visit my aunt Serafina on my mother's behalf, so I thought I would just drop in and see how you were while I was in the neighbourhood.'

Dante, sharp as a tack when it came to reading people, recognised a cover story coming his way and marvelled that Marco believed that he could fool someone as astute as he was. 'Is that so?'

'And as I said since I'm here anyway,' Marco continued, gathering speed like a reluctant man pushing himself towards something he would rather have avoided, 'I saw no harm in calling in for a chat.'

Trying not to laugh at his old friend's transparency, Dante murmured lazily, 'Why not?'

'Have you heard much from your mother recently?'

Dante froze, his keen intelligence taking his thoughts in a different direction. 'She phones and chats most days,' he responded with studied casualness, long black lashes dropping low in concealment over his shrewd gaze as, for the first time, honest tension clenched his big, well-built body.

'Oh, is that so? Good…er…excellent…' Marco countered, visibly not having expected to receive so reassuring a reply. 'But when did you last visit?'

Dante stiffened, wondering if that was a hint of censure. 'I assumed the newly-weds would prefer to be left in peace.'

'Of course…of course,' Marco hastened to reassure him in a tone of apology. 'A natural assumption even at their age. And…er…forgive me if I cause offence, although you have never said anything on the score of your mother's remarriage, it must have come as a surprise to you.'

As he recognised that he might well still be waiting for his overly tactful friend to get to the point in another hour, Dante suppressed his innate desire to keep his every feeling and reaction private and decided to be blunt. 'More than a surprise,' he admitted flatly. 'I was shocked and worried by it. Not only was my mother's decision to remarry very sudden but I was also dismayed by her choice of husband.'

'Yet you said nothing at the time,' Marco groaned. 'If only you could have been more plainspoken with me, Dante.'

'My mother led a wretched life with my late father for more years than I care to recall. He was a bastard. That is not something I would acknowledge to anyone but you. Bearing that in mind, I am the last man alive likely to criticise her bridegroom or interfere in her attempt to, at long last, find a little happiness.'

Sympathy now etched in his kindly brown eyes, Marco visibly relaxed. 'I can understand that.'

A brooding expression on his lean features, Dante was recalling his widowed mother's sudden marriage to Vittore Ravallo. The wedding had taken place only two months earlier. Ravallo was a failed businessman and onetime womaniser, who was as poor as Sofia, Contessa di Martino, was rich. The marriage had been impulsive and improvident but Dante was a loyal and loving son and he had kept his reservations to himself. If need be he would intervene to protect his mother should the marriage prove to be the mistake he assumed it was, but in the short term he would mind his own business. Even so, that considerate restraint had proved a challenge, particularly when the happy couple was still occupying Dante's castle in Tuscany while they waited for renovations to be completed on their new home several miles away. For that reason, Dante had not been back to *Castello Leonetti* for a visit since the small private wedding that had sealed his mother's fate.

Marco compressed his mouth. 'Perhaps you could consider going home soon. There's something strange going on.'

Dante almost laughed out loud at that statement. *'Strange?'*

'I've never been a man to listen to gossip but we've been friends all our lives and I felt I should give you a hint about what has been happening.'

'So…' Dante summed up rather drily, not interested in his friend's penchant for drama, 'what *is* happening at the castle, Marco?'

'Well, you know what an energetic woman your

mother has always been?' Marco remarked. 'Not any more. She's no longer involved in her usual charitable pursuits either, never leaves the castle and no longer even gardens.'

Dante frowned, unable to even imagine his very active mother suddenly abandoning the busy life she had built as widow to that extent. 'That does sound strange...'

'And then there's her new social secretary—'

'Her...*what*?' Dante cut in, taken aback. 'She's hired a secretary?'

'A young English girl, very attractive and apparently perfectly pleasant,' Marco recounted uncomfortably. 'But now she's standing in for the contessa at her charitable engagements and she's often been seen getting lifts from Vittore—'

Dante was very still, an attitude that his employees knew as the calm before the storm, for the inclusion of a young and attractive girl in the set-up that Marco was describing had him seething with anger. Many older men were fools when it came to young girls and Dante's stepfather might very well be one of them. His heart sank on his mother's behalf. He had hoped that if the marriage failed it would do so on less wounding grounds for his parent than that of another woman. His own father's infidelity had already caused Sofia Leonetti so much pain that Dante simply could not stand by and watch it happen again.

'*Is* there an affair going on?' Dante demanded, hands clenching into fists by his side as he sprang upright, unable to stay seated any longer.

'I honestly don't know. There's no evidence of one,

nothing more suspect than the look of things,' Marco responded ruefully. 'And we all know how misleading appearances can sometimes be. But there is one odd aspect to that girl that doesn't quite add up—'

'Go on,' Dante urged in a raw undertone, struggling with his outrage at the image of his mother being humiliatingly betrayed by an employee and her new husband in his home.

'My father was invited to a dinner at the castle for Vittore's birthday. The girl was wearing a diamond necklace that my father swore is worth many, many thousands of euros.'

And both men were well aware that Marco's father was an infallible judge of such things because he was a renowned jewellery designer.

'Of course it *could* be a family heirloom,' Marco conceded fairly.

'But how likely is it that a young office worker would own such an item or even bring it abroad with her?' Dante retorted, unimpressed by that argument. 'As far as I'm concerned, when you take everything else into account, the diamonds are hard evidence of misbehaviour of some kind!'

But even if it was, what the hell was he planning to do about it? Dante asked himself angrily after his friend had taken his leave. Obviously Dante would go home to personally check out the situation and if there was anything questionable afoot *he* would deal with the girl with the diamond necklace.

Topsy suppressed a groan of frustration as her sister Kat continued to challenge her with worried questions on the phone. What were the family she was living with like? Were there any men coming on to her? Did she have a lock on her bedroom door?

The guilt that Topsy had initially experienced about lying to her family about what she was doing and where she was staying in Italy suddenly dissipated like a damp squib. What age did her big sister think she was? A vulnerable teenager? For goodness' sake, she was almost twenty-four years old with a doctorate in advanced maths, scarcely a babe in arms! But Kat, just like Topsy's twin older sisters, Emmie and Saffy, simply refused to accept that Topsy had grown up and had a life of her own to lead.

In Kat's defence, she *had* been acting more as Topsy's mother than her sister since Topsy was six years old and the sisters' birth mother, Odette, stuck all three of her younger children in foster care so that she could reclaim her freedom as a single woman. No, Odette Taylor had had no taste for mothering and Topsy was all too well aware of how much she and her sisters owed Kat for her loving care and loyalty. Kat had taken custody of her younger siblings, whisked them off to her home in the Lake District and raised them to adulthood at her own expense. Kat's sacrifice could never be forgotten or go unappreciated, Topsy acknowledged ruefully.

Yet here she was in Italy having run away from home and lied about her whereabouts just like the teenager she had long since left behind! Her family thought she was simply enjoying an extended break staying with an old school friend and Gabrielle was happy to provide the cover story and pretend—should she ever be

challenged—that Topsy was living with her and her
family in Milan.

Topsy sighed, guilt licking at her conscience again.
Her siblings were so overprotective they regularly drove
her to screaming point. Their marriages to rich and
powerful men had only enhanced their desire and ability
to interfere and control Topsy's every move. She loved
them, she truly did, indeed she *adored* her sisters and
their closeness, but she didn't want a job doled out by
one of their husbands and she didn't want to be landed
with a pre-checked boyfriend either. She had lost count
of the eligible and no doubt thoroughly vetted men pro-
duced for her benefit at parties and dinners. She had
also lost count of the boyfriends she had lost, who had
failed to pass the family vetting procedure. In addition
the insistence on her, at one unforgettably embarrassing stage, having a bodyguard had done nothing to advance her prospects in the romantic stakes.

Either men wanted her purely because of her wealthy
brothers-in-laws' financial and business connections or
all the hoopla of even dating her frightened them off.
Even worse, she was now a trust-fund baby, gifted with
a sizeable amount of cash on her twenty-first birthday
in a generous group gift from her sisters' husbands, so
that she would always be independent and secure. *Independent?* Topsy grimaced at a goal long craved but
always out of reach. What a joke the concept of independence was! That wretched money, which she had
never wanted but which had delighted her anxious and
overprotective sisters, had only trapped her more than
ever in a world in which she didn't feel she belonged.
Now her sisters' husbands would only have an even

better excuse to check out any man she dated for fear he might be after her trust fund!

But then that wasn't the *only* reason Topsy had come to Italy and to this particular household in Tuscany, she conceded sheepishly. Indeed if any member of her family were to discover the true nature of the deception she was engaged in, they would be justifiably furious with her. None of them would understand, she thought sadly, none of them would ever appreciate how powerful a motivation she had had to come to Italy and pretend to be something she was not. But then she was not the same as her sisters: their outlook on certain issues was directly opposed to hers. Right and wrong were not as black and white as they believed, she reasoned uncomfortably. Of course some day if things went as she hoped she would have to tell them the truth. Right now she was at the awkward dishonest outset of her mission and the false image she had set up was already discomfiting her. Before her arrival in Italy, Topsy had virtually never told a lie. She had been a squeaky clean and very logical child who recognised at an early age the inherent consequences of lies. Yet here she was all these years on and supposedly intelligent and mature and she was lying her head off all around her! And to such lovely people too, she reflected even more painfully. Why was it that the drawbacks of her mission had only occurred to her *after* she had taken up residence and started work? How was that for poor forward planning?

Yet how could she simply give up a cause that meant so much to her? Her sisters though would never understand that angle: they would simply fiercely disapprove.

And if they knew the lengths her mother had forced her to go to before she would finally divulge the information that Topsy craved, they would have been outraged, Topsy conceded heavily. But in her opinion, it had been worth it to finally get the truth…if it *was* the truth. Unfortunately she was all too well aware she could not totally trust her mother's word.

Meanwhile she was living in the lap of luxury in a genuine medieval castle, which had been owned by the Leonetti family for hundreds of years. Yet her beautiful surroundings had that wonderful lived-in vibe, which made even the splendid furnishings emanate a warm and cosy ambience. No, she certainly couldn't complain about the standard of her living conditions.

Mid-morning the next day, her dark eyes shadowed by a restless night of troubled thoughts, Topsy was in the garden cutting roses for the contessa to arrange. The superb rose garden basked in the heat of the sun shining down from the clear blue sky above and it was so warm that Topsy was relieved she was only wearing a cool cotton skirt and tee shirt. Vittore, who generally got involved in anything relating to his only recently acquired wife, crossed the bed of roses to extend a particularly lovely rich pink bloom to her. 'It's La Noblesse…her favourite,' he explained, a small, slightly built man in his late forties with benevolent dark eyes and a still-handsome face.

'You're identifying them now?' Topsy teased even though she was touched by his consideration for Sofia. 'Your time with that rose book is certainly paying off!'

Vittore laughed, turned a little red and smiled warmly.

* * *

This was the little tableau that Dante was deeply disturbed to witness as he strode round the corner of the castle to access the side entrance. Like a pantomime lech, his grinning stepfather was extending a rose to a giggling young brunette. Even if Marco hadn't planted suspicion in Dante's mind he would have become suspicious at the sight of such conspicuous familiarity between an older man and a youthful employee.

'Vittore…' Dante breathed, quietly announcing his presence.

Startled, his stepfather whirled round so fast he almost fell over a shrub and, righting himself, stiffened and froze in place still standing in the rose bed. 'Dante,' he acknowledged with a rather forced smile. 'This is Topsy. She's working here to help your mother with her charities.'

Topsy stared at the tall black-haired male who had appeared out of nowhere. So, this was Dante, Sofia's beloved only child, the selfish, unfeeling cad, who had spoiled the older couple's wedding with his cold attitude and even quicker departure. Of course she had seen a photo of him in Sofia's sitting room but no two-dimensional image could possibly have conveyed the devastating effect of Dante Leonetti in the flesh.

He was drop-dead gorgeous from the crown of his luxuriant black hair to the soles of his undoubtedly handmade shoes. His dark suit said he meant business and was faultlessly tailored to his lean powerful frame. He stalked closer like a predator closing in on its prey and she blinked, wondering where that strange comparison had come from. Within six feet of them he came to a halt and the sheer height and breadth of him intimidated her, reminding her of the undeniable drawbacks of being just four feet ten and a half inches tall. His extraordinary eyes made her stare for they were an unexpectedly exquisite shade of green, strikingly luminous and light against his bronzed skin and oddly unsettling. An unfamiliar sense of breathlessness afflicted her.

Her body felt weirdly detached from her brain while a series of bizarre reactions was filtering through her. All of a sudden, her breasts felt incredibly sensitive and an uncomfortable clenching sensation between her legs made her instinctively press her thighs together. Sexual attraction? She refused to believe that it could be. She couldn't possibly be attracted to a male she was already programmed to thoroughly dislike!

Dante studied the tiny brunette with fierce attention. Her glossy mane of curling dark hair fell down her back almost to her waist. She had wide almond-shaped eyes the colour of melted honey, creamy olive skin and a ripe pink mouth. Her beautiful face was the shape of a heart and, for all her surprising lack of height, she had the pronounced curves of a pocket Venus. The ripe swell of her full breasts pushed against her thin cotton top while the opulent flare of the hips below her tiny waist was neatly delineated by the fitted skirt. Dante was startled by the instantaneous swelling sensation at his groin for not since he was an undisciplined teenager had he reacted that strongly at first sight of a woman. Annoyingly, she wasn't even his type, she absolutely *wasn't* his type: he went for tall elegant blondes and always had. But evidently his treacherous hormones had a different opinion and he had cause to be grateful for the suit jacket he still wore.

Topsy extended a slim hand. 'Topsy Marshall.'

'Dante Leonetti,' Dante told her as he grasped her small hand, barely aware of his stepfather still hovering in the background while his keen scrutiny remained welded to Topsy's smiling face.

His brain kicked back into gear. Of course she was smiling at him, of course she was responding with charm! How else would she treat a very rich man? After all, if she was a gold-digger, he was a wealthier and much more rewarding target than Vittore could ever be. On the back of that thought the germ of an excellent idea flared through Dante. He was rich and single and consequently had to be a much more tempting prospect than his stepfather. Possibly, Vittore was still only flirting with the idea of adultery, for Dante was convinced that Vittore would not be going to the idiotic lengths of gathering roses if he had already got into the little brunette's bed. Surmising that nothing very much had yet happened between the couple, Dante recognised that *he* had the power to nip the relationship in the bud and protect his mother in the short term. If *he* showed an interest in his mother's employee, Vittore would have to master his weakness and back off.

'Your mother will be eager to see you,' Topsy remarked.

Her use of fluent Italian surprised Dante. 'You speak our language?'

'I speak several languages,' Topsy admitted lightly. 'But my best friend at school was Italian and we shared a room, so I picked up more colloquial phrases.'

'You have a commendable grasp,' Dante remarked, curious about her for the first time. 'What other languages do you speak?'

'French, Spanish and German. Rather old-fashioned choices,' Topsy commented wryly. 'I wish I'd had the foresight to study Russian and Chinese. Even a working knowledge of those might have been more useful.'

Dante shrugged a broad shoulder as he moved towards the entrance. 'You can't lose with those languages while you're living in Europe.'

'I'll take you straight up to see your mother,' Vittore volunteered, hurrying towards the stone staircase at the rear of the hall.

'And I must deliver the roses before they start to wilt,' Topsy added, her heart beating very fast as Dante momentarily paused to shoot a razor-edged glance at her that was anything but friendly. What on earth was wrong with the man? Had he disliked her on sight?

Dante ground his even white teeth together. He was in his own home and he had not seen his mother for weeks. He needed neither a guide to her rooms nor companions and was immediately suspicious. Vittore slung him an almost apprehensive look over his shoulder as he reached the top of the stairs, his attention shooting anxiously to Topsy. Witnessing that revealing byplay between them, Dante sensed a powerful hint of duplicity that put him even more on his guard.

The contessa smiled warmly as her husband entered her charming private sitting room.

'I have a surprise for you,' Vittore said tautly.

And then, a split second later, as Dante strode through the door the small slim brunette, who had been reclining on the comfortable chaise longue by the window flew to her feet and cried, 'Dante! Why didn't you tell me you were coming?'

'I was scared I would be forced to cancel at the last moment.' Dante kissed his mother's cheek and then grasped her hands to stand back and look at her. 'You look pale, tired—'

Recognising the flicker of dismay in the older woman's eyes at that remark, Topsy spoke up before she could think better of it. 'Your mother's still recovering from the bout of flu she had a couple of weeks ago.'

'Yes…it took a lot out of me,' Sofia confirmed the lie while sending Topsy a warm glance for providing her with that easy excuse. 'Come and sit down, Topsy—'

'I think I should get on with some work,' Topsy protested as Sofia settled back down onto the chaise longue and patted the space beside her. In her late forties, Sofia was still a very pretty woman with the same unusual clear green eyes that distinguished her son.

'No, no,' Vittore argued, reaching for the house phone with alacrity. 'Take a break. I'll order coffee for us.'

Dante watched in silence while Topsy took a seat beside his mother, his handsome mouth compressing with disapproval as he recognised that the older woman was treating the girl more like a favoured niece than an employee. Quite clearly she had no suspicions whatsoever about the younger woman's character or, indeed, her behaviour with her husband. Vittore, meanwhile, hovered beside the chaise longue within reach of his wife, the very epitome of the devoted husband he wanted Dante to believe he was.

In reaction, hostility flared through Dante's lean, powerful frame and he wondered if anger was making him paranoid for, observing the cosy little threesome, he was convinced he was being treated to an act designed to pull the wool over his eyes. Yet what could his mother possibly have to hide from him? Sofia and her son had always been close. His reading of the situation, his conviction that something was badly amiss, *had* to be wrong, he reasoned in growing frustration.

CHAPTER TWO

Topsy got up and walked through to the adjoining cloakroom to put the cut roses in water and then she answered the knock on the door that preceded the housekeeper, Carmela's entrance with a tray of coffee and cakes. The grey-haired older woman reacted to Dante as though he were the prodigal son with a fatted calf to be slaughtered to celebrate his return.

Topsy returned to her seat while Vittore arranged a table beside his wife so that she could pour the coffee. While that was going on, Topsy studied Dante. Those eyes, fringed by long black lashes in that lean dark face were utterly stunning, she conceded grudgingly, unsettled that such a thought should even occur to her for he was not the type of man who should ever appeal to her. He wore his elegant business suit like a second skin and his sleek aura of well-groomed arrogance and command reminded her strongly of her bossy brothers-in-law. Dante Leonetti, she reflected abstractedly, would have all the imagination of a stone and would only think in terms of power and profit. Money was all important to him and undoubtedly the yardstick by which he judged other men. She suspected that had Vittore Ravallo been a rich and powerful man, Dante might well have welcomed him into the family.

How could anyone dislike someone as sweet and inoffensive as Vittore? Even so, although Dante might be offensive he was still, indisputably, a stunningly beautiful man. The shock of that second disturbing acknowledgement almost floored Topsy where she sat, for she had never been the susceptible sort, impressed by outward appearance. After all, her sisters were married to handsome men and she was accustomed to their looks. But no matter how hard she tried to concentrate on something else her attention remained hopelessly locked to Dante, noting the arrow-straight flare of his nose, the level black brows, the spectacular bone structure and the strong stubborn jaw line already darkening with stubble. She shifted uneasily where she sat, shocked by the sensations flooding her treacherous body and appalled to realise that for the first time in her life she was greedily wondering if a man would look as good naked as he did clothed. Her lashes fluttered as she tried to suppress that embarrassingly intimate thought while still guiltily engaged in mentally mapping the impressive breadth of his shoulders, the muscular width of the chest flexing beneath his silk shirt and the neat fit of his expensive trousers pulled taut over his long, powerful thighs.

Dante's handsome dark head whipped round and he met her wide dark gaze in a head-on collision. Topsy felt her face flame red as fire, mortification claiming her entire body in a scorching blush as she literally tore her scrutiny from him, lowering her head as awkward as a schoolgirl caught out, only to find that her wretched gaze accidentally fell on the very last part of him she should be studying: the prominent masculine bulge at his crotch. It was as if Dante Leonetti put out sexual pheromones that fried her brain cells and all she could think about was touching him, tracing that arrogant blade of a nose, caressing that roughened jaw line, smoothing hands in worshipping exploration of places she had never touched before but longed to discover.

'Excuse me...' Dante sprang upright and strode over to the window, turning his back to them and thrusting the latch open to filter in fresh air to the stuffy room. *Madre di Dio...* He had never known temptation could come in such a small unexpected package, had never dreamt that involuntary arousal could seize him when he was in every way an adult in full control of his libido. What the hell was happening to him? Why was Topsy Marshall having this effect on him? It was not as though he were sex-starved or had even had much interest in that direction of recent. He ground his perfect white teeth together in bemused frustration, striving not to picture the diamond-hard pointed buttons of her nipples indenting her tee shirt, the mere hint of a shadowy vee between her creamy thighs as the hem of her skirt rode up. It was like being shot back screaming to the teen years when his control over his own body had been a bad joke. So exactly what was it about her that got to him? A tiny, shapely brunette, years his junior, not a raving beauty by any means but sexy, impossibly, *outrageously* sexy.

'Are you feeling all right, Dante?' his mother asked curiously.

'I was too warm,' Dante murmured flatly. 'Would

you mind if I took a run over to see how the work is progressing on your house? I feel like some fresh air.'

'Of course I wouldn't mind and if you don't mind taking Topsy with you, Vittore and I will be able to have lunch together,' his mother remarked. 'Topsy has to see my decorator and check that he's redone the kitchen the way I wanted it. I don't know what I would have done without her help. For a while there, I had far too much on my plate.'

Dante skimmed a glance in Topsy's direction that didn't linger. 'We'll go as soon as we've had our coffee.'

Not best pleased by the news that she would be visiting the Casa di Fortuna in Dante's company rather than Vittore's, Topsy had stiffened, gripped by the most maddening self-consciousness she had ever experienced. She was afraid to look near the wretched man in case he cast a spell over her again. She wasn't stupid: she knew she was attracted to him and that it was a stronger attraction than she had ever felt before. So superficial of her too, she scolded herself wryly, being physically drawn to a male who was a virtual stranger and with whom she would not have a thought or feeling in common. It was yet another complexity in her life that she really didn't need, but hopefully he was only making a fleeting visit to the castle to see his mother. From what she understood, Dante spent little time in his Tuscan home and much preferred the faster, more sophisticated pace of Milan.

She listened quietly while her companions made polite conversation, Sofia mentioning recent visitors and small domestic concerns at the castle while parrying her son's concerned questions about her mythical bout of influenza. *Oh what a tangled web we weave when first we practise to deceive!* Sir Walter Scott's words were as relevant to Vittore and Sofia as to Topsy. They all had their secrets from which Dante was being excluded but, watching the frown slowly darkening Dante's face, she reckoned he was fully aware of the covert undertones.

Why, oh, why had she walked into the lion's den without thought of what *her* secret might cost others? Self-loathing momentarily gripped Topsy. Her twin sisters had got by fine being ignored by their father after their parents divorced and their father remarried. Topsy's father had not married her mother but she was still desperate to know *who* he was. Perhaps that very desperation was driven by the fact that for most of her life she had mistakenly believed that she did know who had fathered her: a handsome South American polo player called Paolo Valdera, who had enjoyed a brief affair with her mother. After all, over the years she had met Paolo several times when he visited London and there had been the occasional phone call around Christmas or her birthday. Sadly, although Paolo had apparently accepted without question that he was Topsy's father, he had been very little more interested in his supposed daughter than her mother had been.

Then when she was eighteen Paolo had discovered that he was sterile and had finally asked for DNA testing, the results of which had proved that he could not possibly be Topsy's dad. Topsy had had to go to great lengths to get another name out of her mother and the only name she had been given was Vittore's.

Getting close to Vittore and working out exactly what kind of a man he was had been Topsy's main motivation in applying for the job working for Sofia. She had been driven by entirely selfish promptings, never pausing to consider that such a bombshell as the existence of an adult illegitimate daughter could damage his very new and happy marriage. For that reason, while she had learned to like Vittore Ravallo, she had done nothing to check out her mother's story and could not even begin to imagine asking Vittore to subject himself to DNA tests to satisfy her craving to know who she was. Right now, Vittore had far more pressing concerns on his mind and Topsy was very unwilling to do or say anything that might risk upsetting Dante's mother.

Dante rose to his full height, fluid as quicksilver for all his size. 'We'll leave now.'

'Don't pass the work that's been done in the kitchen unless it's perfect,' Sofia warned her firmly.

'Why don't you accompany us?' Dante asked lightly.

His mother tensed. 'I hate the smell of paint.'

Sofia also got horribly car sick, Topsy conceded, happy to stand in for the older woman if it helped her to rest and regain her strength. Struggling to keep up with Dante's long impatient stride, she accompanied him downstairs and out to the rear of the castle where one of the collection of high-powered cars he owned had already been extracted for his benefit from the garage block. It was a Pagani Zonda. Saffy's husband, Zahir, owned one of these high-powered sports cars although as the king of the Arabian Gulf state of Maraban he never seemed to get the opportunity to drive himself anywhere. Boys and their toys, she thought wryly.

'Nice wheels,' she said, reckoning it was another nail in the coffin of her attraction to him, another re-

minder that they would be a poor match in every way.
The gilded extras of life did not impress her although
she would have been the first to admit that since Kat
had assumed charge of her as a child she had never
known what it was to want for anything she needed. In
so many ways she had been spoiled as the baby of the
family and perhaps that was why she had had to run
away to grow up.

'I gather Vittore drives you around quite a lot,' Dante
commented as she slid in beside him.

'I need lifts anywhere I can't walk or ride a bike,'
Topsy admitted. 'I can't drive.'

Dante frowned, his surprise unconcealed. 'That must
make doing the job a challenge.'

'Yes,' Topsy conceded, since it was the truth, watching a lean brown hand glide smoothly round the steering wheel, angling the powerful car through the castle
gates and down through the village beyond the ancient
estate walls. 'But neither your mother nor I thought of
the need for me to drive during our interview.'

'You could learn. I'll fix the paperwork,' Dante informed her.

'I've failed the driving test a few times at home...I
don't really want to try again,' Topsy said truthfully.

'How many times?' Dante asked.

Topsy stiffened. 'Six times. That was enough for me.
I've got poor co-ordination and lousy spatial awareness. Everyone's got a weakness—that's mine and I
can live with it.'

'Any idiot can drive,' Dante retorted, unimpressed,
seeing how she could be detached from Vittore in one
way at least. 'I'll teach you while I'm here.'

Topsy winced at the prospect. 'Thanks but no, thanks.'

'It wasn't a suggestion, it was an order,' Dante told her lethally. 'To fully perform your duties, you should be able to drive.'

Topsy stared straight out of the windscreen at the magnificent scenery as the car descended the hill into the rolling valley studded with shapely cypresses and the serrated green lines of the vineyards, her expressive mouth silently forming a rude word of disagreement. 'I work for your mother, not for you. I don't have to do what you tell me to do.'

His long fingers flexed expressively round the steering wheel and she stole a reluctant glance at him, noting the taut set of his bold bronzed profile while she doubted that he met in-your-face rebellion very often from subordinates. Momentarily, his shimmering green gaze flared in her direction and a crackling energy filled the atmosphere with tension. Topsy breathed in deep and slow, smoothed her skirt down over her slim thighs and tactfully said nothing.

'So, tell me what qualified you for the job,' Dante invited without skipping a beat.

Topsy was more intimidated by his self-discipline than she would have been had he snapped angrily back at her. 'I have a lot of experience with charity committee work, volunteers and functions,' she confided, recalling the long educational summer stays in Maraban while her sister Saffy concentrated her time on benevolent good works as befitted the wife of a ruler, not to mention her sister Kat's ventures in the same line. 'I also speak the language and I'm very versatile and not too proud to do whatever needs to be done. Basically

I'm your mother's gopher. I deal with all the decorating hassles at the new house as well. Your mother has a very clear picture of how she wants every room to look. I'm also handling the arrangements for the fancy-dress ball.'

His jaw line set granite hard. 'Try to understand my surprise at your employment. My mother has never required assistance before.'

'But then she had made her charities and your very extensive gardens into a full-time job,' Topsy pointed out a shade drily. 'And now the contessa wants the time to relax and be with her husband. She's also hired another full-time gardener to help out on the estate.'

If possible, Dante's stubborn chin and firm mouth took on an even more hostile set. 'I know my mother.'

No, you don't, Topsy thought silently. He was out of the inner circle now and evidently not yet to be trusted with the news that had torn Sofia's neat and tidy life apart. Really, that aspect was none of her business either but she had no intention of betraying the contessa's trust. Sofia had been very kind to Topsy and she was determined to be loyal and supportive in return.

The Casa di Fortuna sat on top of a hill, a square, solid stone structure surrounded by garden. It had once been the estate manager's home but the current manager had built his own house and Sofia had decided to make the old house her new marital home. A variety of pickup trucks and vans sat in the driveway announcing the presence of builders and tradesmen.

Dante vaulted out of the car, Topsy falling in step behind him, gazing up at the sheer height and width of him, shaken afresh by the total size of him and the utter impossibility of ignoring him. They had barely walked into the hall when Gaetano Massaro, whose building company was in charge of renovating the house, descended the stairs to greet them. 'Topsy…' He inclined his curly dark head and grinned in his usual friendly fashion before addressing Dante and offering to show him round.

Of course the two men knew each other, not least because Gaetano was also involved in the fund-raising for the local child's leukaemia treatment. In the airy kitchen Topsy dug her phone from her bag so that she could take photos to show Sofia. The tiles had been redone in a different shade and design at Sofia's request. Her employer was very particular about details and Topsy fully understood why. Not only married but also a mother at the tender age of seventeen, Sofia had moved into her husband's ancestral castle and had not been allowed to change anything to suit her own taste. By all accounts, Dante's father had been something of a domestic tyrant and a control freak. The Casa di Fortuna, therefore, was very much the contessa's first real home.

The decorator joined Topsy and took her into the cloakroom to inspect the illuminated mirror that had been installed. Playing safe, Topsy took a photo of it as well and then lingered in the doorway, watching Dante and Gaetano chat. Beside Dante, Gaetano looked small, slight and boyish and yet it was only three days since she had decided that Gaetano was attractive enough to date and she had agreed to have dinner with him in his family's restaurant that very evening. Gaetano was good company, she reminded herself impatiently, which was all she required in a man. He didn't need to send her temperature rocketing as well.

Dante crossed the hall. 'Show me the downstairs reception area,' he instructed, dismissing Gaetano with an almost invisible nod of his handsome dark head.

Behind Dante's back, the builder rolled his eyes in mock amusement at the manner in which Dante had virtually ignored his offer to be his guide and Topsy coloured, narrow shoulders lifting back as if she was bracing herself while she led the way into the very large open-plan area that several rooms had been sacrificed to create. Floor-to-ceiling glass doors led out onto a terrace at the back of the house.

'It's much more contemporary than I was expecting,' Dante admitted lazily, his deep accented voice fingering a trail of awareness down her taut spine. 'For some reason I thought the two of them would recreate the Eighties here.'

'I think your mother's tired of living with the past and looking to the future for inspiration.' Topsy pressed a wall button and the glass doors whirred smoothly back. 'All this took an enormous amount of planning.'

'How much input did Vittore have?' Dante asked.

'Very little…' Strolling outside into the shade cast by the roof above, Topsy laughed softly. 'He doesn't have much interest in house interiors but I think he was also aware from the outset that this was very much your mother's dream and he didn't want to spoil it for her by imposing his views.'

'You appear to have a high opinion of Vittore,' he commented with a derogatory edge to his tone that suggested he didn't share her outlook.

'I speak as I find. I've yet to see or hear him do anything to detract from that opinion,' Topsy responded easily, trying not to resent his judgemental attitude towards the older man, telling herself that was none of her business and refusing to let Dante make her feel uncomfortable.

And yet he managed that feat without even trying, she acknowledged in dismay as she looked up at him, striving to be fearless and frank rather than nervous and wary of her every word. His stunning green eyes glittered with high-voltage energy in the sunlight in which he stood, for he was much more at home in the heat of midday than she was. He looked hostile and intimidating and she was in the act of stepping back from him when his hands came out and closed round her slender forearms, halting her into a startled retreat.

The instant he made physical contact, another kind of energy hummed into being inside Topsy, taking her body out of control and into a dangerous state of extreme awareness. For a split second she couldn't breathe. Her breasts swelled beneath her clothing, the tender tips straining into tight buds while a sensation of heat pulsed almost unbearably at her feminine core. 'What are you doing?' she said breathlessly, struggling to pull air into her depleted lungs as his hands trailed down her arms to close round her wrists instead.

'What I wanted to do the minute I first saw you,' he husked, pressing her back into the cooling shade of the wall. 'Discover how you taste.'

'No, thanks,' Topsy told him thinly, fighting her weakness with all her might even though she was insanely tempted to move forward and sink into the hard muscular heat of him and find out what that mutual tasting would feel like.

A derisive smile that unnerved her slashed his hard, handsome mouth. 'The way you look at me, do you seriously expect me to believe that?'

Shock that he could study her in such a way and yet show his scorn filled her and momentarily she hesitated, struggling to compute that strange combination of desire and contempt. That tiny instant of hesitation, however, was fatal. His mouth swooped down on hers with a hard, hungry urgency that shot every sensible thought right out of her head as though it had never existed. She *felt* as she had never *felt* before, burning waves of reaction slivering through her entire body, whipped up to a storm with every carnal plunge of his tongue. Heat burst low in her pelvis, tightening her nipples to the point of pain and shooting raw stabs of need to the very heart of her. Inflamed by her own response, she strained back against him, just as he bent even more with a growl of frustration to curve his hands below her hips to lift her and pin her in place between his body and the wall behind her. She felt entrapped, excited, *wild* for more...

His hands roved across her back, came up to curve to the sides of her face while her fingers delved happily into his luxuriant black hair, delighting in the springy depths. The scent of him flared her nostrils, clean, hot male laced with an elusive spicy scent of soap or cologne. She breathed him in headily like an addict.

'You're way too small to do this standing up,' Dante complained against her swollen, reddened mouth.

That remark cut through the haze of desire that had engulfed her, innate apprehension gripping her. Do *what*? Suddenly she was aware again, conscious that her legs were pinned round him and that her skirt had

to be somewhere up round her waist. Shock reverber-
ated through her like a hard wakening slap on the face.
'Put me down!' she exclaimed in horror. 'We shouldn't
be doing this!'

Dante lowered her slowly, reluctantly, back down to
the tiles while with frantic hands she yanked down her
skirt to cover her exposed thighs. She was appalled by
her own loss of control and the false message of avail-
ability she had no doubt given him by responding to
him in such a way. She didn't play around and she didn't
tease men either, and as her stomach brushed against
his hard, taut length on the passage back to standing on
her own feet again she knew he was in no mood to be
teased. He was aroused, fully aroused, and a wave of
discomfited pink engulfed her heart-shaped face. Her
brain told her it had only been a kiss, but no kiss, no
man's touch had ever had that explosive an effect on
Topsy before, and even as she stole a glance up at him
she knew she wanted to drag him back into her arms
and have him do it again. Hands unsteady, she reached
for the shoulder bag that had fallen on the patio and anchored it round her shoulder again.

'Is that a "no" in Topsy land or simply a prudent
"not here, not now"?' Dante enquired with terrifyingly
smooth assurance.

'It's a no, never. I'm sorry. That shouldn't have happened. I work for your mother. I don't think she would
like me—'

'I assure you that it is many, many years since my
mother worried about who I take to my bed,' Dante
sliced in very drily.

Flustered and intensely ill at ease, Topsy walked

away from him on stiff legs to the edge of the patio, perspiration beading her upper lip as the hot sun beat down on her. Drowning in mortification and consternation at the passion that had exploded between them, Topsy breathed in jerkily. 'But in the circumstances it's not a good idea, let's face it,' she reasoned steadily. 'I've no intention of going to bed with you anyway so there's no point starting something that won't go to the finish that you expect.'

'I'll take you into Florence this evening…we'll dine out,' Dante declared as though she hadn't spoken.

Topsy froze, registering that she had made a mistake that would bring punishment home to her fast. 'I've already got a date tonight.'

Ashamed as she was of her behaviour, Topsy could not resist looking at him again and the astonishment that briefly flashed across his handsome features in reaction to that admission only increased her embarrassment.

'I don't share—cancel him,' Dante advised, taken aback by her statement while wondering if she was reluctant to dally with him because she already had Vittore in her sights. Certainly she could not hope to keep two men in the same household interested.

'No, I won't do that, not when this was a mistake…but for your information, it's a first date. I haven't cheated on anyone,' she confided on a driven note of pride. 'I wouldn't do that.'

Dante shrugged a broad shoulder as if such restraints had no meaning for him and she was even less impressed by that attitude. 'We're both single. I want you and you want me—'

'For a moment of madness,' Topsy quipped. 'But I'm glad it didn't go any further.'

'Liar…' Dante murmured soft and low.

That fast she wanted to slap him so hard that her palm tingled and she flashed him a flaring look of such seething anger that he looked taken aback. But if Topsy was furious with him, she was equally furious with herself. She had come to Italy with a real purpose and, while she had certainly planned to enjoy the freedom of meeting men without family supervision, a fleeting affair with her employer's son would be as inappropriate as it was humiliating. Her stubborn chin came up just as Gaetano strolled out to join them, flicking her a curious glance as if he had picked up on the tension in the air.

'Anything I can help you with?' he prompted Dante. 'Do you want to see the upper floor?'

'Another time,' Dante deferred with no expression at all. He had known the Massaro family all his life and he was well aware that Gaetano would be out of his depth and drowning with a little schemer like Topsy. Was Gaetano being used as cover for the girl's interest in Vittore? If his marriage crashed and burned, Vittore would be a wealthy divorcee well worth pursuing. But if money was Topsy's goal, and what else could it be, why was she turning down Dante, who was a much more lucrative target? His face set into forbidding lines. Of course Vittore would be easier meat, he reasoned, and some women preferred older men. That suspicion still rankled with a male who had not, in living memory, been turned down by a woman.

Topsy settled back into the Pagani sports car and strove to rigorously ignore the thunderous undertones in the atmosphere. She had said no and he wasn't pleased that she had but she had made the right decision; she *knew* she had. Getting involved with Dante would be disastrous even though she wasn't foolish enough to imagine that he was considering anything more than a brief sexually entertaining fling. Although she had no doubt that he would be seriously disappointed by her lack of bedroom expertise. She knew that rich international bankers didn't seriously date humble employees unless said humble employee was possessed of extraordinary beauty. The only exception to the rule was her sister Emmie, who had ended up marrying her Greek billionaire boss, Bastian Christou.

While Saffy, Zahir's adored queen, and her twin Emmie could stop traffic with their looks, Topsy had long since resigned herself to being the plain one of the family, having inherited neither the height, the flawless features nor the blonde manes bestowed by their mother's genes. Kat was a redhead and stunning as well. At an early age, Topsy had grasped that her own most notable talent was her powerful intellect but that being cleverer than most of the people around her was not so much a gift as a curse. It certainly didn't make you popular, she reflected, thinking of the brutal bullying she had endured at primary school. Being different from the norm could entail paying a high price.

Her mobile phone rang in her bag and she dug it out to answer it.

'It's Mikhail. I'm in Milan and you're not where you're supposed to be,' her brother-in-law told her succinctly, making her lose colour and freeze in dismay at her end of the phone, quite unprepared to deal with the bombshell that her cover story had blown up in her face when she least expected it.

'I had no idea you were coming to Italy,' she muttered, nervous tension gripping her for Mikhail, Kat's husband, was not a man she felt she could lie to with impunity.

'And unfortunately for you your school friend, Gabrielle, decided to confess and admitted that you were actually staying in Tuscany. We'll meet in Florence tomorrow for lunch and you'll explain then *fully* what's going on,' he decreed without an ounce of hesitation, making her feel like one of his many minions who leapt to do his bidding and fulfil his every request.

'I'm afraid that won't be possible,' Topsy said stiffly.

'*Make* it possible,' her Russian brother-in-law advised in a grim tone that brooked no argument. 'I'll send a limo to pick you up at noon.'

'That won't be necessary. I'll meet you if you tell me where to go.'

'I decide what's necessary and don't feed your sisters any more nonsense or tell my wife anything that might worry her,' he told her sternly.

Topsy swallowed her growing ire with difficulty, feeling like a dog being yanked by a choke chain, both powerless and bullied. 'I wouldn't risk doing that.'

'Wouldn't you? It would undoubtedly distress Kat to learn that you felt the need to lie to her,' Mikhail breathed harshly and cut the connection without another word.

Topsy breathed in deep and slow and thrust her phone back in her bag. Mikhail was furious with her, for naturally he would only see the situation from his wife's point of view and he was fanatically protective when it came to her sister. Even so, it didn't matter what he intended to say to her in Florence, she wasn't quitting Tuscany and returning to London on his say-so.

On that rebellious thought she lifted her chin, her innate obstinacy kicking in. Somehow, some way her family had to come to terms with the reality that she was an adult with a right to freedom and independence and if that meant that she made mistakes, so be it! Her sisters had had the chance to grow up and explore the world without interference. Why shouldn't she claim the same right?

'You seem upset…trouble?' Dante prompted softly.

'No…er…not exactly,' she responded tightly.

'Your family?' Dante queried, shooting the Pagani off the road and into a farm track without even thinking about the sharp curiosity driving him to interrupt their journey.

Not even having noticed that the car had parked, Topsy stiffened even more defensively, reminding herself that she owed no one any explanations that she did not wish to make. 'Er…no, an old flame,' she fibbed, determined to retain her anonymity and persuade her fabulously wealthy relations to stay on the sidelines for once.

But a sensation like ice was already trickling down her spine because if Mikhail Kusnirovich knew where she was, she was convinced he would also have demanded an investigative report on her current living arrangements. Would he guess about Vittore? Would he realise exactly what his sister-in-law was doing at the Castello Leonetti? Could *nothing* in her life be considered private? Lunch had been arranged and Mikhail never entered any meeting unprepared. Suddenly ferocious resentment was bubbling up through her tiny body. She had believed she had temporarily escaped her family's suffocating hold but their reach was longer than she had appreciated. It was typical that she had not been warned that her brother-in-law was coming to Italy and planning to visit her.

'Are you scared of this man?' Dante pressed, level black brows drawing together in a frown as he leant closer.

'Of course I'm not scared!' Topsy forced a laugh because she was undeniably afraid of the emotional blackmail her family utilised to make her toe the line, the subtle guilt-inducing reminders that she owed her happy childhood and everything she had become to their love, support and loyalty. She, alone of her sisters and owing only to her young age at the time, had escaped her mother's neglectful care without sustaining any permanent damage and if her siblings were quite unable to accept that she no longer required their guiding hand, was that their fault? Or was it *hers*? Maybe it was some obvious lack in her that had convinced them she still needed to have her every move policed, she reflected worriedly.

Dante's shrewd green eyes were pinned to the fluctuating emotions on Topsy's intensely expressive little face. As someone who didn't *do* emotion, he was fascinated, never having seen anyone betray so many changes of emotion and all within the space of seconds. Dark glossy strands of silken hair fanned her cheek, the exact match of the long flickering lashes framing her anxious amber eyes above the flushed rise of her delicate cheekbones. No, she was not a raving beauty but there was a softness about her, a seeming honesty and vulnerability that had the strangest appeal to a male accustomed to more sophisticated and controlled women. He blinked, disconcerted by that uncharacteristic thought. And that fast desire kicked in hard, tensing every lean muscle in his powerful length with an almost exquisite surge of arousal.

'You may not be scared but you *are* upset,' he contradicted, fighting to stay focused on the conversation but his mind in another place entirely as he imagined igniting all that obvious pent-up passion for his own benefit and riding her raw in his bed to sate the painfully strong hunger punching through him.

'No, I'm not...it was just a stupid phone call...and sometimes I overreact.' Topsy was mesmerised by the force of his stunning green eyes holding hers and she could hardly breathe for the excitement gripping her while she scanned the handsome features above hers. In terms of the physical, he really was the most absolutely beautiful man. A supersonic quiet had fallen inside the car so that she could hear her own breathing, air sawing in and out of her throat as if she had been running a marathon, her heart racing like an express train behind breasts that were swollen and tender tipped, that same terrifying heat rising between her legs.

Dante lifted an elegant hand and slowly and with great dexterity and deceptive calm wound long fingers into the glossy mane of her hair to hold her in place. He was in a car and in broad daylight at a place where anyone might see and recognise him. He didn't know what he was doing but would never ever have admitted that a much more primal drive than intelligence had suppressed his innate caution and freed him from inhibition. The seething hunger was clawing at him like an angry beast, the pulse at his swollen groin threatening to control him as he brought her to him and kissed her with scorching heat, his tongue delving deep, his body firing as she loosed a strangled whimper of response than only made him harder.

Dante reached for her and lifted her out of the seat to bring her down over his spread thighs. He had never wanted anything so much as he wanted the hot, tight, wet heat of her body at that moment and the shockingly new strength of that wanting overpowering everything else inflamed him.

'What are you doing?' Topsy gasped, having got feverishly lost in that passionate kiss. He touched her and every sensible thought, every shred of self-discipline vanished as though it had never been. She studied that perfectly moulded, wide, sensual mouth, which felt so firm and sexy and unbelievably good on hers, and trembled, needing more, every skin cell evidently programmed to want more.

Slumberous green eyes below black lashes surveyed her. 'I think you know the answer to that, *cara mia.*'

His fingers glided up the sensitive inside of her thighs and her heart rate went from fast to racing in seconds. Tell him no, a voice urged in the back of her head, but the craving for him to go further was too strong for her to fight. In conflict with herself, she shivered, breasts with beaded tips pushing against a bra that seemed too tight to contain her, inner muscles she hadn't known she had clenching tight at the very thought of greater intimacy. She tensed as a fingertip eased beneath the lace edge of her panties and she knew she should move, knew she should be telling him, *no*, she wasn't this kind of a woman. But just then, with Dante Leonetti's hand on her all too responsive flesh, she knew she was exactly that kind of woman and she was quite unable to resist the temptation he offered. She trembled, gazed down into glittering emerald eyes as bright as gemstones and he found the place he sought, circled, teased, brushed, stroked while she moaned and tried not to lose herself in the terrible maddening pleasure of his caresses. But her body was on another plane of existence entirely, quivering and burning and leaping with new sensation.

'D-Dante…' she pronounced shakily at her second attempt to find her voice.

'*Sì…*' he purred like a jungle cat, yanking her head down to claim her already reddened mouth with fierce and passionate urgency. 'Let Gaetano down gently— he's a nice boy. I want you naked and hungry in my bed and tonight I will satisfy your every fantasy. Now come for me…'

And with a skilled flick of his hand, the quaking intensity became more than she could withstand and this great whoosh of sensational excitement engulfed her straining body, jolting her with wave after wave of almost unbearable pleasure. She heard herself cry out in ecstasy.

Even though his body was rigid with arousal and self-control, Dante was surprisingly satisfied as he rested his tousled dark head back against the head rest.

He readjusted her panties, smoothed down her skirt where she knelt on his lap. He had put his mark on her: she was *his* now and he had no objection to admitting that she was the most exciting woman he had had in his arms in a very long time. He could not believe that she could be engaged in some sleazy relationship with Vittore at the same time as she was responding to him and, *Dio mio*, that was some response, he savoured sensually.

Shock and embarrassment roared through her in a head-spinning whirl and she scrambled off him in sudden horror, her face red as fire, her eyes momentarily closing in an agony of mortification. What had she done? *What had she done?* As she moved she saw another car parked a few yards away. 'Oh, good grief, there's another car nearby...we've been *seen*!' she gasped, stricken.

Dante didn't bat a single magnificent eyelash. 'My bodyguards, you don't need to worry about them.'

'Bodyguards?' she yelped in even greater dismay, because she knew all about bodyguards, teams of men who operated in all her sisters' lives as protection and supervision.

'I go nowhere without them. The bank insists,' Dante said, unconcerned.

Biting her lip, Topsy did up her seat belt. You *slut*, she told herself, her body still humming with treacherous pleasure and frank astonishment at what he had made her feel. Even so, his erotic approach had made her feel ridiculously virginal and ignorant, so far out of her depth and foolish she could not even bring herself to look at him again. She would certainly never ever look in the direction of his wretched bodyguards, knowing

very well that bodyguards were just as human as everybody else and equally prone to gossip. Had that not been
why Mikhail moved her bodyguard Vlad to other duties
when he considered that they had become too 'friendly'.
Prior to that, she had heard some very amusing tales
from Vlad about his experiences, his Russian reserve
crumpling around her. Mikhail had teased her about
being a femme fatale for mortifying months afterwards
yet nothing had ever happened between her and Vlad.
If only she could say the same thing of Dante Leonetti!

CHAPTER THREE

DANTE WATCHED TOPSY bounce out of the castle and down the steps to greet Gaetano in his Porsche. She looked incredibly young and pretty in a fuchsia-pink dress and ridiculously high heels. He snatched in a breath, teeth clenching as she flashed her shapely legs climbing in. It was ridiculous: she *should* have cancelled the date. The very idea of Gaetano getting close enough to touch her made Dante incredibly tense. Yet he was not a possessive man and had often enjoyed non-exclusive relationships that enabled him to retain his freedom. Possibly it was because he hadn't bedded her yet, he ruminated with brooding intensity.

'Is that Gaetano picking up Topsy?' his mother enquired from where she was still seated with Vittore at the dining table behind her son. 'I hope he behaves himself—not like that Siccardi boy.'

'Siccardi? Bruno Siccardi?' Dante referred to one of their neighbours, a young and handsome playboy known for his wildness. 'She went out with him as well? *Maledizione*, she does get around!'

'And why shouldn't she?' Sofia enquired. 'She's cooped up all day every day with us and we're middle-aged and not a lot of fun.'

'Speak for yourself,' Vittore teased. 'I think I'm just as much fun as the Siccardi boy!'

'What happened to him?' Dante prompted.

'Oh, she had to fight him off, said he had more hands than an octopus and that was the end of him,' his mother supplied cheerfully. 'Topsy's no pushover.'

But she hadn't fought *him* off, Dante reflected with positive relish, using that recollection to suppress his exasperation with her at her determination to keep that date. It was a novelty to be with a woman who wasn't falling over herself to meet his every demand and expectation but that didn't mean he liked it and he was confident that her attitude would soon change.

Topsy was embarrassingly conscious of Gaetano's family's very hopeful and constant scrutiny of their table. So far, she had met his mamma, his papa, one sister and two younger brothers, for the restaurant in the village was a family affair and every one of his relatives was delighted to see Gaetano dining out in female company. Gaetano had already taken her step by painful step through the story of how his childhood sweetheart and former fiancée, Daria, had gone off to study for a further degree and had fallen madly in love with another man and dumped him, leaving him with a half-built marital dream home.

'Your liveliness reminded me of her…a little,' Gaetano had told her, clearly thinking that was a compliment until she advised him that the best thing possible for him would be to seek a woman who reminded him not at all of his lost love. By that stage both of them knew that they would never be anything to each other than friends and Topsy didn't have to feel the slightest bit guilty at not having experienced any romantic spark in his direction.

'Dante seemed…er…attentive,' Gaetano selected, eyes dancing with amusement. 'When he brought you to the house.'

Topsy blushed furiously. 'I don't think we'd have much in common.'

Gaetano nodded thoughtfully. 'You're thinking of his wealth and his fancy title but it would be a mistake to assume that Dante always had it easy.'

Topsy didn't correct his assumption. 'Hasn't he?' she pressed, full of a curiosity she could not suppress.

Gaetano grimaced. 'When he was sixteen, my father found him lying by the side of the road one night. He'd been badly beaten up, broken nose, broken ribs, in fact every finger of one hand was broken. He wouldn't tell my father or the police who had done it.' Gaetano hesitated. 'My parents always believed it was his father, Aldo. The old count had a filthy temper.'

Topsy had paled in shock, mentally picturing one of Dante's long-fingered elegant hands, and she swallowed hard on her nausea. 'If that's true, he must have had a tough time as a child.'

That conversation was still lingering on her mind when she was climbing the stairs at the castle at the end of their evening. Just goes to show, never judge by appearances, she conceded ruefully just as she rounded the corner of the landing and entered the corridor to find herself face-to-face with the very man occupying her brain to the exclusion of all else.

'Dante!' she exclaimed, startled by his unexpected appearance.

Dante scanned her face with intent gleaming eyes of green. 'Your lipstick isn't even smudged,' he commented with unconcealed satisfaction.

'And what the heck is that supposed to mean?' Topsy flung back at him, dark hair dancing round her slight shoulders as she tossed her head in annoyance.

'You didn't let him touch you.'

Topsy sucked in a deep, angry breath that filled her lungs to capacity. 'And that is your business *because*...?'

'Tonight you're mine,' Dante informed her with a level of unmistakable assurance that drove her breath right back out of her lungs again, deflating her when she could least afford the weakness.

A split second later, Dante did nothing to help her condition because he did something even more shocking: bending down, scooping her off her feet as though she were a doll and anchoring both arms tightly round her.

'Have you gone insane? What are you doing?' Topsy exclaimed, keeping her voice low though because she did not want anyone to come investigating, indeed would have done just about anything to avoid being caught in such a compromising position by anyone living at the castle.

'Stop acting dim—you know exactly what I'm doing!' Dante asserted, boldly thrusting wide a door and striding into a room she had never entered before for the simple reason that it was *his* bedroom.

'What on earth do you think you're playing at?'

Topsy yelped as he put her down on the giant four-poster bed with scant ceremony.

'You went on your date to which I very generously did not object.'

'You've got no blasted right to object!' Topsy hissed back at him full volume. 'No right at all!'

His features set rigid, his spectacular bone structure prominent. 'I want you to spend the night with me.'

'And even if you'd asked like any normal man, the answer would *still* be no!' Topsy slung at him furiously, flushed and all of a quiver from the assumption he appeared to have made about her and anything but grateful to be forced to relive those deeply embarrassing and heated minutes in his car, which had led to his misapprehension that she would be so easily available that she would simply fall into his bed the instant he expressed the desire.

Dante dealt her an incredulous look from scorching green eyes. *'No?'* he repeated, as though it was a word he had never heard before from a woman in the bedroom.

Topsy scrambled off his bed, retrieved a shoe that had dropped off and wedged her foot back into it at the same time as she smoothed down her rucked skirt. 'I'm sorry if I gave you the wrong impression this afternoon but I'm not going to sleep with you,' she told him squarely.

She reminded Dante of a determined little bird rearranging her bright-feathered plumage, her slightly snub nose in the air, her heart-shaped face pink as one of his mother's precious roses. 'Yet you want me,' he breathed between clenched teeth, for *all* he had thought about all evening when he should have been catching up on work was his fantasy of getting her in his bed where she belonged.

'This afternoon...er...well that was an aberration and entirely your own fault,' Topsy told him roundly, furious at the situation he had put her in, fighting her mortification that he could have thought she would be that easy. Of course when she hadn't objected to that shameless little session of intimacy in the car, could she really blame him? And it did not help that when she looked at that gorgeous dark angel face of his she felt breathless and boneless and prone to reliving every madly exciting moment of his touch.

'How was it *my* fault?' Dante demanded.

'You shouldn't be so good at seduction,' Topsy responded with every evidence of conviction in that belief. 'If I'd had a moment to stop and consider, it would never have happened and we wouldn't be having this conversation now.'

Dante was furious with her for the ambiguous signals she had fed him, but for a split second he was startled to realise he was also on the edge of bursting out laughing at that response. 'Perhaps we should begin again,' he breathed instead, his hard mouth curling a little, for he had never said that to a woman in his life before, but then he could also not recall ever being quite so hot to have one.

'No, we're not going to begin anything!' Topsy exclaimed, and then bent down as her heel dug into a sheet of paper on the rug, detaching it with careful fingers and lifting it up to see the columns of figures. 'Oh, that's wrong...'

Already detaching from her hand the sheet that had escaped from the file that had fallen to the floor when he put her on his bed, Dante frowned down at her. 'What's wrong?'

Topsy peered over his arm and stabbed a finger at one column. 'It's added up wrong.'

'Of course it isn't,' he responded impatiently, setting the document down on the file beside his laptop.

'Dante, I have a doctorate in advanced maths and the one thing I do know is figures and I assure you that that final entry is a mistake,' Topsy said drily.

'A doctorate in advanced maths?' Dante echoed, studying her with incredulous eyes while wondering what someone with such a background was doing working for his mother.

Topsy nodded, wishing she had kept her mouth shut while carefully edging back towards the door.

Dante stalked her like a fox set on cornering a hen. 'I don't want you to leave. I want you to explain why we can't start again.'

Topsy groaned out loud. She hated these conversations with men, for in her experience they almost always went the same way and the men got disgruntled, unable to understand why she wouldn't just drop into bed with them to scratch a sexual itch. 'Look, all you want is sex and that's not enough for me.'

Dante dealt her a pained appraisal, by which time she was plastered up against the back of his bedroom door, one hand curled round the door knob. 'Doesn't everybody want sex?'

'I'm not looking for love and marriage either but there has to be something more,' Topsy contended, because she had considered the subject in depth and had drawn up a list of desirable male attributes, none of which he met.

An eloquent black brow rose. 'Something...*more*?'

'I'm not into casual sex,' she pointed out, almost adding *any* kind of sex but holding that revealing admission back. 'You don't know me or even care about me and we're not similar or even complementary in character,' she pointed out very seriously. 'I mean, when did you last wear a pair of jeans?'

Not since his student days. Dante was feeling increasingly like a male version of *Alice in Wonderland* who had fallen down the rabbit hole only to emerge into an incomprehensible world. 'Jeans?' he repeated thunderously at what he saw as yet another red herring. Similar or complementary in character? What planet was she from?

'You toured a building site today in an Armani suit and gold cuff links. I don't dress up as a rule, don't like that appearances sort of thing that people get hung up about. What on earth would we talk about or do together?'

Dante was much more interested in the doing than the talking and he leant forward, bracing his hands on either side of her face. 'I don't think entertainment would cause us much of a problem,' he husked in a low-pitched growl that raised colour in her cheeks again, the clean, spicy, male scent of him entrapping her like a covert spell. 'Mentioning stuff like clothing is just so superficial—I'm surprised at you.'

'But superficial, ruthless and mercenary is what you

are!' Topsy protested helplessly, feeling crowded at the few inches that were now all that separated their bodies.

'We would have maths in common,' Dante countered with something that felt dangerously akin to desperation. 'I'm terrific at maths.'

'Oh…' Topsy was also thinking about his reputation as a philanthropist, striving to cram him under an acceptable label on her all-important list of ideal male traits. But there was just no way he would fit there. He wasn't modest or soothing and she seriously doubted that he could cook or clean. All he had going for him was sex appeal and a very immodest amount of it, she reasoned feverishly.

Dante skated a fingertip along the sultry line of her luscious mouth. 'Let me make love to you.'

'Don't use words you don't mean. It wouldn't be making love, it would be grubby sex!' Topsy snapped bluntly. 'And I'm worth more than that!'

Dante frowned, green eyes radiating resolve while his face took on a sardonic edge at her use of that insulting label, 'grubby'. 'How much more?'

'You really don't give up easily, do you?' Topsy framed, her mouth still tingling from his touch, but his bold determination was starting to intimidate her because he was like a guided missile locked onto target. 'It's just we really would be wasting each other's time.'

'I don't *do* grubby, *cara mia*,' Dante whispered. 'I *want* you to waste my time.'

'My goodness, I'm so tired I can hardly stay awake!' Topsy lied in dismay, carefully screening her mouth as though she were yawning in a last-ditch effort to conclude the confrontation.

'Tired?' Dante repeated, unimpressed, but he retreated a disconcerted step.

Mercifully he had moved just enough to unblock the door and Topsy flipped round and opened it fast. 'Night, Dante!' she called over her shoulder and sped off fast.

Dante swore and not under his breath. She was a tease, nothing but a tease, he reckoned furiously. Maybe it was an act, designed to lure him in deeper and increase his desire for her. He could not remember when a woman had last knocked him into pursuit mode. In fact he could not recall *ever* having to pursue or persuade a woman. He needed a cold shower. He flicked a glance at the empty bed and cursed again. Jeans… similar or complementary characters? *Superficial, ruthless, mercenary?* Self-evidently, she was a nutcase. Furthermore, ruthless was a compliment, not a personality trait worthy of censure. He had had a narrow escape, he told himself impatiently, and if she was playing some childish girlie game with him, she would soon discover that she was indeed wasting her time for he wasn't that desperate. She exasperated him. He headed for the cold shower with anger in his glittering eyes. There was a world of women out there, beautiful, sophisticated women, who didn't talk rubbish, insult him or lead him on only to change their minds at the last possible moment.

Having climbed into her comfortable bed, Topsy checked the list in the back of her diary that she had written when she was eighteen and trying to make sense of the almost incomprehensible dating scene at university. She had never fit in, never met her soul mate but had truly believed that he was out there somewhere. Dante met only one of her listed requirements: he was clever. But clever wasn't quite the right word, she reflected ruefully: conniving and unscrupulous came closer to how she would have described him. And she had no regrets, she told herself urgently. She was much too sensible to surrender her virginity to a male who only awakened her hormones and didn't give a damn about her.

A little voice in the recesses of her less scrupulous conscience pointed out speciously that Dante was very probably very good in bed and would almost certainly make a great first lover. After all, it wasn't as if *she* were looking for love or commitment, so perhaps it was a little unjust to blame him for a flaw she suffered from herself. Some day she would fall in love and want commitment, but she imagined that day was very far away and she fiercely suppressed that dangerous little voice in her brain.

Tomorrow, she would be lunching with Mikhail, who was as devious and manipulative as any Machiavelli when it came to delivering what would please her sister Kat most. Topsy knew she would have to keep her wits about her and make sure that she stood her ground.

CHAPTER FOUR

THE FOLLOWING MORNING, Dante used the back stairs to return to his bedroom after a heavy workout session in the basement gym. On edge after a restive night, a freezing-cold shower and the conviction that he had been manipulated by some means he had yet to identify, he was not in a good mood. Almost more infuriatingly when he had finally risen early to concentrate on work instead, he had discovered that she had been correct about that figure being wrong in the file. Yet she had only glanced at the page! How could she possibly have recognised a mistake that fast? He was about to stride through a doorway when he heard Topsy's distinctive voice and Vittore's, both of them talking in low voices somewhere out of his view.

'I can't make it today,' Topsy was telling the older man. 'I should have told you last night but I couldn't mention it in front of Sofia.'

'Of course not. We'll have to go to Florence some other day.' Dante's stepfather sighed. 'As long as Sofia doesn't realise what we're up to, we have nothing to worry about.'

'Would she be annoyed?' Topsy prompted.

'Are you joking?' Vittore groaned. 'After the last

time, she said she'd kill me! I have to get it right this time.'

While Dante hovered with a frown, the voices died away as the couple retreated. What the hell was all that about? His original notion that Topsy might be involved with his stepfather had dwindled, but after that cosy exchange suspicion ran rampant through him again. Why were Vittore and his wife's secretary whispering in corners? Why were they meeting up in Florence in secret? How could that be innocent? What had to be hidden from his mother? *After the last time, she'd kill me!* A previous act of infidelity, Dante decided in disgust. Was that what Vittore had been referring to?

He did not like to think that his mother would even consider forgiving and forgetting such a betrayal, but he could not overlook the fact that she had spent many years married to a man who had *forced* her to close her eyes to his infidelity and accept it. His parent could be slipping back into that unfortunate pattern, refusing to see the truth that this time around she had no reason to feel that she had no choice but to accept such behaviour.

It was ten minutes to midday and Topsy was dressed for lunch in Florence, her curvy figure simply clad in a green sundress with shoestring straps. Tense though she was, Vittore had contrived to put a smile on her face. That cliché about try, try, try again when you got it wrong might have been specially coined for Sofia's husband. Vittore wanted to give his wife a piece of jewellery that she would actually like and wear and, since Vittore had a natural love of bling and sparkle while Sofia preferred plain and elegant, her bridegroom had repeatedly got his gift choices wrong. That was why Topsy was to accompany Vittore to the design studio to choose a piece that her employer might genuinely appreciate for her birthday.

Topsy joined Sofia to briefly discuss the floral arrangements for the fancy-dress ball and then headed downstairs, stiffening as the ancient bell over the massive gothic front door rang noisily and checking her watch: it was five to twelve. When she saw the hulking bodyguard on the step, she recognised him as Danilo, the head of Mikhail's security, and, while she wondered if the forbidding older man had been sent to collect her in an effort to daunt her, her soft mouth firmed.

'Where's your luggage?' Danilo enquired with a frown.

Topsy's heart sank. Had she misunderstood Mikhail? Was he expecting her to simply pack up and go home with him to London? Her chin came up. 'I'm coming back here after lunch. I'm not leaving.'

Danilo made no comment, which didn't surprise her because he was not a chatty man. He stood out on the step instead wielding his mobile phone and talking in Russian, undoubtedly checking up on his employer's expectations.

As she lifted her handbag from the hall chair where she had left it earlier she saw Dante poised in the doorway of his study, lean, strong, dark face taut. At the sight of him, her heart jumped as though someone had closed a hand round the organ and squeezed. His straight dark brows were low over dazzling green eyes thickly enhanced by lashes black as coal as he gazed back at her. He was *so* beautiful. Without warning she

was reliving the touch of his finger on her lips the night
before, the little bristles of dangerous pleasure that had
travelled down her spine to warm secret places, making
her breasts ache and her knees tremble. Colour washed
her cheeks, a hunger she couldn't deny stirring like a
threatening storm.

'Are you ready to leave?' Danilo prompted impatiently.

Topsy spun back to the older man and walked out of
the door. Unfortunately the heat of the summer sun did
nothing to cool her overheated skin.

The limo had barely driven off when Dante crossed
the wide hall, inclining his arrogant dark head in acknowledgement of the younger man waiting by the car
that had just drawn up outside. He had decided to have
Topsy followed. He wanted to know who she was meeting in Florence and why she had been shaken by the
invitation. The more he learned about her, the closer
he might come to working out what was going on at
the castle. Everybody around him was acting weird,
he thought impatiently. His mother was lying about
on a chaise longue like some fragile Victorian lady
suffering from a decline, while Vittore was whistling
under his breath and whispering in dark corners with
the hired help.

Topsy's brother-in-law looked grim when he greeted her
at the door of his hotel suite. A waiter was already setting out food from a heated trolley and hovering. With
a flick of an imperious hand, Mikhail dismissed him
and urged Topsy to sit down.

'So, what's going on? What are you up to?' he asked Topsy baldly before she even got her bottom onto a seat.

'That's my business,' Topsy replied quietly as she tucked into her starter.

'If it threatens Kat's peace of mind, it's mine,' Mikhail overruled without hesitation. 'She's pregnant again, by the way.'

That announcement took Topsy by surprise because her sister suffered from fertility problems and having had IVF to conceive her twins had tried it again but, sadly, without success. 'Oh, my goodness, that's wonderful news!' she exclaimed, knowing how much her eldest sister had longed for another child. 'But...er... how?'

'It happened naturally this time but you can understand why I won't have her upset at the moment,' he pointed out levelly. 'It's cards-on-the-table time, Topsy. If the draw at the castle is Dante Leonetti, you need to be aware of the kind of lifestyle he leads.'

'Dante is not the draw and, yes, I do have a secret but it's private and nothing to do with anyone else in the family, nor would it matter to them,' Topsy proffered with conviction. 'I'm almost twenty-four years old, Mikhail. Don't expect me to explain everything I do.'

Her brother-in-law compressed his hard mouth. 'I still remember you in your school uniform.'

'And how many years ago is that?' Topsy sighed. 'I'm a big girl now.'

'No, you're physically tiny and still very naïve,' Mikhail countered impatiently. 'But don't lay that at my door. Your sisters refuse to accept that baby has grown up.'

At that unexpected admission, which implied some understanding of her plight, Topsy relaxed a tiny bit. 'I know. It's ridiculous to get to my age and have to lie to lead my own life.'

Mikhail sat back into his chair. 'Dante Leonetti?' he queried with a raised brow. 'How is he involved in this?'

'He's not. I don't know why you've got a bee in your bonnet about him.' But Topsy could feel her face burning, her eyes evading his direct look because she knew that she was insanely attracted to Dante.

'He's a player, Topsy. You couldn't handle him,' her brother-in-law told her in a tone of warning. 'At one stage a couple of years ago he was famous in banking circles for keeping three mistresses. One in New York, one in Milan and one in Tokyo.'

Topsy was appalled. '*Three*? Seriously?' she pressed, wide-eyed.

'Seriously, he's the equivalent of a suicide mission for a young woman from a sheltered background,' Mikhail delivered.

'Nothing's going on, Mikhail,' Topsy parried. 'I have a summer job with Dante's mother in a particularly beautiful part of the world. That's virtually all there is to this.'

Dante had or had had *three* mistresses. That sleazy little fact rattled round and round in Topsy's head throughout the drive back to the castle and left her feeling quite nauseous. What sort of a man went from one woman to another like that, treating them like interchangeable sexual utilities? And why did the X-rated imagery now assailing her overactive imagination actually wound and hurt? Why should it matter to her what he did in his bed? It wasn't as though she were planning to have an affair with him. She couldn't possibly be jealous of a man she barely knew. Yet neither could she doubt Mikhail's veracity because Kat's husband employed a highly trained investigative team. Through them, he had unparalleled access to background information about people he did business with and he was even more rigorous in checking out those who might offer a threat to members of his family.

While Topsy was lunching with Mikhail, Dante was entertaining an unexpected guest. Jerome St Charles, a member of the House of Lords and a widower, owned a house nearby where he often spent the summer with his adult children and their families. For a time, Dante had gone to school with Jerome's son, James, and as neighbours of long standing the two families still occasionally socialised. Once, Dante had even cherished the vague hope that his mother might return Jerome's obvious interest and admiration but nothing had come of it. Sad though it was in his view, his mother had remained impervious to male advances until Vittore came along.

'I'm sorry to drop in on you without an invite. I would've phoned first but I didn't know quite how to broach the subject,' Jerome told him, a troubled look on his patrician face as he pushed an uneasy hand through his thick grey hair in a nervous gesture. 'I'm afraid this is likely to be a rather embarrassing interview, but I'm fond of your mother and I felt I *had* to speak up and tell you what I know.'

Disconcerted as he was by that opening speech, Dante frowned at that reference to his parent and his light eyes narrowed with questioning intensity. 'I'm afraid I haven't a clue what you're talking about, Jerome.'

'It's this…' The older man settled a local newspaper down on the table beside the window.

Dante lifted it up and gazed down at a print photograph of his mother with Topsy standing in the background. The picture adorned an in-depth article about the charity to support women who had had miscarriages that his mother had started up about ten years earlier. 'What's wrong with it?'

'That pretty brunette working for your mother— I've…er…met her before,' Jerome divulged awkwardly. 'In London. I spent an evening with her… I…er…*paid* for her time.'

His green eyes darkening and cooling by several degrees, Dante stared back at him in unconcealed disbelief. 'Topsy? You *paid* for her time?'

Colour marking his cheekbones, the older man sighed. 'It's not quite as sordid as it sounds. She's not— as far as I know—a prostitute, but when I spent time with her she was available for the right price as an escort. I took her out to dinner one evening. I enjoy young attractive female company now and again and very pleasant she was too,' he acknowledged ruefully. 'But what's a girl like that doing working for your mother?'

'Let me get this straight…' Dante paused, his strong jaw line now set hard as granite, a tiny muscle tugging at the corner of his unsmiling mouth. 'When you met Topsy Marshall, she was working as an escort? And you *hired* her?'

Jerome nodded. 'We dined out. It was purely platonic. I had the pleasure of an attractive woman on my arm and she, of course, would've received a fee for her time.'

Dante gritted his even white teeth together, a combustible mix of anger and revulsion burning through him. Topsy was an escort; Topsy had worked as an escort! She had fooled him, he reflected rawly. Hadn't he been falling for the vulnerable ditzy act she was putting on? He was not easily shocked but the news that she had worked as an escort did shock him. Nevertheless he had complete trust in the older man, whom he had known all his life. Even though Jerome was embarrassed to admit that he had hired an escort, his sense of honour and his concern for Dante's mother had not allowed him to remain silent and Dante respected the sacrifice of dignity that the older man had made.

Jerome had barely departed before Dante received a call from his bodyguard telling him who Topsy had met up with in Florence. After what he had learned from Jerome he was just a little better prepared for that revelation. Mikhail Kusnirovich, the Russian oil oligarch, her ex-flame? Presumably, she was a former mistress, what else? Dante swallowed hard, knowing he no longer needed to wonder why she had been picked up by a limo or where her reputedly expensive diamond necklace had come from. Those expensive trappings told their own sleazy story. Such a dubious background did, however, make it seem highly unlikely that she had designs on Vittore, who had virtually no money of his own and no hope of any unless he got a divorce.

Had Topsy been summoned to the Russian's hotel suite in Florence simply for sex? Dante, his heart pounding, his hands clenched into fists, green eyes ablaze, paced his study in an ever-deepening rage. What else would she have been doing in a hotel suite but laying herself down on a bed? Mikhail Kusnirovich had made a booty call and she had answered it without the smallest protest. It could not get much more basic than that.

Yet he recalled her dismay during that phone call, his original suspicion that she was alarmed. Certainly, Kusnirovich was a man few women would dare to reject, a man of unsavoury reputation. *Che diavolo!* Was he making excuses for her now? She was a whore; what else could she be from such a background as Jerome had given him? Jerome might not have taken advantage of the situation but other men assuredly would have expected, even demanded, something a good deal less innocent than her company. Under no circumstances should such a Jezebel be working for his mother!

In a reflective mood, Topsy mounted the steps to the castle. Mikhail had not leant on her as heavily as she had feared, his mood doubtless softened by the delightful and surprising news that he was to become a father again without the necessity of Kat having to undergo another gruelling round of IVF treatment. Mikhail had also recognised that it was ridiculous for Topsy's sisters to fuss over her every move as much as they did and hopefully his more realistic attitude would eventually persuade Kat that her constant worrying about her youngest sibling was unnecessary.

Topsy was heading for the imposing main staircase when a door opened.

'I want a word with you in private,' Dante murmured curtly from the doorway.

'Maybe later. I have some stuff to do for your mother,' Topsy replied, shooting a lingering glance in his direction. *Three* mistresses, she was thinking helplessly. The surfeit of sex he was enjoying should surely have prevented him from demonstrating any interest in her. Yet it had not. His face was taut, faint colour edging his exotic cheekbones, his extraordinary eyes unusually bright below his winged brows. *So* beautiful, she reflected before she could suppress and kill that dangerous thought.

'Now,' Dante ground out like a feudal king demanding subservience.

Her chin lifting, Topsy stood her ground. 'But—'

'*Now!*' Dante thundered back at her in full volume.

Topsy was so taken aback by the shattering charge of anger he radiated that her feet automatically made the turn for her and she moved towards him, her smooth brow furrowed with concern. 'What's happened?'

CHAPTER FIVE

DANTE STEPPED BACK to allow her entry to the book-lined room and closed the door with an impatient hand. 'I've received some disturbing information about you.'

Topsy backed away from him towards the window. 'About…*me*?' she exclaimed in astonishment at the claim. 'What on earth are you talking about?'

'Jerome St Charles,' Dante shot back at her. 'He's an old friend and a neighbour.'

Topsy was aghast. That name struck her like a slap on the face for, of course, she hadn't forgotten that unforgettable evening, indeed wouldn't ever forget the indecent lengths she had been forced to go to before she could persuade her mother to give her the information she sought. It occurred to her at that moment that life could be very random and unjust. What were the odds of that man being an old friend and an actual neighbour of the Leonetti family? How could she possibly be so unlucky? On the other hand, she had done nothing to be ashamed of with Jerome and, unless the man had lied about the time they had spent together, she had no need to defend herself or make pointless excuses.

Dante strolled closer, his keen gaze sharp as a laser

beam on her tense and anxious face. 'I see you recognise the name... Care to give me an explanation?'

'I don't have to explain anything I do to you,' Topsy countered without hesitation. 'As I said before, you don't employ me, your mother does.'

'You will not distress my mother with any reference to this conversation,' Dante informed her harshly, his contemptuous attitude patent. 'You will make an excuse, possibly concerning a family problem, and tell her that you are sorry but that you have to return to London immediately.'

Amber-brown eyes wide with wonder at that demand, Topsy stared back at him. 'You're asking me to resign from my job and just go?'

'I'm not asking, I'm *telling* you to leave,' Dante ground out. 'You've worked as an escort. You're not the sort of woman I want working for my mother!'

'My goodness but you're prejudiced,' Topsy declared, her own temper rising. 'Astonishingly prejudiced and narrow-minded for a man in possession of *three* mistresses! I would've assumed that a live and let live mentality would be more appropriate in your circumstances.'

Dante froze where he stood, eyes widening slightly and then veiling below thick black lashes. Dark blood outlined his hard cheekbones while his firm mouth compressed into an unsmiling line. 'Where did you get that information from?'

Topsy flushed and made no reply. He hadn't denied it anyway. Maybe she shouldn't have thrown it but she had wanted to level the playing field. Why should she stand there being force fed his ethical objections when he himself was leading a far from moral life? 'You're a complete hypocrite,' she condemned.

'Mikhail Kusnirovich. He told you,' Dante guessed, struggling for the first time in many years to get a hold on what felt like an ungovernable rage. Dante never ever allowed himself to be out of control.

'If you've found out that I was meeting Mikhail in Florence, you've been spying on me,' Topsy gathered, fierce resentment lancing through her soft brown eyes and hardening them. 'What gives you the right to invade my private life?'

'I have the right to protect my mother from a woman likely to cause her distress and embarrassment. And a woman who has worked as an escort and who responds to booty calls from Mikhail Kusnirovich is not an acceptable employee on my terms!'

So inflamed with anger that she was on automatic pilot, Topsy stalked forward and lifted her arm. 'Don't you dare call me a whore or malign Mikhail!' she snapped back at him furiously.

A hand like an iron vice clamped round her wrist to prevent her from delivering the slap she intended. 'Keep your hands to yourself,' Dante growled soft and low before dropping her fingers again in a gesture of scorn.

The vibration of his accented drawl seemed to hit a sensitive spot somewhere deep down inside Topsy and she quivered in treacherous response, eyes flying wide to connect with his as sensual shock engulfed her. Something about the way he looked at her called up a deep driven response within her. Regardless of how she felt about it, her wretched body was awakening and suddenly awash with sensations she would have done anything to deny. Her breasts were swelling, the heat of awareness surging to her feminine core. An intoxicating mix of shame and mortification gripped her that she could still be so susceptible to him. 'That wasn't what you were saying last night!' she launched back at him accusingly.

'Last night I didn't know that I was dealing with a practised little tart,' Dante fielded grimly.

'Whatever turns you on,' Topsy quipped unevenly, tensing at the straining tightness of her nipples and the warm feeling of sensitivity pulsing like a taunt between her thighs. The atmosphere in the room was as thick and suffocating as the quiet before a thunder storm. 'And although it is absolutely none of your business, I was not acting like a whore with Mikhail. I know his wife and his children well—I was having lunch with him and catching up on news.'

Dante dealt her an unimpressed appraisal. 'I don't believe you.'

Topsy moved towards the door. 'That's your prerogative.'

'You're not leaving…I haven't finished with you yet,' Dante objected vehemently.

'But I've finished with you!' Topsy said sharply, yanking the door wide to make her escape.

Before she could guess what he intended, Dante wrenched the door from her grasp and slammed it loudly shut again in her face. Shocked by that very physical intervention, Topsy flipped round and leant back against the door, needing the temporary support of the solid wood against her spine. She looked up into scorching green eyes that glittered like stars, so bright against his darker skin. He was seething and he couldn't hide it. 'Underneath the bankers' suit, you're not Mr Cool at all, are you?' she murmured in helpless fascination.

'Not when it comes to protecting my family,' Dante traded without apology.

'You're crowding me,' Topsy told him, because he was inside her space, way too close for comfort, the familiar scent of his hot male body distracting her when she could least afford to be distracted.

'Deal with it,' Dante grated unhelpfully.

'No, you deal with your temper,' Topsy advised, shooting straight from the hip. 'Exactly what did Jerome tell you about me?'

'That he hired you as an escort and you went out for a meal. He recognised you from a newspaper photo that was taken of you with my mother and decided that it was his duty to speak up.'

Topsy rolled her eyes in mockery, wishing he would back off, wishing he weren't so domineeringly tall that he made her feel like a ridiculously undersized freak. It was one more way in which they were a poor match: her list of desirable male attributes specified a male no more than nine inches taller. It would be more comfortable for her to be with someone closer to her own size. Her sisters' husbands were *all* tall and whenever she disagreed with any of them she carefully kept her distance, having always understood that her diminutive height almost invited a bullying approach.

'You seem quite unconcerned by what Jerome told me,' Dante noted in a low gritty drawl. 'But my mother would be very much shocked.'

'I think Sofia would be shocked if she thought I'd

slept with him, but not that I once dined out with him in a public place,' Topsy countered drily.

Dante stared down at her radiating frustration. 'That's not the point. He *paid* for your company.'

'And that's all he got. Don't make it sound like I acted like a hooker,' Topsy urged, big brown eyes increasingly defiant. 'I worked as an escort for only that *one* night.'

Dante finally took a step back and she breathed again, peeling her spine off the door, shrugging her taut shoulders to loosen their tension. 'Do you really think I'm going to believe that you only did it once?' he derided.

'You obviously want to think the worst and that's not being fair to me,' Topsy complained, sliding past him in a sudden movement that took him by surprise and walking back over to the window where there was too much space for him to corner her again. 'I went out with Jerome that night as a favour for someone. His usual companion was off sick and I was her replacement. It was totally above board and unworthy of your suspicions.'

'You worked as an escort. I'm quite sure it wasn't above board with *all* your clients,' Dante vented with a curled lip.

A sound of impatience escaped Topsy. 'You just don't listen, do you? Jerome is the only client I ever had because that evening was the only time I ever worked as an escort!' she snapped back in exasperation.

He shot her a look of wounding derision. 'You can't really expect me to believe that…'

'I went out with Jerome as a favour to my mother,' Topsy chose to admit, willing to tell him enough to satisfy him because she did not want to be forced to leave the castle just when she was beginning to get to know Vittore.

Dante frowned. 'Your mother?'

Topsy braced herself. 'My mother owns and runs an escort agency.'

'An escort agency?' Dante repeated in disbelief.

'There's nothing I can do about the way my mother chooses to make her living,' Topsy pointed out curtly. 'Unfortunately, one doesn't get to *choose* one's parents.'

Dante studied her in silence with caustic cool.

'Yes, I can already hear the wheels of your limited imagination cranking into motion,' Topsy told him sourly, her generous pink mouth thinning with annoyance. 'But no, I wasn't dragged up in a sordid household by a depraved mother. Relax—no sob story of that sort is about to come your way. I was raised in a perfectly respectable home by my eldest sister and I only got to know my mother again recently.'

'By the sound of it you should've kept your distance from her,' Dante commented, watching the tip of her tongue flicking out to moisten her full lower lip, angrily registering the stirring of arousal at his groin as perspiration dampened his skin. He only had to look at that luscious mouth and erotic fantasy took over.

Topsy was tense but the pulse of sexual awareness was like a monster running amok inside her body. She was remembering the glory of that hard sensual mouth smashing down on hers, the wonderfully solid feel of his hard, muscular power pinning her against that wall, the indescribable delight of his fingers touching her intimately and finally the waves of wickedly wanton pleasure that had followed. Her knees trembled, her breathing fracturing. 'Stop looking at me like that,' she warned him stiffly.

'You were telling me about your mother,' Dante reminded her thickly, picturing her on his desk, splayed open and ready for him. He knotted his hands into fists of restraint and breathed in deep and slow, struggling to put a lid on his overactive brain and the images flying up there.

'I needed some very important information from her,' Topsy volunteered after a perceptible hesitation. 'My sisters had warned me that she wasn't to be trusted but I knew what to expect from her and I was prepared. If you want to get on the right side of my mother you have to bribe her. She said that if I stepped in for the employee who was sick and spent the evening with Jerome in her place, she would give me the information I needed. We made a deal and she understands deals. I know she was hoping that I would agree to take on other clients and work for her as an escort afterwards but I never had any intention of doing that. I'm not that stupid…'

'What was the information?' Dante queried, wondering if he could believe anything she told him because of course she would try to vindicate herself in any way that she could. Naturally she would swear that she had only ever worked one evening as an escort and had no plans to do so ever again.

'That's private.' Topsy turned her face away from his hard appraisal, guilty colour mantling her cheeks as the movement made her long dark hair fall against her face and tumble in loose glossy curls round her tense shoulders. '*That*…isn't for sharing.'

Especially not with a man who would happily use that information to slam another nail in the coffin of his dislike for Vittore. Dante would become even more hostile if something embarrassing from Vittore's past were to surface to hurt or humiliate his mother.

'I refuse to believe that you only worked one night as an escort,' Dante drawled scornfully.

Topsy flipped back to face him. 'There's nothing I can do about that.'

'I do not keep three mistresses,' Dante told her in a roughened undertone, the denial wrenched from him without his seeming volition.

Topsy shrugged slim shoulders, face carefully nonchalant. 'It's nothing to me if you do.'

'You were angry about it, *gioia mia*. I could see it in your face.' Dante savoured his recollection of the moment. 'Like me, you don't share.'

'The rumour must've started somewhere,' Topsy replied, although she hadn't meant to say something so revealing and cursed her unruly tongue. Now he would think she was angling for an explanation of that story.

Dante closed the distance between them, resting his hands on her narrow shoulders. 'Once upon a time when I was very young and very randy I thought there was safety in numbers. Instead the combined demands of the three of them drove me crazy.'

His hands felt very heavy on her taut shoulders and her mouth had run dry because once again he had invaded her space. 'I wasn't jealous,' she told him vehemently, recognising that that was what he was driving at and furious at the suggestion.

'Neither was I, but the thought of you cavorting with Kusnirovich in that hotel suite outraged every skin cell in my body,' Dante confided huskily, long fingers spreading to smooth the tops of her arms. 'I can't stand the idea of another man touching you.'

'I'm not going to let you touch me,' Topsy pointed out half under her breath, her lungs less than efficient with him so close. And she wanted to touch him back so badly that it literally hurt to deny herself.

'Then say no now,' Dante advised.

'No...' Topsy said flatly.

'Louder and with more conviction,' Dante urged mockingly, setting her temper on fire.

'*No*, Dante *no*!' Topsy shouted back at him furiously, wishing he would learn how to take no for an answer.

A loud knock prefaced the abrupt opening of the door. Dante swung round with angry words on his lips, intending to rebuke the offender, only to see his stepfather standing in the doorway with a frown of indecision stamped on his face. 'I'm sorry to interrupt but I heard raised voices,' Vittore declared. 'Sofia was concerned when Topsy didn't come upstairs.'

Dante vented a soft laugh. 'We were arguing. I want to give her a driving lesson but she's not sure she's willing to trust me,' he murmured smoothly.

Taken aback by the speed with which he had come up with the excuse, Topsy blinked rapidly. 'Er...yes,' she contributed, not one half as smooth as him in a tight corner.

'If she doesn't wish to learn to drive she doesn't have to,' Vittore commented. 'It's not important.'

'I think it is,' Dante overruled. 'It would make her independent. She would be able to work much more efficiently if she could drive.'

'Right…OK, I'll take that on board,' Topsy promised, moving towards the door, desperate to make her escape and willing to use Vittore's arrival to facilitate it.

'And there's no time like the present,' Dante quipped, drawing level with her, one determined hand pressing lightly to the base of her spine to guide her across the hall. With the other he withdrew his cell phone and instructed someone to bring his mother's car out of the garage.

'It's a small and easily manoeuvred car,' he remarked, walking her outside into the sunshine. 'Perfect for the purpose.'

'I don't want to do this,' Topsy told him grittily. 'I don't like driving and I don't want you trying to teach me.'

'All you need to do is concentrate and you can't have got a doctorate in advanced maths without that ability,' Dante countered with assurance.

Topsy chewed her lower lip in vexation. She had never felt less like getting behind the wheel of a car. Her nerves were ragged after the row they had had, her emotions were still reeling from the shock of being called a whore and her temper remained in highly sensitive mode. Virtually everyone who had ever tried to teach her to drive had ended up shouting at her or at the very least raising their voice, convinced she wasn't listening properly to their directions. She was also convinced that domineering, impatient and far from even-tempered Dante was the last man alive to take on such a challenge.

'Climb in,' Dante urged, opening the door of the small hatchback with a flourish. 'Once you've got over your nerves, I'll hire an instructor to take charge. You have an entire estate of private roads here on which to practise.'

Perspiration beading her short upper lip, Topsy accepted the keys he passed her with a hand that already felt damp. He ran through every move she was to make first and then told her to start the car. 'Promise you won't shout,' she breathed before she put the key in the ignition.

'Of course I'm not going to shout,' Dante retorted drily. 'I'm not the excitable type.'

Well, that was a lie for a start, Topsy thought wryly. He had a really bad temper and when he touched her he was decidedly excitable and anything but cool or calm. In fact he already qualified as the most passionate male she had ever met.

'Are you planning to sit here doing nothing all afternoon?' Dante enquired drily.

He also had the patience of a jet plane forced to travel in the slow lane.

Topsy gazed out of the windscreen at the spacious cobbled courtyard and switched on the engine, which seemed very noisy in the rushing silence. A trickle of sweat ran down between her breasts.

'Run through your mental checklist first,' Dante advised.

Her mind was a blank and her teeth clenched together. 'I don't want to do this with you,' Topsy admitted starkly.

'Stop dramatising yourself—just get on with it!' Dante told her impatiently.

Thoroughly fed up with him and keen to get the experience over with, Topsy rammed the car into gear and hit the accelerator. The vehicle shot back so fast a startled gasp was wrenched from her. Dante shouted something and then there was a sickening crunch and a violent jolt that rattled every tooth in her head, the seat belt cutting into her midriff as it clamped tight.

'You total maniac!' Dante roared at her, leaping out of the car as though she had branded him with a burning torch.

Topsy switched off the engine and breathed in deep to ward off the nausea and the dizziness of shock. Detaching the seat belt, she opened the car door and shakily climbed out.

'You didn't even look in the mirror before you reversed!' Dante launched at her incredulously as he bent down to examine the damage to the bonnet of his precious Pagani Zonda.

'I wasn't planning to reverse… It's an unfamiliar car and I went into the wrong gear!' Topsy protested, folding her arms defensively while trying not to stare at the crunched-up metalwork that now marred the previously pristine paintwork of both vehicles.

Dante flung up his hands in a dramatic gesture. 'How could you accidentally go into reverse?'

'You were irritating the hell out of me…distracting me,' Topsy complained.

Brilliant green eyes targeted her. 'Oh, so now it's my fault, is it?'

'You knew I didn't want to get behind the wheel. I made it quite clear,' she argued. 'I'll go and apologise to your mother about her car.'

'Are you going to apologise to me about what you've done to *my* car?' Dante demanded.

Topsy couldn't bring herself to say sorry. The accident was his fault, absolutely his fault. 'You had an argument with me, called me horrible names and then demanded that I drive even though I made it clear that I didn't want to!' she condemned bitterly. 'So, if you ask me, you got what you deserve!'

Sofia handled the news of the damage to her car with complete aplomb, pointing out that she currently wasn't using it and that the local garage would soon have it fixed. Topsy insisted that she would pay for the repairs and apologised again. 'I'm afraid I don't get on very well with Dante,' she admitted.

A wry smile crossed his mother's mouth. 'My son is accustomed to calling the shots. I knew you would clash but don't let it worry you. I'm happy with the way you're handling everything for me.'

For the first time, Topsy asked to have her evening meal on a tray in her room. The prospect of facing Dante across the dinner table was too much for her. She knew she should have apologised. What had happened to her manners? But Dante brought out a side of her nature that she didn't recognise, provoking only an angry resentful response. He *had* called her a whore. How dared he? She didn't feel the least bit forgiving about that. One evening working as an escort did not make a woman a whore. Busying herself checking the guest list for the fancy-dress ball, Topsy made a note of jobs to be accomplished the following day after her trip to Florence with Vittore.

She felt guilty because going to Florence meant she would be taking most of the day off. Vittore worked part time as a financial advisor in the city and generally Topsy went sightseeing while she waited for him to finish and give her a lift back to the castle. Finally, recognising that her shattered nerves were keeping her stress level at an all-time high, she went for a bath to unwind.

When someone knocked on the door about an hour later, she stifled a yawn, knotted the sash of her wrap round her waist and went to answer it.

It was one of the maids carrying a beautiful bouquet of flowers already arranged in a crystal vase. 'For me?' Topsy commented in surprise, plucking the gift card from the foliage as the smiling maid settled the vase down on a table by the window.

Dante.

Topsy frowned in surprise, distrusting the gesture. Why would he send her flowers? What was he playing at? At this season the castle gardens were bursting with flowers and she could have picked an armful without anyone even noticing. Involuntarily she bent down, nostrils flaring on the intoxicating perfume of the roses, straightening with a jerk as yet another knock sounded on her bedroom door.

It was Dante, always, she suspected, quick to take advantage of any window of opportunity, any moment of weakness. He was very much a predator. She collided warily with his stunning emerald-green eyes. Colour warmed her cheeks and her mouth ran dry.

'May I come in?' he asked, smooth as silk, his self-discipline absolute, a faint smile even softening the hard, handsome lines of his lean dark features.

Even so, regardless of appearances, Dante was still recovering from the demeaning realisation that he had hit a hell of an own goal earlier that day. His temper had got the better of him and he still could not explain to his own satisfaction why that had happened. But he knew he should *not* have confronted Topsy about what Jerome had told him. He should have kept that information to himself and used it to his advantage because he could gain nothing by making her into an enemy.

In speaking up without logical consideration of what the consequences might be, he had not only made her hostile but also forced her to come up with the ultimate silly story in an effort to excuse her work as an escort. Could she really believe that he would swallow all that nonsense about her having traded a one-off evening as an escort in exchange for some indeterminate piece of information from her own mother? It seemed that she liked to play the poor exploited innocent and he was willing to play along with that to see where it led.

Topsy measured the risk of inviting Dante into her bedroom against the potential embarrassment of being seen trading words with him in her nightwear and slowly, reluctantly, stepped back to open the door wider, deeming discretion to be the wiser approach.

'I am sorry about your car,' she proffered on the better-late-than-never principle.

Dante expelled his breath on a sigh. 'I did force you

into driving when you didn't want to. Understandably you were in the wrong mood.'

'You called me a whore,' Topsy reminded him bluntly. 'That was completely unacceptable.'

'Sadly, your work as an escort would make you unacceptable to many people. I'm not the only person around here who is prejudiced,' Dante pointed out steadily, noticing the way the fine silk of her wrap defined the pouting swells of her breasts and the luscious curve of her hips. His jaw line clenched in fierce denial of his burgeoning erection. 'But you are correct—working a while as an escort doesn't automatically make you a whore and I should never have called you one.'

'I spent one wretched evening working as an escort!' Topsy exclaimed, out of all patience at his judgemental attitude. 'It shouldn't make you think of me differently.'

'You can't be that naïve.'

As he was the first man to find out about that evening and his reaction was much worse than she had expected, she was beginning to think that she had been just that naïve. She frowned at the thought of how her sisters would have reacted to the news, knowing they would be furious with her, particularly when they had already warned her to be cautious around their mother. But only Odette had had the power to tell Topsy who her father really was and, hurt and bewildered by the discovery that the man she had always believed was her father was *not*, Topsy would have done almost anything for that knowledge.

'But maybe you are, *gioia mia*,' Dante breathed soft and low in continuance, gazing down at her with an intensity that burned.

'I always try to think the best of people,' Topsy declared, her breath shortening in her throat, the undertones in the atmosphere beginning to make her skin prickle with awareness.

'That's asking for trouble.'

'I don't want to look at the world that way!' Topsy protested vehemently.

A sardonic smile slashed Dante's stubborn mouth. 'But to protect yourself, you must,' he told her drily.

Looking up at his handsome features, Topsy was suddenly swamped by such a powerful tide of longing that she felt dizzy. He was gorgeous but so different from her in every way that she could not comprehend the terrifying strength of his appeal. It's just sexual attraction, a little voice said in the back of her head and for once that little voice was a comfort to her, for 'just sex' she could handle while the prospect of experiencing anything deeper unnerved her.

'You shouldn't be in here with me late at night,' Topsy said abruptly, recognising the danger of being alone with him in her bedroom, instinctively trying to protect herself. 'It'll give the staff the wrong idea about us.'

A surprisingly boyish grin slanted his beautifully shaped mouth. '*Non importa, bellissima mia.* I don't care about other people's opinions—'

'I'm not beautiful,' she told him thinly, questioning that endearment. 'But of course you're an Italian male and fully living up to the stereotype with your compliments.'

'I do think you're beautiful and I'm no stereotype.' Dante cradled her cheekbone, tilting her face up to better appraise eyes the colour of warm melted honey and the succulent pink mouth that haunted his dreams.

Topsy could feel her heart accelerating like an express train on a downhill run and, even worse, the instant leap of anticipation that he alone could summon. 'Dante...*go,*' she urged hoarsely.

Instead Dante bent down and pulled her up against him. 'I want you.'

A tiny pulse flickered below her collarbone, her face taut with strain as she fought an urgent need to respond in kind. 'Put me down,' she told him stiffly.

'I'm not a rabid dog. I don't bite,' Dante teased, burying his mouth in the soft silky tangle of dark hair between her shoulder and neck and nuzzling her skin to kiss a trail up her slender throat, which made her writhe and gasp. '*Dio mio!* I *ache* for you!'

Her arms linked across his broad shoulders to steady herself. 'You only ache because I said no. If I'd said yes, you would already have lost interest,' she condemned.

Taken aback by that condemnation, Dante tumbled her down slowly on the bed. 'I'm not a teenager with a score card and I don't do one-night stands.'

'You're not my type,' Topsy argued shakily, looking up at him with wide, accusing eyes.

One knee on the bed, Dante bent down to mould a possessive hand to the swell of her breast, fingers withdrawing only to expertly massage the protuberant bud of her nipple through the fine covering of the silk. 'Your body says otherwise. As for the suits you don't like,' Dante mused lazily. 'Guess what? They come off!'

Her eyes softened at the teasing note in his voice,

her attention arrested by the compelling smile he now wore. 'This isn't a game, Dante.'

'Isn't it?' A doubting ebony brow rose. 'What else can it be between us?'

And the spell of his charismatic presence broke in that same moment because what he said opposed her every thought and feeling and the shock of her recoil gave her the strength to muster her defences. In an abrupt movement, Topsy pulled away and rolled off the other side of the bed, standing up and folding her arms defensively. 'I don't play games, Dante. Please go.'

Dante studied her, taking in the wilful tilt of her chin, the blazing determination in her dark eyes, and wondered if that strength of character and continued resistance was what made her so powerfully attractive. When it came to women Dante very rarely met with a challenge. His clever brain coolly assessed the situation. He decided that on balance even if he hadn't got her into bed and gratified his lust, he was content that he had redressed the damage of their confrontation earlier. He might be back almost where he had started, but at least communication channels were open again.

Topsy got into bed, weak as a twig blown down in a storm: mentally and physically, he exhausted her. In the back of her mind she had been thinking that they could have an affair. He had worn her down, weakened her into thinking such a development could be acceptable. While it was true that she had come to Italy ready to extend her experience of men if the right opportunity offered, Dante Leonetti was so far off her scale of what was acceptable in a lover that he made her think more of disaster than opportunity.

An affair wasn't a game to her and she didn't want to get hurt. Instinct was already warning her that the confusion of emotions she experienced around Dante went dangerously beyond basic attraction. Possibly it was infatuation, she reasoned uneasily, but only children played with fire without fear of getting burned and Topsy didn't want to suffer so much as a scorch mark. So, on that score, Dante was strictly off limits.

CHAPTER SIX

VITTORE TOOK A last dissatisfied glance at the gold pendant. 'It's so plain,' he lamented, clearly longing for a more bold and sparkly design.

'I think Sofia will like it,' Topsy told him firmly.

Vittore nodded and proffered his credit card. 'We'll go for coffee before I head into the office,' he said, casting her a glance. 'My first appointment isn't until ten-thirty. What are you going to do?'

'My plans are fairly loose but I think I'll do the Uffizi again. My last visit felt rushed,' she confided.

'Do you get homesick for London?' Vittore asked her, having ordered coffee at a pavement café opposite the office he used.

'No, I'm enjoying the change of scene.' Topsy hesitated, seeing her opening, moving to grab it. 'When were you last in London?'

'More than twenty years ago,' Vittore told her, looking reflective.

'Was it a holiday?' she prompted, sipping at her cappuccino.

'No. I moved to London to start up a business but it all went pear-shaped,' he volunteered wryly.

'What happened?' Topsy asked quietly.

'I fell in love with the wrong woman and she emptied my bank account,' Vittore admitted, giving her a rueful look when she could not hide her shock at that admission. 'That was the end of the affair and the end of my business venture. I came home to lick my wounds and never went back.'

Topsy was frowning. 'Did you tell the police?'

'No, I wrote it off to experience. I don't think the police *could* have helped me. After all, I trusted her and gave her free access to my account. What happened was my own fault. Back then I was still young and foolish,' he declared with a fatalistic shrug of his shoulders. 'Maturity does have some advantages.'

Topsy wanted so badly to ask if the woman concerned had been called Odette Taylor but if she mentioned her mother's name she would have to come clean and tell all and she wasn't ready to do that yet. Could the woman who had robbed Vittore be her mother? It was a depressing suspicion and only made the challenge of tackling the thorny mystery of her parentage more difficult, for if Odette had been the thief, Vittore would very probably be appalled to learn that he might have fathered a child with her. Already painfully aware of numerous occasions when her mother had been greedy and dishonest with money, Topsy had little difficulty picturing her avaricious parent in such a scenario. Odette had even admitted to her that she had chosen to lie and tell her polo player lover that *he* was the father of her youngest daughter because he had impressed her as a better financial bet than Vittore.

'You look very thoughtful,' Vittore quipped.

Topsy glanced up from her coffee cup and blinked in

consternation at the tall male figure striding across the square towards them: it was Dante as she had never seen him before, his lean powerful thighs sheathed in tight-fitting faded denim, a blue-striped short-sleeved shirt casually open at his brown throat. Black hair ruffled in the slight breeze, strong face cool and calm, he looked breathtakingly beautiful to her stunned gaze. She moistened her lower lip with a nervous flick of her tongue. 'Dante's coming this way,' she warned the older man.

Vittore frowned, his air of relaxation vanishing. 'He didn't even mention that he was coming into town today.'

Topsy was covertly engaged in admiring the gloriously neat fit of Dante's jeans across his narrow hips and long muscular legs and in the midst of that wholly inappropriate appraisal drained her cappuccino in an effort to suppress her thundering pulses and an almost painful attack of self-consciousness. Soft pink highlighted her cheeks as Dante approached their table. 'I thought I'd find you here. According to my mother this is your favourite breakfast bar,' Dante remarked silkily.

'It is and your timing is excellent because I was about to abandon Topsy to keep an appointment,' Vittore remarked, turning his head to smile at Topsy. 'You could find no better guide to this city than Dante. Florence is the original home of the Leonetti Bank and where he embarked on his gilded career.'

'Is it really?' Topsy pushed away her cup and rose upright, keen to stress her independence, reluctant to be foisted on Dante like some hapless tourist in need of guidance and attention. She watched his eyes follow

Vittore as he vanished through a door on the other side of the busy street.

'I didn't even know my stepfather *had* a job until today,' Dante commented.

'Your mother doesn't approve because it takes him away from her but he does only work four mornings a week,' she proffered, instinctively defensive on the older man's behalf. 'I would've thought you would be pleased that he makes the effort.'

'When I consider the size of my mother's income, it strikes me as a pointless demonstration of independence,' Dante said drily.

'Is financial worth your only marker of good character?' Topsy asked with spirit. 'Anyone with an ounce of sensitivity would see that Vittore is very well aware of his position and determined not to take advantage of it!'

His designer sun specs clasped in one hand, Dante gazed down at her, green eyes radiating irritation. 'Why are you defending him?'

'He adores your mother and he makes her happy,' Topsy countered in quiet reproof. 'I like him, I like both of them and it distresses your mother that you so obviously think so little of the man she chose to marry.'

A muscle pulled taut at the corner of his unsmiling mouth, his stunning green eyes silvering with cold anger at the reproof. '*Maledizione!* What right do you have to interfere in the private affairs of my family?' he ground out with disdain. 'Or even to express an opinion?'

Topsy paled and then reddened, feeling both embarrassed and irritated, knowing very well that she should have kept her thoughts to herself. The icy look of hauteur stamped on his face mortified her and she spun away to cross the square. A hand closed over her arm to hold her back.

'Where are you going?'

'The Uffizi.'

He sent her a derisive look. 'At this time of day? It will be a suffocating crush of tourists and you will only gain entry if you have a pre-arranged ticket.'

'I haven't,' she acknowledged ruefully.

'It would be a nightmare. Give up on the Uffizi and I promise I'll arrange a special pass for you some day so that you can browse in peace.' His eyes locked with hers and her tummy hollowed, her muscles pulling tight while her world rocked dizzily on its axis as if someone had given her a sudden violent shove. In the grip of that almost intoxicating sense of disassociation from planet earth Dante was all that mattered, filling her mind with insane thoughts that turned her inside out, filling her body with frighteningly familiar reactions she couldn't fight. She wanted him, *wanted* him in a way she had never wanted anyone before, craved him with every breath that she drew.

A slow, exultant smile slashed Dante's expressive mouth as he flipped down his sunglasses, closing her off from that visual connection that had made her entire body hum with excitement. She blinked, momentarily dazed by the clawing lash of desire unfulfilled and dropped her head, fighting for self-control and staring in surprise at the hand that now gripped hers.

'You haven't even told me what you're doing here,' she breathed unsteadily.

'My mother forgot to ask you to pick up her contact lens prescription,' he said prosaically.

'Oh…I should have remembered. She always has stuff for me to do here but I didn't want to wake her up so early to ask.' Topsy pushed her knuckles against her pounding brow as if she could force logical thought back into being again.

'This is the original home of the Leonetti Bank founded centuries ago by one of my ancestors.' Dante paused outside a tall sandstone building that bore all the hallmarks of ancient Florentine architecture. 'I started work here when I was twenty-one and a few years later we centralised operations in Milan and donated the building to the city to become a museum.'

'Twenty-one? You were young. Didn't you ever want to be something other than a banker?'

'What I would be was set in stone on the day of my birth,' Dante informed her drily. 'My father would have allowed nothing else and, fortunately for me, I inherited the Leonetti business gene and the affinity with numbers. You still haven't told me how you managed to spot the error on that document the other night.'

Topsy flushed. 'I could just see that it was wrong.'

'But you only saw that document for seconds.'

'I can't help it if my brain works like a computer sometimes,' she admitted soft and low, uneasy with the subject of the high IQ that had made her a gifted child and an even more gifted adult. 'Where are you taking me?'

He walked into the lively and very busy little medieval streets between Via Maggio and Piazza Pitti, the artisan quarter of workshops. It was like stepping back in time as she walked past studios displaying the wares of bookbinders, violin makers, metal workers, sculptors and cobblers. Topsy was enchanted because it was a taste of Renaissance Florence as only a local could have shown her. She had spent several mornings wandering round the city with a guidebook in a never-ending crowd of equally studious tourists until after a while the sights began to blur and intermingle and her brain went into overload mode.

In a design studio she chose a pretty enamelled photo frame for Kat in her sister's favourite colours and frowned in surprise when Dante attempted to pay for the purchase.

'It isn't for me, it's a gift for my eldest sister,' she commented as she politely refused to allow him to buy it for her.

He had more success when he bought her a lemon ice cream, so rich and creamy and smooth in texture that she loosed a helpless moan of delight as the icy concoction engulfed her taste buds. Dante lifted a napkin and dabbed at the tip of her nose and the corner of her mouth where ice-cream stains lingered. 'You're worse than a child for making a mess, *carissima mia*.'

Mesmerised by his flashing smile of amusement at her clumsiness, she looked up at him, amber eyes unusually serious. He *could* hurt her and only the night before that fear had held her back but now that pronounced caution felt more like an excuse for not living than truly living and she was regrouping, hungry for new experiences and wildly curious about him and what he could make her feel.

'We'll go for lunch now,' Dante decreed.

'I should be getting back to work,' Topsy protested.

'My mother isn't expecting you back. She has friends joining her for lunch,' he told her.

He walked her back to a Bugatti Veyron surrounded by a small crowd of admiring teenaged boys. He pressed a banknote into the hand of the tallest youth, thanked him for taking care of his car and tucked Topsy into the passenger seat.

'Where's the Pagani?' she finally asked stiffly.

'In a workshop for the foreseeable future.' Dante groaned out the admission and cast her a glimmering sidelong glance. 'You're a menace.'

'At least nobody was hurt,' Topsy parried, a flush on her cheeks. 'Where are we going for lunch?'

'You'll see.'

Her attention fell on a lean, powerful thigh encased in denim and she dragged it away again, struggling to get a grip on the weird, wild promptings assailing her. She might be curious but she wasn't foolish. Nothing was going to happen between her and Dante unless she allowed it to and she was in too much control to make that mistake, she told herself urgently. Her head was all over the place; one minute she wanted him, the next she was telling herself that she had to resist him.

'So, where did you go with Vittore this morning?' Dante asked casually.

'He wanted my advice about a gift he's buying for your mother's birthday,' Topsy admitted, since she saw nothing wrong with sharing that.

'Why would he need your advice?'

'Because he always gets it wrong.'

'Wrong?' Dante pressed. 'How?'

'Vittore likes bling.'

A husky laugh of understanding unexpectedly sounded from Dante. 'I can see that that would be a problem.'

About half an hour later when they were in familiar countryside, he drove up a winding mountain road and, turning into a stony lane, he switched off the engine. When she looked at him in surprise, he shrugged and said lightly, 'I'm afraid we have to walk from here.'

Topsy climbed out into the sunshine and hung over the door, enjoying the view of the forested slopes and the city now far in the distance. 'Where are we?'

'On the edge of the Leonetti estate.' Dante emerged from the boot gripping a substantial picnic basket and he tossed her a rug to carry.

Topsy gave him a startled glance. 'We're picnicking?'

'I think the food will be a cut above the usual picnic. Though I say it myself, my chef is unbeatable.'

Topsy anchored the rug uncertainly beneath her arm. 'I didn't think you were the picnicking type.'

'Blame yourself. I needed a good reason to put on jeans,' Dante quipped, striding off into the cover of the trees and leaving her to follow the rough trail through the long grass.

Her figure-hugging cotton dress rode up her thighs as she broke into a stride in an effort to keep up with him. She smoothed it back down, breathless in the heat, perspiration beading her brow. 'Wish you'd warned me. I'm not really dressed for the occasion.'

'I know but I wouldn't have missed that outfit for

anything, *carissima mia*,' Dante confided. 'Clinging to your truly spectacular curves that dress is a show stopper.'

It was a grey stretchy cotton dress teamed with a colourful scarf but he made it sound like something else entirely and she flushed, unaccustomed to such masculine candour. Spectacular curves? She had long envied her siblings' whippet-slim frames. Clothes hung on her sisters as though they were elegant models while Topsy's infinitely fuller figure was much more of a challenge to dress.

'Why…a picnic?' Topsy asked, drawing level with him in a clearing below a spreading mature chestnut tree as broad in proportion as a bus. Beyond the clearing the ground fell away steeply into dense woods but the view over the quiet valley was amazing.

'I thought it would be more your style than a trendy city lunch.' Setting the basket down, he took the rug from her and spread it.

The silence but for the birdsong crept round her like a cocoon. She kicked off her shoes and sat down on her knees, determined not to betray her nervous tension. 'Where are your bodyguards?' she asked abruptly.

'I gave them the day off. After all, I'm still on the estate and this was a last-minute decision that nobody else knows about.' Pouring the wine, he passed her a glass, the tips of his long elegant fingers briefly brushing hers. 'Drink up…relax.'

Relax? Topsy almost laughed at that impossibility. Being alone with a man who fascinated her to the degree that he did was deeply unnerving. She sipped the wine and let him pile a plate with a selection of the many delicacies he unpacked from the basket. She ate wafer-thin ham, dainty crostini snacks and Panzanella, a refreshing tomato salad. Lemon tart followed by a rich spicy slice of cake finished the meal. Having drained her second glass of wine, Topsy flopped down flat on her back with a sigh to gaze up through the sun-dappled canopy of leaves above her.

'I'll never move again,' she swore ruefully. 'I've never eaten as much at one sitting.'

'My chef will be flattered.'

A window of clarity briefly shone in her sunlight-and-wine-dazed mind. He had brought her into the woods to seduce her. He had even put on jeans. Topsy froze and then hurriedly sat up, deeming it unwise to lie horizontal like a sacrifice and encourage him. She collided with iridescent green eyes and a quiver of response shimmied through her. 'I know why you brought me here.'

Dante shifted fluidly closer. 'We both know why.'

'This is so *not* going to happen,' she warned him ruefully.

CHAPTER SEVEN

A RELUCTANT SMILE tugged at the corners of Dante's beautifully shaped mouth. 'But why not?'

Topsy sighed. 'When I was eighteen I made a list of exactly what I wanted from a man. I watched my sisters get involved with unsuitable men and getting hurt and I swore it would never happen to me.'

'What's on the list?' Dante prompted, silkily confident. 'I love a challenge.'

'Can you cook?' Topsy studied his face and the bemused frown forming there before sighing. 'I can't cook, so I decided I needed a guy who could.'

'I can provide a chef,' Dante pointed out with deadly seriousness. 'And obviously I can microwave stuff but I usually eat out when I'm working.'

'You can't beat the list, Dante. You just don't match. You're not modest or romantic or caring.'

'But I'm also not asking you to marry me,' Dante declared with staggering candour. 'And by the sound of it, your list was drawn up to road test a potential life partner.'

Topsy tilted her head to one side, long black waves sliding over one bare shoulder, dark eyes reflective because she had never thought of that angle before. 'You're right. You don't need to be Mr Perfect.'

'You choose me to have a good time in and out of bed, *gioia mia*,' Dante proposed silkily.

'No, you're definitely not modest,' Topsy commented with a helpless little laugh as she studied his face, marvelling that just looking at that precise arrangement of features could give her such an extraordinary thrill.

'Modest types lose boardroom battles,' Dante confided with immense assurance and leant forward to bridge the gap between them. 'And they probably lie about their performance in the bedroom.'

'How do I know you're not lying?' Topsy asked breathlessly because he was so close now a faint hint of citrusy cologne was tugging at her nostrils, instilling a powerful recollection of what it felt like when she was in his arms with his mouth on hers. An ache stirred deep down inside her and her tummy flipped.

'I aim to prove it.' Knotting one bronzed hand into the hair falling down her back, he eased her closer and sealed his sensual mouth to hers. It was like dying and being reborn in a burst of fireworks and celebration. Her awareness of her body shot from zero to overload in the space of seconds, every part of her reacting to the heat he generated.

Smouldering green eyes scanned her flushed face in the aftermath. 'Together we burn, *gioia mia*,' Dante savoured. Long fingers smoothed up over her taut ribcage to caress the swell of a rounded breast, ensuring that her breath shortened in her throat.

He reached for the hem of her dress and began to lift it and she literally froze at the threat of being naked in broad daylight. Suddenly she wanted lights she could switch off, a bed she could huddle in beneath a sheet.

'*Che cosa hai?* What's wrong?' he asked.

'Nothing's wrong!' Her throat convulsed on the denial as she struggled to get her nerves under control again. A certain amount of clothing had to come off, there was no getting round that requirement, she told herself. She closed her eyes, reached down to close her hands into her dress and tugged it up and off in one determined movement. It made her feel much better than the alternative of sitting there like a doll for him to undress; it made her feel that *she* was taking control. She glanced at him from below the rumpled mane of her hair, dark eyes provocative, her brain refusing to dwell on the reality that she was stripped down to a lacy bra and knickers.

'Time to take your shirt off,' Topsy told him instead.

His stunning eyes gleamed with amusement and he unbuttoned his shirt and shed it. The corrugated slab of his flat abdomen as he stretched took her breath away. He was beautifully built, hard muscles rippling below bronzed skin with his every movement. Her mouth ran dry as he unzipped his jeans and peeled them down with fluid ease, revealing black boxers that clung to narrow hips and a lean waist. She noticed, could not have avoided noticing, the bulge of his straining erection in the boxers and something clenched low inside her and she hurriedly glanced away, a more primal dart of apprehension infiltrating her. She was wondering if the first time would hurt and was realistic enough to assume that there would at least be some discomfort, but there was nothing she could do to avoid that rite of passage. Of course she could tell him she was a virgin but was afraid he would think she was some kind of freak to have stayed untouched until her age and the prospect of that made her cringe.

'Come here,' he husked, all warm tanned flesh and assurance, finding her mouth again, toying with her lips, stroking them apart, thrusting, in truth unleashing a repertoire of moves that disconcerted her because just kissing had never been so good before. Pulsing energy consumed her and she pushed against him, falling into those kisses and the delving of his tongue with shivering enthusiasm, marvelling that the feverish heat in her pelvis could be awakened by even that small intimacy.

'You have the most glorious breasts,' Dante murmured hungrily, moulding the high round globes with appreciative hands, tracing the tightly beaded tips and suckling the pointed peaks into the hot velvet of his mouth, parting her lips on a gasp and sending tiny arrows of need spearing continuously to her core. Almost as if she had spoken, when the hot, tight feeling between her thighs became unbearable, he tugged off her knickers and touched her where she most needed to be touched.

Her awareness of what was happening took a severe hit at that point as her hips squirmed and sensation overwhelmed every other response. His thumb circled her clitoris and a fingertip traced the sweet swollen tightness of her most private place. Her hips shifted and lifted, a whimper of sound torn from her as he explored. She could feel the wet readiness of her own body and the straining eagerness to reach a climax.

Dante shimmied down the length of her and used

his mouth to tease her. Shock at the incredible intimacy of it rippled through her but the tide of pleasure he evoked was too great to withstand. The flick of his tongue across that tiny bundle of nerve endings made her cry out, excitement gathering that was out of her control. He drove her into a frenzy of need, her back arching, her body screaming for satisfaction by tightening and tightening until the wicked pleasure triumphed and an explosion of sensation overwhelmed her body as she reached the highest peak. In the aftermath her body crested down the slope of arousal on tiny aftershocks of earth-shattering delight.

She heard the crackle of foil, knew he was donning a condom and breathed in deep and slow, too shaken by what she had already experienced to feel her earlier apprehension. He rose high over her, pushing her legs over his shoulders and her eyes widened at the sensation of pressure as he pushed the broad thick head of his shaft into her tender flesh.

'You're very tight, *cara mia*,' he groaned. 'I'll stay in control, go slow.'

Topsy could feel herself being stretched, her inner muscles protesting his invasion and she shut her eyes and struggled to relax.

'You feel miraculous,' he breathed as he eased into her.

In the same moment as he pushed a little deeper she felt a burning sensation and then a sharp pain and she cried out, eyes flying wide, surprise and dismay etched there.

Dante froze. 'I hurt you?' She could see his shrewd

green eyes deducing certain things she would have preferred him not to know.

'It's all right now…it's been a while,' she muttered dismissively, her face red and hot as fire.

Dante shifted his lean hips, sank slowly deeper and then withdrew and repeated the manoeuvre. A ripple of excitement gathered in her pelvis as her body clenched around him and he thrust deep with an appreciative groan. The delirious dark pleasure was engulfing her again by degrees, tightening her muscles, making her heart race, filling her with a flood of hunger. He slammed into her harder and faster, the all-consuming urgency of their entwined bodies enthralling her as another climax slowly, steadily began to build. The extremity of that orgasm when it came made her thrash and buck and cry out.

Afterwards, Topsy thought she would never move again because her body was in a blissful state of exhaustion. Dante dropped a kiss on the bridge of her nose and levered off her, releasing her from his weight.

'*Che diavolo!* You're bleeding!' he exclaimed.

And there and then she almost died of mortification, startled eyes flying wide on his shocked expression as she sat up and saw the smudge of blood on her thigh. She burned red from head to toe and folded her arms round her knees. 'It's nothing to worry about.'

'You were a virgin,' Dante breathed in audible disbelief, reprogramming his every former assumption about her.

'We don't need to do a post-mortem on it,' Topsy fielded.

'You should have told me!' Dante censured. 'I could

have made more of an occasion out of it. If I'd known I wouldn't have taken you on a picnic rug in the woods.'

Embarrassed though she was, that had Topsy turning wondering eyes on him. 'You don't find it a turn-off?'

'I think it's the biggest turn-on I've ever had,' Dante told her, his keen gaze studying her with fascination. 'To know that at its most basic no other man has done what I've just done with you is extraordinarily exciting, *gioia mia*.'

In relief she leant forward and kissed him. He nibbled at her lower lip and then kissed her long and hard and before very long all talk ceased and they were making love again.

Topsy surfaced from a long much-needed nap to find that the sun was going down and she glanced at her watch in consternation. Dante was already dressed and the picnic packed away. 'You should have wakened me,' she complained.

'You must've needed the rest.'

Shy of him now, she flipped off the edge of the rug he must have tossed over her while she slept and concentrated on retrieving her clothing and getting into it fast. She felt downright astonished by what had transpired between them and the raw passion that had engulfed them had rewritten all that she thought she knew about herself. She hadn't known she had such a capacity for passion, indeed had often assumed she was more than a little cold in that department, for never before had she found it impossible to resist temptation. And Dante was the very essence of temptation on her terms. With him she was weak, she acknowledged. But was that necessarily a bad thing?

It was a fling, a little holiday fling, nothing more serious. Neither of them was looking for or expecting anything more and on that basis they were a good match. As he had pointed out, he wasn't auditioning as potential husband material. And yet as she glanced at him when they reached the car again and he smiled, a feeling like trapped sunshine expanded inside her chest, making it feel tight. It was an infatuation, she told herself, responses heightened by the heat of the Italian sun and the taste of freedom she was enjoying. She was young and full of hormones, finally exploring a side of herself that had been on a leash for too long. What she was experiencing was normal, she reasoned frantically, not something she needed to worry about.

'You've gone so quiet. I'm used to you chattering,' Dante confided, shooting the car to a halt by the garages.

'I'm making a mental list of all the things I have to check before the ball next week.' Topsy hesitated and then forced herself to continue, 'Don't say anything about—'

'Of course I won't.'

Topsy's tension level dropped a little. 'If your mother or Vittore knew or guessed, it could make for an uncomfortable atmosphere,' she warned him.

She scrambled out of the car in haste, desperate to have a shower and relocate her poise. At that moment she was as awkward as a clumsy teenager around him and it galled her.

'Topsy…' His voice halted her as she sped across the

courtyard towards the servants' entrance at the back of the castle.

Reluctantly, she turned, amber eyes welding to his lean, darkly handsome face and the sardonic expression he wore. 'Yes?'

'I have work to do as well. I'll see you later,' he told her smoothly.

Topsy fled, heart beating as fast as if she were sprinting. He could set her alight with one look, one word, even the rich accented timbre of his beautiful voice. It was as if she had succumbed to the worst possible addiction and the strength of it frightened her.

Dante walked into his study, a dark frown pleating his ebony brows. Topsy was always surprising him. Once he had realised just how inexperienced she was, he had feared she might be a little clingy—and he hated clingy women like poison—but she had taken off like a bat out of hell without even trying to instigate the expected fact-finding dialogue about where they were going and what they were doing. Her restraint had disconcerted him.

It was an affair, no big deal, he reflected impatiently, but the circumstances were not what he would've chosen. She was his mother's employee and, just as he had always ensured that his relationship with his staff at the bank remained strictly above board, he would not have chosen to become intimately involved with anyone working for his family. But then that was before he met Topsy and before he enjoyed a session of amazingly vibrant and satisfying sex that had only left him craving more. There was always an exception to the rule and he could not remember when he had last craved more of a woman so soon after having her.

In retrospect he could barely believe that he had cherished such sordid suspicions of her relationship with his stepfather and with Mikhail Kusnirovich. He was more taken aback by the acknowledgement that he had become so cynical about women that he had automatically distrusted the evidence of his own eyes and had decided, on no very strong evidence, that Topsy was a promiscuous little schemer up to no good. Well, she certainly wasn't promiscuous.

Topsy stood in the shower reliving his every touch and, with a frustrated groan, leant back against the cold tiled wall, angry with herself for being so susceptible. Where was her brain when she needed it? It was a physical infatuation, nothing more threatening and it would run its course soon enough.

Dante didn't join them for dinner and she was guiltily relieved when she heard that he was dining with his old friend, Marco, one of the local doctors, but she was also a tad irritated that he hadn't thought to tell her that he was going out. So, now was she trying to attach strings to him? He didn't belong to her; she didn't belong to him. Their lovemaking in the woods might never be repeated, she conceded, because it was perfectly possible that he might have decided that their intimacy was a bad idea.

On that thought her heart sank as if a giant stone had been attached to it and to give her thoughts a new direction she rang Kat and listened to her beloved sister burbling happily about what a wonderful surprise her latest pregnancy had proved. Kat rang off when Mikhail walked through the door of their London home. That was true love, Topsy reflected wryly, that desperate longing to reconnect after a parting, no matter how brief.

She was lying in bed around midnight reading an absorbing research paper on non-equilibrium dynamics and random matrices when her door opened, breaking her concentration. Closing the door, Dante strode towards her, his tall well-built physique bare but for a towel rather negligently looped round his lean hips. The very sight of him shook her up, her tummy flipping at the explosive effect of him in the flesh. He looked absolutely gorgeous. Her mouth opened but no sound came out.

'I warned you that I didn't do one-night stands,' he quipped, dropping the towel without an ounce of self-consciousness and sliding into bed beside her. He glanced at the article and raised a brow. 'Light reading?'

'One of my favourite fields,' she admitted.

'A doctorate in advanced maths,' Dante recounted. 'You could have an incredible career in a bank.'

'I'm not particularly interested in quantitative finance or statistics,' Topsy told him, settling back against the pillows and striving to seem relaxed even though every nerve ending was jumping at his arrival. 'I think I'd like to go into theoretical research. I want to take my time about choosing where I work.'

Dante pressed his sensual mouth against the remarkably sensitive slope between her neck and shoulder and she shivered violently. 'You *can't*,' she told him baldly.

Luxuriant black lashes lifted enquiringly on emerald-green eyes and her heart lurched.

Topsy turned to face him, her cheeks hot as fire. 'I can't…I'm…um…sore,' she confessed grudgingly. 'Seems there *is* a drawback to being a virgin. I'm off the menu for now.'

'I shouldn't have been so very greedy this afternoon, *gioia mia*.' Dante sighed.

Topsy rubbed her cheek over a broad bare shoulder smooth as golden satin, a small hand travelling across his pectoral muscles and wandering south, feeling whipcord muscles flex and tense every step of the way. 'That doesn't mean we can't do other things,' she told him with a hunger she couldn't hide, couldn't suppress, and simply couldn't deny.

He expelled his breath when she found him hot, hard and ready for her attentions. She loved touching him, literally could not bear to take her hands from him while she watched him respond to her every tentative caress, his inky lashes dropping lower over smouldering, wildly appreciative eyes.

'I might be a bit clumsy at this,' she warned him in advance.

'I'm all yours,' Dante breathed hoarsely, fingers gliding slowly through the silken fall of her hair where it lay across his thigh. 'Experiment all you like…'

And she did, revelling in the reactions he couldn't hide, triumphant only when he finally let go of his ironclad self-control and shuddered and groaned his pleasure. Yet inexplicably it felt even better when afterwards he wrapped his arms round her and, even though he put out too much heat for comfort and took up too much room in her bed, she resisted the idea of waking him and sending him back to his own bedroom and could not understand why she wasn't being more sensible.

Over the breakfast table the next morning she studied his bold bronzed profile, remembering how she had made him feel, how he had made her feel, wondering when the infatuation would start to burn out and let her return to normal. She didn't like the out-of-control sensation he gave her. She liked to know exactly where she was going and what she was doing at all times.

After breakfast, Dante drove Topsy to a coffee morning for his mother's favourite charity, which was being held in a local town. It had been Sofia Leonetti's repeated experience of miscarriage that had first persuaded her to set up a local support group for fellow sufferers and the organisation had eventually become a charity. Topsy left Dante being fussed over by several middle-aged women and plied with coffee and cakes while she sped off to deliver the short speech Sofia had written for her. The older woman had already personally informed the committee members that she was standing down as chairwoman with immediate effect but Topsy gathered that Dante hadn't known because he studied her with frowning eyes when she referred to his mother's resignation.

'So, when are you planning to tell me what's *really* going on with my mother?' Dante enquired, tucking her back into his car.

Topsy directed a strained glance at him. 'What do you mean?'

'Don't play games with me,' Dante advised impatiently. 'My mother's not herself. Stepping down from the charity she struggled to build up is not normal behaviour for her. There's something badly wrong.'

'I don't know what you're talking about,' Topsy said woodenly, knowing it was not her place to reveal what Sofia preferred to keep secret while hoping that the older woman would decide to come clean soon.

'You're a lousy liar. I have sufficient respect for Vittore to assume that he wouldn't be walking around whistling if my mother were seriously ill,' Dante told her, strong jaw line hardening. 'For that reason alone I've kept quiet but I expect *more* from you.'

Topsy paled at that unexpected admission. 'Vittore and Sofia have private affairs about which I know nothing,' she pointed out uncomfortably.

'But you're remarkably cosy with them both. Don't think I haven't noticed that fact, *gioia mia*. And you may work for my mother but I expect your first loyalty to be to *me*.'

Topsy turned stunned eyes to his lean, hard-boned face. 'You can't be serious.'

Dante examined his expectations and realised to his surprise that he was deadly serious. His mother might pay her salary but Dante demanded one hundred per cent loyalty from Topsy when it came to anything that he considered to be important to him. He *expected* to be put first, he acknowledged, possibly he even took it for granted because women had always been so eager to please him, but he saw nothing wrong with his outlook.

'You're not being fair.'

'And you're not being honest or realistic,' Dante condemned without hesitation. 'Reverse our positions and ask yourself how you would feel if I was lying to you about your family. You know more than you're willing to admit.'

'We're having our first row,' Topsy commented stiffly.

'No, we're not,' Dante parried, skimming a forefinger down over her thigh in a teasing gesture. As he smoothly demonstrated his complete sexual power over her, a chill of apprehension assailed Topsy because he made her feel vulnerable. 'When I lose my temper you'll know about it.'

CHAPTER EIGHT

THE FOLLOWING EVENING, Dante gave Topsy a wonderful surprise by keeping his promise to arrange a tour of the Uffizi art gallery for her. He had secured tickets for a private viewing. Sofia surveyed Topsy's glowing face, her mouth tightening as her gaze briefly skimmed to her son's nonchalant expression. 'It'll be a very dressy occasion, Topsy. Those champagne viewings always are.'

Having piled her hair up on top of her head, Topsy dug a sleek black cocktail frock from her wardrobe and clasped her diamond necklace round her throat. Feet encased in fashionable and perilously high heels, she walked downstairs to join Dante.

'Between the hairstyle and the shoes, you've gained about a foot in height, *cara mia*,' Dante commented, the very epitome of designer elegance in a well-cut dinner jacket and narrow black trousers. Superbly elegant, he looked, as always, stunning.

'You suit diamonds,' he added, noting how the white-fire sparkle of the jewels seemed to reflect the brightness of her dark eyes.

Topsy involuntarily touched the diamonds at her throat. 'An eighteenth birthday present.'

'Kusnirovich?' Dante surmised.

'Yes.'

'Obviously you've known him a long time,' Dante commented, oddly irritated by the realisation and resisting an even stranger urge to tell her to take the necklace off. 'It looks like a very generous gift.'

Topsy simply nodded agreement, not wanting to say anything else and encourage more questions. Naturally he was curious about her friendship with Mikhail, who only socialised in the most exclusive circles, and while she didn't want to reveal the truth about her wealthy and powerful relatives neither did she want to lie to Dante.

The gilded event at the Uffizi was a true art lovers' dream. Beautifully dressed people sipping champagne strolled at their leisure through the rooms of magnificent artworks. There was no noise, no queues, no crush to struggle through and this time around she could even appreciate the splendid ornate interior of the building itself.

When she paused rapt before Raphael's Madonna of the Goldfinch, Dante remarked that she seemed to know exactly what she wanted to view.

'This is one of my sister's favourite paintings. She used to be an art restorer in a museum and, when I was growing up, she took me to all sorts of places to see wonderful pieces of art,' Topsy confided. 'She wanted to be sure that I got a really well-rounded education and she didn't quite trust my boarding school.'

'You attended boarding school?'

Topsy sent him an amused look as she paused in front of Caravaggio's Bacchus. 'I was a gifted child and, obviously, I was a scholarship girl. Kat could never have afforded the fees.'

'How gifted were you?' Dante prompted.

'I don't like talking about that, Dante,' she admitted quietly. 'I learn incredibly fast and I have a photographic memory for facts and figures. Let's leave it there.'

A tall beautiful brunette in pearls and black and white polka-dot silk strolled up to them and addressed Dante with the familiarity of an old friend. Her need to ignore Topsy's presence told Topsy all she needed to know about the brunette's true source of interest and she drifted off.

'Why on earth did you walk off?' Dante demanded ten minutes later when he finally ran her to ground in the Titian room.

'She was flirting with you and being rude to me. I don't waste my time with people like that,' Topsy told him without apology.

'We were lovers many years ago,' Dante admitted with a fluid shrug. 'She means nothing to me now.'

As soon I will mean nothing, Topsy's logic supplied, sending a wave of gooseflesh across her exposed skin. Her slim shoulders set back as if she was bracing herself for that day. She knew that their affair lacked the longevity gene. Soon, Dante would head back to the bank headquarters in Milan and Topsy, and having only agreed to work for Sofia for three months, she was returning to London at the end of the summer. He was a holiday fling, she told herself urgently, scanning his perfect profile in a hungry stolen glance. And the end of a holiday fling would sting, not *hurt*.

'That was an amazing experience,' Topsy assured him when she slid back into his car. 'I thank you from the bottom of my heart. Kat will be so envious when she hears that I attended a private viewing.'

'There's something I want to discuss with you,' Dante told her softly. 'I have to fly to Milan tomorrow for forty-eight hours—there's something of a crisis and I have a government minister to advise. I want you to come with me, *gioia mia.*'

Dismayed though she was at the prospect of being without him for even that short length of time, Topsy was very practical. 'That's impossible. There's only three days to go to the fancy-dress ball. I can't possibly leave your mother to deal with any last-minute hitches that might arise.'

'I heard her say that you'd taken very little time off.'

'That's true but that was my choice and it doesn't mean I'm willing to leave her in the lurch. The ball is a huge amount of work and loads of little things could go wrong.'

'She has Vittore.'

Tensing at his persistence, Topsy shot him an angry look of reproach. 'You really don't like hearing the word no, do you? My answer is no, sorry…and thanks for asking…but *no.*'

'It should be yes,' Dante contradicted harshly, making no attempt to conceal his dissatisfaction with her decision.

'Arrogant…*much*?' Topsy quipped. 'You don't get to tell me what I should and shouldn't do.'

'*Non importa*…no matter,' he pronounced with dismissive finality, wide, sensual mouth clenching into a hard line.

Well, at least she was seeing *all* his flaws, Topsy reflected unhappily as she lay alone in her bed for the first night that week. Dante was spoilt by having enjoyed too much attention from over-eager-to-please women. He should not be willing to put her in a difficult position with his mother when they could perfectly well cope with being apart for a mere forty-eight hours.

'Topsy…?'

In the act of crossing the hall the next morning to head into the dining room for breakfast, Topsy spun and raised an imperious questioning brow when Dante beckoned to her from his study doorway. She was still angry with him and it didn't help that he was so extraordinarily handsome in his formal dark suit teamed with a very chic fuchsia-pink shirt and black tie that one glimpse of him literally stole the breath from her lungs.

'A word before I leave?' he added expectantly.

Unimpressed, Topsy stalked towards him, outraged by his infuriating self-assurance. 'When you say, "Jump," I will never say, "How high?"' she swore in a sizzling undertone.

Instead of answering back, Dante swept her off her feet and up into his arms with the easy strength that always shook her. Linking her arms round his neck, he backed into the study and sealed her mouth to his in a passionately hungry kiss that jolted every skin cell in her treacherous body. 'You'll miss me,' he husked against the swollen contours of her lush mouth. 'I'll miss you.'

'But we'll live,' Topsy pointed out prosaically.

'For a woman who wants a romantic male that was a very unromantic comment,' Dante mocked, eyes dancing with amusement. 'You've brought fun back into my life, *cara mia*.'

He lowered her slowly and reluctantly to the floor again. Her fingers curled into fists by her side because for the first time in her life she wanted to hurl herself back into a man's arms but she wouldn't let herself behave like an adoring schoolgirl. Fun, *his* word and very revealing it was, she acknowledged grimly. Fun was never serious and never permanent. Fun was a fleeting thing of the moment and appreciated as such.

The next morning, Topsy had breakfast with Sofia in her private sitting room. With Vittore in Florence, the two women ran over last-minute changes to the seating arrangements for the many celebrities attending the dinner being held before the ball. Topsy noted the name of the woman seated beside Dante.

'Cosima Ruffini?' she repeated the name. 'Why does that name seem familiar?'

The older woman tensed. 'Perhaps you've seen it in a magazine. Cosima is a famous fashion model.'

Topsy nodded, wondering if Cosima was being placed beside Dante to entertain him. Was his mother playing cupid? And if that was the case, it was none of her business. Fun, she reminded herself doggedly, she and Dante were only having fun and temporary fun at that.

'Topsy…? May I be frank with you?' Sofia asked rather abruptly.

Topsy glanced up from the list, her mouth still crammed full of delicious melting croissant, and she nodded agreement, wondering what on earth her employer wanted to say.

'It's about Dante,' his mother volunteered. 'He's my son and I love him very much but I don't want you to get hurt.'

Topsy's croissant suddenly turned to sawdust in her mouth while colour rose hotly to her cheeks. She had thought that she and Dante were being so discreet that nobody would realise there was anything going on and, self-evidently, she had been fooling herself on that score.

'Dante doesn't seem to get involved in serious relationships. I worry that he may be what is nowadays called a commitment-phobe,' Sofia admitted uncomfortably. 'But he wasn't always like that.'

Topsy finally managed to swallow and clear her throat. 'Neither of us is looking for anything serious,' she hastened to declare.

Her companion lifted her chin and gave Topsy a measured look. 'I've seen the way you look at my son and it worries me.'

Topsy paled, not knowing how to answer that for she *knew* she was always looking at Dante, always mesmerically drawn to him when he was around, but wasn't that a physical pull rather than a mental one? She reddened, knowing the distinction was not one she could raise in present company. I only want him for his body would be a conversational killer, she reflected a little hysterically, because Sofia had taken her very much by surprise in opening the subject.

'Dante's wife used to look at him the same way,' the older woman told her softly.

Topsy frowned in disbelief. '*Wife?* His wife?' she repeated.

'I see he hasn't mentioned his marriage.' Sofia seemed unsurprised by Dante's oversight in that regard. 'Dante got married when he was twenty-one. Emilia and he virtually grew up together. She died within a year of their wedding—she walked in front of a car in Florence and she was killed instantly. Dante was inconsolable.'

A tragic experience of first love, Dante 'inconsolable'. That was a challenging image, which disconcerted Topsy for it had never occurred to her that he might be concealing such a past. 'He was very young when he married,' Topsy remarked abstractedly, thinking it typical that Mikhail had chosen to tell her about the three mistresses but not the tragedy that had preceded that change in Dante's private life. 'And no, you're right, he didn't discuss it with me.'

'Why would he have? It's a long time ago. I'm telling you now only because I don't want you to think too badly of my son. I doubt that he's ready for an exclusive relationship,' Sofia opined, 'but sometimes people do know instantly when they've met their perfect match…'

Topsy glanced up again. 'Do they?'

'It may have taken Vittore and I thirty years to finally get together but we first met and fell in love when we were sixteen years old,' Sofia divulged quietly.

Topsy was stunned by that information. 'Why did you break up?'

Sofia looked sad. 'Vittore was the son of the town drunk and I was the daughter of the most successful local businessman. My family would never have allowed us to be together. My father owed Dante's father a great deal of money and when I agreed to marry Aldo, the debt was written off.'

'That must've been horrible for you!' Topsy breathed in horror.

'It was but in those days you did as your parents told you.'

'So, how on earth did you meet Vittore again?'

Sofia grinned. 'I found him on the Internet and do you know? The minute I saw him it was like the thirty years hadn't happened and we didn't want to waste any more time,' she confided.

'What does Dante think of that story?' Topsy frowned. 'You haven't told him, have you? But it's so romantic, Sofia.'

'Dante is not a romantic man,' Sofia declared ruefully. 'He would think us both even more foolish if he knew the truth.'

Touched by that story, Topsy took a while to get back to checking the seating arrangements. Her brain was teeming with busy thoughts. It was a shock to learn that Dante had once been married and that he had gone from losing the wife he loved to taking on three mistresses. Had he tried to bury his pain in rampant sex?

Whatever, Sofia's warning earlier was kindly meant even though Topsy had not needed it for she'd seen from the start that Dante was not interested in anything more than a fleeting affair. And she was content with that, wasn't she? She would return to London a lot less ignorant of men and look back on Dante as her first lover with fondness rather than regret. She had no other expectations, absolutely *none*, she assured herself doggedly, silencing and squashing the cry of pain deep down inside her. If she had accidentally managed to become a little too attached to him she would soon overcome that foolishness.

In Milan, Dante was frowning and tossing his phone on the desk. He had been candid with Cosima and, to be fair, she had matched his candour. Choice didn't come into the situation when the PR power of the ball would have a direct effect on the funds being raised. What was he supposed to say to Topsy? But then why was he worrying about saying anything? He reminded himself that Topsy had refused to accompany him to Milan. He didn't owe her any explanations, nor did he want to take their affair in a direction that implied that he wanted more. *Accidenti!* He didn't like complications and hated hassle, particularly with women. Keep it simple, he told himself impatiently. Saying nothing was wiser.

The night before the ball, Topsy agreed to join Gaetano for a drink in the village café when he rang. She was grateful for the distraction the invite gave because she had repeatedly and pointlessly revisited her decision not to go to Milan with Dante and just as often she had told herself that she would not rearrange her life, ignore her safe boundaries or fall down on the job she was doing simply for Dante's benefit. She had made the right decision and she had no regrets, and in the same way she wasn't sitting around waiting for Dante to come home like faithful Penelope. After all, he hadn't phoned her *once* since his departure.

Dressed in a bright geometric print shift and high

wedge sandals, she skipped down the steps and climbed into Gaetano's car.

'I'd have taken you for a meal but I don't want my family to get the wrong idea and assume we're dating,' the builder confided ruefully. 'Before you know where you are my mother will get the baby albums out.'

'Your mamma already told me that you had gorgeous curls as a baby,' Topsy told him with a giggle.

'Besides, I hear you're seeing Dante,' Gaetano commented.

Eyes wide, Topsy swivelled in her seat. 'Who told you that?'

'My kid brother saw you walking hand in hand through Florence,' Gaetano admitted. 'There's no such thing as privacy around here, particularly not when it comes to love lives. Gossip is the spice of life.'

Topsy seriously hoped that nobody knew about the picnic in the woods and went pink. 'Dante and I...well, we're just a casual thing.'

'I wouldn't want to tread on his toes,' Gaetano confided. 'When I phoned, I thought you'd say no to coming out.'

'I don't even know when Dante's due home,' Topsy admitted.

Gaetano asked her what she was wearing to the ball. 'It's a glorified maid's outfit,' she confided. 'Sofia wanted me to choose something fancy but basically I'm staff and she's the hostess, so I thought it made sense to choose something plain.'

'You could never look plain...'

In a white-hot rage shielded by formidable cool, Dante focused on her vivid little face from across the street. Infuriatingly, she looked as though she was enjoying herself. He had been incredulous when he learned that she had gone out with another man when he was within an hour of coming home and he had been forced to sit through a session of his mother pontificating over whether or not Gaetano could get over his ex quickly enough to properly appreciate Topsy. As far as he was concerned, Topsy needed no other male appreciation. He was convinced that if he left her alone by the side of the road for five minutes he would find her surrounded by men when he came back. Topsy's *je ne sais quoi* sexiness and energy were a magnetic draw for the opposite sex.

Topsy very nearly fell off her chair when Dante strode into the café. Within seconds the proprietor was by his side and hurrying off to serve him. She studied Dante, hopelessly greedy for the sheer rush of seeing him again, her heart rate kicking up, a steady tension infiltrating her every muscle. As she met his remarkable green eyes her surroundings vanished into oblivion. It was a severe overreaction to his presence and she knew it was but she couldn't suppress it. A physical infatuation might have seized hold of her formerly controlled self, but her brain told her she could cope with it as long as she didn't let it take over entirely.

Gaetano was already cheerfully exchanging talk of the ball with Dante as he sat down, a glass of wine arriving magically fast at his elbow. Topsy glanced across the table at him, noting the heavy black lashes that concealed his eyes, the spectacular bone structure beneath his olive-toned skin. Dante had been married, she found herself thinking afresh. He had promised to love, honour and share with another woman and she had died and he had ended up alone. Alone but for the three mistresses, she reminded herself staunchly, keen not to idealise her image of him. Without warning he looked at her and a surge of unwelcome heat and awareness blossomed between her legs. Conscious her breasts were swelling and her nipples tightening, she sucked in a deep audible breath and soft pink warmed her cheeks.

'You won't mind if I take Topsy home,' Dante murmured to Gaetano.

'I've only had one drink,' Topsy objected. 'This is virtually my first break from work in two days.'

'I own a wine cellar. If you want to drink, you can do it with me.'

'And what cave did you emerge from?' Topsy asked sweetly. 'Obviously it was a very recent move.'

Beside her, Gaetano was trying not to laugh but Topsy wasn't amused. She didn't want Dante ordering her around. He didn't own her, he didn't have the right to dictate where she went and what she did and even if she had loved him she would have fought him to the death on that issue.

'*Madre di Dio*...OK, I should've phoned!' Dante ground out the grudging admission between even white teeth.

'Perhaps...' Topsy tossed back, refusing to give ground, her dark eyes veiled as she wondered if he had consciously decided *not* to phone while he was away, if indeed he was as set as she was on respecting the limits of their relationship. And if she was right in her suspicion, why was he behaving that way? And why change course to chase her down when she wasn't immediately available?

'*Venga qui*...come here,' Dante breathed in a driven undertone as he suddenly sprang to his feet, six feet plus inches of rippling impatience, extending a lean, elegant hand to pull her upright.

'See you tomorrow night,' Gaetano told her with an appreciative grin, saluting them both with his glass as Dante closed an arm round Topsy's slight shoulders.

'I hate it when you try and tell me what to do,' Topsy stretched up to mutter in Dante's ear as he walked her across the street to his car.

'It would have caused a scene if I'd just lifted you and carried you out,' Dante parried in a mild tone that suggested his determination to retrieve her at any cost was perfectly normal.

Inside the car she couldn't resist any more: she closed her fingers into his luxuriant black hair and dragged his beautiful mouth down to hers. Fireworks went off inside her, instant blazing, wildly colourful fireworks, and the connection left her weak. He pressed her back into the passenger seat. 'Next time, I'll phone,' he promised.

'Gaetano's only a friend.'

'I know. He's still hoping his ex's marriage breaks down, so that he can get her back,' Dante confided with a sardonic twist of his mouth.

They walked back into the castle. There was nobody about. 'I'm going to get changed,' Topsy murmured.

Dante scooped her up into his arms on the first landing and carried her up the next flight. 'We'll sleep in my room tonight.'

'But I didn't say.'

'I'm so hungry for you, *bella mia*. I didn't know two days could seem so long,' Dante groaned into her hair, the ache in his voice stirring something tender within her.

He settled her down on his huge four-poster bed and she kicked off her shoes, reflecting that it was only a week since he had brought her there and she had walked out again, determined not to succumb. What had happened to that resolve, the strength of her original resistance? Already that night seemed like a lifetime ago. Dante lifted the house phone to order champagne.

'I don't need another drink,' she told him wryly. 'I only meant that I was enjoying getting out and having some company.'

'I'm company,' Dante told her very seriously as he took off his jacket, jerked loose his tie and embarked on his shirt buttons.

'No, you're my lover…that's different,' Topsy contended. 'Gaetano and I are friends.'

'And what are we?'

'Chance acquaintances having sex,' Topsy said a little painfully. 'We fell into this.'

'There's nothing wrong with that,' Dante reasoned, flipping her round to run down the zip on her dress. 'Pre-planning can make life boring.'

'Funnily enough, I would have said that you plan everything right down to the last detail.'

For a split second, Dante hesitated as he lifted her dress off over her head, his attention dwelling on the glorious swell of her breasts seguing down into her impossibly tiny waist and the voluptuous curve of her bottom. She was right: he usually did plan every move he made. But he hadn't planned on her. He was willing to admit that she was an anomaly in his life and didn't fit the usual mould but he wasn't yet ready to finish the affair. It would end when boredom set in as it always did and when his desire for her no longer drove him.

He caught her to him with impatient hands and his mouth burned on hers. Tasting him, savouring him, she shuddered as he unfastened her bra and stroked her achingly tender nipples. She hadn't expected the evening to end like this but she wanted him, *needed* him in a way she had never imagined she would ever need anyone and, even though that was scary, she could not deny herself the incredible exhilaration of being with him again. She pulled off his shirt, her hands relearning the hard masculine contours of his hair-roughened chest, trailing down to cup and tease his urgent erection, already imagining what it would feel like to have him inside her again.

'I never want to wait with you, *bella mia,*' Dante grated hungrily against her mouth, nipping at her full lower lip, making her whimper as he skated a fingertip across the damp silk of her knickers. 'And I don't believe you want to wait either.'

Topsy was trembling with desire, desperate for the passion he unleashed so naturally in her. Suddenly he was kissing her with the driving demand that always fired up her body, sending tiny snaking thrills of wicked anticipation through her. His caresses became a little rougher, just exactly what she craved at that instant because she was every bit as impatient as he was. His teeth grazed a pouting pink nipple as he wrenched her out of her last garment and a long finger speared into her unbearably sensitive depths. She cried out, helpless in the grip of the passionate need he had awakened.

He grabbed a condom, made use of it and flipped her over onto her stomach, startling her. He pulled up her hips and thrust into her lush damp heat with exquisite force. He swore then in his own language. 'Did I hurt you?'

'Don't you dare stop!' she gasped, breathless with delight. Don't stop, don't stop, don't stop—it was like an unquenchable chant inside her head. Every nerve in her body responded to every plunge of his. Her inner muscles clenched around him, wild heat gathering at her core as he used his hand to stroke the most sensitive spot of all.

'Not going to stop,' he groaned, nipping at her shoulder with his teeth. 'I dreamt of doing this all night, having you over and over again until neither of us can move.'

His pagan rhythm filled her with excitement. Breathing was a challenge when the waves of pleasure were gathering intensity in her pelvis and her heart was hammering at an insane rate. As her body was overpowered by the wild convulsions of orgasm he gave a shout of completion and drove deep one last time. She writhed under him, her body flailing out of control as she reached her peak and lost herself in the exquisite ripples of pleasure.

'You were *so* worth waiting for,' Dante breathed with hoarse emphasis against her cheek as he held her close afterwards.

She tensed as a knock sounded on the door. 'That'll be the champagne.'

He vaulted off the bed, pulled up his trousers and zipped them. Shaken, she watched him, wanting him back in her arms again, struggling not to be embarrassed or ashamed that he hadn't even got completely undressed. The sweet spasms of her fully pleasured body were still quivering through her when he passed her a glass of champagne.

'What are we drinking to?' she whispered.

Shimmering green eyes rested on her. Her hair was wildly tumbled round her heart-shaped face, her luscious pink mouth slightly parted, one pouting breast on display, her creamy thighs exposed. His body hardened again and he gave her a shimmering brilliant smile. 'You look amazing. We're drinking to all the pleasure we can handle, *bella mia*.'

She reached out a hand and closed it over his. 'No, we won't be that selfish. We'll drink to staging a very, very successful fund-raiser tomorrow night,' she contradicted gently.

CHAPTER NINE

LATE AFTERNOON THE next day, Topsy was dealing with the reporters and photographers who had arrived to cover the ball and the many celebrities expected to attend.

'You're part of the household,' one of the women remarked thoughtfully, a redhead with a choppy haircut and bright dark eyes. 'Any titbits to offer on La Principessa and the Conte?'

'Yes, their romance is hot news right now,' another woman chimed in, looking hopeful.

'La Principessa? Sorry, I don't know who you're talking about,' Topsy admitted, knowing that there had been no princess listed among the guests that she could recall.

'Cosima Ruffini,' the redhead extended.

'I didn't know she was a princess.'

'A princess and a count. Those two go together like salt and pepper. We were hoping there'd be an engagement tonight. It would be a great time to make the announcement.'

'Er...Mr Leonetti and the princess are dating?' Topsy prompted tightly, an odd whirring sound in her ears as though she had suddenly become light-headed, a surge of perspiration dampening her skin.

The redhead raised her brows. '*Dio mio*, you are out of touch and I can see *you* aren't going to be much help in the gossip department.'

'Dante and Cosima have been seeing each other for weeks,' the other woman informed her with visible impatience. 'In fact right now they're society's hottest new couple and we can't wait to see their outfits.'

Slowly and very painfully, Topsy could feel her facial muscles freezing while her stomach performed a sickening flip. At first she couldn't credit the enormity of the betrayal, could not bring herself to believe that Dante could possibly have done that to her but her companions were already exchanging chatter that made it clear that Dante and Cosima were in an acknowledged relationship, not one suggested by rumour alone. Shock hit Topsy as hard as an unexpected blow to the back of her skull and she felt horribly ill and exposed. Clearly, Dante had been seeing another woman before Topsy even met him and he had had a fling with Topsy behind his girlfriend's back. Her sense of betrayal, guilt and hurt was so intense it felt like a knife blade sinking into her heart.

'Excuse me for a moment,' she muttered, even her voice fading as she sped off for the cloakroom and a much-needed moment of breathing space in which to collect her chaotic thoughts. In truth she wanted to run out of the castle front door and keep on running but that option was not open. Not only was it her responsibility to ensure that the ball ran smoothly, but she also had her pride. It might be battered but no way was she running away with her tail between her legs because a man had treated her badly! She would see out this nightmare evening to the finish and depart with dignity.

When she emerged again, the photographers were already busily at work in the huge hall. A tall and very beautiful blonde clad in a very full turquoise satin and lace ensemble was regally posing, and even as Topsy hovered behind the crush surrounding the other woman Dante came downstairs and Topsy did not have to look hard to see the proof that her worst imaginings were true because the blonde and Dante were a matching pair, outfits co-ordinated in colour, fabric and design, something which must have been organised weeks earlier when the outfits were chosen. Dante was dressed up like Louis XIV, the French Sun King, and Cosima as one of his mistresses. Topsy searched his devastatingly handsome face, noting the tension etched there as Cosima rested a hand on his arm and leant closer to speak to him. *You bastard*, she thought in indescribable pain as the couple posed for pictures and Cosima made the most of the attention.

Dante had slept with Topsy the night before. She had been so desperately busy all day that she had not seen him since and had thought nothing of it. Now she truly understood why Sofia had warned her off her son, for clearly Sofia had known that there was another woman in Dante's life. An engagement was in the offing? Or had that suggestion been only journalistic excess? And what did it matter to her now anyway? After all, whatever happened now she was finished with Dante. There would be no coming back from such a revelation as his infidelity and deceit.

The celebrities were assembling for the meal and the catering staff, clad in plain brown medieval dresses and mobcaps, were moving round serving drinks. Reluctant to risk being mistaken for a waitress, Topsy had picked a similar dress in green and left off the mob cap supplied. As she checked the seating for the guests she discovered that a famous Italian actor had brought two female companions instead of the allocated one and she gave up her seat to one of the women without regret because the last thing she needed to do right then was share a table with Dante and his truly gorgeous girlfriend.

What an idiot she had been not to ask him if there was anyone else in his life! Why had she assumed that there was no competition? Why hadn't she smelled a rat the instant he came after her? As far as looks went she wasn't in the same league as Cosima Ruffini and only a body transplant could have remedied that hurtful reality. Cosima was a classic beauty.

Pain gripped Topsy as she watched Dante lead his girlfriend into dinner, the two of them effortlessly regal and impressive together. She was remembering him touching *her*, kissing *her*, holding *her* throughout the night and she sped off to convene with the caterers in the kitchen and escape the view of the hottest society couple in Italy surrounded by friends and admirers. She was sick with jealousy and the horrendous pain of betrayal and her own misjudgement, she acknowledged dully. She definitely wasn't as clever and cool as she had believed she was because her fun holiday fling had downshifted into a sleazy conclusion and now she would remember Dante with hatred rather than fondness.

* * *

The ballroom was beautifully decorated with flowers and the band was already playing when Sofia and Vittore entered to officially open the public event. Sofia, splendidly glamorous in crackling golden satin, rose behind the podium to give a short amusing speech, closely followed by Dante, who gave the latest figures for the fund along with the expected travel date for the little girl, Maria, suffering from leukaemia.

Thunderous applause and stamping feet greeted the good news and it was a couple of minutes before Topsy noticed the furore at the top table and rose from her chair in the corner to investigate. Sofia had fainted and Dante had lifted his mother into his arms to carry her out of the room with Vittore hurrying anxiously at his heels. Reluctant though she was to go anywhere near Dante, Topsy was fond of his mother and concerned about her and she followed the small procession into the drawing room where Dante laid his already recovering parent down on a sofa.

'What the hell's wrong with her?' Dante demanded of his hovering stepfather. 'You didn't seem surprised when she fainted.'

'Don't blame Vittore, Dante, it was very hot in there,' Sofia groaned, raising herself against the sofa arm with difficulty. 'This is my fault. I didn't want anyone to know until I had to tell them.'

'Tell them what?' Dante prompted tensely, his concern palpable. 'What's the matter with you? Are you ill?'

Well aware of what was about to be divulged, Topsy darted out of the room to fetch Sofia a reviving glass of water and by the time she returned the other couple's secret had finally been brought out into the open.

Dante was tellingly still staring at his mother in stunned disbelief. 'You're pregnant?' he was saying unevenly. *'Seriously?'*

'At least you didn't say, "at your age" but I know you have to be thinking it,' Sofia muttered waspishly. 'And no, it wasn't planned but we're over the moon about it now that it's happened.'

'Why on earth couldn't you simply tell me?' Dante demanded starkly as Topsy presented his mother with the glass of water.

'At first I thought it was the menopause. I never dreamt that I might still be able to conceive in my late forties,' Sofia confided ruefully. 'Of course I was overjoyed that I *had* but I was also very embarrassed about telling people, particularly because I've had several miscarriages. What would be the point of astonishing people with such an announcement if I was likely to miscarry *again*? And initially it did seem quite likely that this pregnancy wouldn't continue either.'

'But Sofia's been seeing a very good consultant and he advised her to rest as much as possible for what remained of her first trimester. She's doing very well now,' Vittore added, gripping his wife's hand as he settled down on the arm of the sofa beside her.

'That's why I scaled back my busy life to such an extent,' Dante's mother explained ruefully. 'I want this baby. I want this baby very much.'

'Yet you couldn't bring yourself to tell me?' Dante breathed tautly.

'I didn't want to worry you. This is a risky pregnancy,' Sofia conceded honestly. 'I knew you would remember how ill I was the last time I miscarried and I didn't want to put you through that again. I was also afraid that you would urge me to—'

'*Dio mio!* I'm not completely insensitive and would play no part in suggesting you terminate my own little brother or sister!' Dante shot back at her in a strained undertone. 'Yes, I'm afraid you will fall ill again but I can see how much this baby means to you both. All that I'm interested in is keeping you healthy and happy.'

'Thank you, Dante,' Vittore said awkwardly. 'I appreciate your generosity. I do not want Sofia to put herself at risk, I have never wanted that, but you understand that the dream of another child is very dear to her heart.'

Deeming her presence unnecessary, Topsy began to tiptoe tactfully back out of the room.

'Topsy…stop right there!' Dante raked at her when she had not even realised that he had registered her. 'We need to talk.'

'I have nothing to say to you,' Topsy told him succinctly.

'Vittore and I will return to our table in a few minutes,' Sofia murmured, smiling tensely at the younger woman as her attention skimmed uneasily to her son's combative stance. 'Go ahead.'

Within seconds, Dante had crossed the room to Topsy's side, gritty tension etched into every line of his face. She stepped away from the guiding hand he put to her back, his proximity acting like a repellent on her because every time she looked at him she was remembering things she didn't want to remember, thinking thoughts she didn't want to think.

'We'll talk out here,' Dante breathed, pushing wide the door next to the drawing room. The lush plant-filled orangery with its highly decorative mosaic-tiled floor and indoor fountain had wide doors standing open onto the sunlit terrace beyond.

'What is there to say?' Topsy enquired curtly, fingernails biting sharp crescents into her palms as if pain could help her stay in full control.

'I've got plenty. For a start, why didn't you tell me that my mother was pregnant?' Dante demanded, sharply disconcerting her with that choice of topic and angle of attack. 'We're lovers. Why didn't you share that with me?'

We're lovers. That statement stung like a whiplash, reminding her only of her stupidity. He spoke as though nothing had changed but her world had fallen apart and she felt as if she were still stumbling round, struggling to stay upright in the midst of the debris. She was having to fight harder than she had ever fought in her life to stay in control. Nothing, she appreciated dimly, had ever really hurt her badly before; her sisters had protected her too well.

'I couldn't share any of it with you. Sofia wanted her condition kept a secret and it would have been wrong for me to interfere in a family matter. I only found out because of certain symptoms she had and her consultant's visits,' Topsy related flatly.

'My mother almost died the last time she was pregnant. I was fifteen years old and I'll never forget it.' Dante raked fingers through his luxuriant black hair, disordering it, his whole bearing illustrating that Sofia's illness had been a very disturbing experience for him. 'I am *very* concerned about her. You *should* have warned me.'

'I work for your mother. My first loyalty is to her and I respect other people's privacy,' Topsy parried in tart disagreement.

'You still should have told me. I was already very worried about her,' Dante revealed for the first time, pacing restively away from her. 'That's why I came home and stayed on. She had suddenly changed her whole way of life and I could see no good reason for it. Pregnancy never even occurred to me as a possibility. I was more afraid that Vittore might be having an affair.'

'Vittore?' Topsy exclaimed, astonishment bringing animation back to the frozen pallor of her heart-shaped face. 'You would have to be insane or blind to suspect him of infidelity. Vittore worships the ground your mother walks on!'

Dante swung back to her, anger brightening his brilliant green eyes. 'Yet *your* intimacy with him caused a good deal of local gossip!'

'I beg your pardon? My...*intimacy* with Vittore?' Topsy queried with sharp and sceptical distaste.

'Suddenly my mother dropped out of sight and Vittore was seen squiring a young beautiful girl round the countryside. Of course there was talk and suspicion!' Dante retorted crushingly. 'You're not that naïve.'

Topsy was feeling slightly sick as she registered what he was telling her and she cringed at the belated knowledge that she and Vittore had unwittingly become the target of unpleasant local gossip. 'You came back home solely because you thought I might be having an affair with your stepfather?' she questioned in disgust.

'When a young beauty and an older man are seen together too often, people assume the worst.'

Topsy was frowning, staring back at him with her chin raised. 'And you thought that too?' she pressed.

'I was worried that it was a possibility. Obviously my overriding desire was to protect my mother.'

'And yet even thinking that dreadful thing of me, you still tried to get me into bed with you,' she reasoned in shock at that truth.

'Better me than Vittore and, let's be honest, you *do* enjoy an unusually friendly relationship with Vittore.'

'Only because Sofia was unwell when I first started work here and the usual barriers came down once I guessed that she was pregnant. My sisters have been pregnant a half-dozen times in recent years and I'm an old hand at recognising the symptoms. I also spent a lot of time talking Vittore out of his frantic anxiety about your mother's health. That Vittore was feeling so upset and guilty about the situation put more of a burden on your mother,' Topsy pointed out grudgingly, refusing to admit that she had deliberately taken the opportunity to get closer to the older man for more devious reasons of her own. She had wanted to get to know Vittore and find out what kind of a man he was before she approached him with her belief that he could be her father.

Better me than Vittore. That crucial little phrase Dante had used bit deep into Topsy's self-esteem. 'Were you willing to sleep with me to take my attention off Vittore?' she asked bluntly.

At that thorny question, Dante compressed his wide,

sensual mouth. 'That was the original plan but it swiftly became much more complicated because I was very strongly attracted to you on my own behalf.'

Her lip curled, her scorn at that claim unconcealed. Obviously he hadn't cared whether or not she got hurt in the process of his seduction. He had targeted her, wanting only to deflect her from his stepfather, and even though he thought that she might be a shameless slut encouraging the attentions of a married man he had *still* gone to bed with her. That did not say much for his morals, but then that could hardly come as a surprise to her, she reasoned wretchedly. He had betrayed both her trust and Cosima's.

But the sense of hurt Topsy was feeling was even greater because she had honestly believed that Dante had been as blindly, instinctively drawn to her from the outset as she had been to him. Now she was appreciating that that was far from the case. Dante had needed her to want him and had succeeded beyond his wildest dreams, plunging them into an affair that she suspected he would never have had with her under any other circumstances.

'You *planned* to seduce me,' Topsy condemned, stricken, fighting to keep the pain and resentment out of her not quite steady voice when she thought of how intoxicated she had been by his attention and how recklessly trusting and naïve to let her head be turned so easily. Not once had she stopped to think that it was more than a little unreal that such a gorgeous male should be in hot pursuit of her! Why hadn't that occurred to her sooner? After all, she did not possess her sisters' beauty. In fact she was distinctly ordinary in comparison, pretty on a good day and, in her own eyes, dumpy with her lack of height and pronounced curves on a bad one.

'By that stage I was already in over my head, *bella mia*,' Dante fielded in a raw undertone. 'Naturally once I realised you were a virgin I knew you were innocent of any involvement with Vittore and that the rumours about the two of you were mere gossip.'

'Don't call me your beauty. I'm not. Cosima is.' Topsy whirled away and stared at the humming-bird fountain fanning down a shower of sparkling water droplets to dapple the surface of the pool below. She was already cursing her unruly tongue for she had not wanted to confront him about Cosima. His relationship with the other woman was an unarguable fact and she was not going to ditch her pride to fight with him over that unhappy truth. Dante had wanted to distract her from Vittore and he had succeeded to a level she couldn't believe, even making her forget why she had come to Italy in the first place. She had come to Castello Leonetti solely to get to know the man she believed might be her father but since Dante entered the picture she had barely seen Vittore.

'It may look like that. Perhaps I should have mentioned her.'

'There's no perhaps about it!' Topsy hissed back at him as she spun back to face him, that casual comment cutting deep. 'I had a right to know that there was another woman in your life!'

'Let's not have this conversation here and now,' Dante urged in an undertone, eyes locked to her distraught face as if he couldn't look away. 'We'll discuss this when the ball is over.'

'Have you forgotten that I'm staying tonight and I'm planning to dance until dawn?' another voice interposed and Cosima Ruffini, looking every inch a princess in her grand turquoise ball gown, strolled deeper into the orangery to subject Topsy to a head-to-toe scornful assessment that left Topsy's cheeks burning. 'She's not your type at all. What could you possibly see in her?'

'Cosima,' Dante growled. 'We have an agreement.'

'And you're cheating,' Cosima pronounced dulcetly, smoky dark eyes hard as jet, scarlet lips pouting in challenge. 'You're with her when you're supposed to be with me and this place is swarming with reporters and photographers...'

As Cosima planted a possessive hand on Dante's arm Topsy walked away fast without another word. Nothing more needed to be said. Cosima evidently knew that Dante had not been faithful and did not seem upset. But then Cosima had mentioned that they had some sort of *agreement*. Thinking about what that agreement might encompass sent a shudder of very moral disgust travelling through Topsy. It was difficult to feel guilty about having slept with Cosima's man when Cosima was such a tough case and seemingly willing to overlook infidelity.

Topsy's cell phone vibrated in her pocket and she dug it out, pinning it to her ear.

'It's Kat. You have to come home immediately,' her sister relayed in a staccato burst. 'Something's happened and you can't be abroad and unprotected while it's going on. You'll be picked up early tomorrow morning. Can you pack up quickly? It *is* an emergency.'

Topsy's head was spinning, her mind buzzing like

an angry wasp, concern building. 'Can't you just tell me what's happened?'

'Not over the phone. It's not a secure line,' Kat warned her. 'So, please don't say anything else.'

Topsy dug the phone back into her pocket. What had happened to which member of her family that could be called an emergency? A kidnapping? Her blood ran cold. It was a reasonable fear with her family circle. She went straight off to find Sofia, waiting until the older woman was free to tell her that a family crisis had arisen and she needed to return to London immediately. She wasn't quite sure that Dante's mother believed the excuse and didn't blame her because the call to come home was a case of perfect timing when Topsy could not face staying in Italy if it meant seeing Dante daily.

CHAPTER TEN

'I'LL BE VERY sad to see you leave,' Sofia confided. 'I've loved having you here, Topsy. You brighten my day and fit in so well with us. If only…' Her eyes veiling, the older woman clearly thought better of what she might have been about to say. 'Perhaps you'll come and visit when we've moved into our new home.'

'I would like that very much,' Topsy said warmly, bending down to enable Sofia to kiss her on both cheeks.

From the back of the room, Topsy watched Dante and Cosima glide round the dance floor while cameras flashed all around them, Cosima occasionally striking a glamorous pose and smiling to display pearly teeth. All the life seemed to be squeezed out of her heart and it was a leaden weight inside her chest, a constant nagging reminder of loss and pain. She wondered then when it had happened, when the fun fling had turned serious for her, serious enough to wound and cause lasting damage.

Last night she had wakened to find herself wrapped round Dante like a vine and she had shifted away until two arms very firmly retrieved her, welding her back into stirring connection with his hot body, refusing to allow her to keep her distance. And she had looked at him in the moonlight, her attention roaming over his superb bone structure, the twin dark fans of his lashes, his beautiful mouth softer and fuller in repose, and her heart had jumped as if she were on a Big Dipper ride of thrills and spills. Well, she had had the thrill, now she supposed she was in full spill mode and it was time to pay the piper for her idiocy. Few women, after all, would ever be able to claim that they had been seduced to keep them out of another man's bed. And when she had wanted Dante so badly, did she even have the right to call it seduction?

She watched Vittore sliding an arm round Sofia, the warmth of his smile for his wife full of the love that Dante evidently couldn't read. She so desperately wanted to speak to Vittore before she left but she could not speak to him while he was with Sofia. And she might never receive another opportunity. Sofia had said she would invite her back to Italy but people often said such things in passing and it was doubtful that she had really meant it.

Topsy was on the way back from the kitchens, having sorted out a slight conflict between the caterers and the castle kitchen staff, when she saw the older man crossing the hall and seized her chance.

'Vittore?' she called. 'Could I have a word?'

He came to a halt with a look of surprise. 'Sofia told me you're leaving. It's very sudden.'

'Family crisis, I'm afraid. Could you give me five minutes to chat to you about something?' Topsy asked apprehensively.

'Of course. I'm sure Dante won't mind if we make use of his study.' Dark eyes frankly curious, Vittore pushed open the door.

'I have a request to make of you,' Topsy confided once they were safe from being overheard. 'But first I should tell you certain things. My mother's name is Odette Taylor.'

Vittore was stunned. He stiffened, that name clearly still familiar to him even after all the time that had passed.

'I suspected she might be the woman you were involved with all those years ago in London.' Topsy compressed her lips. 'She's not a kind or honest person and I won't pretend otherwise. I have virtually no contact with her.'

'I do not understand how you came to be working here. It cannot surely be a coincidence?' Vittore prompted, frowning with concern. 'The world is not that small.'

'It's not a coincidence.' And then Topsy got on with what she had to do and told him in as few words as possible about growing up with the belief that her father was Paolo Valdera and then discovering six years earlier that she was not his child.

'And what does…this have to do with me?' Vittore asked, although she could see he was beginning to suspect by the pleat in his brow and the intent look in his unusually stern gaze.

'My mother lied about my father's identity because she believed Paolo was a better financial bet. She admitted that to me and a couple of months ago I had to do her a favour before she would finally tell me the name of the man she believes—'

'Odette told you that I was your father,' Vittore guessed, his astonishment unconcealed. 'Yes, of course

I can see what way this conversation is going but I really don't think it is very likely.'

'And you could be right. There may be nothing in her claim at all because Odette does tell lies whenever it suits her to do so,' Topsy conceded, perspiration beading her short upper lip, embarrassment almost threatening to swallow her voice alive as she made that lowering admission yet again. 'But as you're the only lead I have I'd be grateful if you would agree to a DNA test so that we can both know for sure. I promise you that I don't want anything from you but information and that I will not discuss this with anyone else. I also appreciate that this is a particularly stressful time for you and I do not want you to tell Sofia and risk upsetting her in any way.'

'I would not take that risk.' Vittore shook his dark head slowly as though to clear it from the shock she had given him. 'I *can't* be your father! I understand that you want to know one way or the other but I do wish that you had come to me with this weeks ago.'

'I was trying to build up to it slowly but events have rather taken over instead and now I have to leave,' Topsy admitted ruefully. 'I really am sorry to bother you with this, especially if turns out to be another piece of my mother's nonsense.'

'For a DNA test you will need to give a sample. I suggest that you get that taken care of here before you leave and inform me of what arrangements have been made,' Vittore pointed out seriously. 'I will agree to the test to put your mind at rest and because I know that I was with your mother around the time of your conception and it is reasonable for you to ask.'

'Thank you. I really do appreciate it,' Topsy told

him sincerely, her heart beating very up tempo as some of her nervous tension began to leak out of her again.

'And if there is anything in this, we will *definitely* be seeing you again,' the older man pointed out with a rueful, utterly charming smile, which was very much Topsy's smile had either of them but recognised it. 'One advantage you do have from my point of view, and please don't take this the wrong way—you bear very little resemblance to your mother in either looks or character.'

Topsy left him again in better spirits because he had dealt with her belief that he could be her father very kindly and he was willing to help, which was almost more than she had hoped for because she had feared he would angrily refuse her request. She went back to supervising the ball, chasing after first a mislaid purse and then a fur stole as some older guests began to depart while the younger ones made the most of the more contemporary music now being played and got up to throw themselves round the dance floor. It was an exhausting evening. Sofia and Vittore went upstairs about one in the morning and Dante took over as host with Cosima still by his side, at which point Topsy decided that she had done her duty and could retreat to her room to pack and check out the Internet for somewhere local where she could have a DNA sample taken.

When she entered her room, she turned the key in the lock. She doubted very much that Dante would approach her with Cosima staying under the same roof but she wasn't prepared to take the risk. She had nothing polite to say to him and screaming at him, revealing how very hurt she was, would only mortify what remained of her pride. She was grateful for the distraction of wondering what the crisis was in London that required her return and was much inclined to think it would prove to be a storm in a teacup.

She found a firm doing DNA testing on the outskirts of Florence and noted down the address, emailing Vittore with the details. She would call in on the way to the airport tomorrow. That achieved, she dragged out her cases and began to pack, wishing she hadn't brought so much with her. After a quick shower she got into bed, rolled over and stuck her nose in the pillow next to hers, scenting the faint elusive aroma of Dante's citrusy aftershave and the husky smell that was purely *him*. Was he right this very minute making love to Cosima? Were women interchangeable to him? Had Topsy merely been a useful outlet for his high-voltage libido when Cosima was unavailable? Did Cosima take other lovers as well?

Topsy tossed and turned, unable to find the blessed oblivion that sleep would have given her. Her thoughts were all over the place but one thing she did know now: she had fallen hard for Dante, fallen madly in love for the first time in her life. That was why she was hurting so much, why the simple image of Dante in bed with Cosima literally tore her to shreds inside herself. Engulfed by pain, she closed her eyes tight, willing herself to calm down and be sensible. It was over and right from the beginning she had known it couldn't last, so what had changed? Loving him only meant that she had accidentally become more attached to him than she should have done, she reasoned feverishly. She would soon get over him again surely common sense would see to that? He had deceived her, betrayed her, used her, hurt her. He could never really have wanted her the way she wanted him and that knowledge cut the deepest of all.

'So what's the big emergency?' Topsy demanded as her sister Kat, a tall slender redhead, greeted her in the hall of her London home with outstretched arms as if she had been abroad for months rather than weeks.

A herd of little boys were dragging a dainty little girl out of the cloakroom where she had clearly been hiding with a teddy clutched to her chest. A sense of warmth and of coming home to where she was safe enclosed Topsy.

'If you give it to me, I won't tear its arm off!' Karim told his cousin Appollonia.

'If you hurt Rags I'll scream,' Emmie's daughter warned him, screwing up her face in challenge. 'And then you'll be in *so* much trouble.'

'If you touch her teddy, I'll shout,' Karim's father, Zahir, announced witheringly from a doorway, turning to say to the other man at his shoulder, 'I think it's time we packed them all off to bed.'

'It's too early for bed,' Karim protested vigorously, his little brother, Hamid, sucking his thumb sleepily to one side of him.

'Yes, it is, it is!' carolled his twin cousins, Dmitri and Stavros.

'I'm not going yet,' Kat's elder twin, Petyr, announced, looking very like his father as he folded his arms and took on an aggressive stance while his sister, Olga, played on the stairs.

Kat rounded on her children. 'When I say bed, you *go* without an argument!' she told Petyr and Olga firmly.

'Or I have to say it,' Mikhail breathed very quietly from the doorway.

'Come on now, children,' the resident nanny spoke from the top of the stairs.

Within the space of a minute all Topsy's little nephews and nieces had vanished and silence had fallen. In the interim her cell phone rang and she pulled it out, her heart thudding at an insane rate when she realised it was Dante. Part of her wanted to disconnect the call as she had been doing every time he tried to speak to her throughout the day she had spent travelling. He must have rung her a dozen times already and her nerves were worn down and this time it seemed easier just to answer it.

'Yes?'

'Why the hell have you gone back to London?' Dante thundered angrily down the line. 'Without even speaking to me? Without even giving me a chance? That has to be the craziest, most irrational thing you've ever done!'

'Dante? Why would I give you a chance after what you've done to me? I'll give you crazy, I'll give you irrational!' Topsy slammed back furiously, forgetting that she had an audience. 'I don't ever want to see you again. So, leave me alone and don't phone again!'

The awful silence around her finally pierced the shell of her utter misery. For the first time she wanted to cry and sob with the sheer frustration of the many emotions attacking her all at once but the combined power of her siblings' questioning stares stifled that desire.

'Petyr's getting very cheeky,' Mikhail complained with unexpected tact to his wife.

'He's a real chip off the old block, then,' Kat told her husband without sympathy.

'Karim started it,' Zahir's wife, Saffy, pointed out wryly.

'But we both know that my daughter loves getting your son worked up,' Saffy's twin, Emmie, countered uncomfortably. 'She deliberately teases him.'

'No matter. Royalty has to learn self-discipline,' Zahir spelled out wryly. 'And Karim is too inclined to get bossy with little girls.'

Topsy gave her twin sisters an awkward hug, avoiding the looks that told her they now had lots of questions to ask, and said, 'Does anyone care to tell me why I had to come home so suddenly?'

Every pair of eyes in the room seemed to meet in mute discomfiture and a heavy silence fell in response to her question.

'It's Odette,' Saffy advanced reluctantly.

'She's been arrested,' Emmie chimed in behind her twin.

'*Arrested?*' Topsy exclaimed in horror.

'Accused of living off immoral earnings from her escort agency,' her brother-in-law Zahir supplied grimly.

Topsy sank down shakily into a seat, appalled by the news, well aware of how much embarrassment such a case being taken to court could cause her relatives. As the ruling King and Queen of a conservative Gulf state, possibly Zahir and his family had the most to fear from being publicly linked to Saffy's mother.

'I couldn't care less what happens to her,' Emmie's husband, Bastian Christou, admitted with unnerving cool. 'After what she did to my wife, it's past time she got her comeuppance and if it takes the law to do it, so be it.'

'But in the meantime we don't want our families or our reputations smeared by her dodgy lifestyle,' Mikhail pronounced in direct disagreement.

Topsy said nothing while the three men in the room began to argue about how best to deal with Odette's arrest. Her sisters clumped together exchanging grimaces until finally the broad terms of a reluctant agreement were thrashed out between the men. They would hire a good legal team to represent Odette in court but in no other way would any of them get more closely involved.

Topsy tried to imagine how Dante would have reacted to the news that her mother was going to be hauled up in court to answer a charge of living off the proceeds of prostitution and she shuddered sickly, grateful he would never know. Her sisters weren't saying anything and neither was she and, sadly, she understood why: they were one and all ashamed to death of Odette and the dubious way in which she made her living. Several attempts had already been made to persuade her mother to sell her business but Odette had demanded so much money in compensation that even her wealthy sons-in-law had baulked, believing that she would continue trying to blackmail them.

'Dante?' Mikhail queried softly to one side of Topsy, his approach having gone unnoticed by her in the state she was in. 'Was that Dante Leonetti phoning you?'

Topsy wrapped her arms round herself, suddenly cold, suddenly exhausted by the mental and physical stress of the past forty-eight hours. In silence she nodded.

'But I warned you about him,' her Russian brother-in-law reminded her.

'It was too late by then,' she muttered, wondering at what exact hour her fate had been cast. The first time she rested her eyes on that lean, devastatingly good-looking face of Dante's? The first kiss? The first time he held her hand?

'But by the sound of it, it's over now,' Kat commented, crossing the room to close a supportive arm round her youngest sister. 'What did he do to you?'

Saffy was the next to move closer. *'Spill,'* she urged.

But Topsy couldn't spill, couldn't bring herself to admit that Dante had had another woman all along. Blanking out her sisters' frustration over her refusal to talk about Dante, she confessed to suspecting that Vittore was her father instead and told her sisters about the DNA testing to take place. That provided a comfortable alternative to discussing Dante, and after dinner when Odette was the main topic of conversation, Topsy took refuge in her bedroom. She needed her own place, she really did need a corner of her own, she conceded ruefully, and she texted Saffy to ask if the couple's town house was free or if they were staying there on this visit. Generally when there was a family conclave, everyone stayed with Mikhail and Kat because they lived in an enormous house. Saffy confirmed that their house would be free but urged her to stay on with the family for company for a few more days.

Three days later, when Topsy was convinced that she was dying from the inside out in the slowest and most painful of ways, Dante showed up at Kat and Mikhail's on an evening when they were entertaining. She had tried so hard not to think about Dante, not to keep on going over the same old pointless ground inside her head. It was done and dusted, finished with no need of a post-mortem to drag her spirits down further. That constant mantra kept her together until above the sound of the jazz pianist playing she heard the sound of raised voices from the hall and then the noisy crash of breaking china. Taken aback, she followed Kat and Mikhail to the doorway.

Four men were engaged in a physical fight in the hall, two of them Mikhail's security guards and the other two she recognised from Italy as working for Dante.

'Dante…' she whispered in astonishment, seeing his tall, powerful figure poised by the front door, which still stood wide open on the night air. And every feeling and sensation she had tried to deny and suppress came flooding back to her in a violent shameful wave. In his charcoal-grey suit, he looked amazing: cool, sophisticated, wonderfully handsome, all the gifts that she had told herself all her adult life were superficial and unimportant. But that awareness did not prevent her from responding to Dante's pure physical charisma.

In a thunderous burst of Russian, Mikhail intervened in the free-for-all of angry men and told his bodyguards to take the fight outside before saying in English to Dante, 'Topsy doesn't want to see you.'

But Topsy *did* want to see Dante; she wanted to see him and speak to him so badly that the prospect of him leaving again hurt and that sudden burst of lowering self-knowledge slashed her pride to ribbons.

'I'm sorry about the fight,' Dante said drily. 'One of

your men took a swing at me when I became insistent on entering and one of mine took offence.'

'You can't see Topsy,' Mikhail retorted harshly.

'I won't let you tell me no,' Dante countered without hesitation, striding forward like man with a death wish.

Topsy leapt into the space between the two men. Mikhail was as tall as he was wide and much more heavily built than Dante. She registered that she could not bear to see Dante physically hurt. She knew she should *want* to see him smashed through the nearest wall and slung from the house, but for some peculiar reason she didn't.

'Don't you dare lay a finger on him!' she warned Mikhail instead.

'Topsy!' Kat interposed in shaken reproach.

'I do not require your protection, Topsy,' Dante growled from behind her as he carefully set her to one side of him.

'Actually, you do,' Mikhail informed him grimly. 'Anyone who hurts or harms Topsy is liable to get damaged here.'

Zahir's handsome and charming kid brother, Prince Akram, walked over and grabbed Topsy's hand without ceremony. 'Let your family handle this,' he advised. 'Let's go and have some supper.'

'And who the hell are you?' Dante suddenly roared at poor Akram like a lion watching someone stroll in to try and steal his prey.

'Exactly what have you got to be all jealous and possessive about?' Topsy roared back at him, losing her own temper with an abruptness that startled her and everyone around her. 'You're the one with the girlfriend you didn't mention!'

'*Kick* him out, Mikhail!' Kat snapped suddenly.

'I do not have a girlfriend. I am not involved with Cosima,' Dante spelled out between clenched teeth. 'Now will you listen to me?'

'I was kind of looking forward to kicking you,' Mikhail told him cheerfully.

'Is your family always like this?' Dante groaned, his emerald-green eyes almost radiant with raw-edged tension in his handsome face. 'Is nothing private?'

'Very little, I'm afraid,' Zahir dropped in gently. 'And cross one and you cross them all.'

'I do want to hear what you have to say,' Topsy admitted tightly, her eyes suddenly stinging with tears because she had thought she would never ever see Dante again and seeing him in Kat's home so unexpectedly was extremely disconcerting and had knocked her right off balance. Had he followed her to London? Or had he been coming to London anyway on banking business? And what did it matter either way? Couldn't she even control her own brain any more?

'We'll go back to my hotel.'

Saffy dug a set of keys from her clutch bag and dropped them into Topsy's hand. 'Use our place. It's more private.'

'You can't just walk out of here with that man,' Kat argued worriedly. 'He's got a bad temper. He looked at Akram as if he was going to hit him. Suppose he loses that temper with Topsy?'

A pained light entered Dante's eyes. 'I am not going to lose my temper or hit *anyone*.'

'You lost your temper when I smashed your car!' Topsy reminded him resentfully.

Mikhail closed a comforting arm gently round his wife's taut shoulders. 'Topsy's all grown up, Kat. It's time to cut her loose.'

'You've got the family from hell,' Dante told her darkly outside the front door. 'I've never met a more interfering bunch of people.'

'But they love me a lot,' Topsy replied ruefully. 'I'm lucky to have them.'

'Not your mother though. I saw an article about her in a tabloid newspaper,' he admitted curtly, a hand at her elbow as he guided her out to the limo parked outside. 'It was only thanks to that article that I was able to track you down. The sole address my mother had for you was your mother's apartment, which is, of course, empty. I assume that was another attempt to cover up your connections with your family.'

'You read about Mum?' Topsy felt totally humiliated by that admission. She had deliberately not read any of the newspaper reports about their mother's arrest. She knew that studying highly coloured revelations about Odette's turbulent life would only upset her because Kat was doing exactly that and had already been in tears over the stories several times. Mikhail had begged his wife not to read the newspapers, pointing out that the inaccurate articles were written to shock, rather than inform, and that Odette's plight would only attract tabloid interest for a few days at most. Fortunately nothing more was likely to appear in the media until the older woman was tried in court.

'Yes,' Dante confirmed with a forbidding jerk of his

stubborn jaw. 'I thought I did badly in the parental lottery but clearly you didn't do very much better.'

'*Your* mother's lovely. How can you say that?' she demanded in bewilderment, sliding into the limousine and leaning forward to give his driver the address of Zahir and Saffy's house.

As he buzzed the partition shut between the front and the back of the car Dante's jaw line clenched hard, his eyes glinting like crushed green ice below the fringe of his black lashes. 'I wasn't referring to her. My father was a violent man, who used my mother like a punch bag,' he confessed, every word seemingly wrenched from him against his will. 'Worst of all, he got away with it because she was too scared of him to report him to the police and when he developed a brain tumour she nursed him right to the end.'

'Couldn't you have done something to help her?'

'I tried. She was terrified of anyone finding out about what went on in our home. She was deeply ashamed of it and blamed herself for everything that was happening.'

'How could she do that?'

'She said she never loved him and he always knew it and hated her for it.'

'I think she was in love with Vittore when she married your father. It wasn't as though she wanted to marry him, so I suppose he got what he deserved when he used his power and influence to get the girl he wanted.'

Dante frowned at her in bemusement. 'Vittore? How could she have been in love with Vittore when my father married her when she was only seventeen?'

And at that point Topsy realised she had spoken out of turn, revealing facts Dante had not been told. At the same time, she felt he should know that story to understand the strength of the ties between his mother and his stepfather. That conviction in mind, she shared what she had learned.

Dante was very much disconcerted. 'I didn't know she knew him when she was young. Why didn't she tell me? They got married so fast. I wouldn't have been as concerned had I known.'

'Well, you know now,' Topsy responded, thinking that in some ways Sofia and Vittore had contributed unfairly to Dante's reserved response to their marriage. Greater candour could well have changed his attitude.

'It's not important now,' Dante breathed in sudden dismissal. 'But the reason my mother almost died during that last pregnancy with my father was because his violence had caused internal bleeding…'

Topsy grimaced in silence.

'Soon after that *I* tried to protect her from him and I hit him but, unluckily for me, I was a weedy teenager, who didn't grow big and strong until I was much older,' he volunteered tight-mouthed.

She wondered if that was the time he had been found badly beaten up by the side of the road and her heart squeezed, the awareness that he had grown up in a profoundly disturbed and unhappy home somehow punching a small hole in the wall of her angry resistance to him. She couldn't forgive him for Cosima and still couldn't comprehend why he had come to London, for what could he possibly hope to achieve by seeing her again?

Yet she felt better for understanding him a little more and could only wonder if his childhood experience of violence and his parents' unhappy marriage had damaged his ability to deeply care for someone else. And then she remembered, with a sense of utter foolishness and sheepish self-loathing, that he *had* married a woman at the age of twenty-one. After that recollection she could only question why on earth her brain should be set on trying to find excuses for *his* inexcusable behaviour!

She unlocked the door of the town house and stepped inside. Lamps were already lit and the temperature made it clear that the heating was on: Saffy must have contacted their caretaker/housekeeper to forewarn her of their arrival.

A gas fire flamed in the grate and Dante examined his surroundings, pausing to glance at a large collection of family photos arranged on a side table. 'There's a lot of children in your family,' he commented.

Topsy breathed in deep. 'Dante?' He swung round, stunning green eyes locking to her with sudden unexpected intensity, the power of his compelling attraction washing over her like a potent drug. 'Will you please tell me what you're doing here in London?'

'I *had* to see you,' he declared.

'But we have absolutely nothing to say to each other,' she reasoned in a voice strung tight with the strain of self-discipline.

'I care about you, Topsy,' he breathed thickly.

'Well, you have a funny way of showing it,' Topsy told him, unimpressed, indeed resenting that statement when his lack of concern for her feelings had been paraded in front of her at the ball. 'Until tonight I don't believe you've ever told me anything really personal about yourself. I even had to find out that you were once married from your mother. We had fun as you once said but it stopped being fun and I want out…*I am out.*'

His spectacular bone structure was rigid below his bronzed skin. 'When I mentioned my father tonight, it was to lessen your discomfort over your mother's arrest. I'm not used to talking about myself. I'm not used to sharing private matters with people.'

'Which only underlines how right I was to walk away.'

'But I'm not the *only* one of us who chose to keep secrets,' Dante countered suddenly, his green eyes ablaze with sudden condemnation.

'And what's that supposed to mean?' Topsy said defensively.

Dante pulled a small envelope from his pocket and extended it to her. 'Perhaps this will explain.'

Brow indenting, Topsy grasped the envelope. It felt like a greetings card but it wasn't her birthday. She tore it open to extract the card and flick it open.

Welcome to the family. Vittore.

Dante crossed the room to look over her shoulder and read the same message.

'What does he mean?' Topsy whispered, afraid to believe that those words meant what she hoped they meant.

'The DNA tests were a match…' He skimmed her with a cool telling scrutiny. 'Yes, Vittore told me that you thought he might be your father but that you only approached him the night of the ball. Were you ever planning on sharing that possibility with me?'

Topsy was reeling, both from the news that the DNA testing had confirmed that Vittore was indeed her father and the wording of the card that seemed to offer to include her in the family circle. It seemed too good to be true. 'How does Vittore feel about it?'

'Since he's had a couple of days to absorb the shock of your existence, he seems pleased. He's also broken the news to my mother. She was certainly disconcerted when he explained about his unfortunate experience with your mother years ago, but *my* mother seems to have spent every moment since finding delightfully sentimental comparisons between you and her husband,' Dante revealed with an edge of derision. 'She says you have the same smile. Frankly I've never noticed.'

'I'm so glad your mother's not been distressed by all this coming out,' Topsy commented breathlessly. 'And of course you won't recognise any similarity in smiles when Vittore so rarely smiles around you. Why *would* he smile? Do you expect him to bask in your disapproval?'

'You realise this makes you my stepsister?' Dante prompted with a sardonic twist of his handsome mouth, ignoring her admonition with regard to his attitude towards his stepfather. 'And that the child my mother carries will be a half-sibling to *both* of us?'

Topsy smiled, thinking that over, and nodded. 'You have no idea what it's like not to know who your father is, particularly when your mother is as uninterested as Odette. Finding out the truth meant a lot to me, and Vittore and your mother are handling this in such a positive way. I'm very, very lucky,' she conceded gratefully.

'The information you required from your mother

that persuaded you to work as an escort for an evening,' Dante recounted in a flat tone that could not hide his disapproval. 'Was that information the name of your father?'

'Yes,' Topsy confirmed, hating the fact that for the first time they were talking almost like polite strangers. Yet she wondered what other relationship they could possibly hope to establish in the wake of their unfortunate fling. At the same time she knew she would have to work on her own feelings because Vittore was her real father and Dante would always be a part of Vittore and Sofia's life.

In pursuit of that objective, she added in a rush, 'I grew up believing that another man, who lived abroad, was my father. I only met him a couple of times but when I was eighteen I discovered that he wasn't my father at all.'

'And finding out who was was *so* important to you that you took a job with my mother…for precisely what purpose?' Dante prompted tautly.

'I wanted the chance to get to know Vittore a little before I decided whether or not to approach him and then everything got so complicated.' She sighed with a wry roll of her big dark eyes. 'Before I came to Italy I hadn't thought anything through. I saw the job offer on the castle website and decided it was a heaven-sent opportunity. But once I arrived, there they were—Sofia and Vittore, a newly married happy couple—and I was scared that if I did turn out to be Vittore's daughter, it would damage their marriage.'

'It could have done,' Dante conceded reflectively. 'Fortunately my mother isn't threatened by the discovery that her husband has an adult daughter but probably more important in this case is the fact that she already likes you, so you're not an unknown quantity she is being forced to accept.'

'Your mother's still been very generous,' Topsy responded.

'But I was quite right to be suspicious of your motives in coming to work for her. You accuse me of keeping secrets but really you kept many more secrets from all of us,' Dante condemned grimly. 'You came into my home and earned my mother's trust on false pretences.'

'That's not a fair criticism,' Topsy objected sharply.

'You know it is. I can understand the reasoning behind your masquerade but you also concealed who your family were and any hint that you were from a privileged background.'

Topsy flushed because that was more or less a true charge. 'I wasn't born into a privileged background. In fact there was nothing privileged about my life until Kat met Mikhail and married him. That was when everything changed and suddenly I was staying in a country mansion with servants at the weekends and Kat was buying me designer jeans.'

Someone rapped on the door of the lounge and Dante went to answer it.

'Would you like coffee?' Dante enquired over his shoulder. 'Or anything to eat?'

'No, thanks.' She didn't think she could get any sort of a drink past her tight throat and she was angry that Dante had put *her* on the defensive by reminding her that she had been downright dishonest when she deliberately took a job working for his mother simply to get close to Vittore. The acknowledgement embarrassed her. She hadn't set out to hurt anyone and, luckily, nobody had been hurt and surely that should be the bottom line that judged her behaviour.

'I wasn't honest about my family circumstances because I didn't want anyone questioning why I should need the job in the first place. I was also trying to take a break from my sisters and their expectations for a while and be independent,' she explained unwillingly, watching an ebony brow quirk. 'I love them all but they do meddle a lot in my life. I've never been allowed to make my own decisions. My sisters made the decisions for me, right down to who I dated and who I didn't date.'

'I wouldn't have even got on the list of potentials,' Dante quipped.

'Don't kid yourself, Dante.' Topsy wrinkled her slightly snub nose. 'You're rich and successful and those are exactly the qualities my sisters and their husbands respect.'

'Kusnirovich knows who I am and he was ready to throw me out of his house tonight,' Dante observed grimly, his passionate mouth tightening into a hard line. 'There was neither respect nor acceptance in my reception. In all fairness, you're misjudging your family, *cara mia*. The instant you accused me of having another woman, it didn't matter *who* I was or *what* I was worth, they didn't want me anywhere near you.'

Topsy could see the truth of that for herself and her shoulders drooped, emotional exhaustion settling in as she sank down wearily on a well-padded sofa, allowing her rigid spine to sink into the cushions. 'I was tired of my family watching my every move, trying to fix me up with a job they picked, and that was another reason to come to Italy, except Mikhail tracked me down there as well.'

'They care about you,' Dante reasoned, oddly hesitant in his delivery, his accent purring along every syllable. 'As do I.'

Topsy froze, her small face rigid. 'I don't want to talk about Cosima. I still don't know what you're even doing here. Are you in London on business?'

'No. I'm here solely to see you,' Dante delivered.

'Why did you get married at twenty-one?' she asked him abruptly, determined to steer him off that subject lest it upset her and she let herself down by getting emotional. Attack, she thought, was the best part of defence. 'And why did you never mention that you had been married?'

Dante was palpably disconcerted by her reference to his being a widower and he breathed in deeply, as if he was bracing himself. 'To say the least, my life as a child and adolescent was dysfunctional. I thought that if I married young I could do it all differently and create the happy home I had never known. I also thought I loved Emilia. I never refer to my marriage because I made a mistake and I still feel guilty about that.' Dante virtually grated that final hard-edged admission. 'Are you satisfied now?'

'Satisfied with what? You're still not telling me what happened.'

'Emilia died, running across a busy road to meet me for lunch. While I was waiting for her...*before* I learned what had happened,' Dante framed jerkily, 'I was wishing she would at least leave me alone during working hours… That's how lousy a husband I was.'

Topsy was frowning, taken aback. 'You didn't love her?'

'I thought I did but with mature hindsight I think it was more a fond friendship on my side than love. Her parents had divorced. We both wanted a stable home life but she wanted too much of me and I felt suffocated, *trapped*,' he explained roughly, guiltily.

'How did she want too much of you?'

'If I wasn't with her she was phoning me constantly and she couldn't stand me leaving her to work. It was as though I had no right to a life of my own any more, but as far as Emilia was concerned that was how you loved someone. It didn't work for me; it was like living in a cage. I knew I shouldn't have married her within weeks. I realised we were too different but I could never have hurt her by telling her that.'

'It's not your fault that she died,' Topsy told him gently.

'I know that…but I wasn't the best husband while she was alive. I was too young and selfish and she was too needy,' he confided tight-mouthed. 'But there's nothing I can do about that now.'

He had regrets and Topsy was appalled to feel a dart of jealousy piercing her even on poor Emilia's behalf because she could not bear to picture Dante having been married to anyone.

'So, after that experience you didn't do serious in relationships,' Topsy guessed.

'I didn't think I was cut out for serious after Emilia and I went for variety rather than quality,' Dante ac-

knowledged, his face forbidding in its detachment as
though he seriously loathed having to tell her such a
thing.

'There's no shame in avoiding what doesn't suit you,'
Topsy mumbled abstractedly. 'We're all different—
we're not meant to be the same. I've never done serious with anyone.'

Dante shot her a literal stabbing glance from glittering green eyes. 'I thought what we had *was* serious.'

'Which just goes to show how mistaken you can be,'
Topsy parried with a strangled little laugh.

'Stop being so obstinate and listen to me!' Dante
growled at her out of all patience, his eyes flashing
with angry hostility. 'I was paired up with Cosima by
her agent! She was not my girlfriend or my mistress or
my lover or anything. She was chosen to publicise the
ball and persuade other celebrities that the event was
fashionable enough for them to attend. We went out to
dinner twice and attended a couple of parties to make
it appear to the press that we were a couple. It is not an
uncommon arrangement when good PR is required...'

Topsy was staring fixedly at him. 'You mean the
hottest society couple in Italy was a fake romance? A
show-mance?' she whispered shakily. '*Totally* fake?'

'Totally fake,' Dante confirmed. 'There was...er...a
casual relationship with someone else at the time but
that was over before I even met you.'

'But the way Cosima spoke to you at the ball...about
your "agreement". What was that all about?' Topsy per-
sisted, frowning, afraid to believe what he was telling
her.

'I explained that I had met someone who would also

be at the ball and she threw a fit at the threat of the paparazzi realising that I had lost interest in her and then assuming that she had been dumped. And Cosima naturally doesn't do dumped as part of her glossy image. She refused to come to the ball until I promised that I would maintain the act of being with her all evening and have nothing to do with any other woman,' he explained heavily. 'If I had had any idea how much grief that promise would cause me, I would never have agreed. But, at least, she turned up and gave the fund the publicity we needed for it.'

'But you *must* have fancied her,' Topsy breathed before she could think better of it. 'I mean, come on, Dante. Cosima's gorgeous and she's got a title like you, and even I have to admit that you look very well together.'

'No, I didn't fancy her in the slightest and she was very irritating company, talks about nothing but fashion and cosmetics,' Dante complained sardonically. 'At one point she called me a dinosaur for not being a fan of guy-liner.'

Topsy was surprised to find herself on the brink of laughing at the thought of that conversation. 'Let's face it, you are kind of conservative.'

'Please tell me you don't want me to wear guy-liner,' Dante urged, almost making that pent-up laughter bubble over inside her. 'I will do almost anything to get you back but I won't use make-up.'

'You don't need guy-liner. You've got great eyelashes,' she told him comfortingly.

Her brain had, however, leapt into a frantic whirl of excited and not particularly logical thoughts. He wanted her back. She wanted him back. For the first time that week the sick, tight feeling of isolation and loss had eased its stranglehold. He said he was serious about her. Could she believe that? Take the risk that he might respond to her feelings for him and give him another chance? But even through the chaos of her over-excited thoughts, there was one question she still had to ask and it was an obvious one.

'So, why didn't you tell me about your arrangement with Cosima *before* the ball?' Topsy asked doggedly, and as his gaze cloaked she immediately saw that it was a question he had hoped she wouldn't ask him.

'I hadn't quite worked out where you and I were going and making a big explanation about Cosima struck me as unnecessarily dramatic,' he advanced with visible reluctance.

'Unnecessarily dramatic?' Topsy yelled, jumping upright, a flush of frustrated fury colouring her heart-shaped face. 'How on earth could it be *unnecessarily dramatic* to explain about Cosima when you were sleeping in my bed with me every night?'

Dante shifted his feet restively, turned away, turned agitatedly back. 'I felt that it would be like making a big statement about our relationship and I was already uneasy about the way I was behaving with you.'

'A big statement,' Topsy repeated, unimpressed by that excuse. 'Why…*uneasy?*'

A deeply pained expression crossed his face. 'Do we have to discuss this now?'

'Yes, we do.' Topsy was sticking to her guns, recognising that she was in a much stronger position than she had appreciated.

'Even that I got involved with you in the first place was unusual for me. You were living in my home and I have never before developed an uncontrollable desire to ravish one of the staff. That felt weird,' Dante recounted flatly. 'And then I was staying with you every night, *all* night and that felt even weirder because I never hang around after sex.'

'My goodness, I was getting a treat and I didn't even know it!' Topsy fired back with spirit. 'What was so weird about being attracted to me?'

'I thought you weren't my type but you're so much my type it's ridiculous,' Dante confessed and, without warning, suddenly stalked forward to reach for her hands with both of his. 'Please tell me that you're willing to move to Italy and live with me for ever, *gioia mia.*'

Topsy's eyes opened very wide indeed, her astonishment at that rapid turnaround unconcealed. 'That's a bit of a tall order, Dante. *For ever?*' she questioned weakly.

'Nothing less than for ever will do and I've already asked your father for his permission.'

'Permission for what?' she echoed.

And Dante got down on one knee in front of her, altogether depriving her of breath and voice, and extended a glittering diamond ring. 'Will you marry me?'

Topsy was so shattered by the marriage proposal that she crumpled back down on the edge of the sofa again. 'You're not serious…you can't be?'

'Why can't I be?' Dante demanded almost aggressively.

'You said you didn't do serious… I mean, you were really clear about that.'

'And then I met you…' A hand braced on her denim-clad thigh like a brand. 'And I fell insanely in love with you so fast I didn't know what was happening to me.'

'But you thought all those bad things about me…that I was chasing Vittore, that I was a regular escort girl.'

'And then you seduced me at the picnic,' Dante slotted in, green eyes glowing with sudden amusement.

'*I* seduced *you*?' Topsy gasped.

'You knew I couldn't keep my hands off you. Letting me take you somewhere that private wasn't a wise move,' Dante reasoned, quietly lifting her left hand and threading the diamond ring onto her engagement finger with a level of satisfaction he couldn't hide.

'But I didn't say yes yet!' Topsy protested. 'I may be in love with you but it's too soon to talk about marriage.'

His hands curved to her cheeks and he leant forward to extract a hungry, demanding kiss that sent the blood crashing through her veins like a tidal wave as her pulses speeded up.

'You can stay the night,' she told him on the back of an ecstatic sigh.

'Not without a yes to the proposal. You get me back in bed only with a wedding ring,' Dante informed her combatively.

'You're the same man who just told me that marriage made you feel suffocated and trapped.'

'I'm not the same person I was a decade ago. You're not the needy, clingy type either. I can see you working away at a whiteboard in maths research and forgetting I even exist for hours at a stretch!' Dante confessed ruefully.

Topsy knew her own flaws. 'That is a possibility and

you're right, I'm not clingy, but I still think it's too soon to be talking about marriage.'

'Without you in my life, I'll get stuffy and ruthless.'

'You're already ruthless and more stubborn than any man should be. You almost lost me because you wouldn't admit what you were feeling for me,' Topsy pointed out while she tangled her fingers lazily in his black hair in a caressing move that might have warned him that losing her was becoming increasingly unlikely.

'I love you,' Dante confided with breathtaking sincerity. 'And it makes me feel insecure. I won't be happy until you tell me that you'll marry me and stay with me for ever.'

Her amber eyes danced. 'The more you talk, the more I'm warming up to the prospect.'

'Do you want to stay here tonight or go back to my hotel with me?' Dante's hands were sliding up and down her slim thighs, rousing tingling heat in dangerous places.

'I think I might ravish you in the car if we leave,' Topsy admitted shakily.

'How do I match up to your list of required male characteristics?' Dante prompted, gathering her up into his arms with great care and tenderness.

'The truth? You don't match at all but you have other more important attributes,' Topsy whispered, smoothing a possessive hand over a high cheekbone that shifted down into a strong jawline. 'You love me. I love you, Dante Leonetti. Now let's go and find a guestroom for two.'

'And you'll marry me?' Dante pressed stubbornly.

'Well, I'm certainly not letting you go,' Topsy laughed, admiring the glitter of her ring in the lamplight.

'I couldn't bear to let you go,' he groaned, tightening his arms appreciatively round her. 'I love you so much I want you on a for ever and ever lease, *amata mia*.'

Topsy gave him a sunny smile, happiness darting and dancing through her like sunlight in the wake of a long winter. 'Oh, I think that can be arranged at no extra cost,' she teased.

EPILOGUE

TOPSY RACED OUT of the research department of the University of Florence, frantically checking her watch. She was late, she was always late, and sometimes it drove Dante, who was punctual to a fault, crazy.

Her husband awaited her in the car park, tall, dark and so breathtakingly handsome that not a female head in his vicinity failed to turn and look in his direction while his entire attention remained pinned to his windblown wife, half in and half out of her coat. He was lounging with folded arms and an air of long-suffering fortitude against the bonnet of his pristine Pagani Zonda.

'Do you know how fine you're cutting this, Dr Leonetti?' he demanded ruefully, beautiful green eyes tracking over her brightly smiling face with a love he couldn't and never tried to hide.

'I just got tied up with something.'

Dante opened the door for her and she slid in, smoothing her tunic top over the very small bump beneath.

'It's very important that you don't miss any appointments,' Dante told her anxiously. 'I want you to have the best possible care and attention.'

'Shut up,' his wife told him, lurching awkwardly into his lap before he could start the engine and kissing him breathless. 'I'm as healthy as a horse and I come from good breeding stock as well. How many nephews and nieces do I have?'

Dante, who had loosened up in his habits since Topsy came into his life, wrapped both arms around her and sighed into her tumbled dark hair. 'I know, but I can't take your casual attitude and I couldn't stand anything to happen to you.'

'It's *you* things are going to happen to!' Topsy warned him cheerfully. 'You're going to have me *and* a mini-me to torment you. Life as you know it has ended.'

'Life as I knew it ended the day I met you, *amata mia*,' Dante retorted with a wide smile of satisfaction, settling her back into the passenger seat and doing up her belt for her. 'Have you ever heard me complain?'

And Topsy had to admit, she had not heard him utter a single complaint in the three years since she had come to live in Italy. She had insisted on a long engagement and, regardless of Dante's eagerness to get to the altar, it was a year before the wedding actually took place. Topsy had wanted both of them to be absolutely certain of what they were doing because she really did want their marriage to last for ever and ever.

Deciding to try for a baby had been a big decision and she had waited until she was twenty-six to do so, confident that she would be a more caring parent than her mother had been and convinced that Dante would make a terrific father. It had been something of a shock when she fell pregnant the first month but she was truly excited about her baby.

She had had no difficulty finding a research job at the university and was currently up for an award following the publication of her most recent maths paper. Her career took up a good deal of her time and she was frequently invited abroad to speak and share her research, as well as continually fending off head-hunters desperate to employ her in more profit-inspired fields. Dante had not been able to tolerate living away from her during the week to be at the bank headquarters in Milan. Nowadays, although he made regular business trips, he mostly worked from home.

The fancy-dress ball that had caused so much trouble between them was now a more positive memory for them both for the little girl suffering from leukaemia had travelled to the USA for highly specialised treatment and was now in recovery with every hope of maintaining her improved health.

On a less important note, Topsy still couldn't drive, had decided she didn't like driving and flatly refused to get behind a steering wheel with Dante beside her but it wasn't really a big problem when Dante had hired a local driver to motor her around instead.

Vittore and Sofia and little Agnese, their daughter, who was now a cherubic toddler, had moved into their new home, Casa di Fortuna. Family contact was frequent and informal and everything that Topsy had learned to enjoy with her sister and their families. Kat had given birth safely to her much-longed-for little daughter. Topsy's relationship with her father was open and affectionate and more than she had ever hoped to have with a parent. Dante had learned to recognise Vittore's deep love for his mother and the awkwardness between the two men had slowly melted away.

Sadly, but not surprisingly, nothing had changed about Topsy's relationship with her mother. Odette had been tried in court and had got off the charges through lack of acceptable proof, but the older woman's jubilation had not lasted long when she realised that all her regular clients had deserted her because they had feared exposure after her arrest. In the end, Odette had closed down the escort agency and retired to the South of France to live on the pension she received from her sons-in-law. Neither Topsy nor any of her sisters had heard from Odette since she had relocated abroad two years earlier and, as the older woman had not written the tell-all book she had threatened to write, her daughters were inclined to think that silence from their mother was a blessing.

'There…we just made it,' Dante pronounced with a touch of superiority as he shot the car into a parking spot beside the obstetrician's consulting rooms.

'I knew we would,' Topsy teased, tenderly stroking the back of a lean brown hand where it still rested on the steering wheel. 'You would hate to miss a scan of our daughter.'

Dante tucked a straying strand of dark hair gently back behind her ear, his reflective green gaze resting warmly on her animated face. 'I never knew I could be so happy…and just to think there's going to be *two* of you. I can't believe my luck, *amata mia.*'

Topsy gave him a knowing look that engulfed him in love. 'I believe we make our own luck.'

* * * * *

DANTE'S UNEXPECTED LEGACY

CATHERINE GEORGE

This one's for Justin.

Catherine George was born in Wales, and early on developed a passion for reading which eventually fuelled her compulsion to write. Marriage to an engineer led to nine years in Brazil, but on his later travels the education of her son and daughter kept her in the UK. And, instead of constant reading to pass her lonely evenings, she began to write the first of her romantic novels. When not writing and reading she loves to cook, listen to opera, and browse in antiques shops.

CHAPTER ONE

ROSE SAT RIGIDLY, every nerve on edge as the plane took off. No turning back now. For years she'd been turning down invitations to Florence, flatly refusing to be parted from her little daughter, or to take her child with her. But this time refusal had been impossible.

'Please, *please* come,' Charlotte had begged. 'Just you and me in a luxury hotel for a couple of days. God knows you can do with a break, and I'll pay for everything and send you a plane ticket, so absolutely no expenses on your part. You know Bea will be fine with your mother, so don't say no this time. I really need you, Rose. So come. Please!' she'd added, and because Charlotte was her oldest and closest friend and she loved her like a sister, Rose had finally given in.

'Oh, all right. If it means that much to you I will. But why a hotel and not your place?'

'I want you all to myself.'

'Fabio can't be cool about this. It's your wedding anniversary, isn't it?'

'He'll be away for it on some business trip,' said Charlotte miserably. 'Besides, he doesn't know about the hotel yet. But I've already booked, so there's nothing he can do about it—not that he would, of course.'

Rose wasn't so sure. A possessive husband like Fabio

Vilari would surely be anything but cool if his wife took a hotel break in Florence without him, even if it was with her lifelong friend and the bridesmaid at their wedding. But from the moment Rose had said a reluctant yes to the trip Charlotte rang every day to make sure that she hadn't changed her mind, and in her final call sprang a surprise with instructions to take a taxi from Santa Maria Novella railway station to the hotel. 'I'll meet you there later in time for dinner, Rose. I can't wait!'

Money, if the hotel brochure was anything to go by, was obviously not part of Charlotte's problem, but if something was going wrong with her marriage Rose couldn't see what earthly help a single parent like herself could give her friend, other than to provide a sympathetic ear. Still, the note of tearful desperation in her friend's voice had been so worrying that Rose had enlisted her mother's willing help, covered her child's face with kisses and made for Heathrow with her shoulder ready for Charlotte to cry on.

On terra firma in Pisa Airport, Rose concentrated on collecting her luggage and finding the train for Florence, but once she'd boarded it the Tuscan scenery passed her by almost unnoticed in her worry about possible problems left behind and the all-too-probable ones awaiting her at journey's end. Her daughter was used to spending time with her beloved gramma while Rose went out to work, but Mummy had always been home before bedtime. Rose blinked hard. The thought of her darling Bea crying for her in the night was unbearable. Yet Charlotte had been there for Rose through thick and thin in the past, and now her friend was the one needing help and support for once Rose had no option but to get to her as quickly as possible to provide it.

Rose came to with a start as the train pulled into Santa Maria Novella and was soon wheeling her suitcase through the heat and bustle of the crowds streaming from the lofty station into the late afternoon Florentine sunshine, so very different from the cool mists left behind. The taxi driver who eventually picked her up took a look at her hotel brochure and whisked her on a fast, chaotic drive past tall old buildings in narrow streets filled with honking cars and scooters en route to the banks of the River Arno. Rose stared, impressed, when they reached the hotel. Charlotte was certainly pushing the boat out for her. A flight of stone steps with a red carpet runner led up to an arched doorway crowned by a fabulous Venetian glass fanlight. Rose paid the driver, wishing she'd worn something more elegant than denim jeans and jacket for her red carpet entrance as she trailed her suitcase past marble statues and urns of flowers in the vaulted foyer. She approached the man behind the reception desk at the foot of a sweeping staircase and gave him her name.

'*Buonasera,*' he said courteously, but to her relief continued in English. 'Welcome to Florence, Miss Palmer. If you will just sign the register? I am to inform you that Signora Vilari has ordered dinner for two in the hotel restaurant this evening.'

Rose smiled gratefully. 'Thank you.'

'*Prego.* If you require anything at all, please ring. Enjoy your stay.'

A porter took charge of the luggage to escort Rose to a lift rather like an ornate brass birdcage. It took them up two floors at such a leisurely rate she could have walked up faster, but she was utterly delighted when she reached her room. She tipped the porter and went straight out onto a balcony looking down on the River Arno, her feelings a heady mix of trepidation and excitement as she recognised the sun-gilded bridge farther upstream as the famous Ponte Vecchio. She was actually, unbelievably, here in Florence at last. She sent a text to Charlotte to confirm her arrival, and then rang her mother.

'No problems, darling; Bea's as happy as a lark,' Grace Palmer assured her. 'She's playing with Tom in the garden before her bath. Do you want to speak to her?'

'I just long to, Mum, but I won't in case it upsets her. If she's happy let's keep her that way.'

'She'll be fine. You know we'll take good care of her, so for heaven's sake, relax and enjoy yourself.'

Rose promised to try, said there was no news from Charlotte yet, but would report tomorrow. She chose a tonic from the minibar and sat back on one of the reclining chairs on the balcony to breathe in the scents and sounds of Florence as she watched the traffic stream past across the river. For the first time in for ever at this time of day she had absolutely nothing to do—but missed her child too much to enjoy it. *Stop it*, she told herself irritably. Now she was here it was only sensible to make the most of her short break in this beautiful city. But what on earth was going on with Charlotte and Fabio? Could Fabio be cheating on her? Rose glowered. In the unlikely event that she ever acquired a husband herself her gut reaction would be grievous bodily harm if the man started playing away. She checked her silent phone again, took a last look at the sparkling waters of the Arno and went inside to soak in the bath for as long as she liked for once.

With still no word from Charlotte, the uneasiness grew as Rose got ready for the evening. To keep occupied, she took longer over her appearance than she ever had time for normally and even coaxed her newly washed hair into an intricate up-do. She nodded at her reflection in approval. Not bad. Her long-serving little black dress looked pretty good now she'd lost a pound or two. Charlotte's clothes were always wonderful, courtesy of a wealthy, besotted husband—Rose bit her lip, wondering if there lay the problem. Maybe Fabio Vilari was no longer so besotted. Or, worst scenario of all, was now besotted with someone else.

She leapt away from the mirror as the phone rang. At last!

'Hello,' she said eagerly, but her face fell at the news that a letter had arrived for her.

A *letter*?

'Thank you. I'll come down for it right away.' And wait for Charlotte downstairs with a drink.

Too impatient to wait for the lift, Rose hurried down the imposing staircase as fast as she could in her kept-for-best heels and crossed the foyer to the reception desk. The bulky envelope, addressed in Charlotte's unmistakable scrawl, was handed to her, along with the information that the gentleman who'd delivered it wished to speak with her.

'*Buonasera*, Rose,' said a voice behind her. 'Welcome to Firenze.'

Her heart, which had taken a nosedive at the sight of Charlotte's handwriting, flew up to hammer Rose in the ribs. To hide her horrified reaction, she turned very slowly to confront a tall, slim man with dark curling hair and a face that could be straight out of a Raphael portrait. A face she had never forgotten, though heaven knew she had tried. Here in the handsome, irresistible flesh was her reason for refusing all invitations to Tuscany—to avoid meeting up with her daughter's father again.

'Good heavens—Dante Fortinari,' she said lightly when she could trust her voice. 'What a surprise!'

'A pleasant one, I hope?' He took her hand, a light in his blue eyes that made her want to turn tail and run. 'I am so very happy to see you again, Rose. Will you have a drink while you read your letter?'

Her first reaction was to refuse point-blank and tell him to get lost, but after a pause she nodded warily. 'Thank you.'

'Come.' He led her to a table in the hushed sophistication of the lounge bar. 'You would like wine?'

She felt in crying need of something even stronger than wine after the shock of seeing him again, but to keep her wits about her opted for water. 'Sparkling water, please. Will you excuse me while I read this?'

Dante Fortinari gave the order to a waiter then sat watching intently while she read her letter. Rose Palmer had changed in the years since their last meeting at Charlotte Vilari's wedding over four years ago. Then she had been an innocent just past her twenty-first birthday, but now she was very much a woman. Hair still the colour of *caramello* was swept up in a precarious knot that made his fingers yearn to bring it tumbling down. Combined with the severe dress, it gave her a look of sophistication very different from his memory of her. His mouth twisted. She had been so irresistible in her happiness for her friend that day, but the carefree young bridesmaid had now matured into a poised, self-contained adult who was very obviously not pleased to see him. This was no surprise. He had half expected her to snatch her letter and walk away, refusing to talk to him at all.

Rose, in the meantime, was reading Charlotte's note in dismay.

You'll want to hit me, love, when you read this—I don't blame you one bit. Fabio woke me up yesterday morning with flowers, a gorgeous gold bracelet, plus tickets for a surprise trip to New York for today of all days.

God, Rose, the relief was enormous. I came across the tickets and hotel reservation by ac-

cident a while ago and immediately pole-vaulted to the wrong conclusion—that Fabio was taking someone else and pretending it was a business trip. And on our wedding anniversary! That was why I needed you so badly.

Sorry to be such a drama queen—I've been a total idiot. I was about to ring you to grovel and cancel your trip when Fabio insisted a little holiday would be very good for you after all your efforts to get away. I agreed wholeheartedly, so take it easy, Rose, and enjoy a taste of la dolce vita before you fly back. Lord knows you deserve it.

Enclosed is some spending money for meals and shopping—and Fabio says don't dare refuse it or he'll be very hurt. Buy presents, if nothing else. I'll fly over to catch up very soon.
Love always, Charlotte.

'Bad news?' asked Dante.

Rose gave him a dazed look. 'I flew here to meet Charlotte for a little holiday, but Fabio's taken her on a surprise trip to New York today instead.' She smiled valiantly to mask her crushing disappointment. 'Never mind. I've always wanted to visit Florence.'

'But in company with your friend, not alone.' Sympathy gleamed in the vivid blue eyes that had haunted her dreams and given her many a disturbed night in the past. Not that she was ever short of those in the present.

Rose shrugged philosophically. 'I'd prefer that, of course, but I certainly won't lack something to do in a city like Florence. I'll explore as many museums and galleries as possible, enjoy glorious meals and gaze into shop windows as much as I like.' And even swallow her pride and spend some of the money sent with the letter.

'But all that is for tomorrow. Tonight, it is time to dine. Charlotte has made a dinner reservation for two here tonight.' Dante reached across to touch her hand. '*Allora*, since she cannot join you, it would give me much pleasure to take her place.'

Rose snatched her hand away. 'Will you bring your wife along, too?'

'*Cosa?*' He sat back, his eyes suddenly arctic. 'You forget. I no longer have a wife.'

Rose winced. Had his wife *died*? 'I…I apologise. I didn't know.'

He raised a cynical eyebrow. 'Charlotte did not tell you that Elsa left me?'

'No.'

'You surprise me! In Fortino it was such a hot topic of conversation I was grateful when my travels took me to the vineyards of California for a while.' He drained his glass. 'But now you know I am *solo* again, and have been for years, may I have the honour of your company at dinner tonight, Miss Palmer?'

She studied him in silence. Her first instinct was to refuse. But she was secretly daunted by the thought of dining alone in such opulent and formal surroundings. Even so, after refusing for years to come to Italy in case she ran into Dante Fortinari again, it would be wiser to have some food sent to her room rather than accept the company of the man who'd caused total upheaval in her life after their first and only meeting. Her brain, which was still furious with him, ordered her to refuse point-blank, but her heart, the unruly organ which had got her into trouble in the first place, was urging her to forget wisdom for once. And, idiot that she was, that was what she was going to do. She would never come here again, so what harm in making use of him?

'You are taking much time to decide, Rose,' Dante pointed out. 'Do you wish for my company or not?'

'Yes. Thank you.' She eyed him curiously. 'How did you get involved in acting as delivery boy for Charlotte?'

He shrugged. 'Fabio offered to deliver a package to a friend of mine in New York and Charlotte requested a favour in return. I was most happy to do this because it meant meeting you again, Rose.' He signalled to a waiter for some menus.

'But do you have a place here in Florence these days? I vaguely remember that you lived in the family home at the Fortinari vineyards.'

'I did at one time, but now I own a house a few kilometres from our vineyards at Fortino. Now my father is retired I help run the business with my brother, Leo. He is maestro of production; I am good at the selling,' Dante said without conceit.

No need to tell her that. 'You came a long way just to deliver a letter.'

'A trip to Firenze is always a pleasure,' he assured her, and held her eyes very deliberately. 'Also, I wanted very much to see you again.'

'I'm surprised you even remembered me after all this time,' she said tartly.

'I have never forgotten you, Rose,' he assured her, and for the first time gave her the bone-melting smile that had caused all the trouble in the first place. '*Allora*, what do you like to eat?'

'Practically anything I don't have to cook myself!'

He eyed her over the top of his menu. 'You live alone?'

'No. I share a house not far from my mother.'

'I remember her well—a very lovely lady who looks much too young to be your mother.'

'That she does.' Rose returned to her menu. 'What do you recommend?'

'If you like fish the salmon will be good here. Or there is the *bistecca alla Fiorentina*, the famous steak of the region. You have travelled a long way today, Rose; you must be hungry.'

'I am, but not enough to attempt a steak. I'll have the salmon.' Her stomach was in such knots that she was sure she'd only be able to manage a bite or two at the most.

Rose listened as he gave the order to the waiter, wishing she could understand the rapid, melodious interchange. She had once fancied learning Italian to add to her schoolgirl French, but studies of a different kind had taken up all her time.

Later, experiencing the effortless service Charlotte had described, Rose was glad of Dante's company among the elegantly dressed diners. She would have felt uncomfortable dining alone. Instead, now she was over the first shock of meeting up with him again, she enjoyed the ravioli in sage-fragrant butter sauce Dante insisted she try for a first course, and ate her share of the exquisite little vegetables served with their main course. But she kept firmly to water instead of the wine he offered.

'You drank champagne the first time we met,' Dante reminded her. 'You were such a delight in that charming dress.'

'It was a long time ago,' she said coolly.

'You do not remember the occasion with pleasure?'

Her eyes clashed with his. 'Of course I do. It was Charlotte's wedding day. She was on cloud nine and I had just left university with a respectable degree. Euphoria all round.'

He held the look in silence for a moment then got up to

escort her to the bar. 'Will you take a little cognac with your coffee?'

'Since I abstained over dinner, I will, please.' Rose needed some kind of stimulant for once. A sip of the fiery spirit helped her to relax a little as she looked across at her companion. Now she could study him objectively without wanting to hit him, he looked a lot older and harder-edged than the effervescent charmer who'd made Charlotte's wedding so memorable for the bridesmaid. There had been other young Italian men among Fabio's relatives and friends at the wedding, but Dante had monopolised Rose so completely she'd had no eyes for anyone else.

'You are very quiet,' he observed.

'It's been a very eventful day.'

'So tell me all about your life, Rose.'

'I run a bookkeeping business from home.'

His eyebrows rose. 'You did not take up your career in accountancy?'

'No, though the qualifications come in very handy in my line of business.' She changed the subject. 'Dante, I know it's a bit late to say this, but I was very sorry about your grandmother.'

'*Grazie*. I miss her very much.'

'Do you miss your wife, too?'

'No. Not at all.' His eyes hardened. 'The marriage was a bad mistake. When Elsa soon left me for another man my brother said I should thank God for such good fortune. Leo was right.'

Rose looked him in the eye. 'Odd you forgot to mention Elsa when we first met.'

His mouth twisted. 'I did not forget. I refused to let thoughts of her spoil my time with you. I was very angry because she refused to cancel a fashion shoot to accompany me to Fabio's wedding.'

'So you made do with me.'

'No! This is not true, Rose. I took great delight in your company.' His eyes held hers. 'Am I too late to apologise for leaving you so suddenly?'

'I completely understood when I heard that your grandmother had died.' She held the brilliant blue gaze steadily. 'Not so much when I was told about Elsa.'

His jaw clenched as he beckoned to a waiter. 'I need more cognac. Will you join me?'

'No, thanks.' She got up. 'I'm a bit tired, Dante, so—'

'No!' He sprang up. 'It is early yet. Stay a little longer with me, Rose, *per favore*.'

Since only sheer pride had forced her to make the first move, she nodded graciously and sat down again, eyeing Dante's glass. 'Should you be drinking that before a long drive?'

'I am not driving. I have reserved a room here at the hotel tonight so that I can be your guide to the city tomorrow.'

Rose stiffened. 'Charlotte asked you to do this?'

'No, she did not. It was my idea.' He lifted a shoulder, his eyes cold again. '*Non importa*, if you do not desire my company I will leave in the morning.'

That would be the best move all round, as Rose knew only too well. But she was a stranger in a city foreign to her and didn't speak a word of Italian, so it was only practical to take advantage of someone native to the place. After all the trouble he'd caused her, he might as well make himself useful.

'I'd appreciate your services as guide, Dante. Thank you.'

'It is my great pleasure, Rose!' He reached across the table to touch her hand, eyes warm again. 'I will try to make your stay memorable.'

He wouldn't have to try hard. In spite of her initial rage at the sight of him, it had taken only a minute in Dante's company again to remember how easy it had been to fall in love with him all those years ago. He'd been a charming, attentive companion who'd shown unmistakable signs of returning her feelings on Charlotte's wedding day, which had made it all the more devastating when she'd learned about his missing fiancée after he'd gone. In sick, outraged reaction to the blow, she had immediately blanked him out of her mind and pretended she'd never met him. And because she'd flatly refused to listen whenever his name came up, Charlotte had eventually given up mentioning him. Yet Charlotte had sent Dante to the hotel with her letter. Rose made a note to have words with Signora Vilari on the subject next time they spoke.

She took her hand away. 'Won't it be boring for you, Dante, showing me round a city you know so well?'

He shook his head. 'Firenze will seem new to me, seen through your eyes. But why have you not been here before, Rose? I had hoped so much to see you again when you visited Charlotte, but you never came.'

'Too much work to get away. And I see her regularly when she comes to visit her father.'

'She told me Signor Morley shares his life with your mother. You are happy with this?'

Rose nodded. 'It's a happy arrangement all round.'

'It was plain that you were all close at the wedding. I am fortunate to possess both my parents, but no longer, alas, my grandmother. I adored her and miss her still.' Dante's eyes lit with sudden heat. 'Only the message telling me she was dying could have torn me away from you so suddenly that night, you understand? But, *grazie a Dio*, because I left immediately I arrived at the Villa Castiglione in good time to say goodbye to Nonna and hold her hand in mine before she…she left us.'

'I'm glad of that,' said Rose quietly. Though at the time she hadn't believed a word of it, convinced the call had been from some girlfriend—a theory which had seemed proved beyond all doubt next morning when she found out about Elsa.

'Nonna left her house to me.' Dante's eyes darkened. 'At first I did not want the Villa Castiglione, afraid I would miss her there too much. But because it was Nonna's greatest wish my parents persuaded me to live there.'

'Alone? You've found no replacement for Elsa yet?'

'No.' He arched a wry black eyebrow. 'You think such a thing is easy for me?'

'I don't think about you at all.' She shrugged. 'After all, I only met you once.'

His eyes narrowed to an unsettling gleam. 'And you did not look back with pleasure on that meeting!'

'Oh, yes, most of it. I had a great time with you all day. But once I knew you were spoken for I never gave you another thought.' She smiled sweetly and got to her feet. 'Now I really must go to bed.'

He walked with her to the ornate lift. 'I shall take much pleasure in our tour of Firenze, Rose.'

'You must tell me what to see.'

'When do you fly home?'

'Thursday morning.'

'So soon!' He frowned. 'But that gives you only one day for the sightseeing. We must meet early for breakfast.'

'I thought I'd have it sent up—'

'No, no.' Dante shook his head imperiously. 'I will take you to breakfast in the Piazza della Signora to begin on the sightseeing as we eat. We shall meet down here at nine, *d'accordo*?'

Rose nodded. 'I'll enjoy the luxury of a lie-in for once.'

'You rise early for your work?'

'Much too early.' She smiled politely as the lift glided to a halt and pressed the button for her floor. 'Which one for you?'

'The same.' He showed her his room number. 'So if you are nervous in the night you can call me and I will come.'

Rose shot him an arctic look. 'Not going to happen, Dante.'

'Che peccato!' When they reached her room, Dante opened the door and stood aside with a bow. 'Now lock your door to show me you are safe.'

Rose nodded formally. 'Thank you for your company this evening, Dante.'

His lips twitched. 'Because it was better than none?'

Rose let her silence speak for her as she closed and locked the door.

Dante made for his room and went out onto his balcony, deep in thought as he stared down at the Arno. Rose Palmer was very different now from the girl he'd fallen more and more in love with as the hours passed during that memorable day. Even in the rush to reach his grandmother's side, and the searing grief that followed, it had been impossible to stop thinking of the girl he'd been forced to abandon so suddenly that night. He had made a vow to apologise to Rose in person when she first visited the Vilaris. But she never came and the apologies were never made.

It was no surprise that she had been hostile at first tonight. Whereas he had felt a great leap of his heart at the first sight of her, and an urgent need to offer comfort when she found Charlotte wasn't joining her. He had seized the chance to propose his own company instead. He smiled sardonically, well aware that Rose had accepted the offer only because it was marginally preferable to spending her brief time in Florence alone. Tomorrow, therefore, he must do everything in his power to make her stay pleasurable before she went back to her bookkeeping. He shook his head in wonder. Could she not do something more interesting with her life?

Convinced, for a variety of reasons, that she'd lie awake all night, Rose fell asleep the instant she closed her eyes. When she opened them again the room was bright with early sunshine, and with a gasp she shot upright to grab her phone, and smiled in relief when she saw a message from her mother. Grace Palmer had come late to the skills of texting, and the message was brief:

Everything fine. Have lovely day.

Reassured, Rose sent off a grateful response and then stretched out in the comfortable bed, feeling rested after the surprise of the best night's sleep she'd had for ages. Eventually, she wrapped herself in the hotel robe and went out on the balcony, face uplifted to the sunshine. Since she *was* here at last, doing the last thing she'd expected to do, pride urged her to make herself as presentable as possible now Dante Fortinari was to be her guide.

In the years since she'd last seen him she'd persuaded herself he couldn't possibly be as gorgeous as she remembered. And she was right. Now Dante was in his early thirties maturity had added an extra dimension to his dark good looks—something her wilful hormones responded to even while the rest of her disapproved. So since a capricious fate—or Charlotte—had brought them together again, she would make use of his escort for a day and then tomorrow, back home in the real world, erase him from her life. Once again.

Dante had worn a suit cut by some Italian master of the

craft the evening before, so if he'd decided to stay on the spur of the moment it seemed likely he'd have to wear the same thing again today. With that in mind, Rose went for pink cotton jeans instead of the denims worn for travelling. With a plain white cotton tee, small gold hoops in her ears and her hair caught back with a big tortoiseshell barrette, she slid her feet into the flats brought for sightseeing with Charlotte and felt ready to take on the day.

Dante was waiting in the foyer when she went downstairs shortly before nine, his look of gleaming appreciation worth all her effort. '*Buongiorno*, Rose. You look delightful!'

So did Dante. She raised an eyebrow at his pale linen trousers and crisp blue shirt. 'Thank you. You've been shopping?'

He shook his head. 'It is my custom to keep a packed bag in the car.'

Her lips twitched. 'Ready for unexpected sleepovers?'

He grinned, looking suddenly more like the youthful Dante she remembered. 'You are thinking the wrong thing, *cara*. I do this to impress the clients. Here in Italy, image is everything.' He looked at her feet with approval. '*Bene*, you are prepared for walking.'

'Always.' As they left the hotel she looked at the sparkling river in delight. 'Though my daily walks at home are in rather different surroundings from these.'

'But the town you live in is a pleasant place, yes?'

She nodded. 'Still, it's good to take a short break from it. My only time away from home before was in university.'

'I remember your pleasure at doing well in your final exams, and the celebrations which followed them.' He frowned as they began to walk. 'But you did not continue with the accountancy.'

'No, I didn't.' She waved a hand at the beautiful buildings they were passing. 'So talk, Signor Guide. Give me names to go with all this architecture.'

Dante obliged in detail as they walked with the river on one side and tall, beautiful old buildings on the other. But eventually he steered Rose away from the Arno to make for the Piazza della Signora with its dominant fifteenth century Palazzo Veccio that still, Dante informed her, served as Town Hall to Florence. He steered her past the queues for the famous Uffizi Gallery and the statues in the Loggia dei Lanzi on their way to the Caffe Rivoire. 'You may look at all the sculpture you wish later,' he said firmly and seated her at an outdoor table with a view of the entire Piazza. 'But now we eat.'

Rose nodded. 'Whatever you say. Breakfast is a rushed affair at home, so I shall enjoy this.' In the buzz of this sunlit square packed with people—and pigeons—she could hardly fail. She sat drinking it all in to report on later.

'I will buy you a guidebook so that you may show your mother what you have seen,' said Dante as the waiter brought their meal. 'You will take orange juice?'

'Thank you.' As she sipped, her eyes roved over the statuary she could see everywhere, and felt a sudden stab of envy for the man sitting so relaxed beside her.

'That is a very cold look you give me,' commented Dante, offering a plate of warm rolls.

'I was thinking how privileged you are to live in a place like this. You probably take all this wonderful sculpture for granted.'

'Not so. I do not live in the city,' he reminded her. 'Therefore, I marvel at it every time I return. And, Signorina Tourist, these statues were erected for more than decoration. The big white Neptune in the fountain with his water nymphs commemorates ancient Tuscan naval victories.'

'How about the sexy Perseus brandishing Medusa's severed head over there? Just look at those muscles!'

Dante laughed, his eyes dancing at the look on her face. 'He is a Medici warning to enemies, while the replica of Michelangelo's *David* represents Republican triumph over tyranny.' He shook his head. 'Enough of the lessons. What would you like to do next?'

'Could we just sit here for a while, Dante?' Rose refused to feel guilty because she was enjoying herself so much. She could go back to resentment and hostility later.

'Whatever you wish.' He beckoned to a waiter for more coffee.

Rose tensed as her phone beeped; she read the text, replied to it quickly and put the phone away. 'Sorry about that—one of my clients.' She smiled radiantly at the waiter who topped up her cup. *'Grazie.'*

'Prego!' The man returned her smile with such fervour Dante frowned.

'It is good I am here with you,' he said darkly when they were alone.

'Why?'

'To keep my beautiful companion safe from admirers.'

Rose shook her head impatiently. 'Hardly beautiful— I'm just reasonably attractive when I make the effort.' But sometimes the effort was hard.

'You are far more than just attractive, Rose,' he said with emphasis, and signalled to the offending waiter. 'I will pay, and then we shall see more of Firenze.'

'Dante,' she said awkwardly, 'could I pay, please?'

He stared at her in blank astonishment. *'Cosa?'*

She felt her colour rise. 'You've given up your time to show me round. I can't expect you to feed me as well.'

'It is my privilege,' he said, looking down his nose. 'Also a great pleasure.'

'But I feel I'm imposing.'

Dante shook his head. 'You are not.' He took her hand and stayed close enough to make himself heard as they threaded their way through the crowds in the Piazza. 'I was forced to rush away from you last time, Rose, with only a brief apology. This time perhaps you will think better of me after we say goodbye tomorrow.'

Less likely to murder him, certainly. 'When you've been so kind, how could I not?' she said lightly. She stood looking up in wonder as they reached Perseus and his grisly trophy. 'Wow! I've seen Renaissance art in books but the bronze reality is something else entirely.'

'Cellini was a master,' he agreed, and moved on to the next, graphic sculpture. 'So was Giambologna, yes? You like his *Rape of the Sabine Women*? It is carved from a single block of marble, but it is flawed, as you see.'

Rose wrinkled her nose. 'I'm not so keen on that one.'

'Then let us go to the Bargello, which was once a prison, but now houses sculpture. Donatello's bronze *David* from a century earlier is there. You will like that, I think. Then you cannot leave Firenze without a visit to the Accademia to gaze in wonder at the greatest statue of all—the marble *David* by Michelangelo.'

Rose found that Dante was right when they arrived at the rather forbidding Bargello. On the upper loggia, it needed only one look at Donatello's jaunty David, nude except for stylish hat and boots, for Rose to fall madly in love. She turned to Dante, her eyes bright with recognition. 'I've seen him before on a television programme.' She grinned. 'The handsome lady in charge of his restoration couldn't help smoothing his bottom!'

He laughed, his eyes alight as he squeezed her hand. 'You have not changed so much after all, *bella*. But now you must have a *tramezzini* and a drink. We may have to wait for some time in the Accademia.'

She shook her head. 'I don't need anything yet after all that breakfast, Dante. Let's go now.'

As Dante had forecast, at the Academy of Fine Arts they had quite a wait among throngs of tourists with cameras and students with backpacks, but when they finally gained entrance to the star attraction Rose stood motionless in pure wonder at the sight of the monumental white figure gazing sternly far above their heads, the sling he would use to kill Goliath at the ready over one shoulder.

'You are impressed?' murmured Dante in her ear.

'How could I not be?' With reluctance, she dragged her eyes from the statue. 'Thank you so much for bringing me here.'

'It is my pleasure as much as yours, Rose. But now, if you have looked at David long enough, we shall go in search of food. Shall we go back to Caffe Rivoire, or would you like to try a different place?'

'The Rivoire again, but just coffee and a snack, please.'

'You shall have whatever your heart desires.'

CHAPTER TWO

To Dante's amusement Rose took surreptitious glances at her phone from time to time when they were seated among the greenery at a table close to the building, a little away from the press of crowds and pigeons in the Piazza.

'You are expecting a call from your lover?' he demanded at last.

'Sorry. Just checking for any client problems,' she lied. No way was she telling him she was checking on her child—who just happened to be his daughter. She thrust the phone in her bag, feeling suddenly cold. Would Dante try to lay claim to Bea if he found out about her? No way was she sharing her child with him. Bea was hers and hers alone.

'You look tense. Forget the work for today,' commanded Dante. 'Let us enjoy this unexpected gift of time together. First you must rest for a while in your room and then later we shall go wherever you wish.'

Rose forced a smile and insisted that she couldn't waste precious time in resting, but after some of the café's famous hot chocolate conceded that Dante's idea was a good one after all.

'*Bene,*' he said as they walked back to the hotel. 'Those beautiful eyes look heavy. We shall meet in the foyer at three, yes?'

She frowned. 'Look, Dante, I'm taking up a lot of your time. If you have other things to do—'

'What could be more important than spending time with you, Rose?'

'If you're sure—' A yawn overtook her mid-sentence, and Dante laughed.

'You see? A rest is good, yes?'

Rose nodded, embarrassed to feel glad of the rococo gilded cage instead of trudging up the stairs. 'If I stayed in Florence for any length of time I'd get very lazy.'

Dante smiled indulgently. 'It is good to be lazy some-times, Rose. I shall see you at three—unless you would like to sleep longer than that?'

She shook her head. 'I'll be ready on the dot.'

Rose rang her mother for a brief update and learned that Tom had collected Bea from nursery school, and af-terwards the three of them had gone for a walk in the park to feed the ducks and buy ice cream.

'Did she cry for me in the night, Mum?'

'No, darling. She told me I wasn't quite as good at read-ing stories as Mummy, but otherwise settled down fairly well, and went off happy to school this morning. So do stop worrying. Enjoy yourself.'

Reassured, Rose had a brief rest on the bed, showered herself awake afterwards and changed the white tee for a navy polo shirt. When she saw Dante waiting for her in the foyer downstairs her unruly heart gave a thump as his eyes lit up at the sight of her. He was too good-looking by half, she thought resentfully as he took her hand.

'You slept, Rose?'

'I had a shower instead.'

'So did I.'

Since he was wearing a fresh shirt, his black curls

were damp and he smelt delicious, Rose had already gathered that.

'Where now?' she asked as they left the hotel.

'To look at shops, *naturalmente*!'

Their first stop was on the Ponte Vecchio to look at the jewellery on display, but with her eyes popping at the prices Rose soon abandoned the jewellers for a shop selling silk ties.

'You want a gift for the boyfriend?' asked Dante.

Tempted to lie and say yes, she shook her head. 'For Tom, Charlotte's father.' She pointed to one in cream-dotted bronze silk. 'What do you think?'

'A good choice. What will you buy your mother?'

'I think I'll go for one of these silk scarves. Which do you fancy?'

Dante pointed to one in colours similar to the tie. 'That one, yes?'

Rose was very pleased with her purchases, sure she would have paid a lot more without Dante's help. Later, window-gazing at designer clothes in the Via da Tornabuoni, they spent fantastic pretend fortunes on a wardrobe for her before Dante took her to the Piazza della Repubblica to browse through La Rinascente, a department store where Rose could have spent hours.

'Next time stay longer and linger here as long as you wish. Also explore the Palazzo Pitti and the Tivoli Gardens,' Dante told her. 'But now, if you are not too tired, let us walk to Santa Croce to visit the Bar Vivoli Gelateria. The best ice cream in the world is made there.'

'An offer I can't resist!' She laughed up at him and saw his eyes light up. 'What?'

'At last you laugh! For a moment I saw the younger Rose again.'

The smile faded. 'A fleeting illusion, Dante.'

Their progress was slow on the way to the Vivoli due to the lure of the small shops in the Santa Croce area. In one of them Rose spotted attractive plaques in papier mâché painted with vegetables and bought a pair for her mother and Tom. 'They both love gardening, and these will be light enough to stow in my suitcase.'

He smiled. 'You have done much shopping for others, but nothing for yourself.'

'I don't need anything,' she assured him. She felt guilty enough about spending Fabio's money as it was. 'I'll settle for this ice cream you promised.'

At the Bar Vivoli Rose rolled her eyes in ecstasy when she tasted her strawberry ice cream. 'It's gorgeous—aren't you having any, Dante?'

He shook his head, smiling indulgently. 'I will protect the shopping from your gelato while you enjoy. Is there more you wish to buy? Or we could explore the great church of Santa Croce here.'

'I'd like to very much, but I'd better leave that for another time.' Not that there would be another time. She looked up at the magnificent facade with regret. 'Shall we go back now?'

'Whatever you wish, Rose. Where would you like to dine tonight?'

So he meant them to dine together again. Irritated by her pleasure at the prospect, she told him that at that moment, her palate still rocking with strawberry gelato, it was difficult to think of food. 'Maybe we could eat in the hotel again?' At least that way the cost of dinner would appear on her hotel bill and she would feel less obligated.

Dante frowned. 'If you really wish to. But there are many restaurants in Firenze. One of my favourites is right here in Santa Croce. We could take a taxi if you are tired. You can decide later when you have rested.'

She nodded. 'Fine.'

'I will see you at nine then, Rose.'

'I'll be ready. Are you taking a rest, too?'

He nodded. 'Also I must make a few phone calls, touch base, as you say. *Ciao.*'

Rose waited to make sure Dante stayed put in his room and then, praying she wouldn't get lost, hurried out of the hotel to make her way back to the Piazza della Repubblica to buy some of the delightful things she'd seen earlier in the department store. It might be Fabio's money, but he would approve of presents for Bea. When she got back she stowed her packages away in her suitcase and, feeling hot and grubby after her rushed, guilty shopping spree, checked her messages, grateful to find a brief but totally reassuring one from her mother. The other, at last, was from Charlotte, so obviously happy Rose felt a searing pang of envy for an instant before stepping into the shower, but afterwards fell into instant sleep so heavy it took the phone to wake her.

'Willow House Bookkeeping,' she muttered sleepily, and bit her lip at the sound of Dante's chuckle.

'You are in Firenze now, *cara.* You obviously slept well!'

She stifled a yawn. 'Very well.' She sat bolt upright after a look at her watch. 'And much too long!'

'*Bene.* You obviously needed this. Sleep longer if you wish.'

'No, indeed. Just give me half an hour and I'll be ready.'

'I shall knock on your door.'

Rose shot off the bed to wash and get to work on her face. Wishing she had something different to wear, she brushed her hair loose to ring the changes a little with the faithful black dress, and flung the scarf bought for her mother over one shoulder.

'You glow, *cara*,' Dante told her when she opened the door to him later.

'Surprising what a little nap can do for a girl.' She smiled guiltily. 'I thought Mum wouldn't mind if I wore her present just once first, but I must be careful not to get anything on it—no more gelato, for a start.'

'Should such a tragedy happen, I will buy you another. So, Rose, do you still wish to dine here, or would you like something more *animado*, where locals eat?'

'*Animado* with locals, definitely. And I'm perfectly happy to walk.' Maybe she could persuade him to let her go halves with the bill.

'Then I shall take you to a trattoria near the bar where you had your gelato. It is basic and traditional, and so popular it is always crowded.'

'Sounds good. Lead on.'

After her hot, furtive dash earlier on it was dangerously pleasant to stroll with Dante through the balmy warmth of the Florence evening. For one night like this she would pretend he was just a friend she was enjoying an evening with, rather than the man who'd once broken her heart and turned her life upside down. The trattoria was packed, as he had forecast, but a place was found for them in a long red-walled dining room filled with laughing, talking, gesticulating diners sitting elbow to elbow, in total contrast to the formality of the night before, and Rose loved it.

After discussion with the waiter who brought their menus Dante ordered wine and mineral water and sat back, amused to see Rose so obviously enjoying the proximity with her fellow diners.

'This is more like it,' she said with satisfaction, sneaking a look at the dishes set down at the next table. 'Will you help me choose, Dante?'

He leaned close to translate the names of the dishes,

and after much discussion about the various delights on offer Rose settled on a mixed grill of fish with spinach. 'I don't cook fish much at home, so this is a treat for me. What are you having?'

'I like your choice. I will have the same.' Dante nodded in approval as he studied the bottle of wine a waiter offered for his inspection. '*Grazie*. Try the wine, *cara*, and give me your opinion.'

'Mmm,' she said with relish. 'Gorgeous. What is it?'

'A Fortinari Classico,' he said with pride. 'I am impressed that they keep this range here.'

'Which means it's very pricey.' Rose drank a little more. 'I can see why.' She raised embarrassed eyes to his. 'I'm putting you to so much expense, Dante. Please let—'

'No!' he said flatly. 'To see you enjoy your dinner is reward enough.'

'I'm enjoying everything.' She looked round the packed, noisy dining room with pleasure. 'I love it here.' Her eyes sparkled as plates were set in front of them. '*Grazie,*' she said to the waiter.

Dante laughed indulgently as she sniffed in rapture. 'Enjoy, *carina*.'

'I will! It's a long time since that gelato.'

'So tell me about this house you live in,' Dante said later, after Rose had refused a *dolce* in favour of coffee.

'It's my own family home. Mum signed it over to me when she moved in with Tom. He wants them to get married,' she added, 'but Mum is happy the way things are, afraid that formalising the arrangement might change it. She believes in the saying "If it ain't broke don't fix it".'

Dante's eyes darkened. 'She is wise.'

Rose looked at him questioningly. 'Were you heartbroken when your wife left you?'

He gave a mirthless laugh. '*Dio*, no! My brother, as al-

ways, was right. I had a fortunate escape—forgive me,
Rose. You cannot want to hear this.'

How wrong could a man be? 'Is Elsa still with the new
man she left you for?'

'Yes, though *new* is not the right word.' Dante's expressive mouth turned down. 'Enrico Calvi is old enough to
be her father, but so wealthy Elsa is now enjoying a life
of idle luxury.'

'She wanted to do that?'

'Oh, yes.' He smiled sardonically. 'Younger faces—and
bodies—were winning the top jobs. She was glad to abandon her career while still known as a supermodel. *Allora*,
I no longer see her face on magazine covers everywhere
to remind me of my folly.'

'Is she very beautiful still?'

He nodded carelessly. 'I have not seen her since she
left, but Elsa was obsessed with her looks and I doubt she
has changed much. Calvi has children from a former marriage and does not demand the babies that would ruin his
trophy wife's perfect body. I, fool that I was, wanted children very much.'

Rose drank some water, suddenly sorry she'd eaten so
much as her stomach lurched at Dante's heartfelt admission.

His mouth tightened. 'She waited until our wedding
night to tell me she had no intention of having babies.
Ever. But no more talk of Elsa.' Dante looked at Rose in
silence for a while, his blue eyes intent. 'Now I must take
you back. I wish you could stay longer, Rose.'

'Not possible, I'm afraid.'

'*Que peccato*! In the morning I will drive you to the airport in Pisa—unless you would prefer the train journey?'
He beckoned to a waiter to bring the bill.

'No, indeed. But won't that take up too much of your time?'

'It is not far out of my way home,' he assured her, 'and will give me the pleasure of more time with you before you leave. But this will not be goodbye, Rose. I shall see you when I come to England again next.'

Her heart lurched. If Dante still wanted babies no way was she letting him anywhere near Bea. He took her arm to steer her past an approaching entwined couple as they walked back, the contact raising her pulse rate even higher.

Rose paused when they reached the foot of the hotel steps, her eyes raised to the handsome, intent face. 'This has been a lovely evening, Dante. Not the kind of thing that features much in my life as a rule.'

'Yet Charlotte told me you have someone in your life.'

'He's a friend from my college days.'

'But surely you will marry one day, Rose?'

She shrugged. 'I doubt it.'

Dante held the door open for her. 'When you see Charlotte so happy with Fabio, do you not wish for a relationship like theirs?' His eyes darkened as they made for the lift. 'I have always envied them their marriage.'

'They're very lucky.'

Dante halted when they reached her room. '*Ascolta*, it is early yet, Rose. I would so much like to sit with you on your balcony and talk for a while longer like old friends. I can order tea. You would like that?'

She looked at him in silence for a moment. 'All right, Dante.' She gave him a wry smile. 'But only because you said the magic word.'

His smile mirrored hers. 'Friends?'

'No—tea!'

Dante laughed and rang room service. After a waiter arrived with a tray Dante tipped him and closed the door behind him then pulled up two of the chairs to the metal table on the balcony overlooking the moonlit Arno. Rose poured tea and the coffee Dante had ordered for himself, and sat back in her chair, eyeing him warily.

'So what shall we talk about?'

'You, Rose. Tell me why you started your own business.'

'I applied for accountancy jobs but didn't get the ones I wanted, so I decided to use my training for something else and eventually hit on bookkeeping.'

'Ah,' said Dante, nodding. 'You went to college again for this?'

'No. I did an eighteen-month home study course accredited by the Institute of Certified Bookkeepers, and managed to complete it in just over three months.' Rose drained her cup and refilled it. 'My mother was a huge help. So was Tom. He found a web designer for me and made sure I informed HM Revenue and Customs, and took out indemnity insurance to cover me while working in clients' offices. I also got a practising licence...' She paused, biting her lip. 'This is probably boring you rigid, Dante.'

He shook his head decisively. 'I am enthralled. You were so young to achieve all this, Rose. I am impressed.'

'I had a lot of things going for me,' she reminded him. 'With such wonderful support from my mother and Tom, a home of my own with a room I can use for an office—and with my brain still in gear from my finals—I managed to get the new qualification quickly. I now divide my time between working at home and in travelling to small businesses grateful enough for my help and my reasonable charges to pass on my name to new clients.'

'You make a good living from this?'

'It was a slow start, but I've now done well enough to pay back the money my mother lent me for the original expenses for certification and optional exams and the web design and so on.' Rose took a look at the clear-cut profile outlined by the light from her room. 'So now you know all about me, Dante.'

He shook his head. 'I think not. One day I hope to learn much, much more—but not tonight. I will leave you now to your sleep.' He raised her hand to his lips. '*Buonanotte*. I shall see you in the morning. Since we must leave early, you would like breakfast brought to your room?'

Rose nodded. 'Will you order it for me, please?'

'*Subito*. And in the morning I shall ring you when it is time to leave.' He went to the door and turned to smile at her. 'Now lock it, *per favore*.'

Rose spent a restless night after the conversation with Dante. His talk of babies terrified her. If he found out that Bea was his child what would he do? What would she do, if it came to that? She eventually lapsed into a restless doze but woke early, and after a horrified look in the mirror stood under a hot shower until she felt, and looked, more human. By the time her breakfast arrived her hair was dry and she was dressed for travelling, her bags packed.

Soon afterwards, Dante rang. '*Buongiorno*, Rose.'

'Good morning. I'm ready. I just have to sort the bill.'

'I will be with you in one second.'

When Rose opened her door Dante smiled at her denim jeans and casual jacket. 'You look so young, like a student again.' He took her suitcase. 'I will put this in the car, which is waiting outside. Forgive me if I stay there with it until you are ready to leave.'

'Of course. I'll join you as quickly as I can.' Armed with her credit card, Rose approached the suave receptionist to ask for her bill.

'All was settled in advance; there is nothing to pay.' He

handed her a receipted bill. 'Signor Fortinari waits outside in the car,' he added. 'I trust you enjoyed your stay?'

She smiled. 'I did. Very much. Goodbye and thank you.'

'*Arrivederci* and safe journey, Miss Palmer.'

Rose felt uneasy as she left the hotel, wondering if she should have asked for an itemised version of the bill for Fabio, but forgot her worries when she saw the car waiting at the foot of the steps. It was sleek and scarlet and as handsome as the man who jumped out of the driver's seat as she approached.

'Wow, Dante, great car!'

He laughed as he handed her inside. 'This is my one indulgence—she's a sports car but also practical. She has four doors, also four-wheel drive, which is of much use to me in some parts of the country. You like her?'

'What's not to like? She's obviously the love of your life.'

'*Davvero*—see how she responds to me?'

Rose laughed and sank back in the seat, feeling the power vibrate through her body when Dante switched on the ignition. 'What more can a man ask?'

He shot her a sidelong glance as he drove away from the hotel. 'Those things a machine cannot do for a man.'

Annoyed to feel her face flush, Rose made no response as she settled down to enjoy the drive, content just to look at the passing landscape as they left the city. She relaxed as she breathed in the aroma of expensive new car, and whatever Dante had used in the shower. 'This is a big improvement on the train journey,' she commented when they were speeding along the *autostrada*. 'I tried to look at the scenery I was passing through on the way here in the train, but I couldn't concentrate.'

'Why not?'

'I was tired after all the effort it took to juggle appoint-

ments and so on before getting away.' Plus her worries that
Bea might be unhappy without her, and the strain of wondering what was wrong with Charlotte.

'If your mother is looking after your business while
you are away she will be pleased to see you back, Rose.'

'Unless she's cross with me for buying presents.'

Dante laughed. 'If so, you may blame me for encouraging your extravagance. But you are very close to your
mother, yes?'

Rose nodded, smiling. 'But we have clashes of temperament sometimes.'

'My mother had many with my sister Mirella in the past,
but now she is Nonna to several grandchildren the clashes
happen only when she spoils them too much.'

'How many nieces and nephews do you have?'

'Five. Mirella and Franco have two sons and a daughter, and Leo and Harriet one of each.'

'Harriet?'

Dante nodded. 'My brother's wife is English. You would
like her.'

Rose was intrigued. 'How did they meet?'

'It is such a strange story I shall leave it until next time
I see you. I must concentrate now as the traffic is heavy.'

Dante insisted on waiting at Galileo Galilei Airport
with Rose until she was ready to board the plane, and took
note of her telephone numbers and her address while passengers surged around them as constant announcements
filled the air. 'I will be in London next month to meet an
old friend of mine, Luke Armytage,' he told her. 'He is a
master of wine and owner of a chain of wine stores which
retail our best vintages. I shall come to see you then, Rose,
but I will consult you first to make sure you are free.'

'Goodbye then, Dante.' Rose smiled at him brightly as
her flight was called. 'And thank you yet again.'

'*Prego.*' Without warning, he seized her in his arms and kissed her full on the mouth. He raised his head to stare down into her startled eyes and then kissed her again at such length they were both breathless when he released her. '*Arrivederci*, Rose.'

Afraid to trust her voice, she managed a shaky smile and hurried away after the other passengers.

Dante stood watching as his heartbeat slowed, his smile wry when it became obvious that Rose had no intention of looking back.

The flight home was tiring. Rose spent most of it convincing herself that there was no danger of falling in love with Dante Fortinari again, even after the electrifying effect of his goodbye kiss, which, from the look on his face, had affected Dante in pretty much the same way. She was human and female enough to find this deeply gratifying, but she would make sure it never happened again. No way could she let him back into her life. She would have to tell him about Bea, and then she would be forced to tell her mother the truth at last, that Dante Fortinari was her child's father. And then Tom would know, and so would Charlotte, and Fabio, and everyone else involved once she started the ball rolling. By the time Rose boarded the Pennington coach at Birmingham Airport, she had decided against any such dramatic upheaval in her tidy little life. If Dante did ring to ask to see her again she would take the coward's way out and refuse to see him.

CHAPTER THREE

WHEN THE CAB stopped outside Willow House the front door flew open while Rose was paying the driver, and a little girl dressed in jeans and T-shirt hurtled down the garden path with the tall figure of Tom Morley in hot pursuit. Rose abandoned her suitcase and swept her child up in her arms, kissing her all over her rosy, indignant face.

'Where you *been*, Mummy?' demanded Bea, struggling to get down. 'You didn't sleep in your bed for lots of nights!'

'Only *two* nights, darling. Have you been a good girl?'

Beatrice Grace Palmer nodded happily. 'Lots of times.' She tugged on her mother's hand. 'Come *on*. Me and Gramma did baking.'

'The cakes smell delicious, too,' said Tom, taking charge of the suitcase. He kissed Rose's cheek. 'You look tired, pet.'

'Only from travelling.' Rose smiled as Grace Palmer appeared in the doorway, looking too youthful in jeans and jersey to be anyone's grandmother. 'Talking of tired, how's Gramma?'

Grace hugged her daughter. 'I'm just fine.' She grinned triumphantly at Tom. 'We coped very well, if I do say so myself.'

Rose allowed herself to be towed straight to the kitchen,

where little iced cakes sat on a wire tray. 'Look, Mummy,' said Bea, bouncing in her little pink sneakers. 'Fairy cakes!'

'They look gorgeous. Let's have them for pudding after our lunch, which is something delicious from the yummy smell coming from the oven.'

'Nothing fancy, darling,' said Grace. 'I offered several menu suggestions to celebrate your return from foreign parts, but cottage pie won the majority vote. So come on, Bea. Let's put the cakes away in the tin so we can lay the table, and we all need to wash before we eat.'

'Bea and I will lay the table,' said Tom, 'and let Mummy wash first.'

'Hurry *up*, Mummy,' ordered Bea. 'I'm hungry.'

'I need another kiss,' said Rose huskily, and picked her daughter up to hug her.

Bea obliged her with a smacking kiss. 'I cried for you last night, so Gramma cuddled me.'

Rose blinked hard. 'Then you were a lucky girl. Gramma's the best at cuddling.'

Tom nodded in vigorous agreement over the curly fair head, winning a flushed, sparkling look from Grace as he took Bea from her mother. 'Come on, Honey Bea. Let's wash those paws.'

Rose hurried upstairs to her room and took a depressed look in the mirror as she hung up her clothes. Far from benefiting from her little holiday, she looked as weary and wan as she felt.

Lunch was a lively affair with much input from Bea about her activities in her mother's absence. 'I went to school *all* day yesterday, then to the park with Gramma and Tom.'

'I bet they enjoyed that!' said Rose, grinning.

'We did,' agreed Grace, and relieved her granddaughter of her plate. 'What a star—you ate the vegetables, too. You liked that, darling?'

'Yummy!' said Bea, and gave Rose a smile exactly like her father's. 'Cake now?'

Rose waited expectantly, eyebrows raised.

'Please!' Bea beamed in triumph.

'Good girl.'

After cakes had been devoured, Rose said casually, 'I'd better find some things I bought in Florence.'

'Where's that?' demanded Bea.

'It's a town near where Auntie Charlotte lives in Italy. I had to fly there on a plane. You can help me carry the parcels.'

Later that evening, after a rapturous Bea had tried on her new jeans and T-shirts, and the exquisite little dress that Rose hadn't been able to resist, the child was finally tucked up in bed with her new cuddly Pinocchio before Rose could finally relax over supper with her mother and Tom and give details of her trip. She told Charlotte's tale with care, not sure how much she was supposed to divulge to Tom.

'Good God!' He eyed Rose in disbelief as she finished. 'Charlotte finally got you there, only to take off somewhere else?'

Grace put a hand on his arm. 'No harm done, love. Rose had her first real break since Bea was born, and hopefully she was able to enjoy it, knowing that her baby girl was safe with us.'

He frowned. 'But the fact remains that Charlotte stranded Rose alone in a strange country while she went swanning off to New York with Fabio. How did you manage, pet?'

Rose braced herself. 'Charlotte asked Dante Fortinari

to deliver a letter to the hotel to brief me. You remember him from the wedding, Tom?'

'Of course I do. Charming fellow—got married shortly after Charlotte.'

'But his wife left him pretty quickly, stupid woman,' said Grace, eyeing her daughter. 'You got on with him very well at the wedding, I seem to remember.'

Rose nodded. 'He was great fun.'

Tom shook his head in disapproval. 'I shall have words with my daughter next time she rings. Now, tell me why she was so determined to get you to Florence. Lord knows she's asked you often enough before, so what made this occasion so different?'

'Tom,' said Grace gently, 'perhaps Rose thinks Charlotte should tell you that.'

Rose sighed. 'I do, but on the other hand, Tom, if it's going to worry you it's pointless to keep you in the dark.' She recounted Charlotte's suspicions about Fabio, followed by her remorse afterwards when she discovered the truth. 'Fabio insisted I should stay at the hotel anyway, all expenses paid.'

Grace shook her head in wonder. 'How on earth could Charlotte suspect Fabio of straying? The man adores her!'

'And spoils her far more than I ever did,' said Tom and raised an eyebrow at Rose. 'So where does Fortinari come into this?'

'He volunteered to show me round Florence.' Rose smiled brightly. 'Which was kind. I would have been a bit lost on my own.'

'I should damn well think you would.' Tom got up to hold out his hand to Grace. 'Come on, love, we must let this girl get to bed. She looks done in.'

'I could stay, if you like, Rose, and get up with Bea if she's wakeful tonight?' her mother offered.

'Absolutely not,' said Rose, laughing. 'You've done more than enough, both of you. Though I'm afraid I'll need you tomorrow afternoon for a couple of hours, Mum, if you can? A client got in touch while I was away so I'm driving to see her.'

'Of course.' Grace kissed her daughter good-night, and thanked her again for the presents. 'You shouldn't have been so extravagant.'

Rose smiled. 'Dante got a far better price for them than I would have done, and in any case it was Fabio's money.'

'Then we'll both enjoy our booty free of guilt,' said Tom, eyes twinkling.

Later Rose checked on her sleeping child, longing to kiss the rosy cheek but too tired to risk waking her up. Yawning, she went next door to her own room, glad to crawl into bed. It had been an odd sort of holiday. The stay in Florence had been too short, the air travel too tiring and her taste of the *dolce vita* with Dante too unsettling. It would take effort to knuckle down to routine again. Not that she had a choice. And though most people, like Dante, thought her job boring, her travels to meet with clients made it far less so than being confined to an office all day. As she reached to turn out the light her phone rang.

'Rose?' said a husky, unmistakable voice.

She sat bolt upright. 'Dante!'

'Did all go well on your journey?'

'It did, and now I'm back where I belong.'

'I do not agree with that,' he said, surprising her. 'In Firenze you belonged there. I shall be in London soon and will drive to see you.'

Rose was about to veto the idea when Dante went on without pausing.

'Now I know you are safe I will let you sleep. *Buona-notte*, Rose.'

'Good night. Thanks for ringing,' she said politely.

His chuckle sent tremors down her spine. 'You knew that I would. *Ciao.*'

Rose switched off the light and slid down in the bed, but thanks to Dante's call she was no longer tired. The mere sound of his voice had conjured up not only his goodbye kiss but all her doubts and fears about keeping his daughter secret from him. But he had no legal right to claim Bea as his daughter, she reassured herself with a resurgence of the old resentment. His sole contribution to her existence was a fleeting episode of sexual pleasure before he'd returned to the fiancée he'd neglected to mention.

When Bea had been dropped off at nursery school the next morning Rose got down to work right away to make up for lost time. Usually she did some household chores before settling at her desk, but Grace had left the house in remarkably immaculate condition for someone in charge of a lively child. Rose sighed. In the beginning, after Bea was born, she had tried hard to transform herself from slapdash student into perfect mother, housekeeper and eventual wage earner. She'd learned the hard way to get her priorities right. As long as Bea was happy, clean and well fed Rose took her mother's advice and kept her brief spells of spare time for taking the baby for walks, or resting while Bea napped. The chores could wait until Rose had time and energy to spare for them. Or, said Grace, she could accept money to pay for a little help in the house.

Rose switched on her computer, smiling at the memory of her indignation at the suggestion. She'd been so determined to be the most efficient single parent it was possible to be. And if she was sometimes desperate for a good night's sleep, or to be out clubbing or shopping with girl-friends again, or even just taking a walk without pushing a buggy, she never admitted it to a soul. She sighed irritably and settled down to work in the brief window of time before she collected her daughter.

Bea's face lit up when she saw her mother waiting for her. 'Mummy! You came today.'

'Of course I did.' Rose took her leave of the young teacher and held Bea's hand. 'I told you I would.'

'You didn't come yesterday.'

'I was away, so I asked Gramma and Tom to fetch you.'

Bea nodded as she was buckled into her car seat. 'They fetched me lots of times.'

'Only two times, darling.'

Bea looked unconvinced by the maths. 'Are you going to work today?'

'Yes, but only for a little while this afternoon. Gramma will stay with you and I'll be home in time for tea. And tomorrow it's Saturday and we can go to the park.'

Rose was soon so firmly entrenched in her usual routine again it was hard to believe the trip to Florence had ever happened until Charlotte rang to grovel with apologies and demand every detail of Rose's taste of *la dolce vita*.

Rose brushed that aside. 'Did you ask Dante Fortinari to show me round, Charlotte?'

'Certainly not. I just asked him to deliver your letter by hand because there was cash in it.' Charlotte paused. 'Though Dante seemed pretty keen on meeting up with you again.'

'He was very kind,' said Rose colourlessly. 'And,' she added with more bite, 'I would have been a bit lost in Florence if he hadn't turned up.'

'I know, I know,' said Charlotte remorsefully. 'But if Dante looked after you it all worked out in the end.'

'As did your problem,' Rose pointed out. 'You were mad to think Fabio would cheat on you!'

'Hormonal, not mad.' Charlotte drew in an audible breath. 'I behaved like a total idiot because—wait for the roll of drums—I'm pregnant at last.'

Rose gave a screech of delight. 'Oh, Charlotte, how *wonderful*. I'm so happy for you. Have you told your father?'

'No. I'll ring him right away now I've told you. I waited until I was absolutely sure before spreading the glad news. I didn't even tell Fabio until we were in New York.'

'But surely he was wondering?'

'Of course he was, but I've been late before so he was afraid to say a word, especially because I'd been a bit standoffish with him due to my crazy suspicions. But now I'm so happy I don't even mind the morning sickness part—at least not too much.' Charlotte came to a halt. 'So, Rose, are you still mad at me?'

'For giving me a luxury, all-expenses-paid holiday in one of the most beautiful cities in the world? No, Signora Vilari, I'm not. Now, hurry up and ring Tom so I can share the glad news with Mum.'

Once the excitement about Charlotte's news had died down Rose was soon back in her usual dual role of mother and businesswoman, until Dante rang one morning to say he would be with her the next day to take her out to dinner. She stiffened her resolve and told him that she was working and wouldn't be available.

'Is this true, Rose, or do you mean you have no wish to see me?'

She sighed. 'All right, I'm not working, but I think it's best we don't see each other again.'

There was silence on the line for a moment. 'I frightened you with my kiss?'

'Of course not. The thing is, Dante, I'm grateful for the time you took to show me round Florence, but it was just a one-off kind of thing.'

'You are refusing to see me any more?' he demanded, his voice hard.

'Yes. I am. You live in Italy and I live here, so it would be pointless, anyway.'

'*Allora*, you have not forgiven me.'

'For what, exactly?' she snapped.

'For making love to you and then leaving you so suddenly that night.'

'Oh, that. No forgiveness necessary. These things happen.'

'If not that, then I demand to know what is wrong, Rose.'

'Do you, indeed! Goodbye, Dante.' Rose switched off her phone and slumped down on the sofa, determined not to cry. She'd done enough crying over Dante Fortinari in the past. But no matter how hard she tried to control them, the tears came pouring down her face just the same and she had to do some hasty face scrubbing in case Bea saw Mummy crying.

Grace popped in later for coffee and frowned when she saw Rose's swollen eyes. 'Darling, what's wrong?'

'Dante rang. He wanted to take me out to dinner tomorrow.'

'But that's good, surely, not something to cry about?'

Rose sniffed inelegantly. 'I turned him down.'

Grace stared at her blankly. 'Why?' Her eyes narrowed suddenly. 'This is about Bea, isn't it?'

'What...what do you mean?'

'You don't want him to know about her. Bea's not a dark secret, darling—it's time you got that idea out of your system.'

Rose's heart settled back into place again. 'You're right. Lord knows, my situation is hardly unusual. I saw the percentages of single parent families in the headlines on my computer only this morning.'

'And, as one of them, you do brilliantly, darling.'

'Ah, but I wouldn't be without help from you and Tom. And,' Rose added with sudden passion, 'don't ever think I forget that, not for a minute.'

'I don't. So why not ring Dante back and say you've changed your mind? We'll have Bea for a sleepover and keep her out of the way if that would make things easier for you?'

Rose shook her head obstinately. 'I'm not going to see him again.'

'Why not? How often will you have a date with someone like Dante Fortinari?' Grace gave a wicked grin as she straightened. 'Your old pal Stuart Porter is very nice, but gorgeous and Italian he isn't.'

Rose laughed ruefully. Her mother had hit the nail on the head. Quite apart from Dante as escort, expensive dinners were not part of her social life. A night out with Stuart meant a trip to the cinema and sometimes coffee or a drink afterwards, all of which she enjoyed occasionally. But dinner with Dante would have been in a different league.

'Look, darling, why don't we have Bea for a sleepover tomorrow anyway, and you have a whole evening to yourself and a good night's sleep afterwards? You look as though you could do with it.'

'I know that.' Rose eyed her mother doubtfully. 'I love my daughter, but a night to myself does sound tempting.'

'Right. We'll come for her about four. She can eat with us as a special treat and we'll take her to school next morning, too, so you can make the most of *your* special treat.'

Bea was wildly excited the next day when she learned about the sleepover with Gramma and Tom. She loved the bedroom they had created for her there, so useful if Rose was ever travelling away overnight for work.

'Are you going out with Stuart?' asked Bea suspiciously as they packed her shiny pink holdall.

'No, not tonight. Why? Don't you like him?' On the odd occasions that she'd run into Stuart while out with Bea his embarrassment had been so plain her bright little daughter had picked up on it.

Bea shook her curly head in disdain. 'He calls me little girl.'

'Ah. His mistake, because you're a *big* girl! Shall I put Pinocchio in here with Bear or will you carry him?'

'Carry him.' Bea hugged the toy to her chest possessively, and then beamed as the doorbell rang. 'Gramma! Can I open the door?'

'Go down slowly,' called Rose. She collected a couple of books and followed with the bag, suddenly aware that it was very quiet below instead of Bea's usual joyful reunion with Grace. She flew down to the hall to find her daughter scowling at the man smiling down at her.

'*Buonasera*, Rose,' said Dante. 'Will you introduce me to this beautiful young lady?'

Struck dumb for a moment, Rose's first reaction was fury because all her cloak and dagger efforts had been useless. Dante was face to face with her child and, as a second strike against him, Mummy looked a mess while he, as always, looked wonderful. 'Why are you here?' she demanded.

His smile faded. 'I hope to change your mind about dining with me. But I make a mistake, yes?'

Dante's English was usually so good it was obvious she'd thrown him off balance.

'Not at all,' said Rose coolly. 'Do come in.'

Bea clutched Pinocchio to her chest, glaring balefully at the visitor.

'My name is Dante Fortinari,' he told her. 'What is yours, *bella*?'

'Beatrice Grace Palmer,' she announced militantly.

'My daughter,' said Rose, in case he was in any doubt.

'You are very fortunate,' said Dante, looking up from the fair curls to meet Rose's eyes. 'Perhaps we could dine early and take Beatrice with us?'

'No!' wailed Bea, incensed. 'I want to go to Gramma's.'

To Rose's relief, the doorbell rang again. 'Go and open the door again then, darling. This time it *is* Gramma; Tom, too, I expect.'

'Mrs Palmer, Mr Morley, I am delighted to see you again,' said Dante, shaking hands with the surprised pair in turn as they exchanged greetings. He smiled wryly. 'I came with hope to change Rose's mind about dining with me.'

'I'm sure she'd be delighted to do that,' said Grace, narrowing her eyes at her daughter as Bea swarmed up into Tom's arms and sat there, secure and hostile, scowling at Dante.

'Are you packed and ready, Honey Bea?' asked Tom. 'If so, we'll take you home to supper.'

'Yes, come along, darling,' said Grace, manfully ignoring the undercurrents simmering in the hall of Willow House. 'It was lovely to meet you again, Dante.'

'My pleasure, *signora*.' He smiled at the little girl in Tom's arms. 'It was a pleasure to meet you, too, *bella*.'

Another scowl was the only response.

'Bea,' said Rose in a tone the child knew well.

'Sorry,' she said and then, to everyone's surprise, gave Dante her most irresistible smile. 'Not Bella. I'm Bea.'

He returned the smile in delight. 'I apologise!'

'Bye-bye,' she said firmly, hugging Pinocchio closer.

'Be a good girl for Gramma and Tom,' Rose reminded her.

'She always is,' said Tom, bending the truth a little.

Rose waved as the trio went down the garden path then closed the door and turned to face her visitor.

'Why did you not tell me you had a daughter?' Dante demanded before she could say a word.

Rose's chin lifted. 'If you're inferring that I'm in any way ashamed of her, I assure you I'm not!'

He held up a hand. '*Pace, pace*. How could you be ashamed of such a beautiful child? Yet if I had not ignored your refusal to see me I would not have met her. You did not want me to?'

'No, I didn't.'

His eyes narrowed. 'Because her father objects?'

'No, nothing like that.' Rose sighed. 'Oh, well, now you're here, come into the kitchen. I'll make coffee.'

Dante shrugged off his suede jacket as he followed her. *'Permesso?'*

'Of course. Do sit down.'

He took a chair at the table, his eyes on the artwork adorning the walls. 'These are by Beatrice?'

Rose nodded. 'Yes. As you can see, she's heavily into red and orange. And, as she informed you, we call her Bea.' She made coffee, then laid a tray and brought it all over to the table. 'Would you like something to eat?'

'Nothing, *grazie*.' Dante's eyes met hers. 'You are angry with me for intruding, Rose?'

'Only because I would have preferred to tell you about Bea before you met her.'

'But since you refused to see me again, when would you have done that?' he demanded, looking down his nose with hauteur. 'You are obviously uneasy because I have come here against your wish. Is there a jealous lover or, worse, a husband, who would object to my presence here?'

'Neither.' She sat down wearily. 'I suppose you may as well know the truth. Bea is the result of a one-night stand with someone who has no idea he's a father. I'm not ashamed of my child, only of the circumstances that brought her into the world.'

Dante sat down abruptly, colour draining from his olive skin. He leaned forward and grasped her hand. 'You were—forced, *cara*?'

'No, nothing like that! I just drank one glass of wine too many one night to celebrate my results.'

'And you did not tell this man what happened?'

'No.' Rose felt her face heat. 'At the time I was work-ing as a waitress while I applied for jobs, and put my lack of energy—and other things—down to being on my feet so much. It was a couple of months before it even dawned on me that I could be pregnant.'

Dante's grasp tightened. 'What happened then?'

Rose drew in a deep, unsteady breath. 'I told my mother and gave her the glad news that I had no intention of con-tacting the father. Tom, of course, was ready to hunt him down and force him to take responsibility. Fabio and Char-lotte too.'

'*Naturalmente,*' said Dante harshly. 'Did they find him?'

'No. I refused to give his name.'

'*Dio!*' He raked a hand through his hair. 'Your mother found this hard, yes?'

Rose nodded. 'So did Charlotte. But she was hugely

supportive, flew over to see me a lot during the pregnancy and even insisted on being present at the actual birth.'

'She is a good friend,' said Dante, nodding. 'She was very unhappy about deserting you in Firenze, Rose.'

'Is that why you volunteered to look after me?'

'No. I was most delighted to do so.' He eyed her narrowly. 'I so much enjoyed our brief time together there, but you think it is a mistake to meet again, yes?'

'I'm sorry I was so rude, but finding you talking to my daughter was a shock.' She sighed. 'When I first found out I was pregnant I was in such a state I begged Charlotte and Fabio to keep it secret from the wedding guests I'd met because there's no father in the picture.'

'Yet there is one somewhere who has no idea he has a daughter.' Dante shook his head. 'Having met your child, I feel sympathy for him.'

'Too late to tell him now; he'd never believe me,' said Rose flatly.

Dante looked at her in silence for a moment, his eyes intent on hers. 'You are going out tonight?'

'No.'

'Yet your child has gone to stay overnight with your mother and Signor Morley, yes?'

'Yes.' Rose coloured. 'Mum thought I could do with some time to myself.'

'So what will you do? Read, watch television?'

'Probably.'

'While I go back to my hotel for a lonely dinner.' He reached across the table and took her hand. 'Change your mind. Dine with me, Rose.'

Now he was here, with the touch of his hand sending heat rushing through her, Rose found it hard to imagine why she'd ever said no to him in the first place. 'All right.'

She ignored the warning bells going off in her head. 'But you'll have to wait while I made myself more presentable.'

His smile took her breath away. '*Bene*! I will go back to the hotel to make myself more presentable also and return for you later.'

'Thank you,' said Rose, wondering if she'd made a huge mistake. At least her mother and Tom would be pleased. They worried about her lack of social life.

'And this time I will be more welcome, yes?'

Her eyes softened. 'Sorry I was so hostile, Dante.'

'*Non importa,*' he assured her, and smiled as he collected his jacket. 'Your daughter was even more hostile, no?'

'It was a new experience for her.'

'The friends who take you out do not call for you here?'

'No. I meet them in town.'

Dante nodded. 'And drive yourself home afterwards so you can leave when you wish?'

'Exactly.'

'I shall return at seven-thirty—and not a minute sooner. *D'accordo*?'

Rose nodded. 'I'll be ready.' She opened her front door and smiled when she saw the sleek hire car. 'Nice wheels again, Dante.'

'Not as nice as my own, though,' he said with regret and returned the smile, his eyes warm again. 'I look forward to our evening, Rose. *Ciao.*'

'*Ciao,*' she echoed as he drove off, and shook her head. Her efforts to keep her life private had been a total waste of time.

Rose hurried upstairs to shower and give herself a makeover. She couldn't compete with Dante's faithless Elsa, but she could look pretty good when she made the effort. When she was ready she eyed her reflection critically and took heart in the fact that even in the clinging caramel jersey of her Christmas present dress her baby bulge was hardly noticeable now, due to constant boring exercises.

She went downstairs, wondering why she was doing this. After the delight Dante had taken in Bea earlier, she should have sent him packing right then to avoid any future danger. But she'd silenced her head and given in to the heart which urged her to make the most of an opportunity that would probably never happen again.

When she opened the door to Dante later the heated look he gave her was worth all her hard work. 'Rose, you are ravishing!'

'Thank you, kind sir. You look pretty good yourself. Nice threads.'

'*Cosa?*'

'Great suit.'

'*Grazie.* I like your dress also.'

'Thank you.'

Rose had expected Dante to treat her to dinner at the Chesterton, the best hotel in town, but she stiffened as she realised he was driving out into the country to a venue they eventually approached down a long tree-lined drive. The Hermitage was so well-known for luxurious comfort combined with the warmth of a family-owned hotel that Charlotte had chosen it for her wedding.

Before Rose could ask why Dante had brought her there, a large, vaguely familiar man came out to greet them, hand outstretched to clap Dante on the shoulder.

'Introduce me, then.'

'This lovely lady is Miss Rose Palmer, Tony.' Dante turned to Rose. 'Rose, allow me to present my cousin, Anthony Mostyn, owner of the Hermitage—also of the Chesterton in town.'

Rose smiled as Tony Mostyn shook her hand. 'How do you do?'

'A pleasure to meet you, Miss Palmer. A shame my wife's taken the children to her mother's for a couple of days. We could have made a foursome for dinner.'

'Give Allegra a kiss from me and tell her we look forward to seeing her next time. What is good on the menu tonight, Tony?' asked Dante.

'Everything,' said Tony promptly, 'including your usual choice. So enjoy the meal. I'll catch up with you later.'

'What is wrong, Rose?' asked Dante when they were seated in the bar.

'This is where we met at Charlotte's wedding,' she said tonelessly, and looked him in the eye. 'I remember seeing Tony Mostyn at the time, and thinking he looked young to run the Hermitage. You didn't tell me you were related.'

'It is not the dark secret. My aunt, Anna Fortinari, married Huw Mostyn, Tony's father, but tragically they were killed in an air crash a few years ago. Tony is now managing director of the company that runs both hotels. His sister used to work in the business with him, but she married a Frenchman and lives in Paris now.' Dante surveyed the crowd in the bar. 'Tony does well.' His eyes were sombre as he turned back to her. 'I thought you would like to come here again, Rose, to the place where we first met. But this is another mistake, yes?'

'Yes,' she said bluntly, her eyes narrowing as a waiter arrived with a bottle of champagne.

'Mr Mostyn's compliments, sir,' he said, and filled their glasses.

Dante told him to convey their thanks and turned to Rose with a frown. 'Why did you look at me so?'

'I thought you were reminding me that I drank too much champagne last time I was here.'

His mouth tightened. '*Dio*, you find it very easy to think badly of me. For which you have good reason.' He lifted a shoulder, his eyes taking on the cold, hard look she'd seen before. The silence lengthened between them. 'This evening is a bad idea, yes?' he said at last.

'No.' Rose felt sudden remorse. 'It's lovely here, Dante, and a great treat for me.' Oh, God, that sounded so pathetic. 'But if you prefer to drive me home right now I wouldn't blame you. I've been utterly petty and graceless—'

'Because I brought you here, where we first met?' Dante moved closer. 'I hoped it would bring back pleasant memories. But perhaps all you remember is the way I left you so suddenly—'

'And then went on to marry the fiancée you forgot to mention to me.' To her angry dismay, her eyes filled with tears.

'For which I felt great guilt afterwards.' Dante gave her a pristine white handkerchief and then filled their glasses. 'Do not cry, *bella*. We must drink some of this champagne or Tony will ask questions.'

Rose dabbed at her eyes, thankful they were seated in a corner where no one would notice. She managed a smile and picked up her glass. 'Has my mascara run?'

Dante checked them out. 'No, Rose. Those beautiful dark eyes are still perfect.'

She raised her glass. 'What shall we drink to?'

'To more evenings together like this, but without the tears!' Dante drained his glass and signalled to a waiter that they were ready to order.

'You know, Dante,' said Rose, thinking about it, 'I've eaten more meals with you recently than with anyone other than Bea.'

'That pleases me very much.' He smiled at her over one of the huge menus. 'What would you like tonight? I always choose roast beef with the Yorkshire pudding when I am here.' He laughed as she looked at him in astonishment. *'Davvero!'*

Now she'd recovered from their disturbing little exchange Rose found her appetite had recovered with it. 'Actually, that sounds really good. Make it two.'

Dante gave the order to the waiter then sat back. 'Perhaps next time we can take your little Bea out for a meal. Would she like that?'

'She would.' Though Rose had no intention of letting it happen.

He smiled and refilled her glass. 'I also. I often take my nephews and nieces out, though not all of them at once! You must bring little Bea to meet them next time you come.'

Rose sighed. 'That won't be any time soon.'

'Because of your work?'

'Partly, yes.'

He eyed her questioningly. 'If the expense is also a problem I would be happy—'

'Certainly not!' she said, so sharply people nearby looked round. 'Sorry,' muttered Rose, crimsoning. 'But I can't take money from you, Dante. I feel beholden enough already because you paid for so much in Florence.'

'Is it so hard to accept things from me?' he demanded in a fierce undertone. 'I ask for nothing in return, if that is your fear.'

'I know that.' She bit her lip. 'The thing is, Dante, ever since Bea was born I've tried very hard to live on what I earn from my business. I refuse hand outs, even from my mother. Though she paid for what I'm wearing today by calling it a Christmas present.'

'She is a clever lady.' Dante relaxed slightly. 'Also I doubt that Charlotte keeps to such rules.'

'No. She comes laden with presents every visit, including the suede jacket you gave to someone to put away.'

'You cannot hurt your dearest friend by refusing her as you refuse me.' Dante got up, holding out a hand to Rose as a waiter informed him their table was ready.

She was thoughtful as she accompanied him to a small, intimate dining room very different from the large one used for Charlotte's wedding breakfast. Had her refusal actually hurt Dante?

The room was full, the atmosphere lively with the buzz of conversation, and though not as loud as at the trattoria in Santa Croce a great improvement on the hushed elegance of her first dinner in Florence.

Dante nodded when Rose mentioned it. 'I was surprised that Charlotte chose that particular hotel for your stay. You liked it there?'

'I was a bit intimidated when I first walked through the doors. But at the time I was so worried about Charlotte—' She halted, biting her lip.

'Fabio told me why,' Dante assured her quickly. 'Charlotte suspected him of taking some other woman to New York on their wedding anniversary. *Incredibile!*' He shook his head. 'There are many men who do such things, of course, but Fabio Vilari, never. And now Charlotte is about to give him a child he is the happiest man alive. What will you drink, Rose?'

'No more wine for me, thanks. I'll have some lovely Welsh water.'

'Because I will drive you home I will drink the same.'

'If you send me back in a taxi you won't have to.'

Dante glared at her. 'You think I would do that so I could drink another glass of wine?'

'Just a thought,' she murmured as they were served with miniature Welsh rarebits.

From then on Rose made sure she was as good company as possible as they ate their appetisers and then watched, impressed, as a huge roast of beef was carved on a trolley at the table and perfect high-rise Yorkshire puddings served to them with locally grown vegetables.

'Do you cook roast beef like this, Rose?' asked Dante as they began eating.

'I've never tried,' she confessed. 'Mum does it on Sundays sometimes, but usually goes for roast chicken, Bea's favourite. At home I cook pasta a lot—and, of course, the inevitable fish fingers, which my daughter would eat every day if allowed.'

'You make the pasta?'

'Alas, no. I buy the fresh kind from a supermarket. But I do make my own sauces.' Rose smiled at him as she went on with her meal. 'I see why you always order this here, Dante. It's superb.'

'Yet I think you enjoyed our meals in Firenze also, yes?'

'I certainly did.' Her eyes met his. 'You made my little holiday there very special, Dante.'

He smiled warmly. '*Grazie*. It was special for me, too. You must come again soon. And this time, perhaps, you will bring your daughter?'

Rose suppressed a shiver at the thought as Dante leaned nearer, the warmth of his breath on her cheek. 'I hope very much that you will come. You have forgiven me at last, Rose?'

'For coming to see me today?'

His eyes held hers. 'No. For leaving you here so suddenly all those years ago, when I wanted so much to stay.'

'Oh, that,' she said airily. 'Of course I have. Forgiven and forgotten years ago.'

Dante's smile was wry. 'You put me in my place, I think.'

Her eyes fell. 'Let's not talk about it any more, Dante. It was a long time ago and we're two different people now.'

'*Certo,*' he agreed. 'You are the successful one with your own business and your beautiful daughter—'

'While you help run the exalted Fortinari vineyards.'

'But I made a bad marriage,' he said bitterly.

She shrugged. 'My record's hardly faultless in one instance.'

'You speak of Bea's father?' He frowned. 'Are you sure you will not search out this man and tell him about her?'

'Absolutely sure. Can we talk about something else, please?'

'I shall do whatever you wish, *carina.*'

Tony Mostyn joined them shortly afterwards for coffee. He showed them the latest photographs of his children and received the news that Rose was a single parent with much interest when Dante told him she ran her own business.

'When you take a day off you must bring your little girl over to meet Allegra and my two,' he told her. 'My wife would like that very much.'

Rose thanked him and looked at her watch. 'And now I'm afraid I must be getting home. It was a wonderful meal, Tony. My sincere compliments to the chef.'

'I'll pass them on.' Tony grinned at his cousin. 'Though next time try something different. Dante here always goes for the same thing.'

'Why not? I eat it nowhere else. Also it is your national dish and your man does it to perfection,' said Dante, unmoved. 'I shall see you in the morning, Tony, but now I must drive Rose home.'

To Rose's surprise, Tony Mostyn asked for her telephone number as they left, so he could get in touch when his wife came home.

'I like your cousin,' she said on the way to the car park.

'He is a great guy,' Dante agreed. 'You will like Allegra also.' He gave her a searching look as he helped her into the car. 'Will you visit her, Rose?'

'If she asks me to, yes, I will.' Rose found she liked the idea a lot. She'd lost touch with most of the friends she'd made in college, mainly because they were now pursuing high-profile careers, or if they had children they also had a husband. And Charlotte, her closest friend of all, lived in Italy.

'You enjoyed the evening, Rose?' asked Dante as he drove off.

'Very much. Thank you for taking me there.'

'Even though it was where we first met?'

'Even so.'

When they arrived at Willow House, Dante switched off the ignition and gave Rose a wry sidelong glance. 'This is where we say goodbye, unless you will invite me in to talk for a while before we part.'

Rose nodded. It was relatively early, and who knew when she would have another evening like this? 'I could make more coffee—'

'I have no wish for more coffee,' he said and smiled. 'But I would very much like more of your company.'

CHAPTER FOUR

ROSE UNLOCKED HER front door and led Dante into the small sitting room, which was unusually tidy, partly due to Bea's absence, and partly because Rose had whirled round it like a dervish in case Dante came in when they arrived home. She took off her jacket and laid it on the back of a chair.

'Are you sure you won't have coffee?' she said, suddenly awkward now they were alone together in the silent house.

He shook his head and took her hand to draw her down on the comfortable velvet sofa that dated from Rose's childhood. 'This is a very warm, welcoming room,' said Dante, surveying it appreciatively.

'All my mother's work,' she assured him. 'I'm lucky. Not many single parents own a fully furnished home, complete with willing babysitters close at hand.'

'Davvero!' Dante smoothed a hand over the upholstery. 'There is a sofa a little like this in my house also, Rose. My grandmother was fond of velvet.'

'Have you kept all her furniture?'

'Yes.' He sighed. 'At first I thought this was a mistake. I kept waiting for Nonna to walk through the door to join me. But now, every time I go home I feel her warmth and love welcoming me.'

'Your wife didn't feel the same about it, obviously,'

Rose said, and wished she hadn't as his face hardened into a mask.

'I do not like to discuss her,' he said, looking down his nose.

She nodded coldly. 'How true. You certainly made no mention of her the first time we met.'

'I have apologised for this already, more than once,' he said wearily and got up. 'I think it is best I leave.'

Rose jumped to her feet, chin lifted. 'So leave.'

For a moment she was sure that Dante, his eyes blazing blue flames, was about to storm out of the house there and then, but with a choked sound he pulled her into his arms and kissed her fiercely. *'Arrivederci, tesoro.'*

By supreme effort of will Rose detached herself, her eyes glittering hotly. 'That's what you said last time.'

He frowned. 'At the airport in Pisa?'

'No. When you left my bed after the wedding.' She smiled sweetly. 'Goodbye, Dante. Thank you for dinner.'

'Tell me, Rose,' he demanded angrily, 'why did you accept my invitation tonight? At one moment I think we are friends, but then in the blink of the eye I am enemy again.' His eyes narrowed. 'It amazes me that you agreed to my company in Firenze.'

It had amazed Rose at the time. 'I was alone in a foreign country, remember?' She eyed him narrowly. 'If it comes to that, why did you offer? Did Charlotte ask you to take pity on me?'

Dante looked down his nose again. 'I felt pity without being asked.'

Rose glared at him, incensed. 'So Saint Dante escorted Charlotte's little friend out of the goodness of his heart!'

He raised a shoulder. 'You could say that, yes. Though I am no saint.'

'No. Neither am I. As you have discovered for yourself

since meeting up with me again, my disposition has deteriorated.' She felt sudden shame. 'So have my manners.'

Dante's smile stopped short of his eyes. 'You have reason. You work hard with no husband to provide for your daughter, and you do well. She is a credit to you.'

'But Bea has a temper, too, which is definitely down to me, because her father—' She stopped dead at the sharp look Dante gave her.

'Her father is of better disposition?'

She nodded, flushing.

'You know this from just one night?' he demanded. 'Rose, I think you know much more than that, so why do you not contact him? He deserves to know the truth.'

She took a leaf from Dante's book and stared down her nose at him. 'It's absolutely none of your business, Dante Fortinari.'

He stiffened, and inclined his head with hauteur. 'You are right. It is not. Goodbye, Rose.'

He strode from the room and straight out of the house. Rose gave a choked sob as she heard the outer door close, and then began to cry in earnest as Dante drove away. She curled up in a heap on the sofa, and for the first time in years gave way to engulfing, bitter tears that only died down at last when she remembered the dress. Head thumping, stomach suddenly unhappy after the rich dinner, she trudged upstairs, hung up her dress and pulled on her bathrobe. She took off her make-up and pressed a wet cloth to her swollen eyes then stiffened, heart hammering, at the sound of the doorbell. Rose raced down the stairs, almost falling in her haste to wrench open the door, and found Dante holding out something that caught the light.

'Your earring, Rose. It came off in the car, I think.'

'Oh. Thank you.' She swallowed convulsively, trying to blink away the black spots dancing in front of her eyes.

'Dante I'm…I'm so sorry, but—' She uttered a sick little moan and would have crumpled in a heap if he hadn't sprung to catch her.

Rose came round on the sofa with Dante leaning over her, an expression of desperate anxiety on his face as he bombarded her with a flood of questions she couldn't understand.

'English,' she croaked, and his eyes lit with a smile so brilliant she closed her own in defence.

'Forgive me, *bella*, in my panic my English deserted me. What is wrong?'

'I passed out.'

'*Certo*! But why?'

'I panicked when you rang the bell.'

'Ah, Rose. I am so sorry. Though it is not so very late.'

'I know. But my immediate thought was Bea. Mothers tend to be wired that way.'

Dante slid an arm beneath her and slowly and very carefully raised her to a sitting position. 'Your head still spins?'

Rose thought about it. 'A bit. Could you hang on to me a little longer?'

He muttered something under his breath.

'What did you say?'

'I will hold you all night if you permit.' He smiled. 'But I will not expect that.'

Her lips twitched. 'I won't, either. I meant until the room stands still.'

Dante sat beside her, holding her close. '*Allora*, you are comfortable like this?'

'Yes.' Much too comfortable.

He looked down into her swollen eyes. 'You have been weeping, *cara*. Because we parted in anger?'

She nodded again and, to her dismay, her eyes filled again. 'And now my head is aching, and I look *awful*.'

'You do not,' he assured her, and gathered her closer. 'You need some of your tea, perhaps?'

Rose managed a smile. 'Do you know how to make tea, Dante?'

He shrugged. 'I put the tea-bag in the cup and pour the hot water, yes?'

'Absolutely. But I won't have any just now.' The scent and warmth and muscular security of his embrace were far more effective than tea. And, unlike tea, were not normal features of her life. 'Sorry I was such a shrew earlier. I enjoyed our evening, Dante. At least until the moment you stormed off and left me sobbing my heart out.'

Dante turned her face up to his. 'You cried because I left?'

'Yes.' She drew in a deep, shuddering breath. 'I was utterly horrible, and you didn't give me the chance to say I was sorry.'

His eyes held hers with a look which turned her heart over. 'We have both made enough apologies now, *bella*, yes?'

She nodded, her bottom lip quivering as she tried to smile. 'Are we friends again?'

Before the words were out of her mouth, Dante's lips were on hers, and she gave herself up to his kiss with a relishing little sound that tightened his arms round her as he kissed her swollen eyelids and her red nose and then returned to her quivering parted mouth with a sigh of such pleasure she melted against him, shivering in response to his urgent, caressing hands. Emotions heightened by the quarrel, their kisses grew wild with such hunger that history repeated itself with inexorable rapture. Hands and lips came together as clothes flew in all directions, restraint gone up in smoke as they came together in a pulsating, overpowering rush of desire that hurled them both to orgasm, and left them panting and breathless, staring at each other in shock.

'*Dio,*' Dante said hoarsely at last. 'From the moment I saw you again in Firenze I have wanted this, but I swear I did not intend it tonight, *tesoro.*'

Rose pushed him away and suddenly hotly aware of her nakedness, snatched up her robe. 'My fault as much as yours, Dante.' She swallowed hard. 'I don't know what to say, so please go now.' Before she did something really insane and begged him to take her to bed and make love to her all night.

Dante pulled on his clothes at top speed and then turned to her, his blue eyes lambent with a light which sent a streak of heat right down to her toes. '*Arrivederci, amore.* But this is not goodbye. I shall return soon. Very soon.' He took her in his arms. 'I have no wish to leave you now, Rose, but it is late and you need your bed.'

She looked at him searchingly. 'Why did you come back, Dante?'

'Because nothing has changed since that first time we met,' he said huskily, smoothing a hand down her cheek as he released her. 'You are as irresistible to me now as you were then. *Buonanotte, carissima.*'

Rose watched him stride down the path to the car at the gate, wishing her heart would resume its normal beat. Dante turned to wave, and she lifted a shaking hand in return, then closed the door and went upstairs to stand under a hot shower to recover. Fool! How could she have allowed that to happen again? Allowed? She gave a mirthless laugh. She could no more have prevented it than stopped breathing.

Grace had insisted on giving Bea her breakfast and then driving her to school so Rose could enjoy the added luxury of a lie-in the next morning, but Rose was showered and dressed and ready to start work by the time her mother called in before going home.

'I've made some coffee,' she said, smiling.

'Good. I need it.' Grace sat down at the kitchen table and watched her daughter filling cups.

'Was Bea all right last night, Mum?'

'Fine. How about you? Did Dante change your mind about going out?'

'Yes. We went to the Hermitage.' Rose set the cups on the table, eyeing her mother narrowly. 'What's wrong? Are you sure Bea didn't play up last night?'

'She was as good as gold.' Grace took a deep breath. 'Look, Rose, there's no easy way to say this, but it's time you told me the truth. Is Dante her father?'

'What?' Rose went cold. 'Why on earth should you think that?'

'Because,' continued Grace relentlessly, 'yesterday when Bea smiled at him and Dante smiled back, the resemblance stared me in the face, not least the blue eyes. Your father's eyes were dark like yours and mine. And I'd better warn you that Tom, not normally observant in such matters, commented on it first.'

'Which doesn't make it true.'

'Doesn't it? I couldn't sleep last night as I thought back to the wedding, how Tom and I preferred to drive home once Charlotte and Fabio left on their honeymoon, but booked a room for you so you could enjoy the party with the other guests. Then Dante Fortinari had to leave in a hurry because his grandmother was ill.'

'So you think he somehow sandwiched in a quickie with me before he took off?' snapped Rose.

Her mother winced. 'I wouldn't have put it quite like that, but it would certainly explain a lot.' Her eyes remained locked with her daughter's. 'I'm right, aren't I?'

The backbone Rose had always managed to keep so rigid suddenly crumbled. Unable to look away, she slumped down on a kitchen chair. 'Yes, you are. But this doesn't change anything. I have absolutely no intention of telling Dante.'

'Why not?' Grace reached to take her hand. 'Can you tell me what happened after we left that night, darling?'

Rose nodded reluctantly.

She had been dancing to something slow with Dante late in the evening when it struck her that Charlotte's home would now be in Italy with Fabio, and her lifelong friendship with Rose would naturally take a back seat. When Dante had asked why she was sad she'd confided in him and blinked away her tears, suddenly desperate to get to bed. Dante had insisted on escorting her to her room, where he'd held her in his arms to comfort her, at which point she'd found she was no longer tired and within seconds they'd been kissing and caressing wildly, shedding their clothes to fall on the bed and join together in a maelstrom of heart-stopping bliss. They had still been locked in each other's arms, breathless as they came back to earth, when Dante's phone rang. Cursing, he had reached over Rose to pick it up, then with a wild exclamation he'd withdrawn to leap to his feet to dress, all the while continuing an impassioned conversation with the caller in Italian. Rose had pulled the sheet up to her chin as Dante, face ashen and haggard, begged forgiveness for his sudden departure, his English erratic in his distress as he explained he had to return home immediately because his grandmother was very ill. 'I will contact you soon. *Arrivederci, tesoro*,' had been the parting words she'd never forgotten.

She smiled bitterly. 'After he'd gone I lay in a rose-tinted afterglow, dreaming of a future relationship with Dante, only to discover the next morning that he had a fiancée he'd forgotten to mention.'

Grace winced. 'And you'd had unprotected sex!'

Rose gave a mirthless laugh. 'Not a bit of it. He used a condom, but it was faulty. In his rush to get away he didn't realise that, so I knew it was unlikely he'd believe he was the father of my child.' She eyed her mother ruefully. 'Not that it was possible to tell him, anyway. By the time I realised I was pregnant I was two months along, as you well know, and Dante Fortinari was well and truly married by then. So there was no way I could name him as Bea's father. Dante is one of Fabio's closest friends, and Fabio is married to *my* dearest friend, so I just couldn't spoil things for Charlotte and perhaps even risk affecting the relationship between you and Tom.'

'So you invented a one-night stand after a college party.' Grace got up and pulled her daughter into her arms. 'My darling girl, what are you going to do now?'

'Nothing.' Rose swallowed hard. 'I was such a fool to go to Florence. I'd been refusing to all this time just in case I met Dante again. And then Charlotte actually sent him to see me at the hotel, and I took one look at him and knew exactly why I'd fallen in love at first sight all those years ago. Because, Mum, if I hadn't fallen so hard for him it wouldn't have happened.' Her face flamed. 'And in case you're wondering, Dante was no way to blame. It was completely consensual.' Not only then but last night, too. Would she ever learn?

Grace stood back and looked at her daughter searchingly. 'Are you still in love with him?'

Rose nodded miserably. 'But I don't *want* to be. Part of me still blames him for what happened, and now and then my resentment gets the upper hand.'

'Did you part on good terms last night?'

'Eventually, yes. But there were a few awkward moments during the evening *and* when he brought me home. In fact, I offended Dante so much he drove off in a strop. But he drove back again later, so we were on good terms again before we said goodbye.' Far too good, damn him. 'It's a pity Bea inherited my disposition, not Dante's.'

Grace smiled wryly. 'He was very taken with her, love.'

Rose shivered. 'I know. But it makes no difference.'

'Are you really sure about that?'

'Yes, Mother.'

'But surely you must have considered telling Dante about Bea once you knew his marriage was over?'

'I didn't *know* it was over. I always refused to listen if Charlotte so much as mentioned Dante's name. You knew, obviously.'

Grace nodded. 'We met him on a visit to Charlotte, but when I tried to tell you about it you shut me up. I understand why now.'

Rose sighed. 'I wish I had listened to you, Mum. I put my foot in it with Dante the first night we met up again in Florence. When he suggested taking Charlotte's place at dinner I practically spat at him and asked if he was bringing his wife along. What a sweetheart I can be when I try!'

Grace gave her a hug. 'I love you just the same.'

When her mother went home Rose got down to work, and did her best to lose herself in it, but it was hard now Grace knew the truth. During the years when the identity of Bea's father had been her own private secret she had hidden it away like an oyster covering a grain of sand. But now it was a secret no longer. She hadn't thought to swear her mother to silence about it, and the relationship between Grace and Tom was so close he would soon know something was wrong and coax the truth out of her. Then probably Charlotte would be the next to know and now she was pregnant and hormonal she was unlikely to be calm and reasonable about it. Rose shuddered as she imagined Charlotte storming into Dante's house, demanding that he did the right thing—whatever that was.

Revelations apart, life went on for Rose in much the same way as usual for the next few days, except for nights disturbed by thoughts of the passionate encounter with Dante, and the fact that her daughter's parentage was no longer a secret. Grace assured her she had not confided in Tom, but found that very hard.

'It's your secret, not mine,' she said unhappily. 'I still think you're wrong to keep the truth from Dante. It would be much better to tell him yourself rather than have him discover it some other way.'

'There is no other way. You're the only one who knows, Mum.' Rose frowned. 'Though you said Tom commented on the likeness. Has he said anything?'

'Yes. But I told him he was imagining it, that Bea's blue eyes came from my grandmother.' Grace pulled a face. 'I just loathed lying to him, Rose.'

'But I'm grateful you did. Think about it! A single mother working hard to provide for her daughter suddenly informs wealthy scion of famous Fortinari wine-producing family that he's her child's father.' Rose's mouth twisted cynically at the thought.

But later than night, when Dante rang after she was in bed, Rose was sorely tempted to tell him the truth when he asked after her little daughter. 'You must be so proud of her. And how is her beautiful mother?' he asked in a tone so caressing Rose's toes curled under the covers.

'Working hard, but otherwise fine. How are you, Dante?'

'I am also working hard, but I cannot sleep for wanting you in my arms again. I need so much to see you, *tesoro*, but for a while this is not possible. I have seen Charlotte,' he added, 'and she is very well.'

'I'm so glad for her and for Fabio.'

'He is looking forward to fatherhood very much—*Dio*, how I envy him!'

A wave of such guilt swept over Rose it was almost like pain. 'You won't when he's walking the floor at night when the baby won't sleep,' she said, deliberately flippant, 'or will he hire a nurse? How do you arrange such things in your world?'

'My world is not so different from yours, Rose. Some people have such help, but if I had a child I would wish to be involved in the caring as much as possible.'

'Sorry, Dante, I must go,' she said breathlessly, 'I think I hear Bea.'

'Then run, little *mamma*. I will ring again soon. *Buonanotte*.'

Rose laid the phone down and slid out of bed to check on Bea, who, as she'd known perfectly well, was fast asleep with Pinocchio and Bear. With her blond curls tumbled over her forehead and the unmistakable blue eyes closed, there was no resemblance to her father at all. But awake it was so marked to Rose that as Bea grew older she had been afraid that everyone involved who knew Dante would some day make the connection. Lying awake afterwards, Rose kept hearing the note in Dante's voice when he spoke of envying Fabio. Her mother was right. It was time to tell Dante he was Bea's father before someone, somehow, got in first. He deserved the truth from her whether he believed her or not.

CHAPTER FIVE

ROSE WAS GLAD to be abnormally busy the following week, with more travelling than usual. By the time she'd played with Bea once she'd got home, given her a bath and shared her supper, then read to her until she slept, Rose was too tired for soul-searching.

Dante rang to inform her that the following week he would be in London again and would drive down to see her. 'I shall take you out to dinner, Rose, but this time you may choose the restaurant,' he assured her, and laughed softly. 'And I will not come too early.'

Rose braced herself. 'Actually, Dante, perhaps you'd like to come to supper here this time. I'll cook.'

'*Grazie*, I would like that very much,' he assured her, surprised. 'But do not tire yourself with cooking. We can send out for a meal.'

Rose rolled her eyes at a sudden vision of a designer-suited Dante surrounded by foil cartons. 'I'll think about it.'

'I cannot sleep at night for missing you. Have you missed me?'

'Yes,' said Rose simply.

'*Ottimo*, I am very happy to hear it. I will be with you at eight on Wednesday evening.'

'Come earlier than that if you like.'

'I like very much, but won't your Beatrice object?'

'No. Apparently she likes you much more than Stuart.'

'And who,' growled Dante, 'is Stuart?'

'An old school friend I go out with occasionally. Bea disapproves of him because he calls her "little girl".'

'So you allow this man to come to your house?'

'No. But we've met him in the town a couple of times. He feels uncomfortable around Bea and she's picked up on it.'

Dante chuckled. 'I will not be uncomfortable with her.'

Rose bit her lip as she closed her phone. He might change his mind about that once he knew the truth. But she would tell him this time, somehow. She had nothing to lose. If Dante refused to acknowledge Bea she was no worse off than before. Besides, she was only taking his advice. It was Dante who'd insisted Bea's father had a right to know.

Grace's reaction to Rose's decision was a mixture of pride and apprehension. 'At least I can now tell Tom. We can provide backup if you like, darling.'

'That's very brave of you, but this is between Dante and me. You can stand by to pick up the pieces if things go pear-shaped.' Rose smiled ruefully. 'I've always been afraid this would happen one day. Every time Bea smiled up at Charlotte and Fabio I was sure the penny would drop, but it never did.'

'Only because they haven't seen Bea and Dante together.'

'True. They're in for a shock.'

'Not as big a shock as Dante.' Grace patted her hand. 'Are you sure you want to handle this alone, Rose? I'm perfectly willing to play the outraged parent. After all, Dante had no right to seduce you when he was about to marry someone else.'

'Mum, he didn't *seduce* me. One minute he was comforting me, the next minute we were so utterly desperate for each other we didn't even hear his phone ring straight away.' Rose sighed. 'He didn't want to answer it but I insisted, and you know the rest.'

Now she'd made her decision to tell Dante the truth Rose wished she could have done so right away instead of having to wait a week. None of her usual travelling was necessary for the time being, which enabled her to get through a lot of work at home and spend more time with Bea, who was delighted by the arrangement.

'But you like it when Gramma looks after you?'

Bea nodded vigorously. 'And Tom,' she assured her mother, and then gave Rose the smile exactly like her father's. 'But I love you best, Mummy.'

'I love you best, too,' said Rose, clearing her throat.

She was reading to Bea on the sitting room sofa later when the doorbell rang.

'Gramma!' cried the child, sliding down.

'I don't think so. She's gone shopping with Tom. Hold my hand while we see who it is.'

Rose opened the front door to find a vividly attractive brunette smiling at them.

'Rose Palmer? I'm Harriet Fortinari. Sorry to take you by surprise like this, but I'm on a fleeting visit to my mother so Dante suggested I look you up.' She leaned down to the child. 'You are Bea, of course. I've heard all about you.' She smiled so warmly she received one of Bea's sunniest smiles in response.

'How lovely to meet you. Do come in.' Rose ushered her guest inside. 'Dante said you were English, but I didn't realise you came from Pennington.'

Bea looked up at the visitor with far more welcome

than she'd given Dante. 'Want a cuppa tea?' she asked hospitably.

'I'd love one, darling.' Harriet grinned at Rose. 'If that's all right with Mummy?'

Rose laughed. 'You're honoured. Bea doesn't offer tea to everyone.'

'So I gather from Dante!'

'Come into the sitting room; I won't be a minute.'

'I'd rather watch while you make it. Bea will show me where.'

'Let's take our guest to the kitchen, then, pet,' said Rose, surprised to see her daughter take Harriet's hand.

'We had to come home from the park,' Bea informed their visitor. 'It rained. Want to see my paintings?'

Harriet assured her she'd like nothing better, and inspected the artwork in the kitchen with due respect while Rose made tea and took a cake from a tin.

'You're a very good artist, Bea—' a verdict which won another smile '—shall we sit here at the table?'

Bea nodded proudly. 'I don't need a high chair now.'

'Of course not. You're a big girl.'

Rose smiled warmly into Harriet's beautiful dark eyes. 'You've been speaking to Dante!'

'Have you got a little girl?' asked Bea.

'Yes, though she's a big girl, too. A bit bigger than you. Her name's Chiara. And I have a son, too; his name's Luca. I couldn't bring them with me because they're in school.'

'I go to school,' said Bea proudly.

'Would you like some cake, Harriet?' said Rose.

'Gramma and me made it,' confided Bea.

'I'd love some,' said Harriet, and sipped her tea with pleasure. 'Wonderful. I can never get tea to taste the same in Fortino.'

Rose loaded a tray. 'Shall we go back to the other room?'

'Let's make it easy and stay here. OK with you, Bea?'

The child nodded happily.

'It's kind of you to spare the time to visit us,' said Rose warmly.

'Charlotte Vilari suggested it first, seconded by Dante, who gave me your number,' said Harriet, and grinned. 'After which, nothing would have kept me away, of course. I should have rung you first, but I'm on a very short flying visit, so I seized the moment. I hope I'm not interrupting your work?'

'You're not, but it wouldn't matter if you were.' Rose smiled eagerly. 'You've seen Charlotte recently? How was she?'

'Blooming! But she told me to say you'll have to fly there to see her because Fabio refuses to let her travel right now.' Harriet looked at her expectantly. 'Will you go?'

'As soon as I can, yes.' Rose smiled at her daughter. 'You can get down now if you like, Bea.'

'Get Pinocchio.'

'Off you go then.'

Harriet smiled as Bea ran off. 'She's lovely. Enjoy her at this stage while you can. They grow up too fast.' She turned, suddenly serious. 'Look, Rose, while we're alone, I just want you to know that Dante had a really rough deal with his marriage. The family was delighted when Elsa the Witch left him but, although he hid it well, the rejection must have been a blow to his pride. Up to the death of his grandmother, whom we all adored, life had been kind to Dante. Then Nonna died, and he married Elsa. She had chased him mercilessly, desperate to marry a Fortinari, but once she had the ring on her finger she refused to have children. Soon afterwards, thank God, she met a man as old as the hills, but so filthy rich the delightful Elsa left Dante flat and took off with her sugar daddy.'

Rose nodded. 'He told me this when I was in Florence. But why are *you* telling me, Harriet?'

'Because I think Dante's lonely. He's no playboy. He works hard and loves his family. My children adore him. So do I. And he cares for you, Rose. Otherwise he wouldn't have asked me to call in on you. How do you feel about him?'

Rose flushed. 'I like him very much. We met years ago, actually, at Charlotte's wedding.'

'So she told me—' Harriet broke off, smiling as Bea ran into the room brandishing Pinocchio. 'Isn't he gorgeous?'

From then on Harriet Fortinari concentrated on Bea, and a few minutes later got up to leave. 'I must go. It's been lovely to meet you both. May I have a kiss, Bea?'

The child promptly held up her face, beaming as Harriet caught her in a hug and gave her a smacking kiss on both cheeks.

'Thank you so much for coming,' said Rose as they made for the door.

'And for the lecture?'

'Is that what it was?'

'I hope it didn't come across that way. I was just putting in a good word. When you come to visit Charlotte we must get together again. It was good to meet you, Rose.' Harriet dropped a quick kiss on her cheek and smiled down at Bea. 'It was lovely to meet you, too, darling. Goodbye.'

'Bye-bye,' said Bea, so sadly that Rose picked her up and cuddled her as they waved their visitor off.

When Dante rang that night Rose thanked him for sending his sister-in-law to see her. 'Bea was very taken with her. So was I.'

'*Bene.* I thought you might like to meet her.'

'She's very attractive.'

'And the light of my brother's life. It was fascinating to watch Leo falling in love with her when they first met. Before that it was the women who fell for him.'

'Is he as good-looking as you?'

Dante laughed. 'However I answer will be wrong. But Leo is an attractive man, yes.'

'So are you.'

'*Grazie*, Rose, I am glad you think so.' He breathed in deeply. 'I am very impatient to see you again, and not just to hold you in my arms again, but because you have invited me to supper.'

'You haven't tasted my cooking yet.'

'The food will not matter if I am with you, *tesoro*.'

'I bet you say that to all the girls.'

'You are wrong. The only ladies who cook for me are my mother, Mirella and Harriet.'

'And I'm sure they're experts. You're making me nervous. It's just a casual kitchen supper. Don't expect haute cuisine, Dante.'

'I will enjoy whatever you choose to give me, *carina*,' he said in a tone which curled her toes.

Rose would have been nervous enough about merely cooking a meal for Dante, but with the thoughts of their love-making fresh in her mind and the spectre of confession lurking to round off the meal she lived in a state of tension which gradually increased until on the day of the dinner she was wound so tight that Grace took Bea off to the park with Tom so Rose could make her preparations uninterrupted.

'We'll give Bea her supper, too,' said Grace as they left. 'And for heaven's sake give yourself time to get ready, and then sit down for five minutes doing nothing. Try to relax, love.'

'And don't forget,' added Tom with emphasis, 'we're just minutes away if you need us.'

Rose smiled sheepishly. 'I know. I let my inner drama queen take over for a minute, but I'm all right now. After all, he can't eat me, can he?'

But when she opened the door to Dante later, for a moment he gave every indication of wanting to do just that. He said nothing for a moment, his eyes gleaming with a look which brought colour to the face which had been pale with tension most of the day. '*Buonasera*, Rose,' he said huskily, and took her by the shoulders to kiss her very thoroughly. 'You look lovelier every time I see you.'

Since Rose had deliberately dressed down in jeans and a by no means new Cambridge-blue sweater she was pleased to hear it. 'Charmer! Shall I take your jacket?'

Dante shrugged out of the butter-soft leather and handed it to her. '*Grazie*. Where is little Bea?'

'Having tea with my mother and Tom. They'll bring her back shortly. In the meantime, come into the kitchen, where I can keep an eye on dinner while I give you a drink.'

'Something smells very good, Rose!'

'It's my signature dish,' she said, handing him a bottle and an opener. 'Will you do the honours?'

Dante inspected the label and laughed. 'A Fortinari Classico! *Grazie tante*, Rose.'

'When he knew I was feeding you, Tom gave it to me.'

'A man of taste!'

'I hope it's suitable as a partner to chicken.'

He smiled at her as he removed the cork. 'You can drink it with anything you wish, *cara*. Will you drink some now?'

'Just half a glass. I must put Bea to bed before we eat.' Rose tensed as the doorbell rang, and then smiled brightly. 'There she is now.'

Dante was the only one at ease when Grace came in with Tom following behind with Bea in his arms. Once the greetings were over, Tom put Bea down and stood tall and formidable as he looked from the child to Dante.

'Over to you now, love,' he said to Rose.

Bea smiled up at Dante. 'Mummy made chicken for you.'

He smiled back. 'I am very lucky, yes?'

She nodded, eyeing him curiously. 'You talk funny.'

'Bea!' exclaimed Grace. 'That's not very polite.'

'But true,' said Dante, chuckling. 'I talk this way because I am Italian, not English like you, *piccola*.'

'Please don't translate,' said Rose swiftly. 'Bea's a big girl, remember.' She looked at Grace. 'Would you two like a glass of wine?'

'No, thanks,' said her mother hastily. 'I put a casserole in the oven so we must get back to it. Nice to meet you, Dante.'

'My pleasure, *signora*.' He turned to Tom. 'I saw your daughter yesterday, and she looks very well. You are thrilled to have a grandchild, yes?'

'I am indeed.' Tom bent to brush a kiss over Bea's curls. 'Though I look on this one as my own, too.'

Grace gave her grandchild a kiss, then blew one to Rose and Dante and hurried Tom away.

'Signor Morley does not approve of me?' said Dante, frowning.

'Of course he does.' Rose looked down to see Bea eyeing Dante in speculation.

'Bath time,' she announced.

He smiled. 'Then perhaps I shall see you later when you are ready for bed.'

Bea looked at her mother. 'I want to show him my ducks.'

'Are you up for that, Dante?' asked Rose.

'I am honoured,' he assured her and smiled down at Bea. 'You have many ducks?'

She nodded importantly. 'Lots and lots.' She held up her arms to him. 'Up,' she ordered, then intercepted a look from her mother and dazzled Dante with her most winning smile. 'Please?'

He lifted her in the practised way of a man used to small children. 'So tell me where to go, *per favore*—that is how I say please,' he informed her.

Rose checked that all was well in the oven and then followed Bea and Dante upstairs to the small bathroom, which felt even smaller with the three of them inside it.

'Down now,' said Bea as her mother turned on the taps. She took a jar from the side of the bath and shook it. 'Bubbles,' she informed Dante. 'You do it.'

Dante smiled, entranced, as he obeyed, then widened his eyes in mock awe when Bea showed him a basket piled with rubber ducks. 'You were right, *piccola*, you have many, many ducks.'

'Right then,' said Rose briskly. 'Clothes off, Bea.'

Dante backed away. 'I will leave now.'

'No!' ordered Bea. 'Play with me.'

'She likes races with the ducks,' said Rose, 'but be careful or you'll be soaked.'

He smiled. '*Non importa.* I have been wet many times bathing Leo's children; Mirella's also.'

After a spirited session with a chortling Bea and a flotilla of ducks, Dante's hair was wet and his sweater so damp Rose took it away to put it in the dryer, and returned with an old sweatshirt acquired from one of her rugby-playing friends in college. 'This will have to do for a while, I'm afraid,' she said, averting her eyes from his muscular bronzed chest. 'Time to come out, Bea.'

'Mummy reads stories now,' the child told Dante as Rose enveloped her in a bath towel.

'You are a lucky girl,' he told her. 'No one reads stories to me.'

She chuckled, shaking her damp curls. 'You're too big.'

'True.' He glanced down at Rose, who was rubbing so hard her child protested. 'Do you think Mummy will let me listen while she reads to you?'

'A'course,' said Bea firmly.

'Then I will wait downstairs until you are ready,' said Dante.

'I'll call down when we are,' Rose told him, willing her stomach to stop churning.

Bea was so impatient to get the drying session over that Rose was feeling even more twitchy by the time her child was propped up in bed with Pinocchio and Bear.

'Call the man now,' said Bea imperiously, but then bit her lip at her mother's raised eyebrows. 'Please,' she muttered.

'I should think so. And our visitor's name is Dante. Can you say that?'

'A'course,' was the scornful answer.

Rose went out on the landing to call down. 'You can come up now, Dante.'

'*Grazie.*' He ran up the stairs two at a time and planted a kiss on her lips on the way into Bea's bedroom.

Bea had a story-book waiting open on the bed and waved a gracious hand at the basket chair drawn up close by. 'There, Dante—please.'

Dante's eyes, which had widened at his name, were lu-

minous as they rested on the child, who looked like a Botti-
celli angel with the lamplight haloing her bright curls. 'You
are most kind, *piccola*. Which story have you chosen?'

'*Goldilocks.*' Bea wriggled more comfortably against
her pillows and smiled as Rose perched on the bed beside
her. 'Ready, Mummy.'

Rose was proud of her steady voice as she read the
story with the animation her daughter always demanded,
with a different voice for each bear and a special one for
Goldilocks. As she read, careful not to miss out a single
word, it occurred to her that, though none of this had been
planned, it was a good warm-up to her big announcement.
Dante was obviously delighting in the interlude as he sat
perfectly still, more handsome than a man had a right to
be, even in the incongruous old sweatshirt. His eyes remained on Bea's face as she drank in every word. Towards
the end her eyelids began to droop and when Rose finally
closed the book the child made no protest when her mother
kissed her good-night.

Dante got up very quietly, a look on his face which
told Rose he would have liked to kiss the child, too, but
he merely said a very quiet good night and left the room
as Rose dimmed the lamp.

Before going down to join him, Rose took a detour to
her room to tidy her hair and touch up her face, then ran
down to open the dryer. 'I hope you're not sorry I asked
you here to dinner now,' she said lightly as she handed
his sweater to him. 'Bath time can be an exhausting experience.'

He stripped off the sweatshirt and pulled on the jersey. '*Grazie*, Rose. For you, bath time with Bea comes at
the end of your working day, when you are already tired.
For me, tonight, it was pure pleasure. Thank you for letting me share it.'

'You're welcome. Will you pour the wine now while I check on our dinner?'

Dante sniffed in appreciation as Rose opened the oven. 'It smells good.' He filled two glasses and with a sigh of satisfaction sat down at the table she'd made festive with a bright green cloth and yellow candles in pottery holders. 'This is much better than a restaurant.'

'Even one as good as your cousin's?'

'Yes.' Dante eyed her flushed face with pleasure as she set a casserole dish on the table. 'Here we are alone with no waiters to intrude. But I can help if you allow.'

Rose shook her head and took a dish of roasted vegetables from the oven. 'No, thanks. All done.' She took the lid from the main dish. 'This is chicken and broccoli in a creamy sauce, finished off with a Parmesan cheese gratin in honour of my guest. Please help yourself.'

'First we make a toast,' said Dante and held up his glass to touch hers. 'To many more evenings like this.' He paid Rose's cooking the best compliment of all by rolling his eyes in ecstasy at the first bite, then clearing his plate and accepting seconds. 'I hope you were not expecting there to be leftovers.'

'No, indeed; I'm glad you enjoyed it. But no pudding, I'm afraid, though I can offer you cheese instead.'

'I rarely eat *dolces*,' he assured her, 'and tonight I have devoured so much of your chicken dish I can eat nothing more.'

Rose braced herself. Confession time loomed. 'In that case I'll just make some coffee to take into the sitting room.'

'While you do that I shall visit your bathroom,' he said matter-of-factly.

She blew out the candles and gathered up the used dishes in a tearing hurry. By the time Dante returned, she had the coffee tray ready and the dishwasher stacked, and could find nothing more to do to delay the inevitable. 'If you'll just take the tray, then.'

Dante eyed her closely as he complied. 'Something is wrong, Rose? Do not worry about little Bea. I took a look through her open door and she is sleeping peacefully.'

'Good.' Regretting the second glass of wine she'd downed for Dutch courage, Rose followed Dante into the sitting room and asked him to set the tray down on the table in front of the sofa.

When they were settled side by side with their coffee Dante eyed her expectantly. 'After such an excellent dinner we should be sitting here relaxed. But you are very tense, Rose. Will you tell me why?'

'Yes,' she said, resigned. 'I will. But I don't know where to start—'

Dante smiled. 'At the beginning is usually the best place, *tesoro*.'

She tensed at the endearment then took in a deep breath. 'Dante, if you'll think back to Charlotte's wedding, you made it plain from the start that you were attracted to me. I was thrilled and excited, and so instantly attracted to *you* I drank so much more champagne than I should have. I was tearful after Charlotte left with Fabio. You comforted me when you took me to my room and you know what happened next.'

Dante brought her hand to his lips. 'The entire day with you had been like the *preliminari* for me. Foreplay, yes? *Allora*, the moment I kissed you I was lost. I have no excuse for what followed. I was no schoolboy to lose control in such a way. But as the climax to that happy day, the joy I felt in your arms, Rose, was sweeter than anything I had experienced before. It was torture to tear myself away from you, even though I was in desperate worry over Nonna.'

He sighed heavily. 'All that day I had banished Elsa from my mind, but later, on the flight home, I felt great guilt because I had not told you about her. When did you learn that I had a *fidanzata*?'

'The next morning, over breakfast. Your friends were worried that your grandmother's illness would affect your wedding.' Rose looked him in the eye. 'The word *wedding* hit me so hard I was numb for a while. Then my temper kicked in. I wanted to punch that face of yours until you weren't so handsome any more. Denied the satisfaction of that, I blocked you from my mind instead, deleted you from my life and refused to listen whenever Charlotte mentioned your name. So she soon gave up trying.'

'And you never knew that Elsa left me,' he said very quietly and took her cup to put it on the tray with his.

'No.'

He frowned. 'Yet Charlotte was most insistent I delivered her letter to you in person in Firenze.'

Rose nodded. 'Fabio sent money for me in the package so she needed someone to deliver it, and you just happened to be on the spot.'

Dante smiled wryly. 'I was most happy to do it, but thought you would refuse to speak to me.'

'I wanted to!'

'Yet you agreed to dine with me.'

She shrugged. 'The thought of eating alone in that rather grand hotel was so daunting I decided to make use of you instead. But why did you offer, Dante?'

'You looked so unhappy when you read Charlotte's letter I longed to take you in my arms and comfort you. Instead, I offered to take her place.' He looked at her steadily. 'You have more to tell me, I think?'

'I do.' Rose sat very erect. 'That was the prologue. Now

we get to the main part. I've decided to take your advice, Dante.'

He frowned. 'What advice, *cara*?'

'To tell Bea's father he has a daughter.'

His eyes blazed in sudden, vehement denial. 'No! I no longer think this a good idea. Do not, Rose. He is probably married by now. You are right; after all this time he will not believe the child is his.'

Rose looked long and hard into the impassioned blue eyes. 'Is that how you would react in such circumstances, Dante?'

'I believe not. I hope I would not. How could any man be sure of his reaction to such news?'

'Now's your chance to find out.' She took in a deep breath. 'Bea is *your* child, Dante.'

He sat like a man turned to stone for several endless seconds, his eyes wild on hers.

'*Cosa*? What are you saying?' His bronze skin drained of all colour. 'It is not a thing to joke about.'

'It's no joke, I assure you. I'm deadly serious.'

'*Dio!*' Dante thrust a hand through his hair as he eyed her incredulously. 'But, even so desperate to make love to you, I used protection that night.'

She flushed. 'It didn't work. After you'd gone I found it had split.'

'Then what you say is really true?'

'You honestly think it's something I would lie about?'

He shook his head in wonder. 'Beatrice is the result of our lovemaking that night.'

Rose sighed heavily. 'I don't blame you for doubting it. I couldn't believe it myself.'

'Why did you never tell me this before?' he demanded with sudden heat.

'How could I, Dante?' she snapped. 'You were already

married by the time I found out. Which is why I was so obstinate about refusing to name the father. But, after seeing you and Bea together for the first time, my mother was sure it was you and said you had a right to know.' Rose slumped back against the sofa cushions. 'So now you do. But don't worry; I'm not asking anything of you.'

He glared at her, incensed. 'You tell me I have a daughter and think I will walk away?'

Rose hugged her arms across her chest, refusing to look at him. 'I don't expect anything from you, Dante. Bea and I have managed perfectly well up to now without you. So by all means walk away if you want. I have no proof that she's your child. If this were a Gothic novel she'd have a birthmark or something to show she was yours, but—'

'I need no proof,' he said roughly and got up to pace the room. 'If you say she is mine I will believe you.'

'Will believe or do believe?' demanded Rose.

Dante turned on her angrily. 'Do not mock my command of English, *per favore.*'

Rose sat very still, gazing at him in such misery Dante sat beside her again and took her hand.

'Why do you look at me so?'

'It was very hard to tell you, Dante.'

'Perche?'

'I was afraid you wouldn't believe me. And it's over four years since that night so you might have forgotten all about it. And even if you did remember you could have thought I was telling you about Bea to get money.'

Dante clenched a fist, as though hanging on to every shred of his self-control. At last he turned to look Rose in the eye. 'I had forgotten nothing. When I saw you again in Firenze I was transported back to the Vilari wedding and my meeting with the entrancing girl who stole my heart.'

'The heart which already belonged to someone else,' Rose said bitterly.

He shook his head. 'Elsa never had my heart. She had no use for it. She wanted my name and my money. But there was less money than she expected. Financially, I was a great disappointment to her.'

'Did you love her?'

'I desired her when we first met. And she desired marriage to a Fortinari.' Dante's mouth twisted. '*Alla fine*—in the end—I was deeply grateful to Enrico Calvi for taking her from me.' He took Rose's hand in his. 'Now, let us talk of important things. How soon can we get married?'

CHAPTER SIX

'Hold on!' She shook her head decisively. 'That's not going to happen, Dante.'

'*Cosa?*' He pulled her to her feet and stood staring down at her. 'We made a child together—'

'But by accident, not because we were in a relationship.' Rose held her ground. 'I didn't tell you about Bea to force you to marry me, Dante. I don't want—or need—a husband.'

'But this is not all about you, Rose,' he flung at her. 'My daughter needs a father. Soon she will be old enough to ask why she lacks one, no? Other children will ask also. You have not considered this?'

'Are you serious? Of course I have!' She sighed wearily. 'I had no way of providing one for her, or even to meet a likely candidate because I had to work from home so I could always be there for her. Besides, I like being in charge of my own life—and of hers. If I married you, Dante, I suppose you would expect me to uproot us to live with you in Italy?'

'*Naturalmente*. I have a home ready for you, also a family who would welcome you,' he said swiftly.

Rose shook her head firmly. 'It's not the basis for a marriage, Dante.'

'You would find it so hard to be my wife?' he demanded, eyes glittering.

In some ways not hard at all, but that wasn't the point. She should, she knew, be grateful that he'd taken the news of his fatherhood so well, with none of the doubts she'd expected. 'I think it's a mistake to rush into anything, Dante,' she said at last. 'You need time to get used to the idea.'

Dante stood with long legs apart and arms folded as he stared down at her. 'If you do not marry me I will demand to spend time with my daughter,' he said harshly.

'Of course,' she said, secretly dismayed. 'But before we descend to bickering about it perhaps you'll listen to what I have to say?'

'*Allora*, talk, Rose.'

'I'm sorry. I shouldn't have been so abrupt with my objection.' She gazed at him in appeal. 'But you must see that we are, in effect, strangers, Dante. Before we rush into something as binding as marriage, it would be sensible to get to know each other better.'

His eyes softened slightly. 'Is that how you feel, Rose? That I am a stranger?' He raised an eyebrow. 'After what happened here between us the last time, how can you say that?'

She felt her face flame. 'It's obvious that we—we're compatible in that way.'

'Compatible!' He gave a mirthless laugh. 'If you mean I want to crush you in my arms and kiss you until you are helpless to refuse me, you are right. Do not look like that,' he added. 'I will not resort to—to physical coercion, this is right? Instead, I give you no choice. You will marry me and make your home in Italy with me and with our daughter.'

'Oh, will I?' Rose cried. 'Just because you've suddenly discovered you're Bea's father doesn't give you the right to turn our lives upside down.'

'You are wrong. It does,' he retorted, a look in his eyes that sent her backing away. 'My child must grow up knowing she has a father who loves and cares for her. If you do not agree to marriage you must share Bea with me. She will like my house, and she will have cousins to play with her, also doting grandparents and uncles and aunts.' He shook his head in sudden wonder. 'I was resigned to the role of uncle. To discover now that I am a father, I feel great joy.' He glared at her. 'Also great frustration because the mother of my child will not marry me.'

Rose thrust a hand through her hair, her eyes troubled. 'Before I took a giant step like that I'd have to be sure that it would make Bea happy.'

Dante held her gaze in silence for a time and then took her hands in his. '*Allora*, this is what we do, Rose. I will go back to Fortino to talk to my brother, also to my parents. Then I will return here to stay at the Hermitage for a while to spend time with Bea. Later, you must bring her to stay at the Villa Castiglione for a holiday to meet my family.' Dante's eyes held hers. 'You agree with this?'

She thought it over then nodded reluctantly.

'*Va bene*. But first she must be told I am her father.' He closed his eyes suddenly. '*Dio*, I still cannot believe it.'

'If you have any doubts on the subject say so now and we forget the whole thing,' said Rose and backed away as his eyes flew open to blaze into hers.

'I meant,' he said very deliberately, as though he was translating as he advanced on her, 'that I cannot believe my good fortune in possessing this child we created together.'

'By accident!' She stood her ground and met his eyes squarely. 'If we did marry would you expect more children?'

'I would hope for them, yes. So if you have some strange idea of a *matrimonio di convenienza*, put it from your mind. You would share my life. And my bed.' Dante drew her into his arms. 'Would that be so hard to do?'

'No,' she admitted, colouring. 'As you well know, Dante.'

He smiled victoriously and brushed his lips in a feather-light kiss over hers, then stiffened at the sound of an anguished cry upstairs.

Rose bolted away from him to take the stairs at a run, Dante hot on her heels as they raced into Bea's room to find her sitting on the floor beside her bed, crying piteously as she reached out her arms to her mother.

Rose scooped her up and ran with her to the bathroom, where Bea threw up copiously. 'On the bed too,' she sobbed, and Rose held her close, murmuring wordless comfort as she glanced round to see what Dante was doing, her eyes scornful when she saw he'd vanished. Fair weather daddy!

But Dante reappeared in the doorway with an armful of bed linen. 'I took these from the bed and shall put them downstairs. Tell me where to find clean sheets, Rose.'

'Airing cupboard on the landing,' she said, startled. 'Bea's things are on the upper shelves.'

Dante eyed the bowed curly head with sympathy. '*Poverina*! Are you better now?'

Bea shook her head mournfully. 'My tummy hurts.'

'You will soon be better in a warm, clean bed,' he assured her.

By the time Bea was bathed, sans ducks this time, and fragrant in clean pyjamas, Dante had made her bed, complete with Pinocchio and Bear.

'A man of many talents,' murmured Rose as she tucked her daughter in.

'Dante, read to me,' commanded Bea, and smiled at him. 'Please?'

Rose blinked hard at the look on his face, and turned away to sort through some books. 'How about *Pinocchio*?' she suggested, clearing her throat. 'He's Italian, too.'

'A good choice,' said Dante huskily as his daughter nodded in approval. 'Where shall I sit?'

'On the bed,' said Bea, and wriggled back against her pillows.

'I'll pop downstairs and get a drink,' said Rose, and escaped before she did something really stupid like bursting into tears at the sight of Bea with the father she didn't know she possessed.

Rose loaded the washing machine with Bea's sheets and pyjamas and stripped off her sweater, which had suffered in the interlude in the bathroom. She pulled on a T-shirt from the basket of laundry waiting to be ironed and went up to Bea's bedroom, but paused in the doorway, her throat tightening as she heard Dante's voice growing gradually softer as he read his daughter back to sleep. Rose stood very still as he finally closed the book and leaned down to brush a kiss over the bright curls. He turned and held a finger to his lips as he followed her downstairs.

Rose felt suddenly awkward, unsure what to do or say next. 'Would you like some coffee, Dante, or maybe a drink?'

'Coffee, *per favore*, to wake myself up to drive. I almost sent myself to sleep with Bea,' he added wryly. 'I will come into the kitchen while you make it, Rose, then I must leave.'

'Thank you for your help,' she said as she filled the kettle. 'I was impressed.'

'I have helped in such ways before,' he said matter-of-factly. 'Perhaps the little one's *nonna* allowed too rich a *dolce* after supper.'

'Actually, Mum's pretty strict. But Tom isn't, so maybe

Bea conned him into giving her an extra sweetie or two.'
Rose smiled. 'He's putty in her hands.'

'Putty? Ah, yes, *stucco*. I sympathise. It must be hard
to refuse her anything she desires.' Dante chuckled. 'He
will find it even harder with Charlotte's child.'

When they sat facing each other across the kitchen table
with mugs of coffee steaming between them, Rose smiled
wryly. 'I thought Italian men were spoiled by *mammas*
who did everything for them, yet you were very efficient
tonight. Thank you.'

Dante shrugged. 'At home, when young, in Fortino,
where my mother was very much in charge, I did little, I
confess. Now I do many things for myself. After Elsa left
me my family bombarded me with dinner invitations.' He
smiled derisively. 'I wished only to be left alone but this
was never allowed.'

'Your family obviously love you very much—'

'They will love you and little Bea also,' he said emphatically and reached a hand across to grasp hers, but
released it and got up when Rose stiffened. 'I will go now
and let you sleep.'

Rose walked to the door with Dante, her mind in tur-
moil. Half of her wanted nothing more than to creep into
bed and pull the covers over her head. The other half, the
part of her savouring the warmth and scent of Dante as
they stood together, wanted to pull him into bed with her
and blot out the world.

'Tell me the truth, Dante—how do you feel?' she asked.
'Now I've told you about Bea, I mean.'

'Amazed, but happy,' he said simply, and took her in
his arms. 'I will be even happier when you are my wife,
Rose. It is useless to fight. It is your fate. We were meant
to be together.' He kissed the mouth which opened to protest and let her go. *'Arrivederci, tesoro.'*

Rose watched him stride down the path to the car, then closed the door and leaned against it for a moment, feeling limp. She pushed away from the door in sudden irritation—time to stop behaving like a character in a romantic movie and do her nightly chores. She had work to do tomorrow. As usual. But maybe a day off would be good for once. She was well in hand with the accounts she did at home and had no visits to make next day. Her mother would be desperate to hear how things had gone tonight, so after she took Bea to school in the morning—so long as she wasn't unwell again—Rose decided she would give Grace a full report over coffee.

To Rose's relief, Bea slept the night through and was even more bouncy than usual the next morning as she ate her cereal.

'I like Dante,' she announced when she'd finished.

Rose's stomach did a forward roll. 'Do you, darling?'

Bea nodded. 'Can he read stories again?'

'I expect so.'

'You like him, too, Mummy,' Bea stated.

'Yes, I do. Now, let's get a move on or we'll be late.'

When Rose got back home from the school run Grace had let herself in and had coffee waiting.

She eyed her daughter anxiously. 'You obviously had a bad night. Dante didn't believe you?'

Rose busied herself with filling mugs. 'Oh, he believed me right enough. He was stunned at first, but when the truth finally sank in he was all for marrying me right away.'

Grace's delighted smile faded quickly. 'But you don't want that.'

'No. As I told Dante, we're virtually strangers. Before jumping in at the deep end I made it clear we would need to know each other better, and I would have to be utterly sure that Bea was happy with the idea.'

'Did he agree?'

'Yes. He immediately made plans to go back to Fortino to arrange some leave, and then come back to stay at the Hermitage to spend time with his daughter.'

'Goodness,' said Grace, blinking. 'I take it you're against the idea?'

Rose nodded vehemently. 'The minute I gave Dante the good news he started giving orders. I was to change my life completely, marry him and take off for Italy to live with him and Bea in his house—the Villa Castiglione, left to him by his grandmother.'

Grace downed her own coffee and got up to refill their cups. 'Good for Dante. After all, love, he could have rejected all idea of Bea's paternity.'

'No chance of that; he was entranced with her from the start,' said Rose moodily. 'He played with her ducks with her in the bath, and afterwards sat with her while I read the bedtime story. Then I softened him up even more by giving him a good dinner before breaking the news that Bea was his child.'

'How did he take it?'

Rose blew out her cheeks. 'As I told you, once the truth sank in he ordered me to marry him. Then when I didn't joyfully and gratefully accept he turned belligerent and demanded time with his daughter whether I married him or not.'

'To take her to his place in Tuscany, you mean?' said Grace, startled. 'So what did you say?'

'Bea started crying at that point because she'd thrown up and we both bolted upstairs.'

'How did Dante cope with that?'

'He stripped the bed and remade it while I cleaned Bea up, then he read her to sleep.'

Grace smiled. 'Bravo, Dante! Tell me, darling, quite apart from Bea, how do you feel towards him now? Are you still bitter?'

Rose shook her head hopelessly. 'Fool that I am, I *love* him. I always have. I tried so hard to forget him, but it was impossible with Bea looking up at me with those eyes of his.'

'How does he feel about you?'

'I wish I knew. He still fancies me. Physically, I mean. But that's not enough for marriage, especially with people from such different backgrounds.'

'It works for Charlotte and Fabio,' Grace pointed out.

'True. But they got married because they really love each other. Dante's motive for marrying me is purely to get Bea.' Rose shivered. 'Last night, when I didn't leap at the marriage idea, he said he'd demand time with his daughter. Could he do that legally, do you think?'

'No idea. You didn't name him as her father on the birth certificate and you've never lived together. Also he's not a British national, so I should think it's unlikely. I'll ask Tom.'

'Dante thinks Tom doesn't approve of him.'

'He's right. Tom can't get past the fact that Dante made you pregnant when he was about to marry someone else.' Grace smiled wryly. 'Yet at the same time he can't help liking Dante either.'

Rose nodded ruefully. 'I know the feeling!'

'Have a cup of tea, then go off to bed for a bit. Tom and I will collect Bea.'

'That sounds wonderful. I didn't sleep much last night after all the excitement.' Rose hugged her mother. 'You spoil me.'

'I prefer to think of it as helping. Take a hot shower and climb into bed. I'll give Bea her lunch before bringing her home.' Grace kissed her weary daughter and pointed her at the door. 'Go.'

Rose felt better after the shower, and even managed a short nap. When she got up, she had come to a decision. This afternoon she would take Bea to the park, and then play all her favourite games with her and later watch her favourite cartoon film with her for the umpteenth time. Rose's teeth clenched. Bea didn't *need* a father! She'd done perfectly well without one up to now, and even had the benefit of a male presence in her life in the shape of Tom Morley.

When Dante rang that night, Rose was ready and armed, waiting for him.

'How are you tonight, *carina*?' he asked in the deep caressing tones which still had the power to raise the hairs on the back of her neck—something that infuriated her in the present circumstances. 'And how is my little Bea? Is she recovered now?'

'*My* little Bea, actually, and we're both fine.'

Silence for a moment. 'What is wrong, Rose?'

'I'm afraid the deal's off, Dante. I'm saying no to your demands.'

'*Cosa? Perche*? What has happened?'

'I've given it careful consideration and decided I can't face the upheaval of making a new life in a strange country. I like my life the way it is. There's no room for a man in it, even one as irresistible as Dante Fortinari,' she added with sarcasm.

'And so you will deprive me of my daughter, and Bea of a father? Can you think only of yourself?' he demanded hotly.

Rose suddenly lost it. 'I had to after you left me pregnant and took off to marry someone else,' she spat at him. 'Goodbye, Dante.'

Dante tried ringing back several times but eventually gave up, which made her even more furious. When her phone rang an hour or so later she snatched it up, ready to tell Dante to go to hell until she saw the caller ID.

'When, Rose Palmer,' Charlotte said belligerently, 'were you going to tell *me* that Dante is Bea's father? I had to hear it from Dad.'

'I didn't tell Dante until last night, so you were next on the list. Not even Mum knew, so don't get angry with me.' Rose's voice broke. 'Please.'

'Oh, love, don't cry; of course I won't! But I demand details.'

'First of all, how are you feeling?'

'At this time of night I feel fine; in the mornings not so much. But never mind all that. You said Bea's daddy was some student, while all the time it was Fabio's best friend! So go on. Talk.'

With a sigh, Rose went through her story yet again, with Charlotte exclaiming in amazement at intervals.

'You were so *brave*, Rose, going through all that and never telling a soul, and all the while working so hard to make a living for Bea. Though, thinking back, the clues were there. You would never listen if Dante's name came up, but I thought that was because of Elsa the Witch. I suppose he never mentioned her when he was charming the socks off my bridesmaid?'

'Of course not,' said Rose indignantly. 'Otherwise—'

'You'd have sent him packing! So now he knows about Bea, what happens next?'

'I am ordered to marry him and take Bea to live with him at his villa.'

'How masterful!' Charlotte waited for a moment then sighed. 'But you're not going to do that.'

'No. With help from my wonderful mother and your equally wonderful father, I've managed my life very well up to now. Dante can issue orders as much as he likes, but I'm staying put. And so is Bea.'

'Damn! I wish I could nip over and see you, but Fabio is adamant about no travelling for a while. And, if I'm honest, I'm not up to it right now, anyway. If I send you the fares will you bring Bea here instead?'

The mere thought of being anywhere in the vicinity of Dante Fortinari made Rose want to kick and scream. 'I can't just now, love. Maybe later on.'

Rose checked on Bea and then stacked her pillows and got into bed to lean against them, waiting for the phone to ring. When it remained obdurately silent she removed two of the pillows and tried to settle down to sleep. Instead of issuing orders, all Dante had needed to get her consent was to tell her—and convince her—that he wanted to marry her because he loved her, not because she came as a package deal with their daughter.

When the phone rang later Rose shot upright and grabbed it, then sank back against the pillows when she saw the caller ID.

'You took a long time to pick up,' said Grace.

'I thought it was Dante again.'

'I gather you won't answer when he rings.'

'How do you gather?'

'Because he rang Tom—he got the number from Fabio—and asked to speak to me. He's desperately worried about you, love.'

'Good!' said Rose viciously.

'I assured him that, healthwise, both you and Bea were

fine, and told him it was best he doesn't contact you for a while.'

'And what did he say to that?'

'That he would try to take my advice, but it would be hard.'

'You should have told him not to contact me at all. Ever.'

Grace shook her head. 'I didn't do that because I know you only too well, Rose Palmer. If I had, you'd be utterly miserable. So I gave you the chance to change your mind when your temper dies down, as it always does, in time.'

'This wasn't a childish tantrum, Mum!'

'I know that. I also heard the pain in Dante's voice, love. When he does ring again, promise me you'll speak to him.'

'I'll think about it.'

This was a promise all too easy to keep. It was impossible for Rose to think about anything else. The nights were the worst part, just as they'd been years before, after her first encounter with Dante Fortinari. Even though she immersed herself in her work and spent the rest of the time with Bea, she existed in a constant state of tension, waiting for a phone call from Dante. A phone call which never came.

CHAPTER SEVEN

IT WAS A relief to spend most of the following Sunday at Tom's house. Bea enjoyed her day so much she protested loudly when it was time to go home. She even refused to wave bye-bye to Gramma and Tom and sobbed when she was secured into her car seat for the drive home, but, much to Rose's relief, fell asleep once the car was in motion.

'Wake up, Bea. We're home now,' said Rose as she turned into the drive, then swallowed, her heart thumping, as she saw a familiar male figure standing on her front porch.

Dante strode forward to help, arms outstretched, as Rose unstrapped Bea. 'I will take her.'

Exhausted after a day spent trying to fool her mother and Tom that she was perfectly happy, Rose yielded his daughter to him without protest.

'This is a surprise,' she said coldly.

'We need to talk; you will not take my telephone calls, so I came,' he informed her, then looked down tenderly as Bea woke up with a smile of delight when she realised who was holding her.

'Dante! Read stories?'

He chuckled. 'Of course, *piccola*.'

Rose unlocked the door and switched on lights. Now

Dante was here, he might as well make himself useful. 'Would you take her straight upstairs, please?'

Once Bea was in bed later, flanked by Pinocchio and Bear, Rose handed Dante a selection of books for Bea to choose from, kissed her daughter good-night and, after a moment's indecision, left them to it.

The sitting room seemed small and chilly after the space and comfort of Tom's house. Shivering with nerves as much as cold, Rose switched on the electric fire and drew the curtains, then went to the kitchen to make coffee and took a tray into the sitting room.

Dante joined her soon afterwards. 'Bea is fast asleep,' he said and crossed to the fire to hold out his hands. 'It is cold tonight.'

'Would you care for some coffee?'

His lips curved wryly. 'Yes, Rose. *Grazie*.'

'Why the smile?' she asked as she poured.

'You are so polite.'

She set the pot down with a clatter. 'Only to hide how worried I feel about the reason for your sudden appearance.'

He lifted a shoulder. 'It is nothing to cause distress, Rose. Because my first proposal did not meet with your approval, I came to make a different proposition.'

Rose sat down suddenly. 'What do you have in mind?' If he had some idea about taking Bea away from her to stay in Italy for weeks at a time he could think again.

Dante joined her on the old velvet settee, careful, she noted, to leave a space between them. '*Ascolta*—listen to me, Rose. I feel much guilt that in the heat of passion after the Vilari wedding I took from you something impossible to replace.'

She raised an eyebrow. 'I wasn't a virgin, Dante! I'd had a steady boyfriend in college.'

Dante's lips tightened. 'I meant that by leaving you with child I robbed you of your youthful freedom.'

Rose nodded as she thought it over. 'I suppose you could say that. I certainly had to grow up in a hurry. But, to be fair, I was an equal partner in what happened between us.'

'But if you had known about Elsa you would not have been, no?'

'Absolutely not! I wanted to beat you up when I found out about her.' She ran the tip of her tongue over suddenly dry lips. 'But the possibility of consequences never occurred to me because you used protection, and even though I later realised there had been a problem with the condom I really thought the chances of anything happening were a million to one. It was a huge shock to find out I was pregnant. There was an equally huge fuss when I refused to name the father.'

Dante took her hand. 'Why did you refuse?'

'You were married by then, so what was the point? You're a close friend of Fabio Vilari, so no way was I going to upset Charlotte's newly wedded bliss by bringing your name into it. Anyway,' she added militantly, 'I was determined to take care of Bea myself.'

He nodded. 'And you have done so admirably. But now I shall help you care for her.'

She eyed him warily. 'How, exactly?'

Dante's grasp tightened. 'The best way is to marry and give our child the love and security of a normal family.' He raised an eyebrow. 'But you do not want this. You value your independence too much.'

'Yes,' she admitted unwillingly.

'Even so, you must listen to my plan.'

'I'm listening.'

Dante smiled in approval. '*Va bene*. The plan is simple. Arrange your work to take time off, and then bring Bea to

the Villa Castiglione for a little holiday. We can visit Charlotte and Fabio, also my family, *naturalmente*.' He paused.
'My mother is longing to meet her granddaughter, Rose.'

She bit her lip. 'I can't believe she's longing to meet
me, Dante.'

'You are wrong. I have told her everything, and she has
much sympathy for you, also admiration for the way you
work so hard to support our daughter.'

My daughter, thought Rose fiercely.

'My house has several bedrooms. You are not required
to share mine,' he assured her suavely. 'A week is all I ask,
to see how Bea likes life Italian style.'

'Are you saying that if she does like it you'll expect me
to let her stay with you there from time to time?'

'She is too young to do that without her mother.' Dante
put a finger under Rose's chin and turned her face up to
his. 'You would come with her.'

Her eyes fell from the searching blue gaze. 'And if she
doesn't like it there?'

'Then I must spend time with her here.'

'You mean stay here in my house?' she demanded.

He gave a mirthless laugh. 'I do not hope for such a
privilege. I shall stay at the Hermitage and come here to
take her out.'

Rose stared at him in defeat. 'Very well,' she said dully.
'I'll bring her to Italy, but only for a week. I can't take more
time off than that.'

'*Bene*. Let me know when you are free.' Dante stood up.
'I will arrange my diary to give me time with Bea. And
with you, of course, Rose,' he added silkily.

'Thank you so much!'

'*Prego*. Now I must go.'

Rose went to the door with him. 'When do you fly
back?'

'Early in the morning. This was a truly flying visit. And I have much more travelling to do once I get back, but by road, for which I am grateful.'

'You prefer roaring around Italy in your car, I imagine.'

'What man would not?' He took her hand and bowed formally over it. '*Arrivederci,* Rose.'

'Goodbye.' She hesitated. 'Dante, I'm sorry you had to come all this way. I should have let you talk to me on the phone.'

He shrugged. 'It was worth it to gain time with my daughter.'

She winced, hoping he couldn't tell how much that hurt. 'But if I come—'

'*When* you both come!'

'All right, when we come, you must make it plain to your family beforehand that this is just a holiday. It doesn't mean I've agreed to anything permanent.'

Dante nodded, his eyes expressionless for once. '*Va bene.* It shall be as you wish. And if Bea likes it there at my home, what then?'

Her chin lifted. 'Let's take this one step at a time.'

'There is one step you must take before you bring Bea to the Villa Castiglione. You must tell her I am her father.' Dante took her by the shoulders, ignoring the hand that tried to push him away. 'Let us be truthful with each other, Rose.'

'I just wish you'd been truthful when we first met,' she snapped, her eyes stormy. She still couldn't get past Dante's deception in the past. The hurt was still raw for her.

'I did not lie,' he said huskily. 'With you in my arms, I forgot Elsa existed—'

'We spent a lot of time together that day before we reached that point. And while you might not have lied, you omitted to tell me you were engaged, which is as bad as lying.'

'*Davvero*! But it was such pleasure to laugh and dance with you, I could not spoil the day by mentioning Elsa.' He pulled her closer. 'I fell under your spell at first sight and went on falling deeper and deeper all that day, until I lost control as we kissed later in your room. It was such agony to leave you that, even frantic with worry over Nonna on the flight home, I was determined to tell Elsa I could not marry her. That I had met someone else.'

Rose stared at him in disbelief. 'You obviously didn't tell her,' she said at last.

'Ah, but I did.' His mouth twisted in distaste at the memory. 'It was a painful revelation to see someone so physically beautiful turn into a *strega* before my eyes. She spat at me that she was expecting my child, which, as she knew well, gave me no choice. Nonna died the next day and in my grief I felt only relief that Elsa abandoned her plans for a big church wedding. She arranged a hasty civil ceremony instead in her determination to become a Fortinari.'

'So what happened to the baby?' asked Rose, stunned.

'There was no baby. Elsa lied. On our wedding night, she told me there had never been a child and never would be.' He dropped his hands and turned away. 'I was an arrogant fool, she told me, to imagine she would ruin her figure that way, even more fool to think I could jilt Elsa Marino, the supermodel all men lusted after. I stared at this beautiful woman saying these ugly things and felt such revulsion I did not touch her that night or ever again.' He gave a mirthless laugh. 'People pitied me when she left me for another man, but I rejoiced.'

'You never told anyone the truth about this?'

'Only Leo. Therefore, Harriet must know also.' He turned to look at her. 'If I had known that *you* were expecting my child, Rose, nothing would have made me go through with the *farsa* of my wedding to Elsa.'

'You must have found it hard to live with her after that?'

His mouth tightened. 'I did not do so very much. With Leo's help, I made sure I was often away on my travels when she was home, which for Elsa meant her flat in Firenze. She hated the Villa Castiglione.'

'But you love it,' said Rose quietly.

'Very much. After Elsa left with Enrico Calvi—and my fervent blessing—the house was my sanctuary.'

'Yet your family tried to get you out of it as much as possible.'

'To show the world I was not heartbroken. My parents were enraged that Elsa had treated me in such a way. It was my mother's greatest wish that I find someone else as soon as possible.' He rolled his eyes. 'Therefore, every time I dined with my parents, or with Mirella and Franco, even Fabio and Charlotte, there was always some woman invited for me.'

'How about your brother?'

'Leo told me I could find my own woman, and Harriet lured me from my house by asking me to do the babysitting for them—which is when I learned to change a bed quickly! I enjoyed this much more than the socialising. But the one I am most grateful to is Charlotte Vilari. She sent me to Firenze to find you again, Rose.' He paused, his eyes searching hers. 'Are you truly sorry that I did?'

Rose eyed him thoughtfully. 'You really told Elsa the wedding was off because you'd met me?'

'Yes.' He raised a dark eyebrow. 'You do not believe me?'

'I want to,' she said honestly.

'But you still have doubts.' He stood back. '*Non im-*

porta. I shall ring you next week to learn when you are free to leave. I will make the travel arrangements.'

'Right. I hope Bea will take to air travel.'

'With both of us to care for her, there will be no problem.'

Her eyes widened. 'You're coming to collect us?'

He smiled bleakly. 'This surprises you?'

'Well, yes; I expected to cope alone.'

'As always. If you prefer to do that—'

'*No*! Indeed, I don't. Thank you.'

'*Prego.* You will permit me to look in on Bea before I go?'

'Of course.'

Rose watched him leave the room with the swift grace that was such an essential part of Dante Fortinari and felt sudden regret, as though she'd somehow missed out on something important. She smiled brightly when he returned. 'Is Bea all right?'

'She is sleeping like an angel, as all children look when they sleep, even Luca, Leo's son, who is more demon than angel when awake. And now I must go. I will ring you early in the week.' His eyes locked on hers imperiously. 'And this time you will answer me and talk to me.'

'Yes, I will. And Dante,' she added quickly before she could change her mind, 'I'm not sorry.'

'*Cosa?*' He frowned.

'That you found me in Florence.'

'*Bene*, I am happy to hear it!' But, instead of kissing her as she'd hoped, he gave her the smile he shared with his daughter and turned to go. '*Arrivederci*, Rose.'

CHAPTER EIGHT

ONE OF THE highest of the several hurdles facing Rose was informing Bea that Dante was her daddy. Grace advised doing it straight away before Dante rang again, so that evening, after reading a longer than usual bedtime story to put off the moment, Rose finally told Bea she had exciting news—they were going on holiday to Italy, where Auntie Charlotte lived, to stay in Dante's house.

Bea, no lover of road journeys, frowned. 'In the car?'

'Only for a little way. Dante is driving us to the airport to catch an aeroplane.'

The blue eyes lit up. 'Tomorrow?'

'No, not tomorrow, darling, but soon.'

'Gramma and Tom, too?'

'No, just you and me. And Dante. Will you like that?'

Bea nodded eagerly. 'Are there stories in his house?'

'I don't know. We'll take ours, shall we?'

'OK.'

Rose took a deep breath. 'Darling, I've got a secret to tell you.'

'What?'

'Dante is your daddy.'

The blue eyes stared at her blankly for a moment then rounded like saucers. 'A real daddy, like Holly's?'

Rose cleared her throat. 'Yes.'

Bea was quiet for several long, tense moments. 'Will he get me from school?' she said at last.

Rose blinked, taken aback. 'Why, yes, I'm sure he will when he's here.'

Bea smiled triumphantly. 'Dante's *much* nicer than Holly's daddy.'

'You like him then?'

'Yes.' Another pause. 'Why didn't he come before?'

The question Rose had been dreading. 'I wouldn't let him.'

'Why?'

'Because I was silly.' Rose bent to kiss her. 'Now, go to sleep. You can tell Pinocchio and Bear your secret if you like.'

'And Gramma and Tom, too?'

'Yes. In the morning.'

After a hectic week spent in bringing accounts up to date and rearranging client appointments, Rose told Dante that the following week was good for her.

'*Ottimo.* I will make all arrangements and ring tomorrow with details.'

'Don't book a hotel room when you come to collect us,' she added casually. 'It would be more convenient to stay here the night before we leave—if you'd like to.'

He was silent for a moment. 'I would like that very much, Rose. *Grazie.* Is Bea happy about the trip?'

'She's wildly excited, though surprised that Gramma and Tom aren't going, too. I told her they had to do my job while we were away.'

He laughed. 'Is your mother happy to do that?'

'Yes, though I've tried to make sure there's very little for her to do.'

'You sound tired, Rose.'

'Nothing a night's sleep won't mend,' she assured him.

'I will ring as soon as I can. *Buonanotte.*'

Rose was in the middle of an endless ironing session when Dante rang to say he would be with her on Sunday afternoon and had arranged a flight to Pisa the following day.

'Is this good for you, Rose?'

'Yes, fine. Mum and Tom have taken Bea out so I can get our things ready.'

'They are much help to you.'

'Always. I'm very lucky.' She paused awkwardly. 'I'll see you tomorrow, then.'

'Yes, Rose. *A domani.*'

When Dante arrived next day Bea flew to the door to open it, beaming up at him. 'Dante, Dante. I've got a secret!'

'A secret! How exciting.' He put down his bag, smiling fondly as he picked her up. 'Will you share it with me?'

'Come inside first,' said Rose, peering past him down the drive. 'Where's your car?'

'I came by taxi.' He leaned to kiss her cheek. 'It is so good to be here, Rose. How are you?'

'I'm fine.'

'*Bene.*'

Dante followed her into the kitchen and sat down at the table with Bea on his lap. 'So, *piccola*, what is this wonderful secret?'

She beamed at him triumphantly. 'You're my real daddy!'

His eyes snapped shut as he hugged her close. 'That is such a wonderful secret. It makes me very happy,' he said when he could trust his voice. 'Does it make you happy?'

Bea nodded fervently. 'I told Gramma and Tom.'

Dante exchanged a look with Rose over the curly head. 'And did they like your secret?'

'Yes.' She looked up at him cajolingly. 'Will you get me from school now?'

'Like Holly's daddy,' explained Rose, busy with the coffee.

Dante took in a deep breath. 'I will like to do that very much, whenever your *mamma* says I may.'

Bea gave her mother a commanding look. 'Every day!'

'Dante doesn't live here, darling,' said Rose rather helplessly.

'But every time I come to England I will fetch you, *piccola*,' promised Dante, and speared Rose with a look which promised discussion on the subject later.

'Mummy was silly,' Bea informed him.

'Because I wouldn't let you come to see us until recently,' explained Rose, wishing she'd explained more to Dante before he came. But she'd been human enough to want to see his reaction when Bea told him her secret.

He smiled lovingly at his child. 'But now we are going to Italy together tomorrow to stay in my house.'

'Is it a big house?'

'Quite big, yes,' he said, ruffling her curls.

'You got children there?' she enquired.

Dante shook his head. 'You are my only child, *piccola*.'

'But you remember Harriet, the lovely lady who came to see us one day?' asked Rose.

Bea nodded with enthusiasm. 'She's got children.'

'You are so clever to remember,' said Dante proudly. 'Their daddy is my brother Leo, and we shall go to his house to play with Luca and Chiara.'

'Tomorrow?'

'No, but soon,' promised Dante. 'Tomorrow we fly in the aeroplane to Italy.'

Due to her excitement, Bea took longer to get to sleep than usual, and later, after a dinner shared with Dante in determined harmony, Rose's tension began to mount as she went upstairs ahead of him. 'You're in my room,' she informed him, ushering him inside. 'I hope you'll be comfortable.'

Dante closed the door quietly behind them. 'Where are you sleeping, Rose?'

'On the sofa bed in my study.'

He frowned. 'I should sleep there and you remain here, near to Bea, yes?'

'Certainly not. You wouldn't fit on it and, besides, I hear Bea wherever I am.' Rose made for the door, but Dante barred her way.

'I cannot take your bed, *cara*. But there is an obvious solution to the problem.' He took her in his arms. 'Share it with me.'

Rose opened her mouth to protest but Dante kissed her into silence. He held her hard against him and her body reacted involuntarily, savouring the scent of him and the pleasure of the contact with a taut, muscular, male body. He raised his head a fraction, but only to rub his cheek against hers and murmur in her ear in his own tongue.

'I don't understand,' she said hoarsely.

'Ah, but you do, *tesoro*,' he whispered. 'I desire you, Rose.'

Desire, not love, she thought bleakly.

Dante drew her closer, his lips against her cheek. 'I think—I know that you want me, yes?'

'Yes,' she admitted, but pulled away, blinking tears from her eyes. 'But not so much that I'll let you turn my life upside down again.'

'Ah, *carissima*, do not cry, or you'll break my heart.'

'Then you'll know how I felt when you broke mine!' Rose flung away and left the room, closing the door softly behind her.

* * *

Rose's second trip to Italy was very different from the first one. A chauffeured limousine replaced the coach trip to Heathrow, followed by a first-class flight to Pisa. The flight attendants were charmed with Bea, the females among them charmed with Dante, too, noted Rose acidly as she listened to melodic exchanges in Italian. She couldn't blame them. Dante was so obviously enjoying every minute of his time with his child, and so far Bea was behaving so well it was hard to remember she was prone to the odd tantrum or two at home. She was delighted with everything, including the pasta she was given for lunch, but Rose, occupied with thoughts of facing Dante's family, could only manage a cup of tea.

'You are not hungry?' asked Dante.

'No.' She managed a smile across her daughter's head. 'What happens when we land?'

'I shall drive you to the Villa Castiglione in my car. Do not worry,' he added. 'I have installed a car seat for Bea.'

'Thank you; how thoughtful,' said Rose, embarrassed because she hadn't thought of it herself.

To her gratitude, the rest of the flight passed quickly, helped by a peaceful interlude while Dante read to his daughter until she fell asleep. Rose sat, trying to relax, but her mind kept returning to the night before.

After her emotional parting shot, she had dreaded seeing Dante again this morning. To avoid him she'd showered and dressed hurriedly in the downstairs bathroom, and after getting Bea through the same process took the coward's way out by sending her to knock on Dante's door to say breakfast would be ready in a few minutes. She needn't have worried. Dante had walked into the kitchen later, smiling as though the biting little exchange of the night before had never happened. But his eyes had smudges of fatigue that matched hers.

Rose tensed as the plane began its descent. She wondered if Dante's family would be there *en masse* at his house to meet them, or if she'd have a day's grace to prepare herself while she explored the Villa Castiligione. A hand reached out to touch hers and she turned to face Dante's questioning eyes over his sleeping daughter's head.

'You feel ill, *cara*?'

'No, just nervous.'

'Of the landing?'

She shook her head. 'Of meeting your family.'

'You will not meet them today,' he assured her. 'I asked my parents to wait until tomorrow.' He smiled as Bea stirred. 'Wake up, *bella*. We are nearly there.'

They left the plane with much waving and hand kissing from the flight attendants for Bea. Dante would have picked her up to carry her but she shook her head.

'Walk—please.'

So Beatrice Grace Palmer made her entrance into the airport, hand in hand with both parents, her father carrying a shiny pink holdall with Pinocchio and Bear peeping out of it. As the trio reached the baggage carousel Rose saw a young man waving vigorously.

'*Va bene*, it is Tullio with my car keys,' Dante told Rose. 'He will help with the luggage.'

Tullio bowed, smiling, as Dante presented him to Rose and Bea, who grew very excited when she spotted her mother's familiar battered student luggage on the baggage carousel.

'Ours, Daddy,' she said, pointing.

Dante gave Rose a look which turned her heart over. 'So it is, *tesoro*,' he said huskily, 'and that is mine beside it.'

The useful Tullio helped stow the luggage in the car

while Rose fastened her daughter into the smart scarlet car seat. She chuckled suddenly and Dante looked round, smiling.

'What amuses you, *cara*?'

'Your car looks faintly ridiculous with a child's seat on board.'

'It must get used to it, yes?' He had a quick conversation with Tullio, who took his leave of them, blew a kiss at Bea and hurried off.

'Where's he going?' asked Bea.

'To take a taxi back to work.'

'What does he do?' asked Rose as Dante helped her into the passenger seat.

'He works for me. He is good at the selling, too.'

'But not as good as you!'

'He soon will be. He is eager to learn. And as an advantage with the selling he is an attractive young man, yes?'

'Very attractive!' Rose turned round to smile at her daughter, who was cuddling Pinocchio. 'Are you comfortable, darling?'

Bea nodded happily.

'Allora,' said Dante and switched on the powerful engine, 'let us go home.'

'Not fast!' ordered Bea in alarm. 'I don't like fast.'

'Welcome to fatherhood,' murmured Rose. 'Soon she'll ask if we're there yet.'

Dante laughed and drove with care as they left the airport. He touched Rose's hand fleetingly. 'Did you hear what she said?'

'She called you Daddy. You obviously liked that.'

'Very much. Did you tell her to say it?'

'No—her idea entirely.'

He let out a deep breath. 'I wanted to buy her many toys, but I did not.'

Rose nodded. 'You need her to like you for yourself.'

'*Esattamente*. You think she does?'

'Oh, yes. Apparently, you're much nicer than Holly's daddy.'

Dante laughed and reached out a hand to touch hers but put it back on the wheel at the look on her face. 'Do not worry, Rose. I will drive safely with such precious cargo on board.'

Judging by the speed of other traffic whizzing past them on the *Autostrada*, Rose found he meant what he said. Even so, she was relieved when they left the motorway at last to take a winding road lined in places with groups of tall cypress trees like exclamation marks which emphasised the breathtaking views of the rolling Tuscan landscape.

'Are we there yet?' came a voice from the back. 'Pinocchio and Bear want to get out.'

'Very soon,' said Dante, smiling at Rose, and after a while turned off on a narrow road which wound up a steep hill in corkscrew curves he negotiated with care she was sure must be very different from his normal approach to his home. As if reading her mind, he slowed down to a crawl to drive through an entrance flanked by stone pillars and on through tiered gardens to park at the foot of steps leading to a terrace edged with small timeworn statues and stone urns full of flowers.

'Welcome to the Villa Castiglione,' said Dante and turned to smile at the wide-eyed child in the back seat.

Rose was as silent as her daughter as she gazed at the weathered golden stone of a lovely old house fronted by an arcaded loggia.

Dante opened the passenger door to help Rose out. 'Do you like my home?'

She nodded dumbly. 'It's beautiful, Dante.'

'Come out!' demanded an imperious voice and Dante

laughed and hurried to release his daughter from her seat. But as he set her on her feet she reached her arms up to him in sudden alarm as someone emerged from the house.

Rose would have given much to do the same as a regal woman with silver-streaked dark hair came out to meet them.

'Mamma!' Dante laughed affectionately as he kissed her. 'You could not wait.'

'No, *caro*.' Maria Fortinari turned to Rose. 'Welcome to my son's home. Dante said I must wait, but I could not let you arrive with no one to greet you.'

Rose smiled shyly. 'How very kind. Thank you.'

'Will you introduce me to my granddaughter, *cara*?'

Bea had recovered from her attack of shyness. From her place of safety in Dante's arms, she eyed his mother with interest.

'This is Beatrice Grace, *signora*,' said Rose, and smiled at Bea. 'This lovely lady is your other grandmother, darling.'

'Another Gramma?' said Bea, surprised.

'No, *piccola*,' said Dante. 'This is my *mamma*, so she has an Italian name. She is your *nonna*.'

'Can you say that?' asked his mother gently.

Bea nodded. 'Course. Down, please, Daddy.'

A look of wonder crossed his mother's handsome face as Dante set his daughter on her feet. She touched the fair curls gently and smiled down into the blue, unmistakable eyes. 'I would so much like a kiss, Beatrice.'

Rose crossed mental fingers, praying that Bea would cooperate, and let out the breath she was holding when her daughter held up her face for the kiss her grandmother placed on both cheeks.

'*Grazie*, Beatrice.'

Since her name sounded even more unfamiliar pronounced Italian style, Bea shook her head. 'I'm Bea.'

Maria smiled lovingly. 'That is a very small name for a big girl like you!'

Wonderful, thought Rose, as Bea accepted her grandmother's hand to go inside.

'Come,' said Dante. 'Let us follow. You would like tea?'

'I would, please. What a lovely house, Dante.'

'I am glad you like it.' He looked up with a smile as a beaming woman came hurrying across the marble-floored hall to greet them. 'I inherited Silvia with the house,' he muttered in English, and in Italian introduced Rose to the woman, who greeted her with a flood of what were obviously good wishes. But she threw up her hands in delight as she saw the child and came out with another flood of Italian, most of which seemed to consist of *bella, bella*, repeated several times.

'This is my son's house,' said Maria Fortinari, slanting a smile at Dante, 'so I must not give orders—'

'Which means I am neglecting you, Rose!' He gave his mother a kiss. 'Just for today, give your orders, Mamma, *per favore.*'

She nodded briskly. 'Rose, what do you desire most? Tea, coffee or to go to your room?'

'Both of us need a visit to a bathroom, *signora*,' said Rose gratefully, and took Bea's shiny pink bag from Dante. 'But, after a freshen-up, some tea would be wonderful.'

'I will take you up,' said Dante firmly, 'while Mamma arranges it.'

'*Subito, caro,*' said his mother, and brushed her hand over Bea's curls as she smiled warmly at Rose. 'It is very good to have you here.'

'It's good to be here, *signora*,' Rose assured her, and to her surprise found she meant it.

'Come,' said Dante. 'Do you need anything from your luggage now, *cara*?'

'No, thanks—' Rose eyed her daughter, who was beginning to fidget. 'Just get us to a bathroom, please.'

The room Dante showed them into was bright with sunshine, held a large bed and, most vital at that particular moment, an adjoining bathroom. Rose hurried Bea inside and a few minutes later mother and daughter, both clean of face and hands, emerged to find Dante pacing impatiently.

'Do you like the room, Rose?' he demanded.

She liked it a lot now she had time to look at the carved furniture and filmy white curtains moving lazily at the open windows. 'It's lovely.'

'Have I got a room, Daddy?' asked Bea.

'Of course, *carina*, but we shall look at it after we have tea with Nonna on the loggia.'

'What's a loggia?'

'The veranda outside, so you must wear your beautiful blue jacket—yes, Mummy?'

Rose nodded. 'I'll wear mine, too.' She hesitated. 'It was kind of your mother to come here to welcome us, Dante.'

'She could not wait to do so,' he assured her wryly, zipping Bea's jacket.

Maria Fortinari was waiting at a table set for tea when they went outside. 'Come sit by Nonna, *tesoro*,' she said, patting the chair beside her. 'You like orange juice?'

'Yes, please,' said Bea, remembering her manners, to her mother's relief.

Maria smiled in fond approval. 'There is English tea for you, Rose, and coffee for Dante, of course.'

Rose took the chair Dante held out for her next to his mother. 'What a heavenly garden,' she commented.

'We've got a garden, too,' Bea told her new grandmother. 'Tom helps Mummy in it.'

'Tom,' Dante explained, 'is Charlotte Vilari's father.'

'Gramma lives with him in his house,' said Bea, and began on her juice.

'She will miss you, *piccola*.' Maria turned to Rose. 'Forgive my English; it is not so good as my son's.'

'It sounds perfect to me,' Rose assured her. 'I can only claim some schoolgirl French, I'm afraid. I wanted to learn Italian when I was younger, but I never had the time.'

'As I told you, Mamma, Rose was too busy qualifying as an accountant,' Dante reminded her. 'And when she had her degree she studied for more qualifications to run a bookkeeping business from her own home.' He met Rose's eyes. 'So that she could stay with Bea while she earned money to provide for her.'

'After such hard work, Rose, you must rest now you are here.' Maria Fortinari smiled down at Bea. 'Would you like one of the *trammezini*, Bea?'

'That is a sandwich, *carina*,' said her father. 'You like ham and cheese?'

'Yes, please.' Bea took one of the dainty sandwiches eagerly.

Rose sat sipping her tea, amazed that this was actually happening. Here she was in Italy with Dante, in his beautiful house and, strangest of all, taking tea with his mother. In the past, when she was facing up to life as a single parent, working hard to provide for her child, this scenario had never entered even the wildest of her dreams.

'Please eat, Rose,' urged Dante. 'You had nothing on the plane.'

'Thank you. The little cakes look delicious.'

'Silvia made them especially for you and your *mamma*, Bea,' said Maria.

'I make cakes with Gramma,' Bea informed her.

'*Che bello*! Your mother lives near you, Rose?' asked Maria.

'Yes. It's a wonderful arrangement for Bea and me.'

'For your mother, also, I think, yes?' She turned to Dante. 'Bea has finished. Would you take her for a little walk in the garden, *caro*?'

Bea looked at Rose in appeal. 'Can I go, Mummy?'

'Of course. Wipe your hands on your napkin first, please—mouth, too.'

Bea obeyed with alacrity then took the hand Dante held out. 'You got lots of flowers, Daddy.'

'*Allora, s*hall we go and count them?'

Maria cleared her throat as she watched her son walk off, hand in hand with his child. 'She is so sweet, Rose. *Grazie tante* for allowing Dante to share her. This is hard for you?'

'In some ways, yes,' said Rose honestly. 'Until a short time ago no one—not even my mother—knew that your son is Bea's father.'

Maria shook her elegantly coiffed head. 'So if you had not met Dante again in Firenze he would never know he has a child.'

'No.' Rose flushed painfully. 'By the time I knew I was pregnant Dante was already married.'

'My heart was heavy the day he married Elsa Marino,' said the other woman forcefully. 'Then one day my prayers were answered and she left him for that wealthy old fool, Enrico Calvi.'

'But until I met Dante again in Florence I didn't know that,' Rose said, and looked Maria Fortinari in the eye. 'It wasn't easy for me to come here, *signora*. I was afraid you'd think I was trying to trap a rich father for my child.'

Maria smiled ruefully. 'I confess I wondered. But then Dante described how you work so hard to make a good life for the little one. I think you are very brave. But now,' she added, suddenly brisk, 'what will you do? Dante says you refuse to marry him.'

Rose felt her colour rise. 'I'm used to running my own life, *signora*. And even though we have Bea as a common factor, Dante and I don't really know each other very well.'

'Yet you were drawn to him in the past, yes? Or Bea would not be here.'

Rose nodded ruefully. 'I fell madly in love with your son the moment I met him, and believed he felt the same about me. I was devastated when I found he had a fiancée, but my world really fell apart later when I found I was expecting his child.'

Maria winced. 'Did you curse him at the hour of Beatrice's birth?'

Rose shook her head sadly. 'No. I wanted him there with me so much I cried. But I still didn't say who I was crying for.'

Maria sighed. 'Your mother must feel much anger at my son, I think.'

'No, *signora*. I've made it very plain that what happened between Dante and me was mutual.'

Rose was glad to change the subject when Bea came running towards them with Dante in hot pursuit. 'Mummy, Mummy, there's a little pool!' Bea launched herself onto Rose's lap, her eyes bright with excitement.

'We shall take Mummy to see it later,' Dante promised.

'And tomorrow,' said his mother, 'you will come to Fortino to meet the rest of the family. We will have a party, yes?'

Bea slid off Rose's lap to look hopefully at her grandmother. 'With balloons?'

'Yes, *carissima*. With balloons!' Maria laughed and

kissed the pink cheeks. 'But now I must go home. *A domani*—until tomorrow.'

Once they'd waved his mother off Dante suggested they go indoors to show Bea her room.

'It's not bedtime yet!' objected Bea as they went upstairs.

He laughed. 'No, *piccola*, it is not. But we must show Pinocchio and Bear where to sleep, yes? Your room is here, between your *mamma*'s and mine.' He threw open the door and waited as Bea ran inside then stopped dead as she saw the doll propped up on the bed.

She looked up at Dante, wide-eyed. 'Whose dolly is that?'

'She is yours.' He caught Rose's eye and shrugged impenitently.

The doll had fair curls and blue eyes and wore jeans and a T-shirt. 'She's got clothes like me,' Bea crowed, picking the toy up to hug her.

'What do you say?' prompted Rose.

'Thank you, Daddy! You get kisses for presents,' she informed him as he picked her up.

'*Davvero*? Then you must kiss me twice because there is another present. Your dolly has a bag.'

Bea obliged with the kisses and wriggled to get down. 'What's in it?'

'Open it and see.'

The holdall, much to Bea's delight, was full of dolls' clothes.

'How lovely, darling,' said Rose, and smiled wryly at Dante. 'You couldn't resist, then?'

He shook his head. 'No. You disapprove?'

'How could I?' Rose smiled as Bea laid out every piece of miniature clothing on the bed, her eyes shining as she showed them to the doll. 'I'm only surprised you had the restraint to wait until now.'

'So am I.' His eyelids lowered. '*Allora*, now I know that presents are rewarded with kisses I shall buy something special for you, Rose, also.'

She shook her head, flushing. 'No need.'

'You mean,' he whispered, moving closer, 'that no gift is necessary for you to kiss me?'

Rose turned away hastily. 'What name shall we give her, Bea?'

Her daughter turned in surprise. 'Dolly, a'course.'

Dante threw back his head and laughed, then seized Bea and spun her round. 'So tell me, *piccola*, do you like your room?'

Bea nodded, giggling as he set her down. She frowned suddenly. 'Is it my room for always?'

Dante exchanged a look with Rose. 'Always,' he said emphatically.

Later that evening, Bea, tired out with all the excitement of the day, made no protest about going to bed in her new room with her growing collection of companions. Once she was asleep, Rose showered and changed into a dress in honour of her first dinner with Dante in the formal dining room, and felt glad she'd made the effort when she found he was wearing a lightweight suit. Dark curls gleaming in the light from the chandelier above a face alight with a smile at the sight of her, he took her breath away.

'You look very beautiful, Rose,' said Dante.

'Thank you.'

'Because this is a special occasion, Silvia has stayed to serve dinner.'

'She doesn't live in?' said Rose, surprised.

'She did in my grandmother's day, but after Nonna died

Silvia surprised everyone by marrying a man she'd known in her youth. So now she comes here for an hour or two in the day, and then goes home to Mario.' Dante eyed her warily. 'She assured me that if we wish to go out any evening she will stay with Bea, but I did not think you would allow that.'

'No, indeed. Not,' added Rose hastily, 'that I don't think she's trustworthy, but—'

'You could not leave your child with a stranger who speaks no English.'

'Put like that, it sounds very cold, but yes, I suppose I do mean that.' She sighed. 'It was a big step for me to bring Bea here at all, Dante.'

'I know this. And now you are here, how do you feel?' The blue eyes lit with heat as they locked on hers. 'For me, it feels so natural, so right, to see you sitting here with me. As we should have done long ago if Elsa had not lied to me,' he said bitterly.

Rose held up a hand. 'Let's not talk about the past.'

He nodded. '*Va bene.* We shall discuss the future instead.'

'No, not tonight, Dante. Let's just sit here and enjoy Silvia's dinner together.'

His eyes softened. 'Does this mean you are enjoying your time here with me, Rose?'

She grinned. 'It beats an evening spent with my computer.'

Having eaten very little all day, Rose was more than ready for the soup Silvia served, and for the chicken roasted with herbs and vegetables that followed. She thanked the beaming woman when she came to clear away, and assured her, via Dante, that the meal had been delicious.

'*Grazie tante*, Silvia,' she said, smiling.

This prompted a voluble response Dante translated as

great pleasure, that coffee and *biscotti* awaited them in the *salone* and Silvia wished them both good night.

Dante led Rose to a sitting room with a painted ceiling and furniture upholstered in ruby velvet. By the abundance of gilt-framed mirrors and pictures, it had obviously remained unchanged since his grandmother's day.

'How lovely, Dante. You've kept everything the same?'

He nodded as they sat down together on the sofa. 'My family says I should buy new things, express my own personality, but I preferred to wait.'

'Until you'd stopped grieving for your grandmother?' she said gently.

'No. Until you and I could make the changes together, Rose. *Perche,*' he said, his voice deepening, 'now I know I have a daughter, nothing will come between us this time.'

CHAPTER NINE

ROSE STIFFENED. 'ONLY because you're so desperate to be her father you're willing to take me as part of the deal!'

Dante stared at her angrily. 'This is not true. When I first saw you at Fabio's wedding I was entranced.' He turned her face up to his. 'It is plain you did not share my feelings.'

'Of course I did,' she said impatiently. 'I fell madly in love with you, Dante. Otherwise, the…the episode in the hotel room would never have happened.'

'The episode that changed your life. When you cried in my arms that night I meant only to comfort you, but the moment we kissed I felt such desperation to make love to you I was lost. When I was forced to leave you so suddenly I felt torn, as though I had left part of myself with you. Which I had,' he said bitterly. '*Dio!* How fate must have laughed when Elsa told me her lies.'

'Tears are something I must try to avoid in future,' Rose said darkly. 'They get me into too much trouble.'

Dante seized her hand. 'You cried the night in your house when we quarrelled, yes?'

'Yes.' She smiled brightly. 'So no more quarrelling, either.'

'This is a good plan,' he agreed. 'So now when I say we must marry you will not argue?'

If he made it clear he loved her for herself, rather than part of the deal that gained him a daughter, there would be no argument at all. He made it crystal clear he wanted her physically, but she would have to be convinced that his heart was involved, too, before she agreed to anything permanent between them. And if that was asking for the moon, so be it. She'd managed without him in her life before and she would do it again rather than enter into a relationship where her feelings were greater than his.

'I still think we should take more time to get to know each other first.'

'Gran Dio!' Dante thrust his free hand through his hair. 'How much time do you need? We have wasted too many years already.' He released her hand and sprang up. *'Scusi!'*

Rose watched, dismayed, as he strode from the room. Did he intend on coming back? But, to her relief, Dante returned quickly, holding out a leather-bound diary.

'Open it,' he ordered.

Her eyes widened as she saw it was dated the year they'd met. As she took it from him, a withered rosebud slid out.

'It fell from your hair at the wedding,' Dante informed her curtly. 'I have kept it all this time, like a sentimental fool.'

She felt her throat thicken and blinked furiously as she carefully replaced the pressed bud. 'I must check on Bea,' she said, getting up, but Dante barred her way.

'I have just done so. She is sleeping peacefully.' He took her hand and drew her down on the sofa beside him. 'You say we do not know each other well enough to marry yet, but the best way for this is to live together, the three of us as a family.'

She looked at him squarely. 'And there's the buzz word. Without Bea in the picture, would you be in such a hurry?'

Dante dropped her hand and moved away, his face

drawn. 'What more can I do to convince you? I even embarrass myself by showing you the rose I kept. You say you fell in love with me at first sight, but now your feelings for me are very different, yes?' He shrugged. *'Non importa.* For Bea's sake, we shall marry, and soon. My child shall not grow up believing I do not want her.'

'But what shall I *do* here?' she said unsteadily. 'You're away a lot. At home I have my work—'

'You could work here also if you wish. Harriet helps Leo a great deal. She is very good at taking visitors around Fortino.'

'She speaks Italian?'

'Yes. She taught it at one time. French also.'

Her face fell. 'I don't do any of that. My sole talent is with figures.'

'You could help Harriet by taking over the English-speaking tourists.' Dante turned to look at her, his eyes bleak. 'Also, I will travel less after we marry.'

Will, Rose noted, not *would*. She had known all along that saying yes to the trip was saying yes to marrying Dante. Which was all she'd ever wanted from the first moment she'd met him; even more so now he'd matured into a man who'd suffered enough, courtesy of Elsa. And so had she. For Bea's sake, if nothing else, it was time to move on. Grow up at last. And surely, once they were married, she could make Dante love her for herself, not just as his child's mother. But what, said an inner voice, if he never does?

'I'll think about it,' she said at last.

Dante eyed her suspiciously. 'What are you saying?'

'I can't just walk away from my life at a moment's notice, Dante. I'd have to sell my business first, for one thing. So you'll have to give me more time.'

He shook his head in wonder. '*Dio*, that is not the answer I wanted, Rose.'

'Take it or leave it,' she said, shrugging, then quailed inwardly at the sudden fire in his eyes.

'I will take it! I will also take this,' he added huskily and kissed her with sudden fierce demand that shook her to her toes. He pulled her onto his lap, his lips and hands caressing her into a response which swept through her with such heat he pulled her to her feet and led her up the stairs to the gallery. At the open door of Bea's room, they gazed at their sleeping child for a moment then Dante took away what breath Rose had left by picking her up to carry her along the gallery to his room. He laid her on his bed and began taking off his clothes. She shot upright in protest.

'Wait a minute!'

He shot her an imperious look. 'No. I have waited long enough.' He knelt on the bed beside her and began undressing her. 'You may not love me, but you want me. Do you deny it?'

'No, I don't.' She took in a deep breath. 'But don't do this in anger, Dante.'

His eyes smouldered as he slid the dress from her shoulders. 'No, *bella*, not in anger.' He took down the hair she'd spent so much time over earlier and buried his face in it. 'I want you, Rose.' He removed the last of her clothes and held her shivering body against his hard male nakedness with a growl of pure male satisfaction. 'Tonight,' he said huskily, 'we finish what we began so many years ago, yes?'

'You've made love to me since then,' she said unsteadily as his lips moved down her throat.

He kissed the pulse he found throbbing there. 'But once again only in haste. Tonight I will show you what loving can be for us, *tesoro*.'

Rose felt his heart thudding against hers and looked up

into the brilliant eyes moving over her in open possession. *Yes*, she thought fiercely. *Show me. I want this.* 'You'll have to make allowances, Dante,' she said unevenly, her breath catching as he slid his lips down her throat.

'For what, *amore*?' he whispered.

'You've obviously done this a lot and I…well, I haven't. As you know, I had a boyfriend in college, but there's been no one since Bea was born.'

Dante held her closer. 'And was he a skilled lover, this college boyfriend?'

'No, he was much better at playing rugby,' she said unevenly. 'But I was fond of him and he made me laugh.'

'It is good to laugh together,' agreed Dante, and kissed her with mounting urgency. 'We shall laugh together many times, I hope, but at this moment, *tesoro*, I want you in all the ways a man wants a woman.'

Rose fully expected an onslaught as he sought instant relief for the tension she could feel building in his body, but instead Dante took infinite pleasure in kissing and caressing every inch of her with clever, inciting hands that tuned her entire body to such a pitch of longing she gave a hoarse little cry of protest as he paused an instant to use protection then took her mouth in a devouring kiss as his body fused with hers in a jolt of such pure sensation she fought for breath, her heart hammering against his. She lay relishing the almost painful pleasure of it for an instant before he withdrew slightly then thrust again to what felt like the very heart of her, his eyes like blue fires burning down into hers as he began showing her exactly what the art of loving should be. He kissed her as he made love to her, the rhythm slow at first until he felt her desire mount to match his, but at last he took her hard and fast towards the culmination that finally overwhelmed them both and, with a smothered cry, she came apart in his arms, and he surrendered to his own release.

Dante drew the covers over them and turned her in his arms to hold her close. 'Rose,' he whispered later, 'I do not wish to move, but soon I must take you back to the guest room. Bea might come looking for you and find the bed empty.'

She nodded, flushing. 'You're right.'

'Tomorrow,' said Dante with emphasis, 'we bring your clothes to my room and tell our daughter you will be sharing it with me.'

Rose braced herself as she shook her head. 'I'd rather not do that until things are more settled between us, Dante.'

'Ah!' His face darkened. 'This is my punishment, Rose?'

'Punishment?'

'For my sins,' he said bitterly. 'I did not tell you about Elsa, I left you with child—'

'Since the child is the light of my life, I wouldn't punish you for that, Dante.' She looked at him in appeal. 'I just want you to slow down a little, to give me more time to get used to—'

'To me?' he said quickly. 'Yet, here in my arms, I thought I made you happy, Rose.'

'You know you did,' she said, flushing, and turned her head way. 'That part of our relationship would obviously be good.'

'All of it will be good,' he said with passion. 'But if you want me to wait until you are also sure of this I will do so.' He gave a mirthless laugh. 'I am good at the waiting. I have been waiting for you for years, Rose.'

She turned on him sharply, her eyes flashing. 'If that's true, why didn't you come looking for me once you were free?'

His chin lifted. 'Charlotte told me you had someone else in your life. She would not say who it was, so I believed, *naturalmente*, that it was a man.' He shook his head in wonder. 'While all the time it was the daughter I did not know I possessed.'

'I begged Charlotte to keep my baby secret. So she did.'

'You were ashamed of Bea?'

She glared at him. 'No, I was not! I was merely afraid that if any of your friends saw you anywhere near my child they would know exactly who her father was. And because you were married, it would have been disaster all round.'

'But Bea resembles you, not me,' said Dante, surprised.

'Not the smile and those eyes of yours. They're a dead giveaway. My mother took one look at you two together and knew straight away.'

'*Va bene*, now the whole world will know,' he said with satisfaction, and slid out of bed. 'No. Stay there, *cara*. I have a present for you.' He licked his lips as he leaned over her. 'So I will get kisses, yes?'

Rose laughed. 'Very probably!'

'I have dreamed of this so often, yet now you are really here at last. Where you belong, yes?' Dante gave her a look that curled her toes then turned away to open a drawer and took out a small box before sliding back into bed.

'You don't have to give me presents to get a kiss,' she remarked, eyeing the box.

'Then I will kiss you first,' he said and did so with such lingering pleasure that Rose kissed him back in kind and melted against him, breathing in the scent of his skin as he nuzzled his lips against her neck. 'Open the box, *tesoro*,' he whispered.

Rose obeyed, and breathed in sharply at the sight of a gold ring set with a baguette emerald between two rose-cut diamonds. 'Oh, Dante,' she breathed, tears welling in her eyes.

He sat upright, pulling her up with him. 'You do not like it?'

'Of *course* I like it,' she said hoarsely, and knuckled the tears from her eyes. 'It's just that I can't accept it just yet.'

'Why not?' he demanded, eyes suddenly cold.

She eyed him in appeal. 'Don't look at me like that! I'm just asking you to wait a little longer.'

Dante closed the ring box with a snap and tossed it on the bedside table. *'Va bene,'* he said shortly. 'But I will wait only until I take you back to England. Tomorrow, you will have a taste of what life could be for us here in Fortino. After that, if you still say no to me it will be the last time. It is against my nature to beg and I will do so no more—but then I will make legal arrangements to share our daughter.'

Rose stared at him in horror. 'Dante, listen—'

'No, Rose. It is you who must listen. It is best we are clear on this. Say yes and we live a normal married life. If not, you know what will happen. *Allora,*' he added silkily, 'since I have you here and now in my bed, I will enjoy the privilege while I can.' And he pulled her closer and made love to her all over again. But in the throes of the climax that engulfed her she waited in vain for the words which would have ended all argument, whichever language he chose. *'Ti amo'* was one bit of Italian she would have understood perfectly well.

CHAPTER TEN

ROSE WOKE TO bright sunshine and found her daughter at the foot of the guest room bed with Dante, shaking her head at her mother in disapproval.

'Up, Mummy. Party time.'

'Not yet, *piccola*,' said Dante, laughing. 'First we have breakfast. So let us leave Mummy to her bath and you and I shall walk in the garden until she is ready.'

Rose blinked in surprise at her daughter, who was wearing fresh jeans and T-shirt, her face shining and curls brushed. 'Good morning, darling. Did you get dressed all by yourself?'

Bea beamed up at Dante. 'Daddy helped me. But I washed and did teeth by myself.'

Rose eyed Dante with unwilling respect. He was diving into the deep end of fatherhood with enthusiasm. 'Then I'd better get a move on and do mine, hadn't I?'

'You are tired, *cara*?' said Dante softly, his eyes gleaming.

'Travelling always affects me that way,' she said, and thrust her hair back from her flushed face. 'Now, give me ten minutes and I'll join you for breakfast—I'm hungry.'

After a swift shower, Rose wrapped her wet hair in a towel to style later, slapped on some moisturiser and pulled on jeans and sweater. Something more elegant could be achieved later on before they left for Fortino. She felt a pang of apprehension again at the thought of meeting the rest of Dante's family. But his mother had been kind and Rose already knew Harriet, so she would have support from a fellow Brit among the alien corn. As she hurried downstairs she could hear Bea chattering away to Dante as they came in from the garden and felt a shamed little pang of jealousy of the man who was making her little girl so happy.

Silvia came hurrying through the hall with a tray as Rose went down, and smiled and wished her good morning, but in a different accent from Dante's.

'Buongiorno,' echoed Rose, hoping it sounded right, and received such a beaming smile in response assumed it did.

'There you are,' said Dante, getting up as she went outside on the loggia. 'Are you dressed warmly enough to eat outside?'

'I asked Daddy if we could,' said Bea.

'And Daddy said yes, of course,' said Rose, smiling.

He shrugged, grinning. 'Naturalmente.' He pulled out a chair for her.

'That means a'course,' Bea told her, and smiled at Silvia as the woman poured orange juice into her glass. 'Grazie,' she said proudly, in exact imitation of Dante. 'Was that right, Daddy?'

'Perfect.' He nodded in agreement as Silvia, smiling fondly at the child, spoke rapidly to him. 'Silvia says you are a clever girl.'

Eating a leisurely breakfast outside in the cool sunlit morning was such a contrast to the normal routine in the Palmer household. Rose suppressed all uneasy thoughts of Dante's threat the night before and smiled as she described their usual morning chaos. 'It takes more effort some days than others, but I always manage to get Bea to nursery school on time.'

'Do you like school, Bea?' Dante asked.

She nodded. 'The teacher reads stories. And we do paint-ing and make things.'

'Did you tell her you were coming to Italy for a holiday?'

'Yes. To Daddy's house.'

Rose eyed her daughter wryly. 'And what did she say?'

'What a lucky girl! Can I get down now?'

By the time Rose had washed her daughter's face and hands and collected Dolly, Pinocchio and Bear, Silvia had brewed a fresh pot of coffee, so Rose sat down to share it with Dante while Bea played with her toys on the steps beside them.

'Sorry about the face and hair,' murmured Rose. 'I'll do something better before we go.'

'I like to see you like this.' He shrugged. 'Elsa drank only black coffee in the morning and refused to leave her room until her face and coiffure were perfect.'

'Who's Elsa?' asked Bea.

Dante shot a remorseful glance at Rose. 'A lady I used to know.'

'Will she be at the party?'

'No, *piccola*. Today is for family only.'

Bea scrambled to her feet. 'Mummy, can I have more juice?'

'Go to the kitchen to ask Silvia for some,' suggested Rose. 'Daddy will tell you what to say.'

'I can get it,' said Dante instantly, but Rose shook her head.

'It's a good way to learn the language.'

He bent down to Bea. 'You must say "*Succo, per fa-vore,* Silvia".'

She repeated it solemnly then went running into the house.

'Forgive me, Rose,' said Dante heavily. 'I did not think. I will not mention Elsa again.'

She shook her head. 'It doesn't matter.'

His eyes flared as he pulled her out of her chair. 'It does matter. Now you and Bea are in my life, I wish to forget she ever existed,' he said, and kissed her fiercely.

But without Bea this would not be happening, Rose thought unhappily, and with iron will managed to keep from melting into his embrace as he crushed her to him.

Dante released her, smiling as Rose picked up the towel she'd lost in the encounter.

She thrust her hair back from her hot face. 'Maybe you should see how Bea is getting along with Silvia.'

'With pleasure!' He went into the house and eventually returned with a plastic beaker of juice, his daughter running beside him.

'This is a special mug for me, Mummy,' she informed Rose, beaming. 'And I said *grazie* to Silvia for the juice.'

'You're a star! Come and sit down by Dolly to drink. Only don't spill anything on her.'

Bea obeyed carefully. 'Mummy, can I wear my party dress today?'

'I've been meaning to ask about that,' said Rose. 'What do you want us to wear today, Dante?'

'My women will look ravishing whatever they wear,' he assured her.

'Only if they're wearing something appropriate and don't feel out of place,' Rose said tartly. 'So are you wearing a suit?'

'No, *cara*. Just ordinary clothes and one of my leather jackets.'

'None of your clothes look very ordinary, Dante.'

'*Mummy!*' repeated Bea imperiously. 'Can I wear my dress?'

'Yes,' said Rose in sudden decision. 'I'll wear a dress, too. But we'll take some jeans and a T-shirt for you, just in case. What time are we due at Fortino, Dante?'

'Noon.'

'In that case I'd better make a start on my hair. You can take a look at the clothes I've brought, Dante, and choose for me.'

'I always do that, Mummy,' said Bea, pouting.

'We shall choose together,' said her father hastily, and snatched her up to give her a piggyback up the stairs.

On the approach to Dante's childhood home through the vast vineyards of Fortino, the house which came into view looked familiar to Rose.

'It's the label on your Fortinari Classico,' she said, impressed. 'I'd assumed it was a reproduction of some Renaissance villa.' She bit her lip. 'It's very grand, Dante.'

'But in bad condition when my parents inherited it,' he informed her. 'Much work was necessary to make it look as it does today. Part of it is used as offices, so Mamma wants a smaller, more private place to enjoy my father's retirement. She would like Leo and Harriet to take over Fortino.'

'Will they do that?'

'Harriet says Leo spends most of his time here anyway, so she is willing to make the change. But Leo is attached to his present house because it is the home he brought Harriet to as a bride.'

'Look, balloons, Daddy!' piped up a voice from the back. 'And lots of people.'

Bea was right. As Dante parked the car, people came streaming out of the house onto a loggia far bigger and grander than the one at the Villa Castiglione, with brightly coloured balloons tied to its venerable pillars.

'Do I look all right?' demanded Rose urgently, and Dante picked up her hand and squeezed it.

'You are perfect,' he said, and got out to help his little family from the car.

Maria Fortinari came hurrying down the steps to greet them and kissed Rose in warm welcome, then planted kisses on her granddaughter's cheeks. 'You both look so beautiful,' she exclaimed, and turned to the distinguished silver-haired man following behind. 'Our newest grand-daughter, *caro*.' She drew Rose forward. 'And this is Rose, her *mamma*.'

Lorenzo Fortinari took Rose by the shoulders and kissed her on both cheeks. '*Benvenuti,* Rose.' He smiled down at the child clinging to Dante's hand. 'Welcome to you, also, *piccola*. May I have a kiss?'

'This is *my* daddy, Bea,' Dante informed his daughter. 'But to you he is *Nonno*.'

Much to Rose's relief, Bea held up her face for her grand-father's kiss, then her eyes lit up and she broke away to dart up the steps to the people clustered there watching. 'Auntie Charlotte, Auntie Charlotte!'

'Honey Bea!' Charlotte Vilari hugged her tightly. 'How's my lovely girl?'

Bea smiled up at her joyfully. 'I got a big secret, Auntie.'

'Have you, darling?'

Bea nodded vigorously. 'Dante's my daddy!'

There was delighted laughter and, to Rose's surprise, a ripple of applause from the people gathered waiting there. Charlotte passed Bea to her husband, Fabio, and hurried down the steps to throw her arms round her friend, both of them too emotional to say a word until Rose drew back, grinning happily through her tears.

'This is a lovely surprise—mind the bump, little mother!'

Dante gave them time to recover then introduced Rose to

his sister Mirella and her husband, Franco. 'This is Rose,' he said with pride. 'And the little angel with Signora Vilari is my daughter—as she has already informed you.'

'And I am his brother,' said a deep voice with a more pronounced accent, and Dante grinned as he turned Rose to meet Leo Fortinari, easily recognisable as an older, more saturnine version of his brother.

'*Il capo*, Rose. My boss,' said Dante, saluting smartly.

'Senior partner, not boss,' said a familiar voice as Harriet Fortinari detached Rose from Dante. 'I'm so glad to see you here. Come and meet my children—they are dying to play with Bea. Will she like that?'

'She'll love it,' Rose assured her, and looked at Dante. 'Will you get her?'

'Yes, *amore*.' He grinned. 'If you think Charlotte will let her go.'

Leo Fortinari issued strict instructions to his son, Luca, and daughter, Chiara, to take great care of Bea, and Franco Paglia did the same with Mario, Renzo and Vittoria, who were older, but just as eager to play with the child as the others, but brought her running back to Rose first.

'I want my jeans,' Bea said urgently, and Maria Fortinari nodded in approval.

'Come with me and your *mamma* to change, *bella*. It would not be good to spoil that lovely dress.'

While the exchange was made, Maria smiled warmly at Rose and patted her cheek. 'Welcome to our home, *cara*.'

Rose blinked hard. 'Thank you, *signora*.'

The striking dark eyes misted over. 'It is so good to see Dante happy again. I am very grateful to you.'

'Nonna!' said Bea, dancing impatiently in her blue trainers. 'Want to play now—please,' she added at a look from her mother.

'*Va bene,*' said Maria, clearing her throat. 'Let us go

out. Come, Rose, join the others for a glass of wine while I return to the kitchen.'

'Can I help in any way?'

Maria patted her hand. 'Not today, *grazie*. I have help in the kitchen. Enjoy the day with the others.'

Rose found it only too easy to enjoy herself in company with Charlotte, Harriet and Mirella on the loggia while she watched a very happy, excited Bea running riot with the other children.

'I'm on lemonade,' said Charlotte, pulling a face as she raised her glass to her husband, who was talking to the other men, but with one eye on his wife.

'It is best for now,' said Mariella with sympathy.

'You still have to keep off the wine if you nurse the baby yourself,' put in Harriet. 'But it's worth it, isn't it, Rose?'

Rose smiled ruefully as she watched Bea trying to catch a ball Luca tossed to her. 'I couldn't do it. I had to resort to bottles.'

'I remember how upset you were about it,' said Charlotte. 'She tried so hard to be the perfect mother,' she told the others.

'You succeeded,' said Harriet, waving a hand towards Bea. 'Just look at the result—oops, she's fallen over.'

Rose surged to her feet but Dante was first to scoop up his daughter and make anxious enquiries.

'Down, Daddy,' she said crossly. 'Want to play!'

Dante obeyed, and exchanged a wry grin with Rose as Bea returned to the ball game. 'It is hard to stand back, yes?'

'Unless they're bleeding you leave them to it,' Harriet advised, and Mirella laughed.

'It took me a long time to learn that.'

'Are you taking notes, Charlotte?' asked Rose.

Her friend smiled contentedly. 'I'm just enjoying the

moment, love. To have you and Bea here like this is just wonderful.'

'Mamma thinks so, too,' said Mirella. 'She has worried much over Dante, but now he is happy, Mamma is happy. I am happy, too,' she added, sniffing hard.

'So when are you going to marry him, Rose?' asked Charlotte bluntly.

'There's a lot to consider before making any decisions. For one thing, I have to sell my business first.' And far more vital than that, before she said yes she needed to be sure that Dante wanted her as his wife rather than just the mother of his child.

'Just put it in the hands of an agent—the house, too.'

'First I need to talk with my mother—and your father, too.' Rose grinned suddenly. 'I was most impressed with *your* mother, Mirella. She didn't turn a hair when Bea told her my mother lives with Tom in his house.'

Mirella laughed. 'She was so delighted her new grand-daughter was talking to her, yes?'

Rose nodded. 'Though to be fair to Charlotte's father, he'd marry my mother tomorrow.'

'Perhaps Grace will finally agree if you marry Dante,' said Charlotte.

'Not "if", Charlotte, "when",' said Dante, coming to join them. 'For me it could be tomorrow, but Rose is making me wait.'

'What for, Rose?' demanded her friend as Mirella and Harriet rushed to settle a squabble among their offspring.

Charlotte's question was hard to answer. Here in Fortino, surrounded by Dante's warm, hospitable family, Rose experienced an urgent longing to become part of it. Grace would understand; it was what she'd always wanted for her girls. 'We've only just got together again,' she said lightly.

'Give me time to get used to the idea. I've been running my own life—and Bea's—for quite a time, remember.'

'But there's a man here who will gladly help you with that if you let him,' Charlotte said. 'Right, Dante?'

'With great pleasure,' he agreed, and smiled fondly as he watched Bea playing with the other children. 'She is a delight. I still find it hard to believe I am her father—'

'You have doubts?' demanded Rose.

'None!' He grasped her hand tightly. 'It is you who have the doubts, not I, Rose. I long to marry you and give you and Bea the life you both deserve. We would be good together,' he added, his eyes boring into hers to remind her how it had been between them the night before.

'So for heaven's sake say yes, Rose,' said Charlotte and smiled up at Fabio. 'If Rose and Dante get married in England you'll just have to let me fly there, darling.'

Fabio flung out a hand to Dante in appeal. 'In that case, *amico*, make it soon, yes?'

'I will do my best,' Dante promised, and sprang to attention as his mother came out on the loggia. 'It is time to eat, Mamma?'

'*Subito, figlio mio.*' She smiled at Rose. 'I have washed the little one's face and hands with all the others. So now we eat, yes?'

A long table had been set up in the garden with a snowy-white cloth obscured by great platters of food and soon everyone was crowded round it, elbow to elbow, and talking non-stop. The children were seated together at one end, with a parent occasionally jumping up to serve them or settle squabbles. Vittoria and Chiara vied with each other to look after Bea, who was so obviously having the time of her life Rose eventually relaxed, enjoying not only the meal but the feeling of belonging.

Lorenzo Fortinari got up when the wine was poured

and held his glass high. 'A toast to welcome Rose and little Bea to Fortino!'

Everyone surged to their feet to echo the toast, and Rose followed suit, smiling gratefully. 'From Bea and myself, *grazie tante*!'

'*Brava, carissima,*' said Dante as she sat down amidst cheers.

She smiled. 'Just look at Bea. She's having so much fun.'

He nodded. 'It is easy to see her gold head among her Italian cousins.'

Mirella leaned forward, rolling her eyes. 'Vittoria will want to dye her hair blond now.'

Harriet groaned. 'And Chiara—maybe the boys, too!'

Franco shuddered theatrically. 'Do not even think of it, *per favore*!'

At the burst of laughter which greeted this Maria Fortinari came to join them to make sure Rose was enjoying herself and to press her to eat more food.

Rose smiled warmly. '*Signora*, I couldn't eat another thing, thank you. It was such a delicious meal.'

'I did not make all of it, *cara*. Letizia, my cook, is still with me, *grazie a Dio*.'

'Ah, but you made the *pollo Parmigiano*, Mamma,' said Dante, and kissed his fingers. 'It was superb, as always.'

'I make it with the identical recipe.' Harriet sighed. 'But it's never the same.'

Leo patted her hand. 'It is good enough for me. And you baked the wonderful English apple pies for us today, *amore*.'

'Much too wonderful,' said Charlotte, patting her stomach. 'I was greedy.'

'It is only natural right now,' said Fabio fondly.

At one time Rose would have been painfully envious as she watched the other couples together, but now that she had the chance of Dante permanently in her life, envy could be a thing of the past. Whatever his feelings for her, perhaps it was time to grasp this opportunity with both hands and make their marriage work for Bea's sake. And for her own, she admitted, her eyes on Dante.

'Just look at him,' murmured Charlotte as he went off to check on his daughter. 'He's besotted with her.'

Mirella watched her brother laughing among the group of clamouring children. 'He is such good uncle, but now he can be wonderful father at last.' She smiled ruefully at Rose. 'My English is not like Dante's.'

'But very good, just the same,' said Rose huskily. 'I must try to learn Italian as quickly as I can.'

'My wife can give you lessons,' suggested Leo Fortinari to her surprise.

'Brilliant idea, darling!' Harriet smiled at Rose. 'Don't worry; I'm a qualified teacher—and you'll be a much easier prospect than a classroom of teenage girls.'

'You have enjoyed the day?' asked Dante on the drive back. 'It was so good to watch you eating and laughing with my family—and with Charlotte. I did not tell you she would be there. I wished to give you a happy surprise.'

'Which you certainly did. Thank you. It was good to see a familiar face, though heaven knows your family's welcome couldn't have been warmer.'

'I am glad you were pleased. Our little one played very happily with her cousins, yes?'

'Bea had such a great time,' Rose assured him, and laughed softly as she glanced over into the back seat. 'She's fast asleep, but still clutching the string of her balloon.'

'It is a pity we must wake her to put her to bed.' He shot her a commanding look. 'I am impatient to have you both with me permanently.'

She nodded. 'I know, Dante.' She hesitated, but couldn't quite make herself take the plunge. 'Thank you for being patient with me.'

'Then I am a good actor.' He turned smouldering eyes on her. 'Inside, I am not patient at all. Sleep with me tonight, Rose.' He touched a slim warm hand to her knee. 'If not your husband yet, you want me as a lover, yes?'

Not much point in denying it. Rose nodded silently.

Dante let out a deep, unsteady breath. 'Then tonight we'll make up for all the nights after you leave me alone.'

Why not? thought Rose. If making love with her would make Dante miss her all the more she was all for it. And for her it would make up for the times she'd cried herself to sleep over him in the past. Besides, she wanted him physically in a way she would never experience with any other man, so why fight it?

The silence between them was thick with sensual tension as Dante carried his daughter into his house. Bea never stirred as Rose sponged her face and hands and put her in her pyjamas, nor when Dante laid her gently in her bed and kissed the sleeping face. Then he led Rose outside onto the gallery and seized her in his arms.

'Now I take you to my bed,' he said huskily.

'I should shower—' she began, but he shook his head and picked her up.

'We shower together—afterwards.'

To Rose it seemed so natural, so right to slide naked into Dante's arms in bed she almost said yes then and there to the prospect of doing so for the rest of her life as he rubbed his cheek against hers.

'*This* is where you are meant to be,' he said as though reading her mind. His arms tightened. 'Where you should have been all these years.'

She had no desire to resurrect the past. 'I'm here now, so do we talk or did you have something else in mind?'

Dante's laugh was so joyous that Rose laughed with him as his lips and hands told her exactly what he had in mind as he made love to her with patience which ended abruptly when for the first time she initiated some caresses of her own. Dante surrendered joyously to his hunger and took her to the very peak of physical rapture and held her there, gasping with her in the throes of it before they returned to earth.

'If we get married—' she said later, lying boneless in Dante's arms.

'*When* we get married,' Dante corrected and turned her face up to his. 'What were you going to say, *amore*?'

'I wondered what kind of wedding you had with Elsa.' So they could do something completely different—if her answer was yes. As it was going to be, she realised. There was no way she could deprive her child of the kind of life she'd experienced today.

'Elsa was in such a hurry after I told her about you she changed her plans for the wedding of the year into a brief visit to the town hall—but with many photographers there to record the wedding of Elsa Marino, supermodel, *naturalmente*.' Dante shrugged. 'I was glad of a civil ceremony. It was easier to end our marriage later when she met Enrico and his money.'

'But you must have been in love with her in the beginning, surely?'

'I was attracted by the outer beautiful shell—also she was very skilled in bed,' he said bluntly. 'We knew each other for so short a time I did not discover the true Elsa until our wedding night, when she told me the pregnancy was a lie, and that she had no intention of having children ever.'

'What on earth did you do?' said Rose.

He took a deep breath. 'For the first time in my life I could have done violence to a woman. To avoid this I did something which injured her far more. I went into the *salone* of our suite and locked the door. She screamed and cursed me for rejecting her but, as I told you before, and I swear it is the truth, I never touched her again throughout the sham of our marriage.' Dante shuddered and hugged her close. 'No more talk of Elsa, *per favore*.'

Rose agreed fervently. 'I just asked so we could plan something completely different for *our* wedding.' She felt the graceful, muscular body tense against hers as she turned her face up to his.

'*Finalmente*! You will marry me?'

'You said it's what you want.'

His eyes blazed with triumph. 'More than anything in my life.' He caught her close and kissed her passionately. 'I promise you will never regret this, Rose.'

'I'll hold you to that.' She kissed him back.

Dante rubbed his cheek against hers. 'Now you have said yes at last we must make plans. We could have the wedding at the Hermitage. Tony does these often. Then after the ceremony we have a party like the Vilari wedding.' He reached out a hand to switch on the bedside lamp and looked down into Rose's face. 'But this time you will be the bride and I shall gain my heart's desire of a child at last.'

Tears welled in her eyes, and Dante caught her to him. 'Do not cry, *tesoro*. If you do not like this idea—'

'Oh, but I do, I do—I love it,' she said thickly, and knuckled away the tears which had welled at the mention of a child. Not, she assured herself, ashamed, that she was jealous of Bea. She just wanted Dante's heart's desire to include her as well as Bea.

Dante slid out of bed to take a handkerchief from his

dressing chest and dried her eyes. 'What can I do to dry your tears?'

Rose sniffed inelegantly. 'Just hold me, please.'

'Always,' he said, and slid under the covers to pull her close. 'So why did you weep, *cara*?'

'Because it's exactly the kind of wedding I wanted but didn't like to ask.'

'Perche?' he said, mystified. 'Rose, surely you must know by now that I would give you and Bea the moon if I could.'

'How lovely,' she said unsteadily and grinned at him. 'But a Hermitage wedding with our families around us is all I want—complete with our own personal bridesmaid!'

Dante laughed and held her closer. 'Bea will enjoy that very much, I think.'

'She will,' said Rose fervently, and then frowned. 'Will your mother mind having the wedding in England?'

'No, because she is so delighted that I am marrying again. And to please her—and myself—we can repeat our vows privately later before a priest in Fortino. But we must arrange our wedding very soon, not only because I am impatient, but so Charlotte can be there.' Dante gave a deep sigh of satisfaction. 'I am sure Tony will be happy to make space in his Hermitage schedule for his favourite cousin.'

Rose smiled at him ruefully. 'I can't believe this is all happening. Pinch me, Dante, so I know I'm not dreaming.' She hissed as he gently pinched a nipple. 'I didn't mean there! You'll have to kiss it better now.'

'If you insist.' He sighed and then eyed her sternly as she punched his shoulder. 'Be still while I obey your command.'

CHAPTER ELEVEN

THE REST OF their stay at the Villa passed so quickly in visits to Dante's parents to ask their blessing, and to Harriet and Leo and the Vilaris to give their news, the day of departure was on them all too soon.

'It seems a shame to drag you all the way to England just to take us home,' said Rose the night before.

Dante shook his head. 'I must make sure you arrive safely, then I will stay the night in your bed and try not to think of all the nights when I'll lie in this bed alone until you come back to me.'

'You spent a lot of nights in it alone in the past,' she pointed out.

'But that was before I knew the joy of sharing it with you, *amore*. Now it will be hard to sleep without you.'

'You haven't slept much *with* me!'

'*Certo*. Why waste time in sleep when we can make love?' Dante held her close. 'But it is not just the lovemaking I will miss. It is having you here to talk and laugh with, to share my life with you and Bea.' He tensed as he heard a cry from his daughter's room and shrugged on his dressing gown. 'Stay there, *amore*. I will fetch her.'

'You're in Daddy's bed,' Bea accused tearfully when Dante brought her to Rose.

'Mummy's going to sleep here with me now,' he informed his daughter.

'When I get bad dreams I sleep in Mummy's bed,' she told him militantly.

Dante laid her down alongside Rose and got in beside them. 'But now I will be there, too, to chase the bad dreams away,' he said firmly and smiled at Rose as their child nodded contentedly and laid her curly head on his shoulder.

With the prospect of parting from Dante looming over her, Rose found it hard to smile for Bea on the flight home as her child chattered about seeing Gramma and Tom again. She felt uneasy and oddly tearful. Stupid, she lectured herself. Soon they would be married and could be together for the rest of their lives. A prospect she'd never imagined, ever. And in the meantime she would have enough to occupy her with her normal workload added to the wedding arrangements and finding a purchaser for her business.

'You are sad, *tesoro*?' said Dante quietly as the plane began its descent into Heathrow.

'Yes,' she said honestly and tried to smile.

He clasped her hand tightly. 'I will miss you both so much,' he said as Bea began to stir from her nap. 'Wake up, *piccola*. We are almost there.'

Since Rose had texted her mother on the car journey from the airport, Grace and Tom were waiting at the front door of Willow House, arms outstretched as Bea ran to them, talking at the top of her voice.

'Gramma,' she cried as Grace snatched her close to kiss her, 'Daddy's mummy is *Nonna*, and his daddy is *Nonno*, and I got lots of cousins, and Daddy bought me a doll. Her name is Dolly.' She turned to Tom, arms up. 'Auntie Charlotte gave me a present for you, Tom.' Beaming, she gave him two smacking kisses as he swung her up.

'Thank you, Honey Bea,' he said, returning the kisses with gusto as Rose hugged her mother. 'How was Auntie Charlotte?'

'She's a lot fatter,' Bea informed him as he put her down. She ran to Rose and picked up her left hand. 'Look, Gramma—Daddy gave Mummy a present.'

Grace took a look at the ring and hugged Rose close again. 'How absolutely lovely.' She smiled warmly at Dante as he brought the luggage. 'Welcome back.'

'Thank you, *signora*.' He kissed her hand and turned to Tom. 'Charlotte is looking very well, sir.'

'Good to know. Any hope of Fabio letting her fly over soon?' said Tom wryly.

'As a matter of fact, yes,' said Rose, and exchanged a smiling glance with Dante. 'Let's go inside so we can tell you why.'

Bea was incensed the next day when she found Dante was leaving, and clung to him in tears when the taxi arrived.

'Soon,' Dante promised as he held his child in his arms, 'we shall be together at the Villa Castiglione, but until then you must help Mummy and Gramma plan the wedding, yes?'

Bea's tears dried a little as she looked at her mother. 'Can I, Mummy?'

Rose nodded. 'Of course, as soon as Daddy arranges the date for the party.'

Bea brightened. 'With balloons?'

Dante laughed as he set her on her feet. 'With balloons, yes! Now I must go, but first I will kiss your *mamma* goodbye.' He held Rose close as he kissed her. 'Do not work too hard, and take great care of yourself, *carina*.'

'You, too,' she said and smiled brightly.

* * *

The period that followed was one of the most hectic of Rose's life, but the soonest wedding date possible for everyone concerned was a month later, which made it still possible for Charlotte to come, but did not please Dante. 'Tony Mostyn could not do it sooner, even for me! But this is good for you, Rose?'

'Yes. It's not long. Actually, I'm glad of time to get everything settled.' Secretly, she would have preferred it sooner, with less time to worry about Dante's motives for marrying her. But every time doubts crept in she thought of Bea, and how she had clung to her daddy as they parted. And as Rose had done since her child was born, she did what was best for Bea, which in this case was to get on with marrying Bea's father.

'Rose?' said Dante in her ear, 'are you still there?'

'Yes,' she said hastily.

'I thought I'd lost you. I shall contact Tony right now to confirm and will ring you again later. Or will you be too tired?'

'No. Ring me whatever time it is.'

He sighed. 'Ah, Rose, I wish I was there with you. It is strange that I have survived for years without you, yet now the wait to have you both here with me is intolerable.'

Both. Rose yearned for Dante to long for her alone for once, and felt mortified because she did. 'By the way, I've had some feelers about my business, but I'm going to wait for a while before putting the house up for sale.'

There was silence for a moment. *'Perche*? You feel the need of a sanctuary to run to if I do not make you happy?'

'No. It's just that the market is flat right now, so I'll wait until things improve.'

Dante sounded unconvinced as he said goodbye. Rose wished she hadn't mentioned the subject, and by the time he rang again later to report on his talk with Tony her headache was making her queasy.

'All is arranged, *cara*,' he told her. 'Tony and Allegra are very happy for us.'

'That's good.' Rose hesitated. 'Dante, are you upset because I'm keeping the house?'

He laughed. 'No, I am not. It is your house to do with as you wish. Now, let us talk of wedding dresses. Please allow me to pay for them, Rose.'

'Thank you, but no, Dante. Mum insists on footing the bill for the bride—*and* the bridesmaid.'

When the wedding day finally came—though at one stage Rose had been convinced it never would—she felt a sense of *déjà vu* as she entered the Hermitage. But today she was the one holding Tom's arm, and of the two strikingly handsome Italian men waiting for her, this time round Dante Fortinari was the bridegroom. *Her* bridegroom.

At first sight of the smiling faces turned towards her in the private room used for the ceremony, Rose's heart filled with such mixed emotions she felt giddy and held on tightly to the small hand of the bridesmaid, who grew very excited when she spotted assorted cousins waving at her.

'Look, Mummy,' Bea said, waving back, then beamed. 'And there's Daddy with Uncle Fabio.'

Dante watched the progress of the bride and bridesmaid with pride blazing in his eyes. He received Rose from Tom with murmured thanks and kissed his daughter lovingly before Tom bore her off to sit with Grace and Charlotte.

Dante made the simple vows with such passionate sincerity Rose had to fight against tears as she responded, hardly able to believe this was really happening at last as Dante drew his bride's hand through his arm afterwards to walk past the rows of smiling guests.

'Who is the fair man with Leo and Harriet?' asked Rose.

'Pascal Tavernier, my cousin's husband. Rosa is not here, much to her wrath, because she is about to give birth. Her absence will save much confusion. She is only distantly related to Harriet, but so strongly resembles her she could be her twin.'

'She must be very beautiful then,' said Rose.

'*Certo*, but not as beautiful as my wife,' said Dante in a tone which transformed Rose into the quintessential blushing bride as their daughter came running to join them in a flurry of organdie frills, the chaplet of flowers still miraculously anchored to her curls as she linked hands with her parents and beamed for the photographers.

Among the festive gold and silver balloons in the Hermitage ballroom, Rose could hardly believe this was happening as she stood with Dante to receive their guests in almost exactly the same places they'd occupied years before at Charlotte's wedding. Something Charlotte was quick to point out while Grace and Tom, and then Maria and Lorenzo Fortinari hugged and kissed the bride and groom.

'I am so happy,' said Maria, dabbing carefully at her eyes. 'You look so lovely, Rose—and so does our little angel.' She bent to kiss Bea. 'That is such a beautiful dress, *bella*.'

'I choosed it myself,' said Bea happily, and tugged on Grace's hand. 'This is my gramma, *Nonna*.'

Maria kissed Grace, and then smiled up at Tom and kissed him, too. 'Now we are all family, *tesoro*,' she informed her granddaughter.

After so much hugging and kissing, Rose left her daughter with her two grandmothers and went off with Harriet and Charlotte before the meal to make repairs.

'That's a very clever dress,' said Harriet as Rose straightened the folds of chiffon.

'More clever than you know,' said Charlotte. 'It's a replica of the one she wore as my bridesmaid. How on earth did you find it, love?'

Rose smiled. 'I was lucky enough to find the right shade of fabric and a dressmaker willing to copy the dress in the photograph.'

'From his reaction when he saw you, Dante believes he's the lucky one,' said Harriet.

'That's because I come part of a package with our daughter,' said Rose, smiling as Allegra Mostyn put her pretty freckled face round the door.

'Get a move on, Signora Fortinari—the bride, not you, Harriet. Dante's getting impatient out there.'

'Coming,' said Rose, surprised as Harriet gave her a fierce hug.

'You are so wrong, Rose. Make no mistake, Dante's in seventh heaven because he's finally got *you*. So off you go, sister-in-law. A wedding day goes by fast—enjoy every minute of it while you can!'

Charlotte smiled triumphantly. 'And today you're the bride, not the bridesmaid.'

Still finding this part hard to believe, Rose held out her arms as Grace joined them to kiss her daughter tenderly, her eyes bright with unshed tears beneath the spectacular hat Tom had bought for her. 'Are you enjoying your day, my darling?'

Rose nodded and hugged her tightly. 'Thank you so very much, Mum.'

'What for?'

'Everything.'

Dante was waiting impatiently in the lobby as the others hurried on their way to let the bride and groom make their triumphal entry. 'You look so beautiful, *tesoro*,' he told Rose, his eyes glowing. 'And so like the girl at the Vilari wedding I thought I was dreaming when you walked towards me today.'

'You like my dress?'

'So much I cannot wait to take it off,' he said in her ear, then laughed delightedly at her heightened colour and took her hand as music struck up inside the ballroom to herald the arrival of the bride and groom. '*Allora*. That is our song!'

Later that evening, when they were finally alone in one of the luxury suites at the Chesterton in town, Dante took his bride in his arms and kissed her with a sigh of relief. 'At last I have you to myself, Signora Fortinari.'

Rose smiled wryly. 'Is that really me?'

He nodded and rubbed his cheek against hers. 'It is a title you share with my mother, also with Harriet, so, to be sure you know who you belong to, *sposa mia*, think of yourself as Signora Dante Fortinari.'

'I will,' she assured him and hesitated, wondering whether to give him her news now. No. Best to keep it for later. 'It was such a lovely day, Dante.' She turned her back. 'I should have changed before we left the Hermitage but—'

'You knew I would want to take the dress off myself,' he agreed, and kissed the nape of her neck. '*Mille grazie, tesoro.*'

'You're welcome! Will you undo my buttons, please?'

Dante heaved in a deep breath. '*Dio*, Rose, my hands are unsteady and you have many buttons.'

'Exactly the same number as last time.'

'I do not remember undoing so many!'

'You didn't undo any.' Rose turned her head to meet his eyes. 'I was so eager I did it myself.'

Dante breathed in sharply and buried his face against

her neck. 'This time,' he said through his teeth, 'even though I want you more than my next breath, *I* will do it, *innamorata.*' He began undoing the tiny satin-covered buttons with speed and dexterity which quickly sent the dress into a heap of caramel chiffon at Rose's feet, and he snatched her up in his arms and carried her to the bed, his eyes dancing as he saw the blue silk garter above one knee.

'My something blue,' she said breathlessly.

Dante slid the garter down her leg and took it off to put in his pocket, then, with maddeningly slow care, removed her stockings and the satin underwear that had cost almost as much as her dress. He looked at her in simmering silence for a moment and then, careless of finest designer tailoring, tore off the rest of his clothes. He pulled her to her feet beside the bed to hold her close and kissed her parted mouth. 'I want you so much, Rose,' he whispered.

Not exactly what she wanted to hear, but for now it was enough because she wanted him just as much.

He bent to pull back the covers on the bed. 'I can wait no longer, *sposa mia.*' He picked her up and gave a purring growl of pleasure as they came together in the bed, skin to skin.

Rose melted against him, luxuriating in contact with the lean, muscular body that to her eyes could have been a model for one of the sculptures she'd seen in Florence. When she told him this between kisses Dante stared at her in astonishment for a moment, then saw by the look in her eyes that she meant every word and kissed her hard on her parted, eager mouth before his lips joined with his seeking hands in a glissando of caresses that transformed her entire body into a trembling erogenous zone.

'I know it sounds silly,' she gasped, 'but this feels new, as though we'd never made love before.'

'We have not done so for an entire endless month, and

never as man and wife,' he whispered, and positioned his taut, aroused body between her thighs. 'Now, *tesoro*!'

Rose clasped Dante close, her inner muscles caressing the hard length of him as he thrust home into her welcoming heat. He kissed her endlessly, murmuring passionate loving words into her ear as his caressing hands and demanding body drew such a wild response. As he possessed her she stifled a scream when the almost unbearable rapture of her orgasm overwhelmed her a second or two before Dante gave a triumphant groan and surrendered to his own.

They lay together afterwards in a boneless tangle of arms and legs, Dante's face buried in her hair.

'A good thing the other guests are all staying at the Hermitage,' said Rose at last. 'Sorry I was so noisy, Dante.'

He raised his head, his eyes blazing down into hers with pride. 'It is the greatest compliment you could pay me, *tesoro*. I feel like a king to know I gave you pleasure!'

'Did I give *you* pleasure?'

'Pleasure,' he said with feeling, 'is not a big enough word. I have made love to other women in my life. You know that. But with you there is rapture I have never experienced before.' He frowned. 'You are crying, *tesoro*?'

She sniffed hard. 'That was such a beautiful thing to say, Dante.' But still not quite the words she longed to hear.

'It is the truth,' he assured her and with a sigh of contentment turned on his back to pull her close. 'I hope our little angel sleeps well tonight.'

To her shame, Rose's pleasure dimmed a little after Dante's attention reverted so swiftly to his daughter. 'Since she's safe in Tom's house with my mother, and Charlotte and Fabio are there, too, Bea will be fine.' She smiled up into his relaxed, handsome face as she stroked the slim, strong hand now adorned with a wedding ring, something, he'd informed her, he'd refused to wear during his former marriage. 'It's time I let you into a little secret. Everyone thinks I named her Beatrice for my grandmother, and in one way this is true, but it was also my own private little joke.'

'Joke?' Dante looked down at her in question.

'Beatrice was the love of your poet, Dante Alighieri, so I named my baby for her as my secret connection to you.'

A look of pain swept over his face. 'Ah, Rose, if I had known!'

'If you had you couldn't have done anything about it at the time, but I thought you'd like to know now we're married.'

'I do like it very much.' He raised her hand to his lips. 'It is much happier than the revelation given to me on my first wedding night.'

Rose took in a deep breath. 'Talking of revelations, I've been waiting for the right moment to give you another one.'

'You have a buyer for the house?'

'No, something far more important than that.' She propped herself on one elbow to look into his face. 'We're going to have another baby, Dante. It must have happened the night you came back after our quarrel…' Her voice trailed away as he shot upright, eyes narrowed as they speared hers. He gazed at her in silence for so long Rose felt cold. 'Say *something*, Dante, please!'

'So,' he said heavily, 'this is why you agree to marry me. You had many doubts about giving up your independence and your home and job here in England, then suddenly you say yes and I do not question it. I thought you had changed your mind because, like a fool, I believed you wanted me.' His mouth twisted. 'But it was only because you were *incinta* again.'

'No, Dante, that's not true, or at least not totally. I'll admit that it was the final, deciding factor.' She flushed miserably. 'I already had one fatherless child. It was a shock to find I was about to produce another.'

'Neither child is fatherless,' he snapped. 'They are both mine. But why did you not tell me until now? Were you afraid I would cancel the wedding? You think I could do such a thing to Bea?' Dante flung out of bed to make for the bathroom.

Just once, thought Rose bitterly, it would have been good for Dante to think of her first, before Bea. Petty it might be, but on this particular night it would have been the perfect wedding gift.

Her nudity suddenly embarrassing, Rose opened the suitcase sitting at the foot of the bed and got into the ivory silk nightgown Charlotte had given her. She wrapped herself in the matching dressing gown and tied the sash tightly, wincing as her headache suddenly returned in full force. She should have kept her secret to herself, at least for tonight. With a sigh, she perched on the edge of the bed to wait. When Dante finally came out wearing one of the hotel bath robes, he sat beside her, leaving a space between them, she noted with a sinking heart.

'So, Rose,' he demanded, his voice stern, 'I ask again. Why did you not tell me sooner?'

Suddenly furious, she shot him a flaying look. 'Because I was naïve enough to keep the news as a wedding present to you—a sort of consolation prize to make up for your previous wedding night. So if anyone's a fool, Dante, it's me!' She jumped up and marched into the bathroom, then slammed the bolt home on the door.

'Rose!' ordered Dante hotly. 'Come back to me. Now!'

Rose gulped, feeling first hot then icy cold as she dropped to her knees and parted with what little wedding breakfast she'd eaten. Tears poured down her face as she cursed the fate which scheduled her first bout of morning sickness for tonight of all nights. Shivering and miserable, she ignored the banging on the door until Dante threatened to break it down.

'*Dio*, Rose!' he exclaimed when she staggered to her feet to let him in. He stared in horror at her ashen, sweating face. 'What is wrong?'

'What could possibly be wrong?' she flung at him. 'I've been sick, I'm pregnant again and, just like the first time, I don't want to be. Go away!' she spat in desperation, but Dante ignored her. He mopped her gently with a damp facecloth and picked her up to carry her back to bed.

He laid her down gently. 'Lie very still, Rose.' He took her hand. 'What can I do for you? Would you like water, or I can ring for tea—'

'You don't have to.'

'Of course I have to,' he said roughly, his grasp tightening.

'I meant,' she said wearily, 'that you needn't ring for room service. There's a tea tray with a kettle and so on over on the table by the sofa. You can make the tea for me.'

The relief in Dante's eyes was so gratifying she warmed towards him slightly.

'You will trust me to make it correctly, Rose?'

'Yes. But not yet. I'll have a glass of water first, please.'

Dante helped her to sit up, then piled pillows behind her and settled her against them with care. 'You feel better now?'

Rose nodded. 'Yes, thank you.'

His lips tightened. 'You need not thank me so politely. I am happy to do anything to help you.'

Except tell her he loved her. 'I'll have that water now, then.'

'*Subito!*' Dante said promptly. He filled a glass with mineral water and sat on the bed beside her, watching her sip very slowly. 'You have been suffering much with *la nausea*, Rose?'

'No. This is the first time tonight.' She pulled a face and put the half-empty glass on the bedside table. 'Bad move to get morning sickness on our wedding night.'

Dante winced. 'I think perhaps it was I who made you ill, not our baby.'

Slightly mollified when he said 'our baby', Rose shrugged. 'Possibly. Your reaction to my news wasn't *quite* the one I expected.'

'Mi dispiace!' he said and took her hand. 'Coming so soon after experiencing such rapture together, I was not thinking clearly.'

'You sounded pretty clear on the subject to me. But let's not talk about it any more. Perhaps you could make that tea for me now?'

Dante got up at once and crossed the room to switch on the kettle. *'Allora,'* he said, 'I pour the boiling water on the tea bag, leave it for a little while, then remove the bag and add a little milk. Yes?'

Rose nodded. 'Exactly right.'

'Bene.' Dante went through the process with care and finally brought a steaming cup over to Rose.

'Thank you.' She eyed him over it. 'Not quite the wedding night you'd hoped for, is it?'

He gestured towards the sofa under the window. 'You would prefer me to sleep there tonight?'

'Of course not,' she retorted. 'I assume you intend me to share your room at the Villa Castiglione?'

Dante's eyes locked on hers. 'My room and my bed,' he stated in tones which left her in no doubt.

'Then we may as well start as we mean to go on. Besides,' she added, eyeing the sofa, 'you'll never fit on that.'

'*Davvero*! But I was happy to make the attempt tonight to let you rest.'

'Very noble, but no sacrifice required.' Rose slid carefully out of bed, stood for a moment to make sure she was steady on her feet, then made for the bathroom. 'Just give me five minutes to brush my teeth.'

When she got back Dante had tidied the bed and left only one lamp burning. He looked at her searchingly. 'Were you ill again?'

'No. I think that was a one-off just now—at least for tonight.' She untied her sash and slid the dressing gown off into his waiting hands. 'That bed looks very inviting,' she told him, suddenly almost too tired to speak as she slid into bed.

He drew the covers over her. 'I will be minutes only, Rose.'

It seemed like only seconds before Dante switched off the lamp and got in beside her. He hesitated for a moment, then lay flat on his back and took her hand. '*Buonanotte, sposa mia,*' he said softly.

'Good night, Dante.' Rose closed her eyes thankfully, well aware that he'd wanted to put his arms round her and hold her close, but had opted for hand-holding instead. Good move, she approved hazily. His unexpected reaction to her news had cut deep. Any attempt at cuddling by Dante right now would have met with short shrift.

CHAPTER TWELVE

THE RETURN TO the Villa Castiglione the next day was physically far less of an ordeal than Rose had expected. When she woke up she felt a moment of panic when she heard Dante in the bathroom, but then relaxed when she found that her digestive system was in good working order. No dash to the bathroom was necessary. When her new husband emerged, towelling his wet curls, he eyed her searchingly.

'*Buongiorno*, Rose. How do you feel today?'

'Good morning. I feel better, thank you.'

'No nausea?'

She gave it some thought. 'None at all.'

He relaxed visibly. '*Grazie a Dio.* You gave me much worry last night. But be truthful, Rose—are you well enough to travel today?'

'Yes, definitely.' Postponing the trip, even by a day, would mean explanations to her mother she would rather avoid right now. And a second round of goodbyes would be bad for Bea—and herself, if it came to that. Rose slid out of bed and stood up, shaking her head as he moved swiftly, ready to help her. 'I'm fine, Dante, really. After a shower I'll feel even better. What time do we leave?'

'At ten. I will order breakfast.' He put an arm round her. 'What would you like?'

'Just toast and tea, please.' She detached herself very deliberately. 'I won't be long.'

Dante stood back, his eyes sombre. 'You have not forgiven me.'

'Not yet, but I'm working on it.' Rose busied herself with choosing clothes to take into the bathroom with her.

'You are shy of dressing in front of me?' he demanded.

She turned in the bathroom doorway. 'Awkward, rather than shy. I'm not used to sharing my life with a man, Dante. You'll have to make allowances.'

He smiled crookedly. 'Then, to avoid further awkwardness for you, I will dress while you shower.'

'Thank you.' Rose closed the bathroom door and got to work, grateful to Dante for not pointing out that there had been no awkwardness last night when he was *un*dressing her. But today, illogically, it would have been hard to put her clothes on in front of him in the new intimacy of married life—which was something she had to get over pretty quickly to make that life successful, if only for Bea's sake. She patted her stomach gently. *For you, too*, she added. After all, compared with life as a single mother, she was living the dream as Dante's wife. His physical response to her, at least, was everything she could wish for. She would just have to work on changing that into the more cerebral love she felt for him. Not that hers was totally cerebral. Otherwise she wouldn't be expecting his second child. Whatever her brain felt about Dante, her hormones were utterly mad about him.

The limousine trip to the airport and the flight to Pisa went just as smoothly as the first time with Dante in charge. Worried beforehand that the nausea would return en route at some stage, Rose survived the entire flight without a qualm, and to reassure Dante even ate some of the meal.

As before, Tullio was waiting at the airport and had taken time out of his Sunday to help them collect their luggage and hand over the car keys.

'*Congratulazione*, Signora Fortinari,' he said to Rose and kissed her hand then shook Dante's and congratulated him in turn.

'*Grazie*, Tullio,' she said, secretly thrilled to bits with her new title.

After a quick exchange with Tullio while he helped load their luggage into the waiting car, Dante helped Rose into the car and, with a quick wave for his assistant, joined the traffic leaving the airport.

'I will not drive fast,' Dante assured her, smiling, and Rose laughed.

'Unlike my—*our*—daughter, I don't mind fast!'

'Nevertheless, I have no wish to make you ill again, *carina*.' He gave her a sidelong glance. 'I asked Silvia to prepare the house and leave food for us, but then take a little holiday so we can begin our new life in peace together. But,' he added when Rose made no response, 'if you want her to come as usual I shall call her back.'

'Of course I don't. When Mum and Tom bring Bea to join us, peace will be hard to come by.' She shot him a wry glance. 'Though I know you can hardly wait!'

He shook his head. 'Much as I love Bea, it will be good for us to have time alone together for a little while, Rose, yes?'

Yes, she rejoiced silently.

'And after a while perhaps you will not feel so awkward with me,' he said with a wry twist to his mouth.

'I'll do my best, Dante.'

'I do not doubt this,' he assured her, and smiled as he saw her eyelids droop.

'Sorry,' she said, yawning.

'Take the little nap, *bella*. I will wake you when we are near home.'

Home, thought Rose, closing her eyes. Not Willow House any more, but the Villa Castiglione. Her lips curved. It would be good to be alone there with Dante for a while...

She woke with a start to a screeching, crunching sound, her heart pounding as something hit the car. Cursing violently, Dante stood on the brakes and her head hit the side window with a crack that knocked her out for an instant.

Rose came round almost at once because Dante was crushing her hand as he called her name in anguish, along with a flood of impassioned enquiries she couldn't understand.

'Answer me, Rose!' he demanded frantically. 'Where are you hurt?'

'Only my head,' she said groggily. 'What happened?'

'Some *bastardo* took a bend too fast and made contact with our front wing, then drove off like a maniac.' Dante leaned over her, his face haggard. '*Dio*, your head is bleeding. I must get you to a doctor immediately.'

'I don't need a doctor!'

'You do,' said Dante inexorably, and wiped her forehead with a handkerchief. 'Stay very still now while I arrange this.' He took out his phone and after a pause spoke to someone at length.

Rose listened to the rapid-fire conversation, but was unable to pick out more than the word *incinta*. At least she knew what that meant. It obviously had the desired effect, since Dante thanked someone volubly and turned to Rose. 'We will be seen immediately we arrive. I just need to check that the car is safe to drive then I will take you to the doctor. I will be seconds only.'

In sudden need of fresh air, Rose undid her belt and got out very carefully, relieved to find her legs steady as she watched Dante make a long examination under the bonnet. She whistled as she saw ugly scrapes along the shining crimson paint. 'How bad is it?'

'It is cosmetic only. The paintwork is scratched but there is no damage to the car otherwise.' He closed the bonnet. 'It is safe to drive, I promise. *Mi dispiace*, Rose. Even when I was young and drove very fast I never had an accident, yet today, when I was taking such care, this happened.'

'Only because some idiot was speeding. It wasn't your fault!'

'*Grazie, tesoro.* Does your head ache?'

'A bit. Do I look a mess?'

Dante pulled her close, his heart hammering against hers. 'You are still bleeding a little, but you are beautiful, as always.' He swallowed hard. 'When your head hit the window my heart stopped. It is good that *bastardo* drove off so fast,' he added, eyes blazing. 'I wanted to kill him.'

'Bad idea! I don't fancy visiting my new husband in prison.' She smiled. 'Thank heavens Bea wasn't with us.'

'Amen,' breathed Dante, and managed a smile. 'Though I was not driving fast!'

Rose chuckled then eyed him searchingly. 'Were you hurt anywhere, Dante?'

He shook his head. 'A few bruises and badly injured pride only. I am mortified that you had to experience such a thing, *carissima*.'

'I'll live. And so, in case you were wondering, will our baby.'

'That is good—but in that terrible moment when you hit your head I had no thought for the baby, only for you, that I might have lost you a second time, this time perhaps for ever.' He blinked hard, but tears, Rose noted in wonder, hung on his enviable lashes.

Oblivious of passing traffic, or anyone in the world who

might be watching, she pulled her husband's head down to kiss him fiercely. 'Well, you haven't,' she said gruffly. 'I don't suppose you have a tissue?'

'This handkerchief only.' He gave it to her, his eyes smouldering. 'That was a wonderful kiss. Do it again.'

'Later,' she said. 'Spit!'

He laughed as he obliged, and held still while she scrubbed a bloodstain from his cheek then gave him the handkerchief.

'Now you do the same for me.'

Once Dante was sure Rose felt composed enough to continue their journey he drove her to the private hospital used by the Fortinari family. As promised, they were seen immediately by a doctor who asked rapid questions Dante translated for Rose while the cut on her temple was dressed. When it was established that Signora Fortinari was not suffering from concussion, and a scan later confirmed that all else was otherwise well with her, the doctor told Dante he could take his wife home on condition that he brought her back immediately if she felt unwell.

When Dante finally drove up the winding road to the Villa later Rose gave a deep sigh of relief as the lovely old house came into view. 'Home at last,' she said thankfully.

'It is so good to hear you say *home*,' Dante said with feeling. He got out to help her out of the car, and then picked her up to carry her into the house. 'This is the custom for brides, yes?'

Rose wreathed her arms round his neck happily, surprised when, instead of taking her into the *salone*, he carried her straight upstairs to their room and carefully laid her down on the pristine bed before casting himself face down beside her, breathing hard, his arm possessive across her waist.

She lay still for a while, but then patted his arm. 'I hate to spoil this romantic moment, Dante, but I'm hungry.'

'I also,' he agreed and sat up, smiling down at her. 'So tonight we will have a picnic up here from whatever Silvia has left for us. I will bring it and you do nothing except lie there and look beautiful.'

Her eyes sparkled. 'Oh, well, if you insist! But I'll have more chance of looking halfway beautiful if I can have a shower first, so could you bring up some of the luggage before you start on the picnic? And I'll ring Mum to report in and check on Bea.'

The euphoria of surviving what could well have been a serious accident cast a magical aura over their first evening together at the Villa as husband and wife. Dante, who prided himself on his driving skills, was obviously mortified about the incident, but Rose was deeply grateful for it. His anguished reaction when she was hurt had removed all her doubts about Dante's feelings. He had no need now to tell her he loved her. She knew.

When Dante returned after removing the remains of their picnic supper he raised an eyebrow as he asked why she was so deep in thought. Rose hesitated for a moment then made a clean breast of her doubts and fears, which won her a stare of utter amazement. 'You did not believe I love you?'

Rose tucked her hair behind her ears. 'You never actually said so, though I knew you wanted me, physically.'

'How could you not? At your slightest touch I am on fire, *amore*!' He sat down on the bed beside her and took her in his arms. 'But that is only part of my love for you, Rose. I want to spend every minute possible of the rest of my life with you, raise our children together, and grow old together. That is how I love you. Is it enough?'

She smiled at him through a sudden haze of tears and

hugged him close. 'More than enough—even though you were so horrible to me on our wedding night.'

Dante winced and rubbed his cheek against hers. 'Forgive me, *carissima*, but try to understand. I wanted you to love me as a husband and lover, and for a moment I thought you married me only to gain a father for another child.'

'While I was afraid that you took me on just to get Bea as part of the package,' said Rose, and grinned sheepishly at the incredulous look he gave her.

'How could you believe that? In Firenze I could not hide my delight at meeting you again. And I knew nothing about our child at that time.' Dante laid his forehead against hers. 'So, to avoid all future confusion, Signora Fortinari, I have loved you from the first day we met. *Ti amo, sposa mia*. Do you understand me?'

'I do, I do. So make sure you understand, too, Dante Fortinari. I married you for exactly the same reason.'

'For which I thank God.' Dante slid the dressing gown from her shoulders and tossed it away. 'You forgive me then, *innamorata*?'

She pretended to think it over. 'I'm working on it.'

Dante pulled her close. 'Always I am the peacemaker, in the business and with my family,' he said bitterly. 'Unlike Leo, who can be abrasive—that is right? I am the one who pours the oil on the troubled waters. Yet on my wedding night I accuse my bride of sins she has not committed.'

'True. You'll just have to spend the rest of our honeymoon making it up to me,' she ordered.

'With much, much pleasure, *amore*! I have given instructions to my family to leave us in peace at the Villa Castiglione for a while when they return from England tomorrow.' Dante raised his head to look down at her. 'They were surprised that you did not want somewhere exotic for our honeymoon.'

'I just wanted to start our life together at the Villa without our little darling for a couple of weeks.' Rose sighed as she stretched against him. 'You know, even with the marriage vows to prove it, I can hardly believe that we're here together at last, Dante.'

He drew her closer. 'To have you here in my arms as my wife is a dream come true, *tesoro*.'

'I never dared to dream anything so unlikely!' She smiled up at him. 'Even though the first day we met I knew who you were before we were even introduced.'

'I knew at first sight that you were the love of my life, *carissima*,' he said huskily. 'So who did you think I was?'

'The man of my dreams. But dreams were all I had for years, Dante.'

'Now we have the glorious reality, yes?'

'We certainly do. Shall I tell you something else, Dante?'

'Anything you wish *amore*.' His arms tightened. 'Will I like this something?'

Rose nodded and rubbed her cheek against his, which, she noted lovingly, was already showing signs of needing a shave. 'I used to tell myself that one day my prince would come, and now here he is at last, right here in my arms.'

'Where he intends to stay,' said Dante with emphasis and then shook his head. 'But I am no prince, *tesoro*.'

'You are in *my* fairy tale!'

He gave her the smile he shared with his child. 'And because I have read many fairy tales to our daughter I know exactly how they end—we live happily ever after!'

By the end of the fortnight, blissfully happy though her honeymoon had been, Rose was in a fever of excitement at the airport in Pisa as she saw her child running towards them with Grace in pursuit and Tom, laden with luggage, following behind.

There was a laughing collision as Rose seized her child, and Dante caught them both in his encircling arms and kissed his daughter's beaming face as she talked non-stop.

Rose gave Bea a smacking kiss and then hugged Grace. 'How's Gramma?'

'Doing fine,' her mother assured her. 'Bea was no trouble at all except for the odd tear when she realised she was missing you.' She turned to Tom. 'We enjoyed having her to ourselves, didn't we?'

Tom dumped down the luggage to kiss Rose. 'We had Charlotte and Fabio's help for the first week, but the rest of it was excellent practice for when the first little Vilari arrives.' He held out his hand to Dante, smiling. 'No need to ask how *you* are!'

'*Davvero,*' agreed Dante, surrendering Bea to her mother. 'I am a very lucky man. Welcome, Tom,' he added, picking up some of the luggage. 'The car is outside.'

Bea frowned as Dante fastened her into her seat. 'I don't like this car, Daddy. I like your shiny red one.'

'It needed painting, so your Uncle Leo lent me this,' he said, kissing her nose. 'But this is your very own red car seat.'

Bea lay back in it like a queen on a throne with Rose and Grace close together beside her. 'Can we go and see Luca and Chiara tomorrow, Daddy?' she demanded.

'Possibly.' He exchanged a gleaming look with Rose over his shoulder. '*Andiamo*, let us go home.'

'Not fast!' warned Bea.

'No, *piccola*,' Dante assured her, laughing. 'I will not drive fast.'

Because he kept his word, Bea soon nodded off, leaving Rose to enjoy Grace's company.

'I've no need to ask how you are,' said her mother, squeezing her hand. 'You glow.'

'I enjoyed these two weeks alone with Dante,' Rose admitted. 'I missed Bea, naturally, but it was good to have time together before we get back to parenthood.'

Bea woke as Dante turned up the steep, winding road to the Villa. 'Gramma,' she said in excitement, 'Daddy's house is up here—ooh,' she squeaked in delight as he drove up through the garden. 'Balloons! Is there a party?' She jumped up and down in her seat. 'Look, Tom, Auntie Charlotte's on the loggia.'

'And not just Auntie Charlotte,' said Grace with misgiving, and grasped Rose's hand. 'Do I look all right?'

'You look gorgeous,' Tom assured her.

'Daddy, Daddy, get me out,' demanded Bea, as an assortment of cousins came streaming from the house. Dante unbuckled his impatient daughter and set her on her feet so she could run to join the youngsters who surrounded her, laughing, then delivered her onto the loggia into the embraces of her *Nonna* and *Nonno*. The senior Fortinaris gave Tom and Grace a warm welcome, smiling as a radiantly happy Charlotte kissed the new arrivals then handed them on to Fabio and Leo and Harriet, and finally to Mirella and Franco.

Rose hung back for a moment with Dante just to breathe in the noisy, laughing chaos of the scene. He put his arm round her, smiling down into her flushed face. 'You are happy, *amore*?'

'Yes,' she said simply. 'At this moment I have everything in the world I never dared wish for. A beautiful home, a loving, welcoming family, and my mother here with me to share it all today—but most of all, Dante, I have you.'

'Ah, *carissima*!' He took her in his arms and kissed her

in passionate gratitude, a move which won much applause and laughter from the crowded loggia.

'Come, *mio figlio*,' said Maria Fortinari, smiling. 'Release your bride for a moment. She will want to show Grace and Tom to their room to do the freshening up, and then we eat, yes, Rose?'

A few minutes later everyone crowded round the table laid in the garden, the noise level high as they enjoyed the food Maria Fortinari and her cook had helped Silvia prepare.

Under cover of the joyful hubbub, Grace took Rose's hand. 'I've no need to ask if you're happy, love.'

Rose gave a deep, relishing sigh. 'I'll be even happier if you—and Tom, of course—promise to come and stay with us as often as you can.'

'I can safely promise that, especially when Charlotte's baby arrives—I won't be able to keep him away!' Grace looked up at the house. 'I'm so glad I've seen your beautiful home. I'll be able to picture the three of you here.'

Rose eyed her husband in surprise as he got up to rap a spoon on his glass.

'Listen carefully, everyone, because I make my speech in English so Grace and Tom understand how happy I am to welcome them both here today and thank them for taking care of Bea these past two weeks.' At the mention of her name Bea left her place between Chiara and Luca and went running to her father. He picked her up and kissed her in a way which brought tears to his mother's eyes and to a few others round the table, notably Charlotte's.

'Hormones,' she apologised, blowing her nose into the handkerchief Fabio had ready.

'So now,' continued Dante, 'I wish to thank my mother-in-law for giving her daughter and her granddaughter into my keeping, also Tom, for taking such good care of Rose and Bea in the past.'

To Rose's surprise, Grace exchanged a look with Tom and got to her feet. 'Thank you, Dante, and everyone here for giving us this wonderful welcome. I shall go home—'

'Not yet, Grace,' called Charlotte.

'Not yet,' agreed Grace, smiling, 'but when I do I shall look back on today and feel happy because I know my girls are happy.'

'Davvero,' said Dante with feeling, and put his arm round Rose. 'After the years apart, it is now time we live happily ever after!'

'Like in my story book,' said Bea with satisfaction, and Dante laughed as he set her down.

'Only this is better because it is our story, yes?'

'Much better,' said Rose with feeling, and smiled all round to lighten the mood. 'Now, then, Harriet's made some gorgeous apple pies and I've made a very British trifle, so hands up. Who wants a *dolce*?'

* * * * *

CAROSELLI'S BABY CHASE
MICHELLE CELMER

To my lovely Facebook friends who cheer me on when my heroes misbehave.

Michelle Celmer is a bestselling author of more than thirty books. When she's not writing, she likes to spend time with her husband, kids, grandchildren and a menagerie of animals.

Michelle loves to hear from readers. Visit her website, www.michellecelmer.com, like her on Facebook, or write to her at P.O. Box 300, Clawson, MI 48017.

Prologue

Once a year since her death, on the day of her birth, December thirtieth, Giuseppe Caroselli honored Angelica, his wife of sixty-eight years and mother of his three sons, by making her favorite cake, raspberry walnut torte with dark chocolate frosting.

Caroselli chocolate, of course.

In less than an hour his family would be there to celebrate with him. To pass photos and share memories. On his request, his grandsons Rob and Tony had arrived early. They each sat on a barstool at the kitchen island, watching him carefully measure the ingredients and mix them together, the way they had when they were boys.

From birth, his three grandsons—Robert, Anthony Jr. and Nicholas—had been groomed to someday take over Caroselli Chocolate, the business Giuseppe had built from the ground up, after emigrating from Italy.

What he hadn't counted on was their being so resistant

to carrying on the Caroselli name. And if they didn't settle down and have sons of their own, the Carosellis would
be no more. At least Nicholas now had the marriage part
taken care of.

"As I'm sure you already know, Nicholas has forfeited
his portion of the thirty-million dollars."

"He told us," Tony said, a perpetual frown on his face.
So serious, that one. He needed to learn to take life in
stride. Have fun.

"That means fifteen million each to you boys if you
marry and produce a male heir," he told them.

"That's a lot of money," Rob said. He was the most
driven of the three, the one who would no doubt take his
father Demitrio's place as CEO one day. If Demitrio would
only put aside his doubts and trust his son.

"It is a lot of money," Giuseppe agreed. Money that he
had no intention of actually giving them. What sort of man
would he be if he singled out only two of his seven grandchildren? And as he had suspected, Nick was so happy to
be married, so content with his life, he had turned down
his share.

One down, two to go.

And Giuseppe didn't doubt that like their cousin, in
the end, Tony and Rob would make the right decision and
do him proud.

In fact, he was counting on it.

One

As he watched his date leave the hotel bar wrapped around another man, Robert Caroselli wanted to feel angry or put out, or even mildly annoyed, but he couldn't work up the steam. He hadn't wanted to come to this party, but he'd let Olivia, a woman he'd been seeing casually, talk him into it last minute.

"I don't really feel like celebrating," he'd told her when she called him around nine. He had already turned off the television and was planning to crawl into bed and with any luck sleep away the next three months or so. It was that or face daily the fact that his family, the owners of Caroselli Chocolate, had lost complete faith in him as a marketing director.

Yes, sales for the last quarter were down, but they were in a recession for Christ's sake. Hiring Caroline Taylor, a so-called marketing genius from Los Angeles, was not only an insult, but also total overkill as far as he was concerned. But against the entire family, his objections carried little weight.

On top of that he had the added pressure of finding a wife. A woman to give him a male heir. By thirty-one most of his cousins, and the majority of his college buddies, were already married. It wasn't as if he'd made a conscious decision to stay single. His dedication to the family business had kept him too busy to settle down. He couldn't deny that ten-million dollars had been a tempting incentive, but fifteen million? That was difficult to pass up. Especially when it meant that if he didn't get his cut, his cousin Tony would walk away with the entire thirty million. He would never hear the end of it.

But if he was going to find a woman to be his wife and bear his children, it wouldn't be in a bar. And it definitely wouldn't be Olivia. Which was why he'd planned to stay home.

"You *can't* stay home alone on New Year's Eve!" Olivia had said. "Who will you kiss? You can't start the New Year without a kiss at midnight. It's…un-American!"

She hadn't seemed too concerned with whom he would kiss when she walked out the door with someone else. Not that he blamed her for bailing on him. He hadn't exactly been the life of the party. When they arrived around ten, he scoped out a counter-height table with two vacant barstools near the back corner, claimed it and hadn't moved since. Now he was on his—he counted the empty glasses in front of him—third Scotch and feeling a hell of a lot more relaxed than when he got there.

Alcohol flowed freely at every Caroselli family function—hell, his family would use any excuse to get together, drink and gossip—but Rob rarely indulged. He never much cared for the out-of-control feeling that came with intoxication. Tonight was a rare exception.

From his table he had a decent view of the entire bar, which was crammed above capacity with people, who, from his vantage point, undulated like the waves off the shore of Lake Michigan. Or maybe that was the liquor playing tricks with his vision.

"Excuse me!"

At the sudden shout, Rob jerked to attention. He blinked, then blinked again, positive he was imagining the angel who stood beside his table. A halo of pale blond hair hung in loose curls that nearly brushed her narrow waist, and framed a heart-shaped face that glowed with youth and good health. His gaze slipped lower and he realized that this particular angel had a body made for sin. She couldn't have been more than a few inches over five-feet tall, but she packed one hell of a figure into her skinny jeans and clingy blue sweater. A complete contrast to the wholesome beauty of her face.

"Is this seat taken?" she shouted over the music. "And just to be clear, I am *not* hitting on you. I've been on my feet all day and there isn't a single other free seat in this entire place."

He gestured to the chair across from his. "Help yourself."

"Thank you." She slid onto the stool, sighing with pleasure as her feet left the floor. "You're a lifesaver."

"No problem."

She offered him one fine-boned hand with short, neatly filed nails. "Carrie—"

Her last name was drowned out by the blare of a noise-maker. She shook his hand, her grip surprisingly firm for someone so petite and delicate-looking.

"Hi, Carrie, I'm Rob."

"Nice to meet you, Ron," she said.

He opened his mouth to correct her, but she flashed him

a smile so easy and sweet, so disarming, she could call him anything she wanted and it wouldn't have mattered to him. "Can I buy you a drink?"

She cocked her head to one side and smiled. "Are *you* hitting on *me*?"

He had never been the type to flirt, but he heard himself saying, "Would it be a problem if I was?"

She leaned forward to study him and his gaze was naturally drawn to the deep cleft at the front of her low-cut sweater. "I guess that just depends."

"On what?"

"Why a man like you would be sitting here alone at eleven-fifteen on New Year's Eve."

"A man like me?"

She rolled her eyes. "Don't even try to pretend that you don't know how hot you are. You should have women crawling all over you."

"I'm alone because my date left with someone else."

She blinked. "Was she blind or just stupid?"

He laughed. "Bored, I think. I'm not in a mood to celebrate."

Although the night was definitely looking up.

"You must have a girlfriend," she said.

He shook his head.

"Wife?"

He held up his ringless left hand.

She paused, then asked, "Gay?"

He laughed again. "Straight as an arrow."

"Hmm," she said, looking puzzled. "Are you a jerk?"

She sure didn't pull any punches. He liked a woman who was direct and to the point. "I'd like to believe I'm not, but I suppose everyone has their moments."

She nodded thoughtfully. "Honesty...I like that. My answer is yes. You can buy me a drink."

"What would you like?"

She nodded to his glass. "Whatever you're having."

He looked around, but the waitresses in the vicinity were overwhelmed with customers, so he figured it would be quicker to go right to the source. "Be right back," he said, heading for the bar.

It took several minutes to navigate through the crowd, and another five or ten before the bartender served him. As he walked back to the table, he half expected Carrie to be gone. He was pleasantly surprised to find her sitting there waiting for him, and suddenly grateful that he wouldn't have to watch the ball drop alone. He might even get a New Year's kiss out of it. Or maybe that would be pushing his luck. Maybe just a quick one, or if she wasn't into kissing a total stranger, a peck on the cheek even.

"Here you go." He set her drink in front of her and reclaimed his chair.

"That took so long, I started to think you left," she said.

"And I wasn't sure if you would still be here when I got back."

"I'm not blind or stupid," she said with a grin, and he felt a tug of attraction so intense, he nearly reached across the table for her hand.

"Do you live in the area?" she asked, sipping her drink.

"Lincoln Park."

"Is that far from here?"

"Not too far. I take it you're not from Chicago."

"West Coast born and bred. I'm here for work. I'm staying in the hotel. That's how I wound up in this particular bar."

"You must have someone back home."

"Not for a while."

"Are the men there blind or just stupid?"

She smiled, and he felt that tug again, only this time

it was lower, and it wasn't her hand he wanted to touch. That New Year's kiss was sounding even more appealing. He would have to call Olivia tomorrow and thank her for dragging him out.

"A lot of men feel threatened by a strong, successful woman," she said.

Rob had quite a few strong, successful women in his family, and compared to them, Carrie looked anything but threatening. His first instinct, when she had approached his table, was to pick her up and hug her.

"I also have the tendency to gravitate toward men who are bad for me," she said.

"Bad for you how?"

"I like jerks. It's my way of sabotaging the relationship before it even begins." She sipped her drink. "I have intimacy issues."

"If you know that, then why don't you date someone different?"

"Knowing what the problem is doesn't necessarily make it any easier to fix."

Well, she had the honesty thing down to a science. The women he met typically played up their good qualities, not their faults. Which he couldn't deny was, in an odd way, a refreshing change of pace. A sort of "this is me, take it or leave it" philosophy.

"When was your last serious relationship?" he asked.

"I've never really had one."

"Really? What are you? Twenty-four? Twenty-five?"

Carrie laughed. "Aren't you good for my ego. I'm twenty-eight."

"I've never met a woman past the age of eighteen who hasn't been in at least one serious relationship."

"Which you clearly find fascinating," she said, looking amused.

"I do." In more ways than just that. She was like the perfect woman. Sexy, desirable, with a decent sense of humor and completely uninterested in a relationship. Had he hit the jackpot or what?

"How about you?" Carrie asked. "Ever been in a serious relationship?"

"Engaged, but that was a long time ago. Back in college."

"What happened?"

"You could say that we wanted different things."

"What did you want?"

He shrugged. "Marriage, kids, the usual stuff."

"What did she want?"

"My roommate, Evan."

She winced. "Ouch."

"Better I found out what she was like before we were married than after. At that point I decided to focus on my career."

"So you're married to your job?"

"More or less."

"It's not unusual for me to work fourteen-hour days, so I totally get that."

She would be the first woman who ever did. And he found himself wishing she were staying in Chicago longer than a few days. She was someone he wouldn't mind getting to know better.

After talking for a few minutes more, and some serious flirting, they had both drained their glasses, so he hailed a waitress for two more drinks. There was more talking, more flirting—but mostly flirting—then Carrie had a third drink, and by then it was nearly midnight. At one minute till, the music stopped, and everyone focused on the big-screen television over the bar to watch the ball drop.

"So," Carrie said, "because neither of us has anyone to kiss…"

"I was told that it's un-American to start the New Year off without a kiss," he said.

"I guess that doesn't leave us much choice, then."

With a grin, he held out his hand and she took it. She slid down off the stool, and didn't show a bit of resistance as he tugged her closer. He should have been watching the ball drop, but he couldn't seem to peel his eyes away from her face. Standing this close he would have expected to see at least an imperfection or two, but her skin was flawless, her eyes such a clear gray they appeared bottomless. His eyes dropped to her mouth, to lips that looked full and soft and kissable.

Only an hour ago he had been dreading the arrival of the New Year, now he could hardly wait for those last thirty seconds to pass. Then it was twenty seconds, and when it reached ten, everyone in the bar started to count. Except for him and Carrie. Their eyes locked, and they stood so close now that her warm breath feathered against his lips. They waited in anticipation. Five…four…three…two…

Unable to wait another second, he slanted his mouth over hers and the cheers and hoots, the shrill of noisemakers and the chorus of "Auld Lang Syne" being sung—it all faded into the background. Her lips parted under his. He heard her sigh as he sank his fingers through the silky ribbons of her hair, felt her melt against him when he pulled her closer. The softness of her lips, the sweet taste of her mouth, were more intoxicating than any drink. And he wanted her, knew he had to have her, even if it was for only one night.

He wasn't sure how long they stood there kissing, their arms wrapped around one another, but when he finally broke the kiss, they were both breathless and Carrie's cheeks were rosy and hot.

"At the risk of sounding too forward," she said, "would you like to come up to my room?"

Of course he wanted to. "Are you sure that's what you want?"

That must have been the right answer, because she smiled and took his hand. "I am now. I figure, why not start the year with a *bang?*"

He grinned, squeezed her hand and said, "Let's go."

Two

Start the year off with a bang indeed, Carrie thought as the cab inched along in bumper-to-bumper traffic through the slushy streets of Chicago. Two days later and her neck still ached, there was a bruise on her shin where she had banged it on the headboard, and she had angry-looking rug burns on her knees, but it had been *so* worth it. She hadn't been *banged* so well, or so many times in a row, in years. The man was insatiable, and gave as good as he got. Better even. And as she had imagined, he looked just as good out of his clothes as he did in them. She would even go so far as to say that it was the single most satisfying, fun and adventurous sexual experience of her life. Then he had to go and ruin it by skulking off in the middle of the night without even saying goodbye.

He hadn't left his phone number, which she could have looked up if she had caught his last name. But all evidence pointed to his not wanting to be found. For all she knew,

Ron wasn't even his real name, and he had been sitting there alone looking for someone just like her, someone to *bang* in the New Year with. Maybe all he'd really wanted was cheap sex.

Oh, well. At least it had been really *good* cheap sex. And in her own defense, she'd hit the minibar in her room before she had even ventured downstairs and had been more than a little drunk. It was possible that he wasn't even as good-looking as she thought. Or that great of a lover.

She wasn't sure if that should make her feel better or worse.

She had been in Chicago barely forty-eight hours, and already she'd invited a strange man up to her room, had sex and had gotten dumped. That had to be some kind of world record.

But Ron—if that was really his name—wasn't totally to blame. She did have the tendency to come on a little strong, and sometimes men took it the wrong way. Under normal circumstances she was outspoken. Get her a little tipsy and she had the tendency to say things she probably shouldn't. According to her stepfather, her sassy mouth had been her biggest problem. And his cure for that had always been a solid crack across said mouth with the back of his hand.

She didn't recall everything she and Ron had discussed that night, but she seemed to remember some of it being very personal in nature.

"This is it," the cab driver said as the car rolled to a stop outside Caroselli Chocolate headquarters. As soon as the contracts were signed, and a timetable set, she would look for an apartment or condo to lease. There was nothing she hated more than living out of suitcases for extended periods of time.

She paid him, grabbed her briefcase, climbed out of the cab and walked to the revolving front door, the damp cold seeping through her coat, the heels of her pumps clicking against the slushy pavement. She pushed her way inside, into a lobby of glass, stainless steel and marble, and walked to the guard station, the alluring scent of chocolate drawing her gaze to the gift shop at the other end of the lobby.

"Caroline Taylor. I'm here for a meeting," she told the guard.

"Good morning, Ms. Taylor. They're expecting you." He handed her a name badge that said "Guest," which she clipped to the lapel of her suit jacket. "Take the elevator behind me up to the third floor and see the receptionist."

"Thank you." She walked to the elevator, back straight, head high. There was no lack of security cameras, and it was critical to make a good impression the second she walked in the door. Despite her reputation, and her impeccable record for getting the job done, some people, men of a certain era in particular, sometimes doubted her abilities. And this being a family business, she had no doubt that she would be working with several generations of Carosellis.

As she rode up to the third floor she shrugged out of her overcoat and draped it over her arm. When the doors slid open she stepped out of the elevator into another reception area. A young woman whose nameplate announced her as Sheila Price was seated behind a large desk, and beside her stood an attractive, older gentleman in a very expensive, exquisitely tailored suit. Considering his age, and the air of authority he exuded, she was guessing he was one of the three Caroselli brothers, the sons of Giuseppe who now ran the company.

She walked to the desk, nervous energy propelling her steps. She hadn't planned to expand her business outside the West Coast area for another year or two, but Caroselli Chocolate was the largest and most prestigious company to approach her thus far, and when they called, it was too good an opportunity to pass up. Of course, if she botched it up, it would decimate her reputation and probably destroy her career.

But that wasn't going to happen.

"Welcome, Ms. Taylor," the man said, stepping forward to greet her. "I'm Demitrio Caroselli."

"It's a pleasure," she said, shaking his hand, a little surprised that the CEO himself was there to greet her.

"Can I take your coat?" Sheila asked.

"Yes, thank you," she said, handing it over.

"Everyone is waiting for us in the conference room," Demitrio said, gesturing down a long hallway lined with offices. "It's this way."

Being a private contractor, Carrie answered to no one, and being in such high demand, she walked into every meeting knowing she had the upper hand. That didn't mean she wasn't slightly nervous. But she seriously doubted they would have shelled out the expense of a first-class plane ticket and a five-star hotel if they weren't seriously planning to sign the contract.

"Do you prefer Caroline or Ms. Taylor?" he asked.

"Caroline or Carrie," she told him.

"We appreciate your coming to see us on such short notice," he said. "And so close to the holidays."

"I'm happy to be here." The assignment back in L.A. that she was supposed to have started this week had been cancelled when the company went under last month; otherwise she wouldn't have been available until much later this year.

"Is this your first visit to Chicago?"

"It is. From what I've seen it's a beautiful city. The snow will take some getting used to, though." The hall was silent and most of the offices they passed were dark. "Is it always this quiet?"

"We're not technically back from the holiday break until next Monday," he said. "The holiday season is a very busy time for us so we give everyone the first week of the year off."

At the end of the hall he opened a door marked "Conference Room" and Carrie held her breath as they stepped inside. In front of a bank of windows that spanned the entire length of the room stood a strikingly beautiful young woman who looked more suited to a fashion runway than a company boardroom. On one side of a marble-topped table long enough to seat a dozen-plus people sat two dashing older men and opposite them, two younger men, who frankly buried the needle on the totally hot-and-sexy scale.

Well, *damn,* the Caroselli family sure did grow them tall dark and sexy.

She assumed one of them was Robert Caroselli, the man whose department she was there to analyze and pick apart. In her experience, that didn't typically go over very well, and resulted in a certain degree of opposition. Especially when the person in charge was a man.

"Caroline," Demitrio said, "these are my brothers Leo, our CFO, and Tony, our COO."

The two older men rose to shake her hand. Tony was shorter and stockier in build. Leo was the tallest of the three and very fit for a man his age. Despite their physical differences, there was no mistaking the fact that they were related.

"Nice to meet you, gentlemen."

"And this is my niece, Elana. She heads up our accounting division."

Elana sauntered over to shake Carrie's hand. Her firm grip was all business, her smile cool and sophisticated, but her dark eyes were warm and friendly. Carrie was fairly adept at reading people, and if she had to guess, she would say that Elana was incredibly intelligent, though underestimated at times because of her beauty.

"On this side we have my nephew, Nick," Demitrio said. "He's the genius behind our new projects."

Nick, the one on the left, rose to shake her hand. He was charmingly attractive in a slightly rumpled I'm-sexy-and-rich-therefore-I-can-wear-a-wrinkled-shirt sort of way. The twinkle in his dark eyes, and slightly lopsided grin as he shook her hand said he was a flirt, while the wedding band on his left hand said he was very likely a harmless one.

"And last but not least," Demitrio said, while Carrie braced herself, "this is Tony Jr., director of overseas production and sales."

What about Robert?

Tony Jr. stood so tall that even in three-inch heels Carrie had to crane her neck to meet his eyes. His professional nod and distracted smile said that he had something other than the business at hand on his mind.

"Please have a seat," Demitrio said, gesturing to the empty chair beside Nick. "We're waiting for one more, then we can get started."

She'd barely settled in her seat when behind her she heard the door open, and a deep voice say, "Sorry I'm late. My secretary isn't back today, so I had to pick these reports up on my way in."

Something about that voice made the hair on the back of her neck shiver to attention. She'd definitely heard it before. But where…

The breath she had just inhaled backed up in her lungs. Oh no, it *couldn't* be.

She glanced up at him out of the corner of her eye as he approached the table, his attention on the pile of folders he carried, and when she focused on his face…

She swiftly looked away, heart pounding. He had the

same smoldering black eyes, the solid, square jaw, the full lips that had kissed her senseless. At first glance the resemblance was uncanny. But it couldn't be him. Could it?

He mumbled an "excuse me" as he laid a folder in front of her. On his right hand was a college ring identical to the one she had seen the other night, and as the scent of his aftershave drifted her way, the wave of familiarity was so strong that her heart skipped a beat.

She stared at the folder cover, unable to focus. Hell, she could barely *breathe*.

It's not him, she assured herself. *It just looks like him, and smells like him, and* sounds *like him...and wears the same ring as him.* But it *had* to be a coincidence, her mind playing tricks on her.

She had a strict rule of never sleeping with a coworker. Especially one she would be working with directly. And definitely not one whose work she would be putting under the microscope. She'd made that mistake once before, on her first high-profile job with a previous client. Previous because the affair had ended in disaster, the aftermath ugly.

It wasn't necessary for the entire team to like her, but maintaining their respect was crucial. When she recalled the things she and Ron had said to one another, the things she let him do...the sheer mortification made her want to curl inside her own skin and hide, or slide down out of her chair under the table.

As he rounded the table she kept her eyes on the folder, pretending to read, afraid to lift her head. Maybe if it was Ron, he wouldn't recognize her. They had both been pretty drunk.

"Rob," Demitrio said, "this is Caroline Taylor. Caroline, this is my son Rob, our director of marketing."

She had no choice but to look up, to meet his eyes, and when she did, her head spun and her heart sank.

Unless "Rob" had an identical twin, he was in fact Ron, her New Year's bang.

Rob blinked, then blinked again. In the conservative suit that hid her pinup model figure, with her granny hairstyle, he almost didn't recognize Carrie. But the slightly too-large clear gray eyes were a dead giveaway.

She sat frozen, watching him expectantly, and his first thought was that this had to be some sort of prank. Were Nick and Tony screwing with him? He'd bragged to them about the blonde beauty he'd spent the night with. Which his cousins knew was completely out of character for him. He didn't do drunken one-night stands. Typically, he didn't do drunken *anything*.

Was this some twisted practical joke? Had they gone to the hotel to look for her, maybe paid her to pose as Caroline Taylor to mess with Rob's head?

He looked from Nick to Tony, waiting for someone to say something, for everyone at the table to burst out laughing. And when they didn't, when they all watched him, looking increasingly puzzled by his lack of a response, he began to get a *very* bad feeling.

"Rob?" his dad said, brow creased with concern. "Is everything all right?"

"Fine," he said, a bit too enthusiastically, and forcing a smile that felt molded from plastic, he told Ms. Taylor, "It's a pleasure to meet you."

Not.

When he'd slipped out of her bed, he'd had no intention of ever seeing her again. Talk about dumb freaking luck.

Caroline nodded in his general direction, her head held a little too high, her shoulders too square and her back too straight, as if she'd been cut out of cardboard and propped up in the chair. She was clearly no happier to see him than he was to see her.

"Well, why don't we get started," his dad said, and everyone opened their folders. Rob tried to concentrate as they went over the contracts, and discussed Ms. Taylor's credentials and her projected time line, but he found his mind—and his eyes—wandering to the woman across the table. She downplayed her looks for work, he assumed in an attempt to gain respect from men who might otherwise objectify her or see her as too pretty to be smart. But he knew what she was hiding under that shapeless suit. The siren's figure and satin-soft skin. He knew the way her hair looked cascading down her bare back in silky ribbons, pale and buttery against her milky complexion, and how it brushed his chest as she straddled him. Even though parts of that night were a bit fuzzy, he knew he could never erase from his mind the image of her lying beneath him, wrapped in his arms, her breathy moans as he—

"Rob?" his dad said.

Rob jerked to attention. "Yeah, sorry."

"It seems we've covered everything."

Already?

"Why don't you take Caroline on a tour of the building while the rest of us have a short discussion. I'll call you when we're ready."

They had covered everything, and he hadn't heard a word of it. Now they would make the final decision, and they were going to do it without him. He'd been clear from day one that he considered her presence there a waste of time and money, and he had never once swayed from that opinion. Still it was a slap in the face to be excluded, not just for him, but for the entire marketing staff that he represented.

Or maybe, getting her alone for a few minutes wasn't such a bad idea. And meeting her wasn't "dumb luck" after all. Maybe a little time alone would give him the opportunity to make her see reason. See that she didn't belong here. Then she would no longer be his problem.

With a smile—a genuine one this time—he rose from his seat and said, "If you'll follow me, Ms. Taylor."

She stood, spine straight, shoulders back, flashing the others a confident smile, as if she already knew she had it in the bag. "I look forward to your decision."

Rob held the door for her, then followed her out, closing it firmly behind him. He turned to her and said in a low voice, "I think we need to talk."

Her eyes shooting daggers, her voice dripping with venom, she said, "Oh, you think so...*Ron?*"

He gestured down the hall. "My office is this way."

They walked there in silence, but he could feel her anger reverberating against the walls like an operatic vibrato.

His secretary's chair was unoccupied as they walked past, and when they were in his office he shut the door. He turned to face her and thought, *Here we go.* "I can see that you're upset."

"Upset," she said, her voice rising an octave. "Not only did you *lie* about your name, but did you have to skulk away in the middle of the night?"

If that's all she was mad about, he considered himself lucky. "First off, I did not lie to you about my name. I said it was Rob. You called me Ron and I saw no point in correcting you."

"I can't believe you didn't make the connection. Carrie Taylor, Caroline Taylor? You didn't at least suspect we might be one in the same person?"

"It was loud in the bar. I didn't even hear your last name. And we never discussed what we do for a living, so how was I supposed to guess who you were? I've met a lot of people named Carrie. You don't have a monopoly on the name."

"And as for skulking off in the middle of the night?"

"It was not the middle of the night. It was early morning and I didn't want to wake you. You were so drunk I'm not sure I could have if I tried. And I did not skulk. I got dressed and left, end of story."

"First off, I wasn't *that* drunk. And didn't it occur to you to at least leave a note?"

"Why would I? We agreed it would never be more than one night. It was over."

She rolled her eyes. "You know *nothing* about women do you? You could have said goodbye, told me that you had a good time."

"I assumed, in our case, actions spoke louder than words."

She didn't seem to have a snarky reply for that one. She couldn't deny it had been damned good for her, too.

"What I don't understand is why we're in here," Rob told her, "when you should be in the conference room telling them you can't work here."

Her brows rose. "Why would I do that?"

"Well, first, despite what my family believes, your services are not required or desired by anyone on my staff. And considering the circumstances, I don't think your presence here would be appropriate."

"What circumstances are those?"

Was she kidding? "The ones we've been discussing

since we stepped in here. It's unlikely either of us could be objective in light of what happened the other night."

"I don't know about you, but now that I know what a macho jerk you are, it isn't going to be an issue for me. In fact, I think I'm going to enjoy it."

He had been accused of being inattentive, arrogant and at times insufferable, but macho jerk was a new one. "Are you sure about that?"

"Absolutely."

"You can remain completely objective?"

"Yep."

Rob was not the type of man to behave rashly. He never made a move before he'd had time to completely think through a situation, weigh the pros and cons. So maybe it was pride that propelled him forward, or the satisfaction of proving her wrong, or just compromised judgment that motivated him to take her by the arms, pull her to him and crush his mouth down on hers.

Carrie made an indignant sound and pushed at his chest. She resisted for all of three seconds, then her fingers curled into the lapels of his jacket and her lips parted beneath his.

Having made his point, he should have let go. Instead he wrapped his arms around her, pulled her closer. It had been just like this on New Year's, his brain shutting down the second he kissed her, his body reacting on pure instinct, a carnal need to overpower and dominate. One that he'd never felt with a woman before her. Because despite her claim, he was not a macho jerk. Of all his cousins and uncles, he was probably the least chauvinistic man in the family. Her gender had no bearing whatsoever on his professional opinion.

Carrie slid her hands up his chest, tunneled them through his hair, taking two fistfuls and jerking his head back so she could kiss—*ow*—make that *bite* his neck.

Growling, he backed her against his office door, cringing as her head hit the surface with a *thunk,* cushioned only by the ugly bun in her hair, but it only seemed to fuel her desire.

"I want you right here, against this door," she said, her eyes locking on his as she slid her hand between their bodies, gripping his erection through his slacks.

Sucking in a breath, he grabbed the hem of her skirt and shoved his hand underneath, sliding it up her leg, and—damn—she was wearing a garter. He had just reached the top of her bare inner thigh, his fingers brushing the crotch of her panties, when his cell phone started to ring.

Damn it. Talk about lousy timing.

Carrie grumbled unhappily as he pulled his hand from under her skirt and backed away from the hand that had been busy unzipping his fly. "Yeah," he answered.

"We're ready for you," his father said.

"Be right there." He hung up without saying goodbye, so his dad wouldn't hear his labored breathing, and told Carrie, "They're ready for you."

She nodded, her cheeks rosy, pupils dilated. "I just need a minute to catch my breath."

He shoved his phone back in his pocket and zipped his pants. "Now do you see what I mean?"

"That you have pitiful lack of self-control?" Carrie said, straightening her jacket and smoothing the wrinkles from a skirt six inches too long for her height. "I definitely noticed that."

"I didn't see you trying to stop me."

She looked up at him, her lipstick kissed away, a stubborn tilt to her chin. "You enjoy being right, don't you?"

"Not always." Not this time. They had chemistry, but

that was about it. With fifteen million dollars riding on his choice, she was the exact opposite of what he was looking for in a woman. Not only did he consider her the enemy, but she'd said herself that she had intimacy issues, and she had never been in a serious relationship. Rob needed a woman with baby fever, someone to marry and pop out a male heir. She wasn't it, and having her around to tempt him would only make a difficult situation that much more tense.

"So, have I made my point?" he asked Carrie.

"You certainly have," she said. "We should get back to the conference room."

They walked side by side down the corridor, an uncomfortable silence building a wedge between them. There was nothing left to say. It had been fun, and now it was over. She would go back to California, and he and his team would work out a plan to beef up sales. And hopefully, sooner rather than later, he would find a woman to give him a son, and everyone would be happy.

The conference room was silent as they stepped inside. Carrie took her seat, and Rob returned to his.

"Sorry to make you wait," his dad told her.

"I completely understand," she said.

Rob waited for her to break the bad news, but she just sat there.

"After going over the final numbers," his uncle Leo said, "we're pleased to tell you that we agree to your terms and we would like you to start first thing next Monday morning."

Rob waited for the big letdown, wondered how everyone would take her turning down their offer.

"I don't come cheap," she said, then looked directly at Rob. "But I don't disappoint."

She may as well have drawn her sword and challenged him to a duel. And clearly she had only been humoring him. She had never intended to turn down the assignment.

If that was really the way she wanted to play this, fine. *You want a fight, sweetheart? Well, now you've got one.*

Three

After the contracts were signed, everyone filed out of the conference room, shaking Carrie's hand, congratulating her and welcoming her to the company. Rob watched, gathering the binders—a task typically left for an assistant—growing increasingly impatient as Elana stopped to admire Carrie's briefcase of all things, and they launched into a conversation about women's purses and accessories. When he'd run out of ways to stall, he flat-out asked Elana, "Could I have a minute with Ms. Taylor?"

Flashing him a knowing look and a wry smile, Elana said, "Sure, Robby. See you Monday, Carrie."

Elana knew that there was no faster way to irritate him than to address him by his childhood nickname. The first half of it anyway. It had been years since anyone dare uttered the phrase that had been the bane of his existence from kindergarten to his first year of college.

She left, closing the door behind her, and Rob turned to Carrie, who was sliding papers into her briefcase.

"Well?" he said.

She closed the case and smiled up at him. "Something wrong...*Robby?*"

That was it—Elana was dead meat. "Why did you lie to me?"

She smiled, the picture of innocence. "When did I lie to you?"

"We agreed that in light of what happened, working together would be a bad idea."

"No, *you* said working together would be bad, and I commented on how you enjoy being right. I never said you *were* right."

"So you were just screwing with me?"

She propped her hands on the conference table, leaning in. "Not unlike the way *you* were screwing with *me*."

She definitely had him there. And he had best be going, before he told her what he really thought of her. "I'll see you Monday."

She smiled brightly. "Sure thing, Robby. Oh, and by the way, the first step will be analyzing your marketing data. I'll need a few things from you."

Gathering his patience, he said, "All right."

"I'll need all the data you have for the past twenty years."

He blinked. "*Twenty* years?"

"That's right."

He wondered if she really needed to go that far back, or if she was trying to make his life a living hell. Probably the latter, and could he blame her if she was? But that, she should realize, was a two-way street.

"It could take some time to compile everything. We've

been in the process of digitizing our older files. Some of it might still be in hard copy."

"That's fine. Just have it on my desk Monday morning."

"If you hadn't noticed, there's no one here. Everyone is on holiday vacation until Monday."

"Well," she said, the sweet smile not wavering a fraction. "Who better to do it than the director himself. Which reminds me, I'll need you available, and at my disposal at all times in case I have any questions."

Gritting his teeth, he nodded, then turned and walked to the door.

"Hey, Robby?"

Jaw tense, he turned back to her.

"I'm not the enemy. This will be as productive or as difficult as you make it. I think you'll find that I can be very pleasant to work with."

"So I noticed," he said, his eyes raking over her. "Will we be meeting for a quickie in my office daily, or just once or twice a week?" He didn't even like her, but his libido didn't seem to notice or care. It was telling him to rip that shapeless, ugly suit from her body, to pluck the pins from her granny hairstyle so he could watch her silky blond curls cascade down her shoulders.

She sighed and shook her head, as if she felt sorry for him. "Robby, is that the best you can do? You think I haven't heard worse? During the course of my career I've been called sweetie and sugar and pumpkin. I've been groped and fondled, objectified and demoralized. I've seen it all, and in the end I always get the job done, and I manage to do it with dignity."

She slung her case strap over her shoulder and said, "We can do this the easy way or the hard way. If you think you'd like to take me on, by all means give it your best shot. But

I should warn you, I always get what I want, and I'm not above fighting dirty."

He should have anticipated that. No one got as far as she had in the business world without being tough as nails. And shame on him for underestimating her.

She walked out, the heels of her shoes clicking as she marched down the hall. He had no plan to demoralize or objectify her, or to call her condescending names. And the only physical contact they might have would be totally at her discretion. He had every intention of treating her with the utmost respect, because he didn't doubt that she had earned it. His cooperation, however, was another matter altogether.

Rob walked to his office and sat down at his computer to send his staff and his secretary an email dictating what Carrie would need—one they would see Monday when they returned to work. He refused to make his people work a weekend they had been promised as vacation.

There was a knock on his door, and he looked up to see Tony and Nick standing there.

"Hey." He motioned them in, and Nick shut the door.

"So what was that all about?" Tony asked him.

"Yeah," Nick said, "what the heck did you say to her when you two left the conference room?"

"You probably wouldn't believe me if I told you." Rob could barely believe it himself. "Do you think my dad noticed?"

"Dude, *everyone* noticed," Nick said. "You looked as if either you wanted to kill each other, or tear each other's clothes off."

It was a little bit of both. "Remember the woman I told you about? The blonde from the bar?"

Tony nodded. "What about her?"

Nick being Nick, he was way ahead of Tony. He started to laugh. "No way. No one's luck could be *that* bad."

"Apparently it can."

Tony looked from Nick to Rob, and then he laughed. "Are you saying that Caroline Taylor is Carrie from the bar?"

He glared at them both. "I'm glad you find this so amusing."

"More ironic than amusing," Tony said.

"Yeah," Nick agreed. "But still funny as hell."

If it were happening to anyone but him, Rob probably would have thought so, too.

"So what are you going to do?" Tony asked.

"What can I do? I already asked her to leave, said it would be a conflict of interest for her to stay, and you can see how well that went."

"Did you see how much we're paying her?" Tony said. "Can you blame her for not walking away?"

"Well, I'm going to make sure that she earns every penny."

Tony shook his head, like he thought that was a bad idea. "You know that if you screw with her, your dad will be pissed."

"Not if he doesn't find out."

"You don't think she'll rat you out?" Nick asked.

"Only if she wants the entire family to know how she and I first met. If it gets around that she picks up men in bars for one-night stands, her credibility will be in the toilet. Every potential future client will believe that a bedroom romp is included in the contract."

"You don't think that's a little harsh?" Nick said.

If she could play dirty, so could he. "I'm not the one who declared war in front of the entire family. And you can damn well bet she plans to discredit me and my team every opportunity she gets."

"Are you sure? She comes off as smart and savvy but not vindictive."

If Nick had just heard her in the conference room, he might feel differently. And if she could be ruthless, so could Rob. She was on his turf now, and she would play by his rules.

"Nick and I are getting a late breakfast at the diner," Tony said. "Are you going to hang around and work, or do you want to come?"

He thought of all the work Carrie expected him to complete before Monday and smiled. "Breakfast sounds good."

He was getting ready to stand when his office phone rang. It was his sister Megan. "Give me fifteen minutes and I'll meet you by the elevator."

"We'll get our coats," Tony said.

"Hey, Meggie," he said. "What's up?"

"I just heard from the real estate agent," she said, her voice squeaky with excitement. "They accepted my offer! The apartment is mine!"

"Congratulations," Rob said. His younger sister had spent the past nine months looking for exactly the right place, and had been outbid on the first two. "And you're sure it's within your budget?"

"That's my other good news! You know Rose Goldwyn?"

Rob had met her briefly at work, then a few times at family gatherings. She was a recent hire. The daughter of the woman who had been *Nonno's* secretary for the better part of his career.

Rose seemed nice enough, but there was something about her, something just a little...off. "What about her?" Rob said.

"She's going to be my roommate."

"But you hardly know her."

"Actually we've been talking a lot lately. We have a lot in common."

"Isn't she like twenty years older than you?"

"What difference does that make?"

"I don't know, Meg. Something about her…"

"What?"

"I don't trust her."

"Robby, I'm twenty-five" was her plucky response. "It's not your job to protect me anymore."

It would always be his job to protect her. She was an infant when his parents adopted her, and although he was six years older, they had always been close. He'd set her classmates straight when they made fun of her for look-ing "different" than the rest of her family. "Do me a favor and at least have legal do a background check on her. Just in case."

Her sigh of exasperation meant she was giving in. "Fine, if it makes you happy."

"It does." From the hallway he heard a door slam, then after a two- or three-second pause, raised voices. One of them definitely belonged to their father.

What the hell?

"Meggie, I have to go. I'll call you later."

"Love you, Robby!"

"Love you, too, Megs."

He got up and walked past his secretary's desk into the hall. At one end, near the conference room stood his dad and his uncle Tony, and his dad looked furious.

"I was never given a choice," his dad was saying, to which his uncle Tony answered, "You gave that up when you left her."

Whatever that meant, his dad's face flushed deep red

and he gave his brother a firm, two-handed shove that sent him stumbling backward several feet into the conference room door.

Rob had seen his dad and uncles argue, and at times it could get heated, but he had never seen them come to blows. Uncle Tony was stocky and muscular, but Demitrio, Rob's dad, was taller, younger and trained by the military to fight. That apparently wasn't going to stop Uncle Tony because he looked as if he were about to lunge.

From behind him, Rob heard his cousin Tony yell, "What the hell is going on?" and turned to see Nick and him running down the hall toward the older men. Rob followed them.

Both older men, red-faced and out of breath, jaws and fists clenched, stopped and turned to him.

"What the hell, Dad?" Tony said. "What is with the two of you lately?"

Demitrio turned to Tony Sr. "Why don't you tell him, Tony."

"I'd like to know, too," Rob said. The last time Uncle Tony had been to their house, Rob showed up to find his mom in tears. He wanted to know why.

"Boys, this is between me and my brother," Tony Sr. said. "There's no need to be concerned—"

"Dad!" Tony said. "You were two seconds from beating the crap out of each other."

"It wouldn't be the first time I beat the crap out of him," Demitrio said, glaring at his brother.

"When you were kids maybe," Rob said, "but you're in your *sixties*. You could have a heart attack."

"Did I miss the fun?"

Rob turned to see Leo, Nick's dad, walking toward them.

"They're fighting," Tony said, as if he still couldn't believe it. "*Physically* fighting."

"It's nothing to worry about, boys," Leo said, laughing heartily. "You wouldn't believe how many times I had to get between these two when we were kids. It's that middle-child curse, I guess." He stepped strategically between his brothers and gave each of them a slap on the back. "Come on, gentlemen, let's go in my office and settle this." He turned to Rob and his cousins. "You boys can head on out. I've got this."

Reluctantly the three cousins walked to the elevator.

"So what do you think that was about?" Tony asked him.

"I don't know," Rob said. "But it's been building for a while now. Things have been tense for a couple of months."

"Don't forget, Tony's mom was arguing with your dad at Thanksgiving," Nick told Rob. Sarah, Tony's mom, used to date Rob's dad before he joined the army. The fact that Tony Sr. married her shortly after he left had been a minor source of friction among the three of them over the years. Certainly, it was nothing they would come to blows over now, unless the dynamics of those relation-ships had changed....

"Tony, you don't think that your mom and my dad…"

"Honestly, Rob, I don't know what to think anymore. But things have seemed off with my parents, as well. I went to a New Year's party with them and they seemed…I don't know, out of sync, if that makes sense. They're typically very physically affectionate with each other, and I barely saw them touch."

"Maybe my dad can help them figure it out," Nick said.

"Is your dad still sleeping with your mom?" Rob asked him.

Nick made a face. "Yeah. It's bad enough knowing about it, but to actually see them…you know…" He shud-dered involuntarily. "Talk about scarring a person for life."

"That'll teach you to barge into your mom's house without knocking," Tony told him.

"I think it's pretty cool that after being divorced for so long, they reconnected," Rob said.

"They do seem happy," Tony told Nick. "Maybe I shouldn't mention this, but they were at the New Year's party, too. They couldn't keep their hands off each other, and they disappeared long before the ball dropped."

"Regardless," Nick said, "I'll never get how two people who despised each other, and had a messy and uncivilized divorce that scarred all three of their children, could suddenly change their minds and hop in the sack."

"I'm sure that if they'd had a choice, they would have preferred to be happy the first time around," Tony said.

Nick shrugged. "Yeah, I guess. So long as I don't have to see my dad's bare ass again, they can be 'happy' all they want."

"So, breakfast?" Tony said.

They said goodbye to Sheila as they passed the reception desk, then rode the elevator down to the lobby. Dennis, the security guard, nodded as they walked past.

"Who are you betting on in the playoffs?" Nick asked him, walking backward to the door.

"Steelers-Lions," Dennis said. "And the Lions will take it."

"No way! The Lions haven't won a championship since what, the fifties?"

"Fifty-seven," Dennis said. "But this is the year."

Nick laughed. "Dream on. I say Steelers-Chargers, and the Steelers will take the championship."

Dennis grinned and shook his head. "Keep dreaming, boss."

Nick laughed as they walked out the door into the bitter wind. Parking was a bitch downtown, so they pulled up their collars and walked the three blocks to the restaurant. The pavement was slick, so it was slow-going, and by the time they got to the diner it was already filling up with the lunch crowd. Every seat was taken and there was a line of people ahead of them.

"Feel like waiting?" Tony asked.

Rob shrugged. "Could be a while."

"I say we wait," Nick said. "It's too damn cold to go back out there."

"Hey, Caroselli!" someone called. Rob followed the voice, cursing under his breath when he realized whom it belonged to.

Four

"Is that Carrie?" Nick asked.

"That's her," Rob said. She sat alone in a booth near the back, and she was waving them over. She was still wearing the ugly suit, but she'd lost the shapeless jacket. She'd let her hair down so it fell in soft waves over the shoulder of a rose-colored shirt made of some sort of stretchy nylon that clung to her curves.

Tony's mouth dropped open. "Holy hell. No wonder you picked her up. Look at her."

"Yeah," Nick said. "Her body is…wow."

Yes, it was, and as much as he didn't want to, Rob couldn't help but look. Just as he couldn't help it the other night either. In her clothes she was smokin' hot, but out of them she was a goddess. A work of art.

But that was where the attraction ended.

"Looks like she wants to share her table," Nick said.

"I'd rather wait for a table," Rob told him. She had ruined enough of his day.

"Stop being a baby and go," Tony said, giving him a shove from behind. "You're going to have to get used to being around her."

But not outside of a work scenario, Rob thought, grumbling to himself all the way to her booth. And while he could have turned and walked out, he refused to show defeat, to let her win. To drive him from a restaurant he'd eaten in weekly for the past ten years.

She smiled up at them as they approached. "Hello, gentlemen. I saw you walk up and thought rather than wait, you might like to share. I stood in line about twenty minutes myself."

"We'd love to join you," Nick said, flashing her his "Charming Nick" smile. He and Tony slid into the empty side of the booth, leaving Rob no choice but to slide in beside Carrie, which earned each of them a malevolent look.

The booths weren't exactly spacious, and with her briefcase on the seat next to the window, there was no hope of putting any real space between them. She was so close he could feel her body heat, and every time either of them moved, their shoulders or arms bumped.

This day was going from bad to worse.

He refused to acknowledge the scent of her perfume, or shampoo, or whatever it was that had driven him mad the other night, or the lusty urges he was feeling as her leg brushed against his. The desire to run his hand up the inside of her thigh again, until he reached the garter holding up her stockings, had him shifting restlessly in his seat.

"Are we a little antsy?" Carrie asked him, but thankfully, before he had to come up with a viable excuse, the waitress appeared.

"Hey, boys," she said, stopping at the table with a pot

of coffee and four beat-up plastic cups of iced water. What the place lacked in class, it made up for in good food and quality service. "What can I getcha?"

Without even looking at the menu, they all ordered their usual breakfast, and after reviewing the menu, Carrie ordered the special, which was a lot of food for a woman her size.

"I take it you gentlemen come here often," Carrie said, reaching across the table for a coffee creamer, her shoulder bumping against Rob's.

"Best greasy spoon in the greater Chicago area," Tony said. "How did you stumble across it?"

"On my way out I asked Dennis where I could get a decent breakfast." She added a packet of artificial sweetener to her cup. "He told me to come here."

If Dennis wasn't such an exemplary employee, Rob might have considered that grounds for termination.

"So what do you think of Chicago?" Nick asked her.

"It's very cold. And windy."

"They call it the Windy City for a reason," Tony said.

"I'll bet you can't wait to get back to the West Coast," Rob said, and she shot him a sideways glance, as if to say, *Don't you wish.*

"I think I'll like it here," she said. "Though probably more when it warms up a little."

"Do you know where you'll be staying?" Nick asked.

"Not yet. I'm hoping to find a rental. I don't suppose you know a good local agent?"

"My brother-in-law David is in real estate law," Tony said, pulling out his phone. "He could probably give you the name of someone reliable."

He found the number in his address book, and she entered it into her phone.

"I miss the days when we used to write things on paper," Nick said.

"Have you got a piece of paper?" Rob asked, and grinning, Nick held up his napkin. "Pen?"

Nick felt his pockets, then frowned and said, "I used to carry one all the time."

"I would be lost without my phone," Carrie said. "My whole life is in this thing. Of course I keep it all backed up on my laptop, which I also could not live without."

"So what kind of place are you looking for?" Nick asked.

"A two-bedroom apartment or condo, preferably furnished, in a building with a fitness room and a pool, or close to a pool. I like to swim every morning."

"I think I may know just the place," Nick said. "My wife, Terri, has a condo that she's been thinking of putting on the market, but it would probably mean taking a loss. She had entertained the idea of renting it out, but she's heard so many horror stories about bad tenants that she's been hesitant. It has pretty much everything you would need, and there's a fitness center with a pool a couple of blocks away. And it's not too far from work."

It also wasn't too far from Rob's loft, which didn't exactly thrill him.

"It sounds perfect," Carrie said. "I can pay her the full three months up front."

"I'll talk to her today and give you a call."

"Sounds great," she said, exchanging numbers with him, which irritated Rob even more. It was bad enough that she would be around for three months. Did she have to pretend to be so nice to everyone? Which she was clearly only doing to make Rob look like the bad guy.

"So, on the rare occasions that I might have a free day," Carrie said, "what attractions would you gentlemen recommend? There are so many things to do in the city, I wouldn't even know where to begin."

His cousins tossed around suggestions like the planetarium and the aquarium and the Museum of Contemporary Art.

"How about you?" she asked Rob. "What would you suggest?"

"The Museum of Science and Industry."

"Really," she said, looking thoughtful. "For some reason I imagined your preferring someplace a little less… academic. Like a sports museum."

"And you assumed that because, why? You know me so well?"

She looked amused, as if this was some big joke to her.

The waitress dropped their food off at the table and when Rob looked at Carrie's plate, he could feel his arteries tighten. The special consisted of three eggs, four sausage links, hash browns, white toast and a stack of pancakes six inches high. A heart attack on a plate, his fitness instructor would call it. Which was why Rob had ordered his usual egg white vegetarian omelet, lean ham, tomato slices and dry whole wheat toast, of which he would allow himself half a slice. Unlike some people at the table, his goal was to live past his fortieth birthday.

"Do the three of you live in the city?" she asked them, and when her leg bumped his, he wrote it off as accidental, until he felt the brush of one shoeless foot slide against his ankle.

Was she coming onto him?

He shot her a sideways glance, but she was looking at Nick, chewing and nodding thoughtfully as she listened to him describe where each of them lived in relation to Caroselli Chocolate.

Okay, maybe it had been an accident. But what about

the way she just happened to get syrup on her fingers, and instead of wiping them with a napkin, sucked it slowly from each digit, one at a time. Which of course reminded him of her sucking on something else.

He grabbed his iced water and guzzled half the glass.

"Not hungry?" Carrie asked, looking over at his untouched food. He'd been so busy obsessing over her that he hadn't even thought about his breakfast.

"Letting it cool," he told her, forking up a large bite and shoveling it in, burning the hell out of his tongue in the process.

"So I'm under the impression you three aren't just cousins, but good friends," Carrie said.

"What makes you think that?" Tony asked.

"I'm very intuitive about things like that."

"Not so much when we were younger," Nick said. "Mostly because of the age difference, but our family is very close-knit, so we saw each other constantly. But, yeah, we're all pretty close now."

"So, then I guess Robby told you that we had sex on New Year's Eve."

Rob dropped his fork halfway to his mouth, Nick choked on his eggs and Tony nearly sprayed the table with a mouthful of coffee.

"What makes you think I would do that?" Rob said, even though that was exactly what he had done.

She smiled serenely. "As I said, I'm intuitive about that sort of thing."

"He may have mentioned it," Tony said, shrugging apologetically to Rob.

"I hope he also mentioned that we didn't know who the other was until this morning."

"That was fairly obvious," Nick said. "And you really don't have to explain."

"I prefer to get things out in the open. I wouldn't want anyone getting the wrong impression."

"Of course not," Tony said.

"Carrie," Rob started, and she held a hand up to shush him.

"I'm not angry," she said. "Men like to talk about their conquests, I get that. Hell, I called my friend Alice first thing the next morning. It's not as if we ever expected to see each other again. I'd just appreciate if it didn't go any further than this table."

"No one will hear it from me," Tony said.

"Me neither," Nick piped in, looking amused. "What you two do in your free time is no one else's business."

Was she doing this here, now, only so that she would have witnesses? So that if he promised not to say anything, then did, it would make him look like an even bigger jerk than he already might be.

She was good at this. But so was he.

"While we're being so honest, should we tell them what happened in my office this morning?"

Tony shot him a look. "Really not necessary."

"You mean what didn't happen," she said and told Nick and Tony with regret, "We ran out of time."

Both men looked to Rob, waiting for his reply, because obviously he hadn't gotten the response he'd hoped for by putting her on the spot. Did nothing rattle her?

"And it won't be happening again," he said, establishing that he was the one to end it, not her.

"And of course I understand why," she said. "I've learned from experience that it's a terrible idea to engage in a physical relationship with a coworker, especially a subordinate."

Subordinate? She was the subordinate, the temporary

consultant. Did she honestly see herself as ranking higher than him?

"I'd like your opinion on something," Carrie said, leaning forward to address Nick and Tony. "Say you have a one-night stand with a woman. You both know that it's never going to be more than one night. Now, it's the wee hours of the morning, she's asleep and you decide to go. Do you wake her and say goodbye, or maybe leave a note? Or do you just leave without a word?"

Nick glanced over at Rob. "I might get my ass kicked for saying this, but I would definitely wake her and say goodbye."

Carrie turned to Tony. "And you?"

"I would at least leave a note."

Carrie looked over at Rob and gave him a "so there" look.

"Boy, would you look at the time," Nick said, glancing at his wrist when, ironically enough, he wasn't wearing a watch. "Tony, we've got the thing we need to get to."

For an instant Tony looked confused, then he said, "Oh yeah, right, that *thing*. Of course. We wouldn't want to be late for that."

Nick grabbed the check that the waitress had left on the table.

"Here, let me give you cash for mine," Carrie said, reaching into her bag.

"Oh no, this one is on me," Nick said as he and Tony slid out of the booth.

"Thank you," she said. "I'll buy next time."

If there ever was a *next time,* they could count Rob out.

"You two enjoy the rest of your breakfast," Tony told them. As if Rob had any appetite left.

As soon as they were gone he switched to the empty side of the booth, which was actually worse than sitting beside Carrie. The deep cleft of cleavage at the low-cut collar of her top drew his gaze like a moth to a flame. The dull light leaking through the open blinds gave her pale gray eyes an almost-translucent quality.

"Well, that was fun," Carrie said.

"Amused yourself, did you?"

She smiled, sliding her empty plate to the edge of the table as the busboy cleared the dirty dishes and utensils. She sure could put away the food. She had stopped just shy of licking her plate clean.

"Tony and Nick seem like really nice guys," Carrie said. "I take it Tony isn't married."

"No, he isn't."

"Single?"

"Why? Are you interested?"

She cocked her head slightly. "Why? Are you jealous?"

"He just came out of a relationship, and the last thing he needs is someone like you messing with his head."

"Is that what I'm doing?" she asked, resting her elbow on the table and propping her chin in her hand. Then he felt a shoeless foot sliding up his left calf.

Damn her.

When she'd made it up to his knee, and clearly had no intention of stopping, he grabbed her stocking foot and removed it from his leg with a warning look, thankful for his long wool coat to hide anything that had *sprung up*. "You're taking cheap shots."

"Am I?"

"You don't really believe that I'm your subordinate."

The head cocked again. "When did I say that?"

"Just a minute ago. You said it was especially bad to get involved with a subordinate."

"So, from that you assumed I meant you? Had you considered that I was talking *to* you *about* me? Or that maybe

I was speaking in general terms, and not about anyone specific."

Actually no, he hadn't considered that.

"Are you always so hyperdefensive?" she asked.

"Never." Only when he was with her.

"Like I said, this will be as easy or as hard as you decide to make it." Her brow lifted slightly, but by the time he recognized the devilish look on her face, it was too late. He sucked in a surprised breath when he felt her still shoeless foot slide into his lap. "Hard, it is," she said with a smile.

"Would you stop that," he hissed, shoving her foot away from his crotch, hoping no one sitting nearby noticed. Did the woman have no shame? And why could he not think of anything but getting her back to her hotel room, out of her clothes and into bed? "Is this your idea of acting like a professional?"

"I'm simply trying to illustrate a point."

"What point? You're certifiable?"

"That when it comes to our relationship, work or otherwise, you do not always call the shots. Because, Robby, you have some *serious* control issues."

"*I* have control issues? This from the woman who can't keep her foot out of my crotch?"

She just smiled, as if she found the entire situation thoroughly amusing. "I'm going to go. I'll see you bright and early Monday."

"Unfortunately, yes, you will."

She pulled on her suit jacket and coat, and he watched her as she grabbed her bag, slid out of the booth and walked to the door. She stepped outside, her loose hair flying wildly in the brisk wind. She hailed a cab, and only after she climbed inside could he drag his gaze away from the window.

Unpredictable. That's what she was. And while he was

nowhere close to the control freak she'd painted him to be, he did prefer a modicum of consistency.

And if today's behavior was a preview of what he had to look forward to, maintaining control of the situation was his only option.

Five

Carrie sat at the hotel bar, having a celebratory margarita, which at 12:04 p.m. was completely acceptable, even though her internal clock still thought it was two hours earlier.

Even though there had been a few kinks in the process, all in all, she considered this morning's meeting a success. And though she had the tendency—in her stepfather's opinion—to be "mouthy," she felt that under the circumstances, she'd been impressively diplomatic. If she'd left out the part where they attacked each other in Rob's office.

The memory made her cringe. But she had regrouped, damn it, then gone back into that conference room and kicked some major Caroselli ass.

She'd found that in business, her impulsive nature could either be an asset or a liability, with very little gray area. This assignment could be a raging success, or a knock-down, drag-out disaster. So far so good, but honestly, it could still go either way. She had broken the cardinal rule of not sleeping with a coworker. And even though she had done it unknowingly, that didn't make the situation any less complicated.

As much as she hated to admit it, that stunt she'd pulled in the diner could have easily backfired. If he hadn't pulled her foot from his crotch, if he'd instead smiled and suggested they go back to her hotel room, she probably would have dragged him there by his tie. And though the cab ride there would have given them both time to come to their senses, the damage would have been done, and the ball would be in his court now.

Fortunately, the next serve was hers, and she was going for the point.

She licked salt off the rim of her glass and took a sip of her margarita, letting the tangy combination of sweet and salty roll around on her tongue. She glanced over at the businessman three barstools away, who she suspected had been working up the nerve to talk to her.

"Buy you a drink?" he said the instant they made eye contact.

Not only was he twice her age with thinning hair and a belly that sagged over his belt, but he also wore a chunky gold wedding band on his left hand.

Seriously? Did she really look that desperate?

She shook her head and gave him her not-in-this-lifetime look.

Her phone rang and, happy for the interruption, she dug around in her briefcase to find it, smiling when she saw her best friend Alice's number on the screen.

"So how did the meeting go?" Alice asked, and Carrie could picture her stretched out on the sofa in the trendy SoHo loft she shared with her sister, her glossy black hair smooth and sleek and tucked behind her ears. She never sat on a piece of furniture so much as draped herself across it.

At five feet eleven inches, and no more than one hundred and twenty pounds soaking wet, to say that Alice was wispy was an understatement. Hence her very lucrative career as a runway model. In college, where they'd been thrown together by chance as roommates, they had been like Mutt and Jeff. Two women could not have been more different in looks or personality, but with their similar backgrounds involving alcoholic parents, they had instantly bonded and despite living on completely opposite ends of the country, had remained the best of friends. Alice was her only *real* friend.

Normally Alice would be calling her from Milan or Paris or some other fashionably hip location, but a healing broken foot would be keeping her off the runway until the fall.

"They signed the contracts," Carrie told her. "So I'm in Chicago for the next three months."

"That's fabulous!"

"They didn't haggle over money either, which you know I hate. As far as business goes, the meeting itself couldn't have gone more smoothly."

"But?"

"What makes you think there's a but?"

"Gut feeling. I'm right, aren't I?"

She sighed. "I broke my cardinal rule. But it was an accident."

"I must be thinking of a different cardinal rule, because I fail to see how it's possible to *accidentally* sleep with someone."

"Nope, that's the rule. And I'm living proof that it is possible."

"Oh, I can't wait to hear this," Alice said, and Carrie

could just picture her catlike grin, the spark of amusement in her violet eyes—colored contacts of course, although she would deny it if asked.

"It's a little hard to believe," Carrie told her.

"Honey," she said with a laugh, "coming from you, I'd believe just about anything."

"That guy I told you about—Ron."

"Mr. Steamy Sex from the bar?"

"Yeah, well, apparently I heard him wrong. His name was actually *Rob*."

"Oh. And that's a problem because?"

"His name is Rob *Caroselli*. And he's the director of marketing at Caroselli Chocolate."

Alice was a tough person to shock, so her gasp was almost worth the mess Carrie was in.

Okay, maybe not, but it was at least a slight consolation.

Carrie told her the whole story, from the minute Rob walked into the conference room until lunch when she had her foot in his lap.

"Well, you were right about one thing," Alice said. "If anyone but you had told me that story, I doubt I would have believed them. But as impulsive as you are—"

"I'm not *that* impulsive," she argued, signaling the bartender for another drink.

"Your first night in a new city you picked up a total stranger in a bar and invited him back to your room."

Carrie cringed. "Yeah, there was that."

"Not that I'm saying you could have or should have anticipated this happening. That part was just dumb luck. Really, really bad dumb luck."

"But on the bright side, I think that now I've got him right where I want him."

"Until you wind up in bed with him again," Alice said.

"I can't sleep with him again."

"You mean you *shouldn't* sleep with him. Yet you almost went for it in his office this morning. Correct?"

"A moment of weakness. I was still getting over the shock of seeing him again."

"And in the diner?"

"I was making a point."

"And did you make your point?"

"I sure did." Below the waist anyway. "Why do I get the feeling I'm going to regret telling you any of this?"

"Because you know that if I think you're acting like an irresponsible moron, I'm going to tell you."

"And you think I am?"

"I think that you might be backsliding a little. Just remind yourself, you are no longer that lonely little girl who pulls fire alarms and stays out past curfew to get attention. You are a strong, mature woman who is in control of her own destiny."

"I know." But that little girl was still in there, and occasionally she persuaded the confident, mature woman to do some not-so-mature things. "The weird part is that I don't even like him very much. But then I get close to him and I just want to rip his clothes off and touch him all over."

"Probably not a good idea. You know, Rex and I used to have chemistry like that."

Alice's boyfriend, Rex, was an up-and-coming fashion designer whose rising star seemed to be keeping him out of the country more than he was in it lately. And even when he was in town, she didn't seem truly happy.

"When will he be back in New York?" Carrie asked.

"Two weeks. This time he promised."

He had promised her lots of things, and so far he hadn't exactly come through. Alice was beautiful and sophisticated and smart, but had miserably low self-esteem. Because of that, she let the men in her life walk all over her.

All types of men clamored for her attention, yet she always picked the aloof, distant ones whose attention she had to beg for. A fact she was quite aware of. But as Carrie had told Rob, a person could recognize the problem and still not know how to fix it.

"How's the foot healing?" Carrie asked her.

"Slowly. The physical therapy is helping. My doctor assured me that I'll be back on my feet before the shows next fall. It's crazy how you can be walking down the sidewalk, minding your own business, then *pow,* out of nowhere everything changes."

The *pow* in that scenario being the bike messenger who knocked her off the curb into the path of a moving taxi. She was lucky to be alive.

"And speaking of therapy," Alice said, "I have an appointment in an hour, so I should let you go. But I want you to make me a promise. If you get even the slightest urge to jump Mr. Steamy Sex again, I want you to call me immediately so I can talk some sense into you. Anytime, day or night."

"Okay."

"You promise?"

She sighed.

"Carrie?"

"Okay, okay, I promise," she said, hoping it wasn't one of those promises that came back to bite her in the butt.

Two days later Carrie hopped in a cab to meet Nick's wife, Terri, at the condo she hoped would be her new temporary home.

She was pleasantly surprised when the cab pulled up in front of a row of attached, newish-looking, charming brick homes with two-car garages. So far so good.

The homes were still decorated for the holidays. All but

the one the driver stopped at. Which wasn't so unusual considering no one was living there. Still, it looked so forlorn and neglected. But thankfully very well-maintained. At least on the outside.

She paid the driver, realizing that if she didn't want to blow her entire earnings on cab fare, it might be more cost effective to lease a car while she was there. She didn't exactly relish the thought of taking public transportation in the dead of winter either.

She climbed out of the cab and paused on the sidewalk to look up and down the street. All the residences were well-maintained, and a large group of children of various ages played in the snow several doors down, which led her to assume the neighborhood was family-oriented and safe.

She headed up the walk and as she stepped up onto the porch, the front door opened and a woman appeared to greet her.

"Hi. Caroline?"

"Carrie," she said, shaking her hand.

"I'm Terri. Come on in." Like her husband, Terri was tall and dark. She was also very attractive in an athletic, tomboyish way, and not at all the sort of woman she would have pictured Nick with. "Drop your coat anywhere and I'll give you a tour."

Carrie's first impression, as she stepped inside and shrugged out of her coat, was *beige*. Beige walls, beige carpet, beige leather furniture. Even the lamps were beige. And the air smelled like pine cleaner.

"As you can see, I left almost everything here when I moved into Nick's place," she said. "It's nothing fancy."

Carrie draped her coat over the back of the sofa beside Terri's and set her purse on top. "It's nice."

"According to Nick, to say I have the decorating sense of a brick is an insult to bricks."

"I'm no decorating genius either. I paid someone to do my place in Los Angeles. This is simple. Elegant."

"It's boring," Terri said. "And if you don't like it, don't be afraid to say so. You won't hurt my feelings."

She wasn't looking for anything fancy. Just something functional and low-maintenance that wouldn't break the bank. "So far so good."

Terri looked surprised. "You want to see more?"

"Absolutely." She could hate the rest of the condo and she would probably rent it anyway rather than hurt Terri's feelings.

Carrie had a way of reading people, and her first impression of Terri was that she had a tough outer shell but was soft and vulnerable on the inside.

The master suite had slightly more color. A queen-size bed with a pale rose duvet, a chest of drawers in a warm honey pine and a roomy walk-in closet that led to a very clean—and yes, beige—en suite bathroom that smelled of bleach and glass cleaner. The only color was pale pink towels and a pink bath mat. The countertops and walls were bare.

"There are towels, sheets…everything you'll need in the linen closet. I just changed the sheets on the bed and scrubbed the bathroom." Terri smiled sheepishly. "I'm slightly fanatical about keeping things clean and tidy."

"Linen closet?" Carrie asked, gesturing to a pair of louvered doors.

"Laundry." She pulled the doors open to show Carrie a stacked washer and dryer.

"Nice." She didn't miss the days before she had money, when she had to haul her dirty laundry down three flights of stairs and either sit in a dingy little laundry room down below the building in the parking structure, or drive two miles to the nearest Laundromat.

The second bedroom was set up as an office, with a desk, bookcase, file cabinet and printer stand. Again, nothing fancy, but very functional, and the window overlooked a postage-stamp-sized backyard.

"This is perfect," she told Terri.

"This room, you mean?"

"No, the whole place. It's exactly what I need."

"You really think so?"

"I do. Can I see the kitchen?"

"Of course. Right this way."

The kitchen, which was—surprise—also on the pale side, was as clean and organized as the rest of the house, and separated by a wall from the living space. She preferred a more open concept, but how much time would she be spending there really?

"I don't cook, so it's not very impressive," Terri said. "Just your basic pots and pans, dishes and utensils."

"I don't cook very often either," Carrie told her. "I like to, but I never have the time. I typically work eighty-hour weeks."

"I used to be like that, too, but my ob-gyn thinks all the stress is screwing with my cycle, and we're trying to get pregnant. So, I cut my hours way back. Used to be, when you opened the freezer it was full of frozen dinners. Thank goodness for husbands who love to cook. Although I've gained about ten pounds since the wedding."

"How long have you been married?"

"Less than two months."

"Oh, so you're still newlyweds."

"Technically. But we've been best friends since we were nine years old. And I don't want to be one of those moms in her fifties carting her kids to grade school, or pushing seventy when they graduate high school. For a process that's supposed to be so natural, you would not believe how complicated it can be."

It wasn't something Carrie had ever thought about. She didn't know much about pregnancy, or even babies. She just assumed that when you were ready, you had sex at the right time and *poof,* you got pregnant. That was the way it seemed to work for her college friends who had gotten married and started families. Hell, there were even a handful of girls in high school who seemed to have no problems getting themselves knocked up. A few of them multiple times.

"So what do you think of the condo?" Terri asked. "Again, I won't be insulted if you don't like it, or if you'd like to look at other places before making a decision."

"I think," Carrie said with a smile, "I'll take it."

Six

"You're sure?" Terri asked.

Carrie laughed. "Yes, I'm very sure. Did you bring a lease agreement?"

"It's in my coat. I'll get it."

They took a seat at the kitchen table and went over the paperwork. When it came to filling in the price of rent, Terri looked over at her. "So we're talking rent plus utilities, including cable TV and internet."

"Name your price," Carrie told her, and she offered up a sum that seemed awfully low for all of that, especially in the heart of a major city. "Are you sure you don't want more? I don't expect any sort of special treatment. I want to pay what's fair."

"Nick and I talked about it. We're not looking to make a profit, just cover expenses."

"You're positive?"

She nodded. "That's the way things are done in the

Caroselli family. They're a very generous bunch. They suck people into the fold."

"Is a personal check okay?"

"If it bounces, I'll know where to find you," Terri joked.

Carrie wrote the check out for three months' worth of rent, tore it from the book and handed it to Terri, feeling guilty to be paying such a low sum.

"Are you sure you want to pay all three months up front?"

"It's just easier for me that way. One less thing I have to worry about remembering." She slid her checkbook back into her bag. "So when you said that the Carosellis *suck* people in, what exactly did you mean by that?"

She must have looked apprehensive because Terri chuckled and said, "Don't worry, it's nothing creepy or weird. Take me, for example. When I moved to Chicago, I was nine. I had just lost my parents and I was living with an aunt who wasn't exactly thrilled to play Mommy to some bratty kid she had never met before. I guess you could say that I was a lost soul. Then I became friends with Nick, and I met his family, and it was like they adopted me. Nick likes to joke that if his mom had to choose between the two of us, she would pick me."

"That's really nice," Carrie said. "Everyone should have family."

"Do you have a big family?"

"I have a few cousins, and a couple of aunts and uncles spread out across the southwest, but I haven't seen them in years. Mostly it's just me and my mom."

"You're close?" she asked, and when Carrie didn't answer right away, Terri said, "I'm sorry, it's really none of my business. The Carosellis are also very nosy, and I guess it rubbed off on me."

"It's okay. It's just that my relationship with my mom

is a little...complicated. We don't really see each other very often. I work a lot and she spends most of her time in a bottle."

Terri nodded. "Ah, I see."

"There's a lot of resentment from my end, and apathy from hers. I have the typical characteristics of a child with an alcoholic parent." She paused and said, "Was that too much information?"

"No, not at all. I didn't even know there were typical characteristics. Which ones do you have, if you don't mind my asking?"

"I'm super-responsible and I take myself way too seriously. Your basic overachiever. When I'm trying to have fun, I feel as if I should be doing something more constructive. But due to a lack of self-esteem, I feel that nothing I do is good enough. I also have trust issues, so I have trouble forming intimate relationships. And telling you all of this is probably just some unconscious way of mine to push you away before I'm able to form any sort of friendship or bond."

"Wow, that's intense," Terri said.

"Yeah, those psych courses I took in college were a real eye-opener. Up until then, under the circumstances, I figured I was fairly well-adjusted. Psychology was actually my major for a while, until it dawned on me that no one as screwed up as I was had any right to be counseling anyone else. That's an enormous responsibility and there was no way I could trust myself to be completely impartial. So I switched my major to marketing. I'm still using what I learned about psychology, without the possibility of screwing with someone's head." She paused and said, "Well, not in a bad way at least. I just encourage them to buy stuff."

"It seems as though you aren't so screwed up that you

didn't realize you're screwed up." Terri frowned. "Does that make sense?"

"It does, actually."

"Hey, do you have plans for tomorrow night?"

Her first thought was of Rob, which was wrong in so many ways. "Nope. I don't really know anyone in the city."

"Nick and I are having some friends over and I'd really like you to come."

"Really? After everything I just told you?"

"Oh, don't worry. You'll fit right in."

Carrie wasn't quite sure how to take that, then decided it was probably meant as a compliment. "In that case, I'd love to."

"It's at seven," she said, writing down the address. "Do you have a way to get there?"

"I can take a cab."

"Or I could ask Rob to swing by and pick you up. It's on his way."

"Oh, I think it would be better if I took a cab."

"If you're worried about getting home safe, Rob isn't much of a drinker. Come to think of it, I don't recall ever seeing him drunk."

"The night I met him he drank a lot," Carrie said, not even realizing what she was saying until the words left her mouth. Everyone was supposed to think their first meeting was in the conference room.

"Yeah, I heard," Terri said.

She blinked. "You did?"

"Word of advice, if you don't want me to know something, don't tell Nick. We're one of those couples who actually tell each other everything."

"Good to know." Carrie recalled the way she had announced to the entire table at the diner about her and Rob's affair, *and* what happened in Rob's office, meaning Terri probably knew about that, too.

Way to go, genius. What had Alice said about her impulsive tendencies? She really needed to think things through before she opened her mouth. She wondered how many others in the Caroselli family knew.

"Did he happen to tell anyone else?" she asked Terri.

"I doubt it. And I don't think Tony would tell anyone either."

She hoped not. She didn't want people to get the impression she slept around, because nothing could be further from the truth.

"For the record, that's not typical behavior for me," she told Terri.

"And for what's it worth, it's not typical behavior for him either," Terri said. "You must have made quite an impression on him. Personally, I think you two make an adorable couple."

"Oh, but we aren't. A couple, I mean. I make it a rule not to date people I work with. If I'd had even the slightest clue as to who he was when I met him in that bar—"

"Carrie, I understand. Believe me. Maybe it was just… fate."

If it was, fate had played a very cruel trick on both of them. "We couldn't be more wrong for each other. In more ways than I can even count."

"Six months ago, if you had told me I would be married to Nick and trying to have a baby, I would have thought you were nuts. Yet here we are."

"So what happened? What changed?"

"That is a very long story, and I promise to tell you about it when you come to the party tomorrow."

"I hardly know you and you're already blackmailing me?"

Terri smiled wryly. "It's the Caroselli way."

"I'll definitely be there, but I'll find my own ride."

"Well, I should go," Terri said. "If there's anything you need, or if you have a question, just give me or Nick a call."

"It was really nice talking to you," Carrie told her.

"I think so, too," Terri said, looking a little embarrassed. She struck Carrie as the type who probably had more male than female friends. While Carrie had very few of either.

"And thanks for the advice," Carrie said.

"Anytime." Terri pulled on her coat, then fished a set of keys from her pocket and handed them to Carrie. "Those open the front and garage door."

"Thanks. See you tomorrow."

When she was gone, Carrie started to explore the kitchen cabinets, feeling a little like a snoop. But she was sure that Terri would have removed anything of a personal nature before she rented out the condo.

She opened the refrigerator and smiled. On the shelf sat an unopened half gallon of low-fat milk, a dozen organic eggs and a loaf of organic nine-grain bread. One shelf down was a bottle of very expensive champagne.

Terri had gone above and beyond to make her feel welcome, and Carrie hoped they would have time to get to know one another better.

Carrie returned to the hotel to collect her things, then took a cab back to the condo, doing her best to memorize the street names so she could find her way around when she had a car. It had begun to snow, so rather than have the driver track it through the living room and potentially ruin the carpet, she had him leave the bags in the garage.

She opened the door to total darkness, cursing herself for not remembering to leave a light on. She felt around on the inside wall for a light switch. She found it and as she was flipping it upward, she felt a cold hand settle on top of hers.

She shrieked and yanked her hand back, the bright light temporarily blinding her. She blinked hard and when she opened her eyes again, no one was there. She peeked around the corner, but the only thing there was a door. Probably to the basement.

She took a slow, deep breath to calm her pounding heart. It was just her imagination. No one was there. She'd clearly been watching too many episodes of *Ghost Hunter*.

She turned to grab her bags, nearly colliding with the very large person standing there. She shrieked again, then realized that it was only Rob.

"You scared me half to death!" she said.

He wore a long black wool coat and black leather gloves…and an amused grin. Fat flakes of snow dotted his dark hair and he'd left snowy footprints on the garage floor. "A little jumpy?"

"What do you want?"

"What made you scream?"

"*You* did!"

"No, the first time."

"Nothing. I was imagining things."

"Imagining what?"

She shook her head. "*Nothing*. It wasn't real."

He narrowed his eyes. "What wasn't real?"

She blew out an exasperated breath. "If you must know, when I reached around for the light switch, I could swear somebody put their hand over mine, but when I turned on the light, no one was there."

"It must have been the lady in the basement."

She blinked. "The *who?*"

"We call her the lady in the basement. Not everyone senses her. Terri and Nick never did, but a lot of other people have. Sometimes she touches people, some people hear her walking up and down the stairs. Some hear her crying. I smell her perfume."

She couldn't tell if he was being serious or just messing with her. "Really?"

"I can smell it from the instant I step in the garage door until I step into the kitchen. Maybe three feet. Then it's gone. I've felt her brush against me, and once I felt a hand on my shoulder."

"No way." She leaned into the doorway and sniffed, but all she smelled was pine cleaner and bleach.

"You have to actually step inside," Rob said. "Or it doesn't work."

She eyed him skeptically. Had she honestly just rented a house with a dead lady living in the basement? And wasn't that sort of thing supposed to be disclosed before the lease was signed? Or was Rob just full of it?

Of course he was.

"You're lying," she said.

"I'm dead serious. Try it if you don't believe me."

It was walk in this door or walk around to the front door, which would make her look even more ridiculous than she probably did now. So basically she was damned if she did and damned if she didn't.

Promising herself that no matter what happened she would not react, she lifted her foot and stepped up over the threshold, then followed with the opposite foot, and the second it touched the floor—

A hand clamped down over her shoulder, and even though deep down she knew it was Rob, a startled screech ripped from her throat.

Heart pounding, she spun around and gave him a hard shove. "You're an *ass*."

"And you are *way* too gullible," he said, laughing and shaking his head. "I can't believe you fell for that."

"I didn't think it was possible, but I like you even less than I did before."

"It was worth it to see the look on your face."

She stomped into the house and switched on the kitchen light, expecting him to follow. And he did, hauling two of her bags inside with him.

"What are you doing?"

"Where do you want them?" he asked.

She was about to tell him she would do it herself, then thought, what the heck. He might as well get used to following directions from her. "They all go in the bedroom."

He had clearly been there before, because he seemed to know where all the light switches and the bedrooms were located.

She shrugged out of her coat, wondering if she might find a box of tea bags somewhere.

On his second trip through to the bedroom, Rob asked, "Are you sure you packed enough stuff? These things weigh a ton."

"You try packing three months' worth of stuff," she called after him as he disappeared down the hall. "That's a long time to be away from home."

Two of the smaller bags had nothing in them but shoes. One was filled with casual clothes, though she realized now that much of it was too light for the cold weather. She would have to do some clothes shopping, and soon. The rest was work clothes, some of which were also inappropriate for the season. Living in a warmer climate, it was difficult to imagine how cold Midwestern winters could be.

"What are you doing here anyway?" she asked on his final trip back to the garage. "And how did you even know where I was?"

He walked back in with the last two bags. "I talked to Nick."

Of course he would know, because Terri told Nick everything. Not that it was some big secret. She just didn't want Rob thinking it was okay to come by and hassle her whenever he felt like it.

This time she followed him into the bedroom. He set her bags down with the others by the closet, then turned to her.

"Which doesn't explain why you're here," she said, folding her arms, giving him her stern look.

"To give you this." He tugged his gloves off, pulled a flash drive out of his inside coat pocket and handed it to her.

"What is it?"

"The financial reports you asked Elana for."

"Oh. She could have given them to me Monday."

He shrugged. "I figured you would probably want to get an early start on this."

Actually, no, she planned to start Monday, when her contract started. But it was interesting that Rob chose to bring it when he didn't have to.

"Thanks," she said, and crossed the room to set it on the nightstand. But when she turned back around, Rob was no longer standing by the closet. He was in front of the bedroom door, blocking her only exit from the room. And he was wearing that *look*.

All the parts of her that had been craving his touch shivered to attention. What on earth had possessed her to follow him in here? If there was a single worst place for them to be together, it was a bedroom.

Rolling her eyes in response to the visual overture, she walked over to her bags and grabbed one that was filled with shoes. She went into the closet with it, found a good place to put them, then bent at the waist to unzip the bag—

and not just because she was trying to make her butt look good either. One by one she pulled the shoes out, pairing them together on the floor.

She heard him in the bedroom, just outside the closet, the hiss of his arms through the satin lining of his coat sleeves. Okay, so he was taking his coat off. That didn't mean he would try anything. He had been the one to proclaim that it was over the other morning. What was he going to do? Break his own rules? Although it would be fun to turn the tables again and turn him down.

She could do that. Right? All she had to do was call Alice and she would talk her out of it.

Before she could make up her mind, she felt his hands slide around her hips, his fingers gripping as he rubbed his crotch across her behind. He was already noticeably turned on, and she wasn't faring much better.

"Really," she said, looking back at him. "This is so… cliché."

"You're one to talk." He slid his fingers under the hem of her sweater, brushing them across her bare skin. "Besides, you didn't seem to mind it like this the other night."

No, she hadn't, had she? And it was very cliché of him to remind her.

Where the hell was her phone? She needed to call Alice pronto.

As she straightened up, he slid his hands around to her belly, pulling her back against him. Oh, that was nice. But not half as nice as when his hands slid up to cup her breasts a second after.

She sighed and let her head drop back against his chest. "I distinctly recall your telling me that this was not going to happen again. And you were right."

"Well, I changed my mind."

"You can't do that."

"I just did." He tucked her hair to one side, kissed the back of her neck, the heat from his body melting her brain.

"We're coworkers," she reminded him.

"Technically we're not. Not yet. Your contract doesn't officially begin until Monday."

He made a valid point. And because they had already slept together, the pre-working-relationship part was already a lost cause. Right?

So what was the big deal if they did it one more time? If she held it up beside the "big picture," it was a tiny, tiny thing. Barely a blip. And why bother Alice when this was clearly going to be the last time?

His hands were under her sweater now, his hot palms scorching a path across her skin. He nibbled the side of her neck, then sucked hard.

A guy hadn't given her a hickey since she was fifteen, but it was unbelievably erotic to think that he was marking her, branding her as his.

She turned to face him, sliding her arms around his neck. "Okay, but just this one time, and that's it."

"Agreed. Unless we have to do it again tomorrow, because it's only Saturday. Then of course there's Sunday..."

"But not after Monday."

"Definitely." He lifted her right off her feet and carried her to the bed. There was no better way to make a house feel like a home than to have really awesome sex in it.

Seven

Rob tossed her not so gently onto the mattress and pulled his shirt up over his head.

She pulled her shirt off, too, then her bra. "For the record, I still don't like you."

"I know," he said, red-hot lust in his eyes as he unfastened his pants. "Take off your jeans."

She unfastened them and shoved them down, and his dropped to the floor. His pants *and* his underwear.

"This is just sex," she told him, as he tugged her panties down her legs. "We're not friends."

"Definitely not." He knelt at the end of the mattress and began to kiss his way up her legs, pushing them apart as he worked his way higher, and when he reached the apex of her thighs, he kissed her there, then took her into his mouth.

She had forgotten that he had such a talented tongue. But as good as it was, she wanted him inside her when she came, and he must have been thinking the same thing. He moved over her, settled between her open thighs, his weight pressing her into the mattress in the most appealing way.

He took her hands in his and pinned them over her head. "Tell me you want me."

"This was your idea," she said. "So clearly you're the one who wants *me.*"

He lowered his head to lick her nipple, then suck it into his mouth. *Hard.* She gasped and pushed up against his grip.

"Tell me you want me," he said, and the devilish look in his eyes said he would take whatever measures necessary to make her cooperate…like slide his erection against her, teasing her with the tip, until she was restless and needy.

"Fine, I want you," she said, shifting underneath him.

His deadpan expression said that wasn't exactly what he'd had in mind. But there was something else, an undercurrent of emotion that made her wonder if he actually *needed* to hear it.

She looked into his eyes and said, "I want you."

With a swift and not-so-gentle thrust that stole her breath, he was inside of her. Then he pulled back and thrust again and pleasure rippled through her like a shock wave. A few more of those and it would be all over for her. She held her breath, anticipating the next thrust, but instead Rob stopped, cursing under his breath.

"Something wrong?" she asked him.

He looked down at her. "Are you using any kind of birth control?"

She shook her head.

"At present, neither am I, so before it's too late…"

She shoved him off her. "Yes, definitely. Please."

Thank goodness he'd noticed in time. She couldn't even imagine what a disaster it would have been if he hadn't. She was at the worst possible time in her cycle to be taking chances.

If there was a world speed record for rolling on a condom, she was sure he broke it. But this time, as he lowered himself over her, he took things a bit slower. Fast, slow, she didn't care, so long as he was touching her.

"You're so beautiful," he said, his eyes searching her face, as if he were trying to memorize her down to the tiniest detail. Hot friction burned at her core, mounting with every slow, steady thrust. She could feel the pleasure coiling tight, the pressure building. She was going to tell him that they needed to slow down, but it was already too late. Her body, her entire being was sucked under into a whirlpool of pleasure. Rob growled and tensed as he came.

And as good as it felt, she was almost sorry that it was over, that it hadn't lasted longer. Of course, if this was anything like that night in the hotel, they weren't anywhere near finished.

Carrie woke the next morning and sat up in bed, disoriented by the unfamiliar room. Then she remembered that she was living in the condo now. In Chicago.

And last night…

She looked over at the empty spot beside her and sighed. The son of a bitch had sneaked out on her again. She looked around for a note, but once again, he hadn't bothered to leave one.

It figured.

In a huff, she tugged on her robe and trudged sleepily to the kitchen to make a pot of coffee. There was a handwritten note stuck to the refrigerator door with a magnet:

*Sorry, had to work. I had a great time last night.
Left at 7, no skulking involved. Wanna not be friends
again tonight after the party?*

It was silly, but the fact that he'd listened, and really
heard her, that he remembered to leave a note this time,
and especially one so sweet and funny, made her dislike
him a little less. And that scared her. What they were
doing now was simple and impartial. It didn't mean anything, which made it very, very safe. But what if they really started to like each other?

Oh, what was she worried about? The next time she saw
him he would say something rude or chauvinistic and she
would be back to hating him.

Carrie showered and dressed, and was standing in the
kitchen getting ready to call a cab to take her to the nearest mall when she heard a creaking sound, as if someone
had opened the inside garage door. Expecting to see Rob,
or even Terri, she stepped around the corner, but there
was no one there and the door was still shut and locked
from last night.

What the—

That was when she looked over at the basement door
and realized it was open. But it had been closed and latched
when they came in last night. She recalled feeling the hand
over hers and her heart skipped a beat. It was possible that
Rob had opened it this morning before he left. But why?

The more likely and logical explanation was that the
door wasn't latched all the way and had drifted open.

She grabbed the doorknob and pulled it closed, making sure that it really latched this time. Feeling better, she
called the cab and left to go shopping. She found herself
some nice casual things, and most of them from the clear-
ance rack.

She forgot all about the basement door until she was in the kitchen fixing herself a cup of hot tea later that evening, and she had the sudden, eerie sensation that someone was watching her.

She knew she was just imagining things, but feeling the tiniest bit apprehensive anyway, she edged her way over and peered around the edge of the wall…sighing with relief when she found the door firmly latched.

Of course it was still closed, and the hand she'd felt had just been her imagination. She felt silly for believing it could be anything else.

The kettle whistled, and she shut off the burner. She poured water into her cup, and was about to take a sip when she heard it. The distinct creak of a door.

No way. She had to be imagining it.

She forced herself to walk over and peek around the wall.

"I'll be damned," she said into the silence. The basement door was open again.

Rob knocked on Carrie's front door at ten minutes to seven.

She opened the door a crack and peeked out, blinking with surprise. "What are you doing here?"

"Picking you up for the party."

She narrowed her eyes at him. "I'm confused."

"The party at Nick and Terri's. You are going, aren't you?"

"Yes, but I told Terri I would find my own ride."

"Well, I didn't talk to Terri."

"Oh. So why are you here?"

"To save you cab fare. Because it was on my way. To be nice." He shrugged and said, "Pick one."

"To get laid."

"That would work, too." He stamped his feet to keep the blood from freezing in his veins. "Whatever it takes for you to let me inside before my feet freeze to the porch."

She hesitated. "We are not friends."

"I'm well aware of that."

She finally moved back to let him in. He stepped inside and she shut the door. When he saw what she was wearing, he nearly swallowed his own tongue. In a figure-hugging denim miniskirt, knee-high spike-heeled boots and a clingy pink sweater, she clearly had no qualms about showing off her figure. "Wow. You look nice."

"You don't think it's too much?"

Even if it was, he would pay her to keep wearing it. Each time he thought he'd seen her at her sexiest, she managed to outdo herself.

"If we drive there together, people are going to get the idea that we're a couple," she said.

He shrugged. "Does it really matter what anyone thinks?"

"It's different for you. You're a man. If you score with a woman at work, you're a stud. If I do that, I'm a slut."

"Really. Was there a particular woman at work that you're interested in?"

She rolled her eyes. "You know what I mean."

"We could just tell people the truth, and say that I picked you up because it was on my way. Or, if it makes you feel better, you can go in first, and I can come in a few minutes later."

"That could work," she said. "And even if people suspect we're together, they'll eventually get the idea that we don't like each other. At all."

"Exactly. Get your coat."

She hesitated. "Before we go, I have to ask you something."

"Okay."

"You have to promise not to make fun of me."

Oh, this should be good. "All right. I promise."

"When you told me that thing about the lady in the basement, you really were kidding, right?"

"Of course I was kidding. Why? Did you feel the hand again?"

"No, I did not."

"But something happened, didn't it?"

"At first I thought it was a fluke…"

"What?"

"The basement door has been sort of…opening by itself."

He cast her a disbelieving look.

"I'm dead serious. I close it, then check it a little while later, and it's open like an inch or two."

"You probably aren't latching it all the way."

"No, I most definitely did latch it."

"If you did, it wouldn't have opened."

She propped her hands on her hips, glaring at him. "Are you honestly suggesting that I am incapable of latching a door?"

It was more plausible than the door opening by itself. "Let's take a look at it," he said. She followed him through the kitchen, her heels clicking on the tile floor. The basement door was open about an inch.

"See?" she said. "I closed and latched it less than fifteen minutes ago."

She was letting her imagination get the best of her. He pulled it closed and made sure that it was latched securely. He tried to open it without turning the knob and it wouldn't budge. There was no way that door would open without someone physically turning the handle. "Okay," he said, watching the knob. "Let's see it open."

"It doesn't work that way. I sat and watched it for like fifteen minutes and it didn't move, so I walked away. Five minutes later it was open again."

"Then let's go in the other room."

"I have to finish getting ready."

He looked her up and down. "You look ready to me."

That earned him another eye roll. "If you want to drive me, you'll have to wait."

It wasn't that he wanted to drive her. It just seemed rude not to. And if it increased his chances of getting her naked again tonight, why the hell not?

Knowing how long women could take getting ready, he shrugged out of his coat and made himself comfortable on the sofa. After a moment or two, curiosity got the best of him. He pushed himself up from the sofa and quietly sneaked through the kitchen to look around the corner. The basement door was as he'd left it. He tried the knob and it was securely latched.

As he suspected, there were no supernatural forces at work here. She had probably been in a rush and hadn't latched it, or maybe she really didn't know how to properly latch a door.

He went and sat back down on the sofa to wait for her, checking the door two more times with the same results. It was still closed tight.

Carrie reemerged several minutes later, pulling on her coat. If she'd done anything different to her appearance, he couldn't tell. Maybe she was one of those women who just didn't feel the night was complete unless she made a man wait for fifteen or twenty minutes.

"So, did you check the door?" she asked him.

"Three times. It didn't budge."

Looking discouraged, she said, "I *swear* it opened by itself."

He shrugged. "I don't know what to say. If it had mysteriously opened I would have told you."

"I *did* close it all the way."

"Okay."

"But you don't believe me."

"I didn't say that."

"You didn't have to." Exasperated, she looked over at the clock and said, "We had better go."

She grabbed her clutch from the coffee table. "I want to go out the garage door so I can grab the opener. If we're going to 'not be friends' after the party tonight, I want you to put your car in the garage."

"Why?"

She shot him a look.

Clearly she didn't want anyone to know he was there. Like he would argue over such an inconsequential detail when sex was involved. "Fine. Paint it camouflage for all I care."

He grabbed his coat and was tugging it on as they walked through the kitchen to the garage door, and she stopped so abruptly that he actually ran into her.

"Rob, that's really not funny," she said, looking at the basement door. Someone or something must have been making a point because the door wasn't open an inch or two this time. It was open all the way.

Eight

"It opens by itself?" Terri looked as skeptical as Rob had when Carrie told him about the basement door. They stood in Terri and Nick's kitchen with several of their friends, including Tony's sister Elana, and a guy named Mark who was making no secret of the fact that he found Carrie attractive. He was cute in an average way. Average height, average weight, naturally blond hair that was thinning a bit on top. And though he went a little gung ho with the aftershave, he seemed very nice, if not slightly forward in his intentions. But when he stood close to her, the air didn't crackle with energy, and her heart didn't beat faster, and when he touched her arm, her skin didn't shiver with awareness. In other words, he was no Rob.

She had already formed a gentle rejection in case Mark asked her out. Which seemed inevitable at this point.

"I take it that never happened when you lived there," Carrie said.

Terri shrugged. "If it did I never noticed. Far as I remember, the door was always closed. I hardly ever go down there. I mostly just use it for storage."

"Storage of what?" Elana asked. "Human remains?"

Terri shot her a withering look. "Old furniture."

Lisa, who worked in Nick's department at Caroselli Chocolate, asked, "Haunted furniture?"

"Not that I know of. But some of it is pretty old. Things my aunt had in her attic when she died. Stuff that has been in the family for a couple hundred years. I doubt I'll ever use any of it, but it seemed wrong to sell it."

Carrie glanced over to the living room where Tony, Rob and a very attractive Asian woman Carrie hadn't yet been introduced to stood by the sofa talking. The woman had come to the party late, and whoever she was, Rob seemed utterly enthralled by what she was saying, hanging on her every word.

Abruptly, as if he'd sensed her eyes on him, Rob looked over at Carrie and caught her staring. The corner of his mouth tilted into a wry smile.

Even though they had arrived together, they hadn't said more than ten words to each other in the two hours they had been there. A few times when he'd walked past, his arm had brushed hers, and once, when they reached into the chips bowl at the same time, their fingers touched. He'd given her his "look" and all she'd been able to think about since then was how they would go back to her place and "not be friends" all night long.

As far as she had seen, Rob had been nursing the same drink since they arrived, confirming what Terri had told her about his not being much of a drinker. Carrie on the other hand was on her fourth glass of wine. Each time she drained her glass, Mark would automatically refill it.

She was beginning to think that he was trying to get her drunk. He seemed a bit tipsy himself.

"Anything else weird happen?" Terri asked her.

"There was one other thing. I was in the garage and reached inside to feel around for the light switch, and I felt a hand settle on top of mine. A very cold hand."

"Eew," Elana said with a shudder, rubbing her arms. "That just gave me goose bumps."

"Me, too," Terri said. "I definitely never experienced anything like that, and if I had, I think I probably would have moved. In fact, if you want to look for a different place, I totally understand."

"The idea that someone or something is there is a little creepy," Carrie admitted. "But I don't get a negative vibe. I don't feel threatened at all. Or even scared."

"Have you been down in the basement?" Mark asked.

"I don't know if I'm that brave," she said.

He slipped an arm around her shoulder, grinned down at her and said, "I'll protect you."

The strong scent of liquor on his breath actually burned her eyes. She waited for him to remove his arm, but he left it there. It didn't feel *awful* exactly. Just a little…awkward. And not sexually stimulating in the least. Which had her automatically looking over at Rob, who was leaning in somewhat close to the Asian woman. He laughed at something she said, then slipped an arm around her shoulder.

Carrie tried to ignore an annoying little jab of jealousy. Whom he did or didn't hook up with at a party was none of her business. Although at the rate things were going, she might be taking a cab home and spending the night alone. Which was fine. He hadn't promised that they would spend the night together. In fact, it was probably better if they didn't.

And if that was true, why did she feel so crummy?

"We should call a medium," Elana said.

"As opposed to a small or a large," Mark joked, but no one laughed.

Elana rolled her eyes. "Like the one on that cable show who talks to the dead."

"I've seen that show," Terri said. "But isn't she in New York?"

"Long Island," Elana said. "I wonder if there's a reputable one in Chicago?"

"Or maybe you need an exorcist," Mark joked, the weight of his arm making her shoulder ache. It seemed that now he was leaning on her more for support, to stay upright.

"Whatever it is, I don't think it's evil," Carrie said, shifting away, only to have him lean more heavily on her. She glanced over at Rob. He laughed at something the Asian woman said, then kissed her cheek.

Yep, she was definitely on her own tonight. She tried not to let herself feel too disappointed. It would have ended Sunday anyway.

"We should have a séance," Elana suggested. "Do they still sell Ouija boards? I used to have one when I was a kid. Until *Nonna* found it and freaked out. She was very superstitious."

"Did you ever actually talk to the spirits with it?" Lisa asked.

"We used to pretend we did to scare each other, but I'm pretty sure everyone was moving the little plastic thing on their own."

"Whatever it is down there, maybe disturbing it would be a bad idea," Terri said.

And because she was the one who lived there, Carrie added, "I agree. I have no problem sharing, as long as it stays in the basement. I'll stay out of its way if it stays out of mine."

She had that feeling of being watched, but when she turned to look at Rob, his attention was on his companion. All this talk of ghosts and the supernatural was making her paranoid.

The weight of Mark leaning on her shoulder was not only uncomfortable, but it was also starting to grate on her nerves, and his cloying aftershave was giving her a headache. At the risk of him falling over, she swiftly ducked from under his arm. He teetered, then caught his balance on the edge of the counter.

"Bathroom?" she asked Terri. She didn't have to go, but she needed a minute or two of fresh air.

"Down the hall on the left," Terri told her, "and if that one is busy, there's one in my office and another in the master bedroom, through the closet." She lowered her voice and said, "If Mark is annoying you, just tell him to back off. He's a decent guy when he's not drinking. Unfortunately, that isn't very often."

In that case, Carrie was less worried about hurting his feelings. The last thing she needed or wanted was another alcoholic in her life, complicating things. "Thanks, I will."

As she headed down the hall, her phone started to ring. She checked the display and saw that it was Alice. Again. Out of guilt she had been avoiding her calls. She would talk to her next week, when she could honestly say that she wasn't sleeping with Rob. It was just too difficult to explain.

The first bathroom was occupied, so she tried the door on the right at the end of the hall and found herself in the master bedroom. Feeling a little weird being in someone else's bedroom, she crossed the room and walked through the closet to the bathroom. She stepped inside and was about to close the door, when someone on the other side pushed it open. She felt a sudden stab of alarm, thinking it was probably Mark. But it was Rob who stepped inside.

"You startled me," Carrie said, a hand pressed over her cleavage, in the exact spot he wanted to bury his face.

"Were you expecting Mark?" Rob asked, closing and locking the door behind him. "You two were looking awfully cozy."

She folded her arms and stuck out her chin. "Jealous?"

"Not at all, because we both know he's not half the man that I am."

"Maybe I think he is," she said, but her eyes betrayed her, just as they had in the kitchen, when Mark was hanging all over her. He could tell that she was as annoyed as he had been.

"No, you don't. That's why you couldn't keep your eyes off me."

"What are you doing in here anyway? Shouldn't you be out talking to your girlfriend?"

He paused for a second, then said, "Don't worry, she'll be along in a minute. All three of us disappearing at the same time would be way too obvious."

All *three* of them? She blinked, then glanced at the door. "That had better be a joke."

"What's the matter?" he said, walking toward her, grinning when she backed away from him. "You don't like to share?"

"You're not funny, you know."

"My 'girlfriend' is Megan."

"Okay."

"Megan Caroselli. My sister."

She blinked again, looking confused, then said, "Oh."

"My *adopted* sister."

She nodded and said, "Okay," as if it suddenly made sense.

He stepped closer, backing her against the countertop. "I like that you were jealous, though."

"I was not jealous," she said, jutting that chin out again.

He wasn't buying the tough act. "You want me," he said.

She rolled her eyes. "Could you be more arrogant?"

He grinned, reaching up to cup her cheek in his palm, swiping his thumb across her lower lip. All he'd been able to think about since he showed up at her place was getting her out of her clothes and back into bed. Staying away from her all evening, pretending he wasn't lusting after her, had been torture. And apparently he hadn't done a very good job of hiding his feelings where Nick was concerned.

Nick had cornered him about an hour ago and said, "Why don't you go over and talk to her?"

"Who?" Rob asked.

"You know damn well who. You two can't keep your eyes off each other."

He didn't see any point in lying to his cousin. "She doesn't want people to think we're involved."

"Anyone with eyes and half a brain is going to eventually notice that you two are lusting after each other. Hell, the temperature in the room rises a good ten degrees when you get within five feet of each other."

Rob honestly hadn't realized it was so obvious, and had been diligent about not going near her or even looking at her for the past hour or so—which had been a lot more difficult than he would have anticipated. Especially when Mark started to put the moves on her. But it seemed as though the more Rob ignored her, the more he lusted for her. When she finally brushed Mark off, Rob had been about ten seconds from punching him in the nose. And though he hadn't actually planned to follow Carrie to the bathroom, his feet had carried him there.

"We can't do this here," Carrie said, yet when he leaned in and kissed the side of her neck, she put up zero resistance. "Someone will hear us."

"We'll be quiet," he said, nuzzling her ear, breathing in the scent of her perfume. "You smell good."

"Rob, stop."

He should have cared who heard, but he didn't. He turned her so she was facing the mirror, watched her over her shoulder. "Say that like you mean it and I will."

"I mean it," she said, but he could tell that she didn't. She just didn't want to admit it. Didn't want to let down her guard and surrender herself to the desire that was eating them both alive.

He reached around to cup her breasts, squeezing the firm mounds. She moaned and her eyes rolled closed. Her hands fisted stubbornly rather than touch him, but they didn't push him away either. He couldn't be in the same room with her for very long without putting his own hands all over her. Which could be a major problem come Monday when they were forced to work together.

He pulled her against him, grinding his erection against her backside, and when she still wouldn't give in, he shoved his hands up under her sweater. He freed her from the lace cups of her bra, and as he palmed her bare breasts, she lost it. She moaned and slid her hands up, hooking them around his neck, pulling his head down for a hot and hungry kiss. He yanked the hem of her miniskirt up her thighs, growling when he saw her bare bottom and realized she wasn't wearing panties.

"I didn't have a clean pair," she said, which they both knew was a lie.

"Sure you didn't." He slipped a hand between her

thighs, watching her in the mirror as he stroked, as her cheeks flushed a deep crimson. "Still want me to stop?"

She clearly had lost the will to fight, grinding her ass against the front of his jeans. "Make it fast, before someone realizes we both disappeared."

He unfastened his pants, pulled out the condom he'd put in his pocket and rolled it on. He bent her over the vanity, grabbed her hips and slammed into her. She cried out and bucked her head back, bracing her hands on the vanity edge, meeting him thrust for thrust. Never before had he been so rough with a woman. In his mind women were soft, delicate creatures who required the utmost sensitivity. But with Carrie…he didn't even know how to put it into words. He wanted to dominate her and…*take* her. Make her scream in ecstasy, surrender her body and her mind to him. Her soul. And the more she resisted, the more determined he was to break her.

Their difference in height was making his calves cramp up and throwing off his concentration. He turned Carrie around to face him, lifted her up off her feet and pinned her against the wall next to the shower. Her legs clamped around his hips, nails dug into his shoulders as he thrust inside of her. She murmured encouragement, words like "harder" and "faster," and a few others that he would never use in mixed company. She let him know exactly what she wanted, and how she wanted it. And he couldn't stop now if his life depended on it. Some repressed, primal need had taken over, was driving him past the boundaries of decency. He wanted to put his hands all over her, make her writhe and scream and beg him for more. He'd been with his share of women, yet until that night in her hotel room, he'd had no idea that sex could be so intensely erotic. That he could not just want a woman, but *need* her. In a way that was so primal even he didn't understand it. For a man who thrived on staying in control, being trapped under the spell of a woman, especially one as independent as Carrie, was a place he had never imagined himself. And as hard as he tried he couldn't seem to fight it.

Hell, he wasn't even sure that he *wanted* to anymore.

When he had reached the absolute limit of his control, as sweet release pulled tight in his groin, Carrie smothered a moan against his shoulder and shuddered in his arms, her body clamping around him like a vise, milking him into ecstasy. His orgasm was so intense and draining, his legs so shaky afterward, he had to set her down for fear of dropping her on the hard tile floor.

They were both sweaty and breathless, and crimson blotches stained Carrie's cheeks.

"What is the matter with us?" Carrie said in a harsh whisper, tugging her skirt back down. "We just had sex in your cousin's *bathroom.*"

"I know," he said, cleaning up before he zipped himself back into his pants.

Carrie adjusted her bra, tugging the cups back into place. "And you don't see anything wrong with that?"

"I'm just as baffled by this as you are," he said, tucking his shirt in.

"So what are we going to do about it?" she demanded, finger-combing her hair, smoothing away the just-had-sex look.

"Well, right now, I'm going to walk back out to the living room. After a minute or two you'll follow me. You'll tell me you aren't feeling well, and ask me if I'll drive you home. I'll roll my eyes and act indignant, then we'll leave and go to your place. And when we get there we're going to do this again, only this time we can make as much noise as we'd like."

She paused to consider that for several seconds, and

must have determined that it was a good plan, because she gave him a not-so-gentle shove toward the door and said, "What are you waiting for? Get out there."

Nine

The most intense sexual experience of Carrie's life was officially over.

Or so she and Rob had established this morning before he went home to get ready for work. And now, as she walked from the cab to the Caroselli building, after spending nearly twenty-four hours together in bed with him, they had to make everyone believe that they were nothing more than coworkers. At first she didn't think it would be a problem, because she didn't even like him—which she couldn't deny was what had made him so appealing. As a rule she didn't date nice guys. In fact, she avoided them like the plague. She dated jerks. Men who treated her like crap.

Rob seemed to have so much "creep" potential, but then everything had changed. Not only could they burn up the sheets together, but she was beginning to suspect that he was a genuinely nice guy. Under normal circumstances she just wouldn't see him again. If he called or texted, she would ignore him until he got the hint and gave up. That wouldn't be so easy with Rob. Not when she had to interact with him daily, five days a week or more, for the next three months.

He'd even offered to pick her up and drive her to work, because it was on his way, and she'd had to gently remind him that they couldn't be seen together outside of the office. She'd taken a cab instead, and planned, during her first free moment, to arrange for a rental or short-term lease. And because she was a novice at driving in the snow, preferably something four-wheel drive and built like a tank.

Dennis nodded and smiled as she walked past him to the elevator and pushed the button for the third floor. Feeling just the tiniest bit apprehensive she rode up. When she entered the reception area, Sheila greeted her with a smile and said, "Rob would like to see you first thing."

"Thanks," she said, returning the smile. Did Rob not realize that until he gave her a place to work, she had nowhere to go but his office?

She walked down the hall and stepped inside his outer office, where a stern-looking secretary sat. She glanced up from her computer, gave Carrie a quick once-over and seemed to determine that she didn't like her—or so her sour expression would imply. "Go on in, he's expecting you."

Definite tension with this one, which undoubtedly meant that she was loyal to her boss, the one whose work Carrie was here to criticize.

"Thank you, Ms...." Even though the woman's name-plate was in plain sight on her desk, it didn't hurt to break the ice.

"*Mrs*. White," she said, icicles dripping off each word.

Ignoring her frosty introduction, Carrie smiled. "It's

a pleasure to meet you, Mrs. White. I'm Caroline Taylor, but everyone calls me Carrie."

"Ms. Taylor," she said with a curt nod.

This one would be a tough egg to crack, but Carrie would do it. She had a way of putting people at ease, winning them over. Look how well it had worked on Rob.

A little *too* well.

Only as she approached his office door was Carrie hit with a sudden and intense wave of apprehension. Which was silly given their history. Or maybe what she was really feeling was exhilaration. She could barely go five minutes without thinking of him, without recalling the way he touched her, how he looked tangled in the sheets, ripples of muscles under smooth, sweat-soaked skin.

But it was over now and she would just have to learn to rein in her wandering thoughts.

Steeling herself, she knocked sharply on the door, then let herself in, melting when she saw Rob sitting there, tapping away at his keyboard, a steaming cup of coffee beside him on his desk.

"You asked to see me?" she said, catching the subtle scent of his aftershave, wishing she could run her hand over his smooth, freshly shaved cheek. Even though she couldn't deny that the rasp of the dark, wiry stubble he'd woken up with this morning had been a turn-on.

Without looking up, he nodded and said, "Be with you in just one second...."

She stood waiting while he typed a bit more, manipulated the mouse for several seconds, frowned, then started typing again. All she could see was the back of the computer monitor, so she had no clue what he might be working on. Or if it even was work. For all she knew he could have been updating his status on Facebook, or corresponding with his online sweetheart. Even though he swore he didn't have a girlfriend. Maybe this would be easier if he did.

While she waited she gazed around his office, which she hadn't really taken the time to notice the last time she was there. In her own defense, it was tough to concentrate on the decor when Rob's hand was up her skirt.

The room was neat, with an unmistakable masculine feel, but not so macho that she had the urge to stuff a wad of chewing tobacco in her cheek. The dark mahogany furniture gave the space a rich, professional feel, but a collection of family photos hanging on the wall and various live plants created a casual atmosphere.

When Rob finally seemed satisfied with what he'd typed, he pushed the keyboard tray in, rose to his feet and greeted her with a very professional "Good morning."

"Sorry I wasn't here sooner. The cab was late picking me up." She waited for him to say something about how, if she'd accepted a ride from him, she wouldn't be late.

He didn't. He just shrugged and said, "No problem."

"What's on the agenda this morning?" she asked, eager to get to work, to keep her mind busy on other things.

"We have a meeting in the conference room in five minutes." He eyed the coat draped over her arm and the briefcase slung over her shoulder. "Why don't I show you to your office first."

He led her down the hall toward the conference room, the scent of his aftershave intoxicating, the casual confidence in his movements mesmerizing. She imagined that once they were in her office he would close the door and pull her into his arms. He would kiss her and tell her that he couldn't keep his hands off her, that he couldn't live without her and that he would die if he couldn't have her again.

When they reached the end of the hall, he hung a left

and gestured to the first office on the right-hand side. "Here it is."

Not only did he not pull her into his arms, but he also didn't even step into the room with her. He waited in the hall while she looked around.

"Will it suffice?" he asked.

It was about half the size of Rob's office and generically outfitted with a desk, bookcase and metal file cabinet. The walls were white and bare, and the carpet an office-gray Berber. Nothing special but functional. "It'll do just fine."

"Great. While you settle in I'll be in the conference room."

He started to turn and before she knew what she was doing, she heard herself say, "Rob, wait."

He turned back to her. "Yes?"

Okay, now what? She wanted to say something, she just didn't know what, or if she even should.

He was standing there, waiting patiently for her to continue, so she blurted out, "I'll need a few things, like Wi-Fi passwords, and I'll need access to a printer."

"We'll discuss all of that in the conference room." He paused, then said, "Anything else?"

Yes, there was something else, she just didn't know how to put it into words. Not without making herself look clingy and pathetic. She forced a smile and shook her head. "No, nothing."

"Then I'll see you down there."

Feeling disappointed for no good reason, she hung her coat on a hook behind the door and stowed her purse in the bottom drawer of her desk. She would need everything in her briefcase for the meeting, so she held on to it.

She had never before questioned her ability to do her job, but as she walked down the hall alone to the conference room, nerves jabbed away at her confidence. Maybe it was the complicated nature of her relationship with Rob that was getting in the way. Yes, they had ended their sexual relationship, but there were still feelings there. It would take time for them to go away completely. And maybe it was a little late to consider this, but what if the past few days hadn't been about sexual attraction as much as his using her to learn her weaknesses? Maybe he would use that information against her to discredit her in front of the people in his department.

Maybe all the while that she had been gushing over what a nice guy he was, it had been an act to lull her into a false sense of security.

A possibility she probably should have considered before she surrendered to him body and soul.

She stopped just outside the conference room door, suddenly convinced she had made a horrible mistake. That by letting her emotions get the best of her, she was about to walk into her worst nightmare. It was imperative that no matter what, she not let anyone see the pain that such a betrayal would cause her.

Taking a deep breath, she stepped into the conference room, head held high, shoulders squared. Rob and three other people sat around the conference table. Her first surprise was that he wasn't sitting at the head of the table, where she would have expected him to be. Her second was that she was greeted with smiles and not scowls when Rob said, "Everyone, this is Caroline Taylor. Over the next three months I expect you to give her your full cooperation."

Huh?

Full cooperation? He wasn't going to give her a hard time? Make her feel unwelcome as he had last week? He was actually going to be nice about this? And why did it suddenly make him about a million times *more* appealing.

Now she was thinking that it would be better if he'd been a jerk. But it was still early. He still had time to knock off some rude or scathing comments. Hell, he had three whole months to prove what a creep he really was. Maybe she had just seen him on his best behavior.

He introduced his team—Alexandra "call me Al" Lujack, Will Cooper and Grant Kelley. They each looked to be in their mid to late twenties and couldn't have been more than a few years out of college.

"Have a seat," Rob said, gesturing to the head of the table, surrendering his authority to her. Crap, he was even nicer than she thought.

She chose the chair beside Al instead and pulled what she needed from her case. "First, I'd like to say that I'm very happy to be here, and I'm looking forward to working with all of you. I want everyone to know it's not my intention to come in and take over the department or diminish anyone's authority. I believe that teamwork is the only way to accomplish goals, and that means I like to hear ideas from everyone. The first six to eight weeks we'll spend analyzing the data, longer if we have to, then we'll discuss our findings, and together outline a viable plan. Does that work for everyone?"

Looking skeptical, Grant asked, "Will it really take that long?"

"It will if we're thorough, and bear in mind we'll be going back twenty years."

There were looks of surprise all around.

"Why so far?" Al asked. "Wouldn't data that old be irrelevant?"

"Not at all. There are many factors we need to consider, and I don't want to risk missing a thing. This will explain my methods." She passed around the folders she had created, outlining all the data they would need and why.

Several minutes passed as they reviewed the material, and Grant said, "As deep as you're digging, compiling data that old could be tricky."

"I have complete faith in everyone."

"As do I," Rob added, going to bat for her once again.

They spent the rest of the day in the conference room, calling in for lunch. She hadn't exactly been sure what kind of leader Rob would be, but from what she could tell so far, he was firm but fair, and it was obvious that his employees respected him. And while they may not have trusted her, they definitely trusted him. And he seemed to, if not trust her, be giving her the benefit of the doubt.

The meeting broke up at six, and everyone went home, or so Carrie assumed. She planned to work only another hour or so, then head home, but when she checked the time later, it was nearly eight-thirty.

"Planning on staying all night?"

Startled, she looked up to find Rob leaning in her office doorway, jacket off, tie loosened, looking too darn yummy for his own good. The dark shadow of stubble across his jaw gave him that I'm-too-sexy-for-my-suit look.

There probably wasn't anyone left in the building....

Carrie, don't even go there.

"I thought everyone had left for the night," Carrie said, and Rob struggled to keep his gaze above her neck, and not on the pillows of cleavage pushing against the form-fitting nylon top she wore under the suit jacket that was now hanging on the back of her chair. Her suit was another story altogether. Unlike last week's shapeless, unflattering garment, this one had a fitted jacket with a tapered waist, and a hip-hugging skirt that reached only midthigh. Her hair was up, but this time it looked looser and sexier somehow. Or maybe it was the same and he was seeing her differently now.

She managed to look both professional and sexy as hell.

It had been torture, not to mention distracting, but he'd managed to keep his hands and eyes off her all day. Well, maybe not his eyes, not completely, but he was careful not to be too obvious.

"I'm here until eight or nine most nights," Rob told her.

"No wonder you don't have a girlfriend," she said, closing her laptop.

That was part of the reason. A fairly large part, actually. "I'm heading home and I thought you might like a ride. No one is here to see us in my car together. Unless that's not the real reason you turned down a ride this morning."

"Of course it's the reason," she said, looking indignant. "What other reason would there be?"

He shrugged. That was the million-dollar question.

She had insisted that they end their affair, that it was the only way to keep a civilized work environment, and claimed she would have no problem with pesky residual feelings. Because while she admitted that they were incredibly good in bed together, she still didn't "like" him. But when he'd asked how she could sleep with someone whom she didn't even like, she'd admitted that she didn't actually dislike him either. He had the feeling that she liked him more than she was letting on.

He could honestly say that he had never met anyone quite like her. And because they had such an intense sexual attraction, and neither was looking for any kind of commitment that extended past the bedroom door, he didn't see the harm in continuing to fool around the full three months that she was here, or at least until they grew tired of each other. But he was honoring her wishes and keeping his distance. For the most part.

"If there is no other reason, then you have no reason to say no to a ride home," he said, and he could see that he had her.

"I guess that would be okay, as long as it's just a ride."

He shrugged. "What else would it be?"

She gave him that look, like he knew damn well.

If someone would be making a move tonight, or any other night, she could rest easy that it wouldn't be him. When he was through with her, she would be begging for it.

"In that case, I'll meet you by the elevator in ten minutes."

"Make it fifteen," he said, just to be difficult. Even he had to have a little fun.

"Fine, fifteen," she agreed, looking exasperated.

Rob went back to his office and finished up a few things, and about twenty minutes later walked to the elevator. She was already standing there waiting, but to her credit she didn't point out that he was late, though he could tell that she wanted to. She had no idea just how easy it would be to ruffle her feathers.

They rode the elevator to the garage, and as the doors opened they stepped off into a wall of icy-cold air.

She shivered under her heavy coat. "I don't think I'll ever get used to this cold."

"Try wearing a hat," he said. "And invest in a well-insulated pair of boots."

"I might just try that," she said, hurrying along beside him to his car. Which was hard to miss being the only one in the lot.

"What happened to the Mercedes?" she asked, as they approached his Escalade.

"They were calling for snow today. This handles better."

When they buckled in with the engine running and the seats warming, she told him, "I wanted to say thank you. For today."

"No problem." He pulled the SUV around to the parking garage entrance and lowered his window to swipe his key card and open the security gate. As he pulled onto the street, he asked her, "Out of curiosity, what did I do today?"

"You showed acceptance when I walked into the conference room, and displayed confidence in me. In doing so, the team will be that much more likely to work well together. It was a nice thing to do."

"I didn't do it to be nice," he said. Mostly he just did it to get laid. He wouldn't seal the deal again by making her life hell.

"Whether you meant it or not, you were."

"I'm still not convinced that just isn't a big waste of time and money. Your methods—"

"Have never failed me before. Just ask my previous clients."

"However," he continued, "you're here, and you're obviously not leaving until the job is done, so there's no good reason not to cooperate." And after going over her plan today, he was slightly less skeptical than he'd been before. Not to mention that now that he really knew her, he couldn't work up the will to disrespect her in front of his team. It just didn't seem right.

"To be honest, it's a bit annoying," she said.

"What's annoying?"

"Your niceness."

"I could act like an ass if it would make you happy."

"That's the thing, I don't think you know how to not be nice."

"And that's annoying?"

"A bit."

There was no doubt about it, Carrie was in a class all by herself.

Ten

Rob glanced over at Carrie, wearing a look that suggested she was just slightly left of center. Or maybe a little more than slightly.

"So, you prefer men who aren't nice?" he said.

"I didn't say that. I just said your niceness is annoying. It's probably that I'm not used to it. I date a lot of jerks."

"And you do this, why?"

She shrugged. "I just do. They're the kind of man I naturally attract. It's an inherited trait. With the exception of my biological father, my mom had lousy taste in men, and so did her mom."

"Why do you think that is?"

"I'm sure the drinking hasn't helped. Although my grandma has been sober since I was little."

"And your mom?"

"She drinks every day. My real dad was killed in the Gulf War, which was when my mom started really drinking. As much as I love her, she was always very fragile. When she lost my dad, she just couldn't handle it. We ended up moving in with my grandma because my mom couldn't pull herself together. She would go to the bar after dinner, stay out until closing, sleep until I got home from school, then after dinner it was back to the bar. It was like that until she met my stepfather, Ben. He was older than her, with an ex-wife and two grown kids in Arizona."

"And he was a jerk?" Rob asked.

"At first he was a godsend. He took care of my mom, and he paid attention to me. He took me to movies and out for ice cream and he would help me with my schoolwork. They were together for only a month when we moved in with him. That was when things started to change."

"I'm assuming for the worse."

"He was an alcoholic, too, but a functioning one. He only drank after work and on the weekends, but when he did drink, he drank a lot. And he was a mean drunk. I learned just how mean the first time I mouthed off to him."

"What did he do?"

"Cracked me across the mouth."

Rob glanced over at her. "He *hit* you?"

"It was backhanded, and only hard enough so that it stung. But as I'm sure you've noticed, I'm not the kind of person who keeps her opinions to herself, so it happened a lot."

"Didn't your mom stop him?"

"She tried once, but he got so mad that she never said anything again."

"Did he hit her, too?"

"There was no need. She did whatever he asked, never argued. I guess in that respect she was the perfect wife."

His grip seemed to tighten on the steering wheel. "Did you tell your grandmother?"

"No way. She was so relieved when Ben came along. She was sick a lot of the time and she didn't have the energy or the patience to take care of my mom. She thought Ben was an angel sent down from heaven. I knew that if I told her what he was really like she would worry. I figured I could handle him on my own. And I did for the most part. My mouth did get me in trouble with my teachers occasionally, but I was an excellent student. It was my ticket out."

"So you stayed there until you graduated?"

"Not quite. When I was sixteen he and I got into a huge fight. I came home three hours past curfew on a school night and he met me at the door."

His brow furrowed, as if he were expecting something unpleasant. "And?"

"Words were exchanged, my mouth got away from me as usual, and I won't deny that I said some pretty horrible things. Nothing that wasn't true, though. He came unglued. He slapped me that time, his full palm against my cheek. It rattled my brain and split my lip and left a bruise the shape of his hand on my face.

"I told him I was going to call the police. He knew he'd crossed the line, so he jumped in his car and took off. He was gone all night. The police showed up around 6:00 a.m. to let us know that he'd been in an accident. He hit a tree and died instantly. There was an open booze bottle in the car, so they assumed it was a DUI, but after the autopsy they discovered that he'd had a heart attack. And he had advanced cirrhosis. He would have been dead in a couple of years anyway."

"How did your mom take it?"

"Surprisingly well. The half-million-dollar insurance payout helped. Plus he had another fifty thousand in investments. She sold the house, bought a condo close to the beach. As far as I know, she's happy."

He shot her another glance. "As far as you know?"

"As you can imagine, there's a fair amount of resentment there on my part, and me being me, I have a tough time putting a filter on it, so when we do talk she walks away from it feeling guilty, which just makes her drink more. Which makes me feel bad. We're both better off if we don't talk often, and when we do, we keep the conversations short. It's not an ideal situation, but it works for us."

"I couldn't imagine not talking to at least one of my parents every day," Rob said, stopping at a red light. "But I guess that comes with being a part of a family business."

"How long have you worked for Caroselli Chocolate?"

"Since birth practically. But I wasn't officially hired until I was thirteen and I started working part-time in one of the stores. When I graduated from college I moved to the main office."

"What did you do then?"

"I started out in the mail room, then worked my way up to the marketing department."

That surprised her. "You had a marketing degree and they started you in the *mail room?*"

"Everyone in the family pays their dues. There's no special treatment and it's very competitive. That includes salary. I could leave the company and go to a marketing firm and almost double my salary. I make most of my money in profit sharing."

"Is there anyone in your family who doesn't work for Caroselli Chocolate?"

Rob pulled down her street. "Tony's sister Christine is mostly a stay-at-home mom. Same thing with Nick's sister Jessica, but they both help out in the stores when they're short-staffed, or around the chocolate holidays."

"Christmas, Thanksgiving, Halloween, Easter and Valentine's Day," she said.

"Very good."

She smiled smugly. "I do my homework. You would be stunned by how much I know about the chocolate industry."

Rob swung the SUV into the driveway, and right away Carrie noticed that something was off. It took several seconds to realize what it was.

"The light is on in the living room."

Rob peered through the windshield to the front of the condo. "So it is. Do you keep it on a timer?"

"No. And it wasn't on when I left this morning."

"Are you sure?"

"Of course I'm sure." First she couldn't close a door, now she was incapable of remembering if she left a light on? Or was she reading way too much into every little thing he said, trying to make him into a bad guy even if he really wasn't? And if so, what did that mean?

Nothing very good, she was pretty sure about that.

She pulled the garage door opener out of her purse. "I planned to go in through the garage, so I left the kitchen light on."

"Maybe the ghost turned it on," he said, and she shot him a scathing look. He shrugged. "Or maybe not."

"I know you think you're funny, but you're not."

Opening doors was one thing, but lights that turned themselves on? It was more likely a burglar than anything supernatural…which was even worse now that she thought about it.

She hit the button for the garage door opener, thinking that whoever it was, if they heard it, would come flying out the front door.

No one did. Still, she was uneasy about just waltzing inside. What if someone was in there waiting for her? Someone too stupid to shut off the light that would alert her to his presence. Just because he was stupid didn't mean he wasn't dangerous.

"You look worried," Rob said.

"Wouldn't you be?"

"Not if I had a poltergeist living in my basement."

She didn't justify that one with a verbal response, but her eye roll said it all.

"You want me to come inside with you just in case?"

She hesitated. The last thing she wanted was Rob, with his sexy stubble, smoldering eyes and ripped muscles, coming into her house and oozing sex appeal all over the place. Sure, he'd been a perfect gentleman all day, but what if he suddenly decided that the platonic arrangement wasn't working for him and he made a move on her?

And suppose there was a deranged psycho in her house waiting to chop her into little pieces and feed her to his pet python? Or make a coat out of her flesh? Which was worse? Death and mutilation or really good sex she shouldn't be having?

Wow, that was a tough one.

"Would you mind?" she asked. "Just in case."

"If I minded I wouldn't have asked. Although if there really was someone in there, hearing the garage door opening probably would have scared them off."

"I'm not sure that's a chance I'm willing to take."

"Let's go." He shut off the engine and they both got out. "Let me go in first," he said as they walked through the garage. To do otherwise would sort of defeat the purpose of asking him in, but she followed close behind him, stopping just shy of clinging to the back of his black wool coat. So close that when he stopped just before the door, she nearly ran into him.

"Key?" he said, holding out his hand.

"Oh, right." She dug through her purse and pulled it out.

She grabbed her phone, too, just in case she had to make a quick call to 9-1-1.

He unlocked the door and pushed it open. The kitchen light was on, just as she had left it, and of course the basement door was open. She followed Rob inside, closing it as she walked past. For all the good it would do. The next time she walked back here it would probably be open again.

As they stepped into the kitchen, the first thing she noticed was the open, half-empty bottle of wine on the counter.

"Did you leave that there?" he asked.

"Why yes, I always have a glass of wine with my breakfast."

He was the one giving the look this time.

"When I left this morning it was in the refrigerator."

He pulled off one leather glove and touched the bottle. "It's still cold."

Who would break into her house and drink a glass of wine?

"I don't suppose you've started smoking," he said.

"No, why?"

He pointed to the kitchen table, where a pack of cigarettes and an old, beat-up silver Zippo lighter lay. She hadn't seen that particular lighter in something like eight years. She gave a sigh of relief to know that they weren't in any imminent danger. At least he wasn't. But Carrie had the feeling she was in for the lecture of her life.

"Alice!" Carrie shouted. "Get in here."

Alice?

Rob looked over at Carrie. Who the hell was Alice?

Before he could ask, a woman appeared in the kitchen doorway. She was nearly as tall as Rob and thin to the point of being gaunt. Silky, pin-straight, jet-black hair framed a face that was as long and thin as the rest of her. She was more striking than beautiful, the kind of woman who would stand out in a crowd.

Dynamic.

"Rob, this is my best friend, Alice," Carrie said. He recalled her mentioning a friend of that name when they were at the diner. He didn't realize that she lived in Chicago.

"Rob?" Alice said, looking him up and down, her crimson lips curling into a slightly lopsided, wry smile. "As in Rob Caroselli, aka Mr. New Year's Eve?"

"The one and only," he said, noticing, as she stepped over to offer him a delicate yet long-fingered hand to shake, she seemed to be walking with a slight limp. She wore black leggings and a long black tunic top. Even her shoes, well-worn ballet flats, were black.

"What are you doing here?" Carrie asked her.

"I haven't been able to reach you in days and assumed you were up to something, which—" she looked pointedly at Rob "—clearly you are."

"He just gave me a ride home. I haven't had a chance to lease a car yet."

Skepticism narrowed Alice's eyes, which were slightly turned up in the corners and an unearthly shade of violet. "Does he always walk you inside?"

"We thought someone had broken in! And by the way, how *did* you get in?"

"How long have we known each other?" Alice said. "You always keep a spare near the front door. It was just a matter of finding it."

Rob looked at Carrie. "You keep a spare key by the *front door?*"

She shook her head and said, "Not now, please."

Alice folded her long, skinny arms under her nearly nonexistent breasts. "You *promised.*"

Promised what? Rob wondered.

"I see you're smoking again," Carrie shot back.

Nice deflection.

"I got *dumped*," Alice said. "What's your excuse?"

Whatever Alice was referring to, it would seem that Carrie had no excuse. Or she couldn't think of one just then.

"That's what I thought," Alice said. "You clearly need supervision."

"It's over," Carrie said, then looked up at Rob. "Tell her it's over."

He looked from one woman to the other, and though he had a pretty good idea of what she meant, he said, "I decline to answer on the grounds that it might incriminate me."

"Did Rex really dump you?" Carrie asked her.

Alice tossed her satiny black hair. "I guess I should have seen it coming. He was never home. And when he was, he was never really there. When I told him that my runway career is officially over, he must have figured the gravy train was drying up for good."

"What do you mean it's over?" Carrie asked, setting her purse and briefcase on the kitchen table. "I thought you just needed time to heal."

"I may have been overly optimistic when I told you that. They said there was a slight chance I wouldn't get full mobility back. But the physical therapy isn't helping and my doctor thinks I might need *another* surgery."

"Oh, honey," Carrie said, shrugging out of her coat. "I'm so sorry."

"I can still do face, or some catalog work, as long as I'm not on my feet for too long or I get a cankle on the left side."

Carrie turned to Rob. "Alice is a very successful runway model."

"Was," Alice said.

"How long will you be staying?" Carrie asked her.

"I guess it just depends on how long you want me around."

"Stay as long as you like. I can easily turn the office into a bedroom."

"You don't have to do that. I'm perfectly comfortable on the couch. It will be like we're in college again," Alice said, trying to sound cheerful, but her smile looked stiff and forced. Then she looked Rob up and down and added, "Are we going to do the hair band again?"

Rob blinked. "*Do* the hair band?"

"When we were roommates in college we had a system," Carrie explained. "If one of us brought a guy home, we would loop a hair band around the door."

"Oh, like a band for your hair," he said. "That makes more sense."

"Than what?"

He shook his head. "Never mind."

Even if there were any '80s hair bands left, those guys would be ancient by now.

"There won't be a need for the hair band because as I said, it's over." Carrie turned to him. "Would you please tell her that it's over?"

"So you brought guys back to your room a lot in college?"

Carrie rolled her eyes. "Ugh! You're no help."

"I don't know," Alice said, looking him up and down again. "Now that I see him, maybe you should sleep with him again. You could do a lot worse."

"True," Carrie said, giving him the same critical once-over in a way that made him feel a lot like a slab of meat. "But he's kind of…well…*nice*."

Alice's horrified look said she had the same distorted ideas about men that Carrie did. "Never mind."

"On that note, I'm going to go…I don't know…mistreat a kitten or something," he said. "Alice, it was a pleasure to meet you. Carrie, I'll see you at work tomorrow."

"Thanks for coming in with me," she said, walking him to the garage. He recalled specifically that she had closed the basement door on the way in, yet it stood open again.

"It was no problem. Are you sure I can't pick you up on my way in tomorrow?"

"I'm good, thanks."

He wanted to kiss her goodbye, but he didn't. Even though he was pretty sure she wouldn't object. But she was going to come to him this time. And when she was ready, she would. He just had to be patient.

He did know one thing for sure as he got in his car and headed for home: having someone like Alice around was going to be very interesting.

Eleven

On her way down to the break room for coffee, Carrie had to pass Rob's office, and though she had promised herself she wasn't going to go out of her way to see him unless it was completely necessary, it seemed rude not to stop in and thank him for walking her into her condo last night.

So instead of going straight down the hall, she hung a sharp right and stepped into the outer office where Mrs. White sat. Only it wasn't Mrs. White sitting there today. This woman was much younger—in her mid to late forties—and very beautiful. She wore her pale blond hair shoulder-length and pulled back from her face. She was sitting down, but Carrie could see by the long, slender legs encased in cream-colored wool pants that she was tall. *Elegant* was the first word that came to mind.

Maybe Mrs. White was out sick and she was a temp from another department.

"I'm looking for Rob," Carrie told her.

"That makes two of us," the woman said, in a husky voice with a slightly watered-down French accent. "Shall we fight over him?"

Carrie blinked. Fight over... Was she joking? Who did she think Carrie was?

The desk phone rang and Carrie waited for her to answer, but she ignored it. Probably not a temp.

"I just needed to talk to him for a second," Carrie said. "I can come back."

"You're Caroline Taylor?" the woman said.

"That's right." *And who are you?* she wanted to say. She was stunningly beautiful. For all Carrie knew, Rob had a thing for older women.

"I've heard so much about you. From Robby and his father. You're here to save the company?"

"I'm certainly going to try." Unsure of what else to say, she told the woman, "When you see Rob, can you tell him...you know, never mind. It wasn't important."

"I was only teasing you. He is with his father. He should be back any minute." She gestured to the chair opposite the desk. "Sit, wait with me."

Before she could decide to stay or leave, Rob walked in.

He looked from the blonde woman to Carrie and said, "Oh, hi. I see you two have met."

"Well, we didn't actually—"

"Is your father ready?" the woman asked him.

"He said to give him a few more minutes."

"Always a few more minutes," she said with a sigh, telling Carrie, "Husbands, they *always* make you wait."

Husbands? If Demitrio was her husband, that meant she had to be Rob's mother. Carrie never imagined that a woman so fair could give birth to such a dark child. Rob clearly favored his father's side of the family.

"I'm sorry, did you need something?" Rob asked Carrie.

"No."

Then why are you here? his look said.

"I just wanted to talk to you for a second. It's nothing that can't wait." In fact, she never should have come to his office in the first place.

"You two talk," Rob's mother said. "I think I will go see if I can pull Robby's father away from his work."

She stood, and Carrie was right. She was tall—barely an inch shorter than her son. It seemed to be about the only family resemblance Carrie could see. And she must have been older than Carrie thought, unless she'd had Rob when she was twelve.

"It was nice to meet you," she said, shaking Carrie's hand. Then she kissed Rob's cheek and sauntered out.

At the risk of sounding like a dope, Carrie said, "Am I correct in assuming that was your mother?"

"She didn't tell you who she was?"

"She just asked me if I wanted to fight over you."

He smiled and shook his head. "She has a bizarre sense of humor."

Carrie had a sudden, terrifying thought. If Rob's mom knew who Carrie was, did she also know what they'd done? "She doesn't know, right?"

"Know what?"

Duh. She lowered her voice to a loud whisper, just in case someone happened to be in the hall. "About New Year's. About you and me."

He looked at her funny. "You honestly think I tell my mom about my sexual conquests?"

"I don't know—hey, wait. A sexual *conquest?* Is that what I was?"

"You know what I mean, and *no,* I didn't tell her anything," he said, looking offended.

"Sorry. I just thought the French were more open about that kind of thing."

Rob sat on the edge of his desk. "She's not from France. She's from Quebec."

"Six of one, half a dozen of the other."

"Whatever. Point is, no, I didn't tell her. I *never* tell her. As far as I know, she thinks I'm still a virgin."

As if. "I'm sure she knows you're not."

He rubbed his hand across the stubble on his cheek. "Did we ever determine why you came to my office? Because I specifically recall your saying that when we're at work we should pretend not to like each other. Did you change your mind? Did you want to *not like me* in here for a while?"

Oh, so tempting…

"It was something work-related," she told him. "But I've completely forgotten what."

He grinned. "I think you just missed me."

"As if," she said, hating that he was right. From now on, no visits to his office unless it really was work-related.

"Well, when you remember what it was, you know where to find me. Or anything else you might need me for."

"Thanks," she said, and oh, did she wish she could take him up on that.

Rob sat at the conference table three days later with Will and Al, waiting for Carrie and Grant so they could discuss the data they had been compiling, thinking about what Carrie and Alice had said about nice guys. He wasn't sure why he found the idea so annoying, but it continued to nag at him.

"Would you two say I'm a nice guy?" he asked Will and Al.

"Sure," Will said.

"Eh." Al shrugged. "You're okay."

He shot her a look.

She grinned and said, "I'm kidding. Of course you're a nice guy."

"Under what circumstances would you consider that a bad thing?"

Looking confused, Al asked, "Why would that ever be a bad thing?"

"That's what I was wondering," Rob said. "Why would a woman prefer to date a jerk over a nice guy?"

"Does this have something to do with Carrie?" Will asked.

Rob blinked. "Why would you think that?"

"Because of your affair."

"Will!" Al said, giving him a shove.

When Rob got over the shock of his statement, which took a good thirty seconds, he said, "Did Nick or Tony say something to you?"

"They didn't have to," Al said apologetically.

"Yeah," Will agreed, "it's kind of obvious."

No way Rob was that transparent. "Obvious how? We hardly say two words to each other."

"Exactly," Will told him.

"I think what Will is trying to say is that you and Carrie try too hard to act like you *don't* like each other. But when you look at each other…"

"What?" Rob demanded.

"*Major* heat."

Before Rob could confirm or deny their suspicions, Grant rushed in, still wearing his coat. "Sorry I'm late. Traffic was hell this morning."

"It's okay," Al said. "Carrie isn't here yet either."

"Actually she walked in right after me, so she should be along any minute." Grant shrugged out of his coat and hung it on the back of his chair. "She probably stopped in her office."

"We were just talking about Rob and Carrie's affair," Will told him, which earned him another shove from his coworker.

"What about it?" Grant asked, taking a seat.

In response to Rob's blink of surprise, Will said, "Like Al told you, *heat*."

If it was so obvious to them, what about everyone else?

"Good morning!" Carrie said, gliding through the door, her usual cheerful self, and everyone went dead silent.

She set her coffee and a folder down on the conference table and took a seat. Then noticing the lack of conversation, she looked around and asked, "Is something wrong?"

No one seemed to know what to say. Including Rob.

So of course he blurted out the absolute worst thing he could under the circumstances. "Apparently everyone here thinks we're having an affair."

Carrie blinked. "Excuse me?"

"It's not just us, Rob," Al said apologetically. "Pretty much everyone thinks so."

"Why would people think that?" Carrie said, sounding equal parts offended and nervous.

"I'm pretty sure you didn't give yourself that hickey on the back of your neck," Will said.

"Will!" Al said, glaring at him.

Carrie slapped a hand over her neck and cut her eyes to Rob, and her look clearly said, *Oh no, you didn't.*

Oh yes, he had. Their last night together. At the time he had no idea that she wore her hair up for work every day, or he would have branded her somewhere slightly less obvious. He hadn't even realized that anyone else had noticed.

"I must have burned myself with the curling iron," Carrie said, using the same lame excuse his sister Megan had in high school, and Rob could see that no one was buying it.

"Even if it weren't for that, Rob's attitude adjustment made it pretty obvious," Will said.

"Attitude adjustment?" Carrie asked him.

"It's no secret that he didn't think your services were required," Will said. "Then suddenly he was all gung ho to have you here. Everyone just put two and two together."

Carrie went stone-still, and a red blush stained her cheeks. Rob knew exactly what Will was getting at. So did Al. She shoved him hard and shot him a look that said, *Are you kidding me?*

Will just shrugged, as if he didn't have a clue what he'd said wrong.

Al rolled her eyes in disgust. "My *brainless* coworker here did not mean to imply that you were trying to win Rob over by sleeping with him," Al said. "Right, Will?"

The color drained from Will's face and he actually looked as if he might be sick. "Oh…God…Carrie, no, that was not what I meant. Not at all."

"Don't worry about it," Carrie told him, but Rob could see that her feelings were hurt, and even worse, her pride had taken a huge hit.

He had been hoping that by getting their suspicions out in the open, he could have made light of the situation. Even passed it off as a joke. He should have kept his damn mouth shut.

"We haven't seen Rob this happy in a long time," Grant said, joining the painful conversation, which Rob had to admit took courage. "We simply assumed, because your presence here was the only thing different in his life, it probably had something to do with you. I sincerely apologize if we were out of line."

"Then let me say, for the record, Rob and I are *not* having an affair." Carrie sounded calm, but there was an undercurrent of anger in her voice that had Rob worrying that she might blow. That or dissolve into tears, which would probably be worse.

"People, could you give us a few minutes," Rob said.

"Absolutely," Al said, and they practically ran from the conference room. Not that Rob could blame them.

He got up and closed the door behind them, and when he turned back to the table, Carrie was on her feet and standing by the window, her gaze on the street below.

"Well," she said, "that was unbelievably humiliating."

"I am so sorry. I shouldn't have said anything."

"No, I'm glad you did. It's always good to know when people are laughing at you behind your back."

"That's not what they were doing."

"Now do you see?" She turned to him, anger leaking into her voice. "Do you understand why I didn't want anyone to know about us?"

"I honestly don't think Will meant it like that. He has the tendency to put his foot in his mouth." In fact, he was the one who had started this stupid conversation.

"Maybe he didn't mean it that time, but you know they all thought it at some point. That's the way it is in business for a successful woman. No one believes you got there on your own merit."

"You are extremely good at what you do, and everyone knows it. They told me that you and I have obvious chemistry, and that's basically how they knew about us."

"Terrific," she said.

"They're right."

"I know they are. And we can't do a damn thing about it."

"I know." If he really cared about her feelings, cared about *her*, he would back off. Which was exactly what he planned to do. Which sucked, because he honestly believed they could have had something really good, if Carrie could just let her guard down. Even if it was only temporary. Or hell, she could have wound up being the mother of his fifteen-million-dollar heir. Even if it had been a possibility, it would never happen now.

"We could still be friends," he said.

"No, we can't, because people will always wonder if it's more than that."

He shrugged. "So what? Does it really matter that much what other people think?"

"To me it does. I know that probably seems silly to you, but I can't help it. I'm a people pleaser. It's in my genetic makeup. I wouldn't expect someone like you to understand."

"Someone like me?"

"You're rich and handsome and successful. And nice. And fantastic in bed. You're the closest thing to a perfect man that I've ever met. Do you have any idea how intimidating that is? And how inferior it makes me feel?"

"That's ridiculous."

"Yes, it is. And I know that, but it's still how I feel."

"No," he said, taking out his wallet. "What I mean is, it's ridiculous to think of me as perfect. I'm not. Not even close."

He pulled out the small stack of photos that he always carried with him, the ones he looked at every time he was tempted to put something unhealthy in his mouth or skip his morning workout. It was a reminder of just how far he'd come, and how much he didn't want to go back to being that unhealthy, pathetic person.

"Here," he said, handing the pictures to her. "This kid is far from perfect."

As she looked through them, Carrie's eyes grew wide

and her mouth forming a perfect O. "Oh, my gosh, is this *you?*"

"Roly Poly Robby. That's what they used to call me."

"You were so…"

"Fat?"

"I was going to say chubby."

"No, for the better part of my childhood, until I started college, I fluctuated between being twenty-five and fifty pounds overweight. I was *fat*."

"Slow metabolism?"

He laughed. "No, I liked food. I still do. But back then I didn't have much in the way of self-control, and no interest whatsoever in exercising. I was the uncoordinated, unpopular fat kid who got picked on in grade school, and chosen last in gym class. In middle school I learned I could make the other kids laugh with me instead by telling self-deprecating jokes about my weight, which didn't make me any less miserable. But I convinced my friends and my family that I was confident and happy looking the way I did. I pretended not to mind that girls I liked dated my buddies, when with me they were only interested in being *friends*."

"But you did mind."

"What teenage boy doesn't?"

"Did you ever try to lose the weight?"

"I don't think there was a time when I *wasn't* trying to lose it. There was always some new diet fad to try. I would do okay for a few weeks, drop ten or fifteen pounds, but I always fell back into my old habits and gained it back. I loathed myself for being so weak. It took me a long time to figure out that diets don't work. That I was just setting myself up to fail, and losing the weight meant completely changing my lifestyle. Becoming healthy."

"And look at you. Your body is…amazing. That must make you proud."

"Sure it does. But the work doesn't end when you reach your goal weight. There isn't a day that I don't struggle with it. The pathetic little fat kid is still in there."

"The exterior doesn't change who you are on the inside. That's what matters."

"Tell me honestly, if we had met in high school with me looking the way I did, would you have been the least bit interested in dating me?"

"I told you, I only date jerks. But if I did choose to judge someone based on their looks or their weight, that's my problem, not theirs. And I apologize for judging you, and calling you perfect before I knew the whole story."

"I've been called worse."

"You do realize what a great guy you are, right? And I'm not just talking looks or physique. You're the entire package. Take it from someone who has met her share of creeps. And I would be the luckiest woman in the world to be with you."

"Yet you're not going to be with me."

"The truth is, you deserve better. I would eventually screw it up. I always do. I would hurt you, and I don't want to see that happen."

For a woman so well put together, who seemed to know just what she wanted, her lack of confidence was astonishing. And the last thing he wanted was to be responsible for making her feel even worse than she already did.

"I'll see to it that everyone is set straight about our relationship," he told her. "I don't foresee anyone hassling you about it, but if anyone does, I'll take care of it."

She shook her head. "That will only make matters worse. If there's a problem, I can deal with it myself."

"Whatever you want. Should we call the others back

in so we can get this progress report started? My dad and Uncle Tony would like to see something from us by end of day and I don't want to rock the boat right now."

"This is probably none of my business," she said, "but I sense a definite rift between your dad and your uncle Tony."

"There's always been a bit of animosity between my uncles and my dad, but in the past couple of months...I don't know. Something is up. My dad keeps saying that nothing is wrong, but it's obvious that he and my uncle Tony are at odds."

"Why is there animosity, if you don't mind my asking? I mean, dysfunctional family relationships are kind of my specialty."

"When my dad was a kid, he was the black sheep of the family. The brilliant-but-bored type. He was constantly getting into trouble in school, and then later with the law. My *nonno*—"

"*Nonno?*"

"It's Italian for grandfather."

"Giuseppe?"

He nodded. "He came here from Italy, and he brought with him a lot of old world traditional values. My dad rebelled against them all, and even worse, he wanted nothing to do with the family business. Finally *Nonno* got fed up. When my dad was twenty-five he was arrested after a bar fight and *Nonno* gave him a choice—sit in jail or join the army. He chose the army."

"Tough love."

"The toughest. Though it was a toss-up as to who was tougher, him or *Nonna*."

"Your grandmother?"

He nodded.

"It obviously did your dad some good."

"Definitely. He went to college and graduated top of his class. After that he came to work for Caroselli Chocolate and shot up the ranks. When *Nonno* retired he made my dad CEO, which both his brothers resented. Plus there's always been some added tension between my dad and Tony."

"Why is that?"

"When my dad went into the army, Tony married his girlfriend, Sarah."

"Yikes."

"Yeah. You can't say that my family history isn't colorful."

"I've learned that most are. But as close as your family is, I'm sure everything will work out."

He hoped she was right. Or everything *Nonno* worked for could crumble around them.

Twelve

Carrie loved what she did for a living. As long as she'd been a consultant, there had hardly been a morning when she woke dreading the workday, even though in the past there had been individuals she dreaded working with.

Usually it was the challenge of saving the company that thrilled her. The act of solving the puzzle. But the past couple of weeks she had begun to realize that this time it was more than that. This time it was the people working for the company that she cared about. It really was like a big family, and hard as she had tried to keep her distance, they had sucked her right in.

As coworkers she and Rob got along exceptionally well together. Their management styles were similar, and what differences they did have seemed to complement each other rather than clash. It was as if he could anticipate her next move before she even made it, and they were so in sync that they'd even begun finishing each other's sentences. If ever she had to choose her favorite assignment, hands down this was it. Yet she was torn between loving it, and the fear of getting *too* close.

When Carrie wasn't working, most of her free time was spent with Alice—who wasn't nearly as blasé about her breakup with Rex or her career change as she'd let on. But there were times when she found herself wishing she could be with Rob. Sometimes at work they would stand close to one another and she would get that soul-deep longing to touch him, or he would look at her a certain way and her knees would go weak. She missed the intimacy of their physical relationship—and not just the sex. She missed the way they would lie in bed, side by side, fingers entwined, and just talk. Usually about nothing in particular.

He could be intense at times, and was passionate in his convictions, but his dry wit appealed to her snarky sense of humor. He didn't take crap from her or anyone else, and when someone gave him a hard time he didn't hesitate to call them out on it. He had integrity, and radiated a confidence that was infectious. With a few simple words of praise he could make a person feel as if they were something really special, because while he wasn't a negative boss, he only handed out compliments where they were earned. Which seemed to make his employees strive to please him. Hell, even she felt a little nervous about possibly letting him down, when as a rule she never let herself become emotionally invested in a client. And she typically never formed attachments. But so far, nothing about this job was what she would call typical.

She even began to think that Rob being a nice guy wasn't such a bad thing after all and if there was a man out there who could ever put up with her, he might have actually been it. Which of course scared the living hell out of her. Alice had once accused Carrie of being afraid to be happy, and Carrie was beginning to wonder if maybe she was right. Maybe she was worried that with happiness came the possibility of losing that happiness. It was so much easier to have low expectations, and hurt less when the inevitable letdown came.

Alice used to be her number one supporter when it came to Carrie's hang-ups, but lately she seemed to be defecting to the other side.

"You're an idiot," she said after Carrie hung up from a work-related phone call to Rob that had turned into a two-hour-long conversation that had absolutely nothing to do with marketing reports.

Carrie looked up from the work spread out on the bed. "We've been friends for over ten years and you're just now noticing this?"

"Do you honestly not see how good you two are together? How much he cares about you? And I mean *really* cares. You just talked for two hours. I was lucky if I could get Rex to talk for ten minutes."

"He deserves better than someone like me."

"Isn't that up to him to decide?"

Alice wasn't in any position to be passing judgment. She excelled at snagging emotionally unavailable men. Which always landed her where she was right now. Miserable and alone with shattered self-esteem.

"We're coworkers," Carrie said. "I don't date coworkers."

"You told me yourself how well you guys work together, so that lame excuse is not going to cut it anymore."

"I live in Los Angeles, he lives in Chicago. Talk about a long-distance relationship."

"Other than your mom, who you barely even talk to, what do you really have in Los Angeles that you couldn't have here?"

The answer should have come immediately, and it surprised Carrie to realize that she had no answer. What did she have in Los Angeles, other than work, which frankly she could do anywhere? Her best friend lived all the way across the country, and she worked so much she didn't have time to make other friends. Or at least, that was what she liked to tell herself.

"I'm tired of sleeping on the couch," Alice said out of the blue.

"I told you before that I could turn the office into a bedroom."

"You're not tired of me yet?"

"Of course not. I was sort of hoping that you would stay here with me until I go back to L.A."

"In that case I should probably order some bedroom furniture."

"Renting it would be a lot cheaper."

She sighed. "As much as I love to shop, you're probably right. Until I decide what to do with my life, I should probably watch my spending."

"I'll call Terri tomorrow and make sure it's okay."

"I'll look online for a furniture rental place."

Carrie called Terri from work the next afternoon.

"Of course you can turn the office into a bedroom," Terri said. "Just stick what's in there down in the basement."

"Perfect! Thanks, Terri."

"And by the way, I was going to call you. We're having a get-together next weekend. We would love it if you would come."

And she would love to be there, which was exactly why she shouldn't go. She was letting herself get too close. This was just supposed to be a business trip. "My friend Alice is visiting and I would feel bad leaving her alone."

"Bring her with you."

Terri was making it very hard to say no gracefully. "The thing is, she just got out of a relationship and I'm not sure if she's ready to put herself back out there just yet. But I will ask."

"I hope we see you."

Carrie wished she could.

A few minutes after she hung up with Terri, Alice called. "Did you talk to Terri?"

"She said it's fine, and we can move the furniture that's in there down to the basement."

"I already picked out the furniture. I thought I would have them deliver it Monday. We can move the office furniture tomorrow. Unless you're planning to work again this weekend."

"I think I've earned a Saturday off," she said. It was hard to believe that today would mark the end of her fourth week in Chicago, and her third at Caroselli Chocolate. And they still had so much work to do.

After they hung up Carrie immersed herself in work until Rob appeared in her doorway later. With his sleeves rolled to his elbows and his tie loosened, he looked too yummy for words. She longed to undress him, and run her tongue over every conceivable inch of his delicious body.

"Tony and I are packing it in and going out for a burger," he said. "Care to join us?"

She looked at the clock, surprised that it was already after seven. "I can't."

He folded his arms. "You're not still worried that people will think we're a couple, are you?"

"No, not anymore." Everyone seemed fairly clear on that concept now. Though it wouldn't take much to get the rumor mill spinning again. If there was one thing the Carosellis loved more than chocolate, it was gossip. "I'm taking the weekend off, so I want to finish this report before I go. It's going to be at least another hour or two."

"You sure? Dinner is on me."

"Maybe next time."

He shrugged. "Okay, see you tomorrow."

"See ya."

He was already long gone when it occurred to her that she wouldn't be there tomorrow, so she in fact would not see him. Which was probably a really good thing. She was very careful to stay safely behind the border she had set for herself. Yet every now and then she caught her toes inching past the line. That was when she knew she had to back off, recapture her perspective.

She worked until nine, and was gathering her things when she swore she heard the sound of footsteps out in the hall. It was rare that anyone worked past six on Friday, and for a split second she wondered if Rob had come back.

She got up from her desk and peeked out of her office, just in time to see someone turn the corner at the end of the hall, where it dead-ended at Demitrio's office. Someone too small to be Rob or any other man.

Had his secretary come back for something maybe?

She walked quietly down the hall and peeked around the corner. Whoever it was, she was messing with the door to the outer office.

What have we here? she wondered. A little interoffice espionage?

"Excuse me," she said and the woman in question squealed with surprise, dropping whatever was in her hand. As it clinked against the granite floor, Carrie realized that it was a large silver paper clip that had been straightened out.

Was she *picking* the lock?

The woman spun around and Carrie recognized her immediately. "Rose?"

"Carrie," she said, slapping a hand over her heart. "You scared me. I thought everyone had left."

Carrie only knew Rose from the break room, and though she found her to be a bit odd, she'd never had a problem with her. But something was definitely going on. "What are you doing?"

Her cheeks blushed bright red as she bent down to grab the paper clip. "I realize how this looks," she said nervously, "but it's not what you think."

"You're picking the lock on the CEO's office door."

"Demitrio's secretary has a binder full of old reports for me that need to be digitized. She left early, but said it would be on the corner of her desk. I lost track of time, and by the time I came down to get it, Demitrio had left and locked up. I tried to reach her, and when I couldn't, I panicked. I thought maybe I could pick the lock."

She looked sincere, so why did Carrie get the feeling she was lying through her teeth. "Would you like me to call Rob? Maybe he has a key to his father's office."

"Oh, wait! My phone is ringing. Excuse me."

Carrie didn't hear a phone ring, but supposed Rose could have had it set on silent.

She scurried several feet away before answering it. "Hello," she said. "Oh, thank goodness you got my messages…are you sure it can wait?" She paused, then said, "Okay, see you Monday." She turned to Carrie, shoving the phone back in her pocket. "It's okay. She said I can do it Monday."

Carrie found it awfully convenient that she called at that exact moment. A little *too* convenient. Not only that, but

Mary, Demitrio's secretary, was a talker. They'd never had a conversation that lasted less than ten minutes.

"Would you mind if we keep this between us?" Rose said, her cheeks crimson. "I would be mortified if anyone knew what I did."

"Sure," Carrie said, fully intending to tell Rob the entire story the next time she saw him.

At noon the next day, when she and Alice were supposed to be moving furniture to the basement, Carrie found her draped on the couch half-asleep instead.

"Are you ready?" Carrie asked her.

"Ready for what?"

"To move the office furniture."

Alice blinked. "With my healing ankle? I couldn't possibly."

"Then why did you tell me you would?"

"I never said *I* would do it personally."

Did she think Carrie would be able to do it alone? "I need help."

"Don't worry." She sat up, stretching like a cat. "I called for reinforcements."

"Reinforcements?" Who did she even know in Chicago? Or had she hired professional movers?

As if on cue, the doorbell rang. Alice put her foot down, wincing as she tried to push herself up from the couch. "Be a dear and get that for me, would you?"

Be a dear?

She walked to the door wondering why Alice was acting so odd. She pulled it open, surprised to find Rob standing there. Tony was behind him.

"We're here," Rob said.

Thanks, Captain Obvious. "I see that. *Why* are you here?"

Confused, the two men looked at each other, then Rob turned back to her. "Alice called. She said you needed help moving furniture."

"Oh, did she?" Carrie turned to give her friend the evil eye, but the sofa was empty. She'd set Carrie up, now she was going to bail on her? How many times had Carrie specifically said that she didn't want to see Rob outside the office?

"Come on in," she said, letting the men inside. She couldn't leave them out in the cold while she murdered Alice. Besides, she really did need their help. They might even lend a hand disposing of Alice's body.

Under his wool coat Rob looked like something out of a handyman fantasy in faded, threadbare blue jeans, a flannel shirt with the sleeves rolled up and well-worn work boots. The kind of ensemble that would be fun to tear off him with her bare hands. Which was exactly what she wanted to do.

Yep, Alice was dead meat.

Wearing black jeans, a black long-sleeved T-shirt and sneakers, Tony wasn't looking too shabby either.

"If you two will excuse me a minute, I need to have a word with my roommate."

"You want us to get started?" Rob asked.

"Nope," she called over her shoulder as she headed down the hall. "I'll be right back."

Her bedroom door was closed, and when she tried to turn the knob, it was locked. She had locked Carrie out of her own bedroom?

"Alice!" she hissed. "Open the door."

"I have a terrible migraine," Alice said weakly. "You'll have to manage without me."

"Migraine, my ass," she mumbled as she walked back to the living room, where Rob and Tony were still waiting.

"Everything all right?" Rob asked.

"Fine. Alice is…resting in my room."

Rob's brow rose. *"Resting?"*

The last thing she wanted was for Rob to realize that this was a setup. He might actually believe that Carrie had something to do with it.

Carrie lowered her voice and said, "Actually, she's hiding. She's taking the breakup pretty hard. And the career stuff."

"Tony is a recent dumpee, too," Rob told Carrie.

"Dude, really?" Tony said, looking irritated. "Tell the whole world, why don't you."

Rob grinned, and Carrie wondered if that had been payback for past fat jokes.

"Alice said you're clearing out the office," Rob said.

"We're making it a bedroom." They followed her down the hall. "So this is it," she said as they stepped into the spare room. "It all has to go. Terri said to put everything in the basement."

"The haunted basement?" Tony said.

She couldn't believe that a big burly guy like him could possibly be afraid of a door-opening spirit. "Whatever or whoever it is down there, it's harmless," Carrie assured him.

Both men took an end of the desk, carried it out of the room and down the hall.

"Where in the basement do you want it?" Rob asked her.

"Oh, anywhere there's room," she said.

"Nowhere specific?"

She shrugged. "Just any old place is fine."

Rob stopped just shy of the basement door, wearing a wry smile. "You've never been down there, have you?"

"Why would you assume that?"

Tony looked down the stairs, then back at her. "Have you?"

"Yes," she said indignantly, then paused and added, "Sort of."

"Sort of, how?" Rob asked.

She'd once made it about halfway down the stairs, but the creak of the door moving behind her had propelled her back up. She'd moved so swiftly, in fact, that she could swear her feet never touched the stairs. "Even if there is something down there, it's not as if it can hurt us."

"Then you won't mind going first," Rob said, gesturing her down.

Unwilling to admit just how nervous she was at the prospect of going down there, she raised her chin a notch, met his challenging gaze and said, "Of course I'll go first."

"We'll be right behind you," Rob said.

She switched on the light and peered down. Worst-case scenario, she might see or hear something unusual. And because whatever kept opening the door seemed inclined to stay in the basement, she had nothing to worry about. Plus she had two strapping men to protect her.

Yet she was still edgy.

She started down, forcing her feet forward, growing colder as she descended, unsure if it was due to a lack of heat or the presence of something unworldly. She was hesitant to hold the rail, lest she might feel that disembodied hand settle over hers again. Her heart was pounding double time when she reached the last step and her foot hit the concrete floor.

She realized, with no small degree of relief, that the only things down there she could see were boxes and old furniture. *Extremely* old furniture and lots of it. Pieces that she was guessing were from the late nineteenth century. It must have been worth a small fortune.

"I guess we should put the stuff from the office off to

the side over there," she said, gesturing to the only relatively vacant area.

They set down the desk and Rob asked, "Are you coming back up with us?"

"I think I'll stay down here," she said, curiosity out-
weighing her fear.

"Okay, we'll be right back."

She wove her way through the maze of different pieces,
checking them out. Some were plain and functional, others ornately embellished and fragile-looking. She knew
next to nothing about antique furniture, but the variety of
grains and colors said the pieces were built from several
different types of wood. Whoever owned all of this must
have been a collector.

There were several dining room and bedroom sets, and
a fair share of living room pieces. She ran her hand across
the surface of a beautifully carved sideboard, expecting
to find a layer of dust but either the air in the condo was
unprecedentedly clean, or Terri sneaked in while she was
at work and dusted everything.

"Find your ghost?" Rob asked as he and Tony appeared
with a large file cabinet.

"Not exactly. But doesn't it seem unusually clean down
here? There isn't a spot of dust on this furniture."

"Terri is a little fanatical about keeping things clean,"
Rob reminded her.

Yes, but a basement? Besides, she hadn't been there
in a month.

"We just have to grab the bookcase and we'll be done,"
he said.

"Okay," she answered distractedly, entertaining a third
possibility, but it was a little creepy to contemplate that
not only was the ghost fanatical about keeping doors open,
but it was a clean freak as well. Could a ghost have OCD?

Carrie heard a soft creaking sound, and she could swear the very faint wail of a baby crying.

No way. It must have been something Alice was watching upstairs, and the sound was leaking down through the floorboards.

And what if it wasn't?

"Do you guys hear that?" she said, turning to where Rob had been standing. But apparently they had already gone back up the stairs for the next load.

She listened hard and the sound seemed to be coming from the far end of the basement, where the bedroom pieces were stored. Coincidentally, right under the bedrooms.

Screwing up all of her courage, she made her way through the furniture, following the sound, and the closer she got, the less it sounded as if it were coming from upstairs. She finally made it to the end of the basement, in the darkest corner and found, stored behind a wide chest of drawers that was desperately in need of refinishing, a child's cradle that looked hand-carved. As her eyes adjusted to the low light, and she got a better look at it, the hair on her arms and back of her neck shivered to standing and her heart skipped a beat.

The cradle was rocking.

She blinked, then blinked again, sure that her eyes were playing tricks on her. But it really was rocking. Not only that, but the crying was louder now, as if it were right in front of her. Loud wailing that wasn't really loud at all. It was all around her, but almost as if she were hearing it on the inside of her head. She stood there mesmerized watching it move back and forth, back and forth, and as she did she felt herself reaching out to touch it…then a hand slammed down on her shoulder and a blood-curdling scream ripped from her throat.

Thirteen

"It's just me!" Rob said as Carrie whipped around, losing her balance and falling against the bureau she'd been looking behind.

"Are you trying to give me a heart attack?" she shrieked, giving him a shove.

"I'm sorry," he said, holding his hands up to ward off another attack. "I called your name three times and you didn't answer me. I came back here to see what you were looking at but I tripped on a table leg."

From behind them he heard the thud of footsteps on the stairs, and turned to see Tony descending two steps at a time. Following him by only a few seconds was Alice, who once again was dressed all in black.

"What the hell happened?" Tony and Alice said at the same time, then turned to each other in surprise, as if they had completely missed one another on the stairs.

"Nothing," Rob said. "I just surprised her."

"Surprised me? You scared the crap out of me."

"I told you, I tripped."

"Did you see it?" she demanded.

"See what?"

"The cradle. It was rocking. And I could swear I heard a baby crying."

Uh-oh. Had he scared her so thoroughly that she had lost touch with reality? "What cradle?"

"Back there." She pointed to the spot behind the bureau she'd been staring at when he fell into her.

He peered behind it, and though the light was dim he could definitely see the outline of something small and low to the floor, wedged between the bureau and the wall.

"Is it still rocking?" she asked.

As far as he could tell it wasn't moving. "Let me see if I can…" He leaned over the bureau, his stomach resting on the top, reaching…

He grabbed the side of the cradle and pulled it up off the floor. It was light, and looked to him to be almost small enough to be a child's toy rather than a functional piece of furniture, but as he held it up to the light he could see that it was handmade and very old.

Her concerns suddenly gone, Carrie started making her way back to where Tony and Alice stood, gesturing him to follow. "Bring it over here!"

He had never known Carrie to be anything but level-headed and rational, but she was neither right now.

He held the cradle up over his head and carried it through the maze of furniture. When he reached the other side, where the three of them stood waiting for him, he set it on the cold concrete floor. It was simple but functional, and looked surprisingly well-kept considering its age, but probably not very safe by modern standards.

"Watch it!" Carrie said excitedly. "I swear it was rocking all by itself. And I heard a baby crying."

"A *human* baby?" Rob asked, which Carrie's exasperated look would suggest was a stupid question.

"Of course a human baby," she said. "Didn't anyone else hear it?"

Rob shook his head, and they both turned to Tony and Alice, who were ignoring them and busy giving each other the once-over. Rob realized that they hadn't been introduced yet. "Tony, this is Carrie's friend Alice, from New York. Alice, this is my cousin Tony."

"A pleasure," Alice said, shaking Tony's hand, a catlike grin curling her lips.

"The pleasure is all mine," Tony said, and they looked utterly enthralled by one another.

"How about a drink?" Alice said, her eyes never leaving Tony's.

"I'd love one," Tony said, gesturing to the stairs. "After you."

As they disappeared up the stairs, Carrie turned to Rob and said, "What the heck just happened?"

Rob shrugged. "I guess they liked what they saw."

"In that case, maybe it's a good thing that you made me scream." She looked down at the cradle, which as far as Rob could see, wasn't moving at all. Sounding defeated, she said, "It's not going to do it for you."

"It might."

They stood in silence and watched it for several minutes, but nothing happened.

"I swear it was moving," she told him.

"I believe you. If doors can open by themselves, why would a self-rocking cradle be such a stretch of the imagination?"

"Either that, or I'm losing my mind."

"It *was* a little weird that you wouldn't answer me. At first I thought you were upset about something. And then I thought maybe you were getting sick."

"Eew," she said, nose wrinkling.

"But as I got closer, it seemed as if you were in a trance or something."

"I guess I sort of felt like I was. And when you fell against me, I think I was reaching down to touch it. But I wasn't doing it consciously. Does that make sense?"

"Not really."

"I could see my arm moving, but I didn't feel as if I was controlling it."

"Are you saying that you were possessed?"

She shrugged. "Maybe I was. I sure didn't feel like myself."

If she were anyone else, he would think she was either nuts or looking to get attention, but that wasn't Carrie. She was one of the most down-to-earth, sane people he'd ever met, despite all her hang-ups. A genuine straight shooter. She looked so damn adorable in her skinny jeans and a UCLA sweatshirt, her hair pulled back in a ponytail that bounced when she walked. And he wanted her just as much as he had in the hotel bar that night. He'd racked his brain trying to come up with a way to make her see that she was wrong. He didn't deserve better than her, because there was no one better. Not that he'd ever met. The problem was making her believe that.

"I guess we should get back upstairs," she said.

"You want me to bring the cradle up?"

She looked at all the furniture piled there, then at the forlorn little cradle on the floor. He thought of the children who might have slept in it and actually felt guilty for leaving it down there. It looked so small and lonely.

Small and lonely? Where the hell had that come from? Now *he* was acting possessed.

"Bring it up," she said. "I'll clean it up. Maybe someone can get some use out of it."

He lifted the cradle off the floor, and as he did, he could swear he felt a rush of cold air brush past him. Clearly he was imagining things.

He followed Carrie up the stairs, holding the cradle, and when they stepped through the door, she pushed it closed behind him.

Just before he heard the knob latch, from the basement below, he could swear he heard the sound of not a baby, but a woman crying.

"They bailed on us." Carrie held up the note she found stuck to the refrigerator and showed it to Rob.

Went for a drink. Back later.

"I guess Tony forgot that we came here together in his car," Rob said.

Carrie wasn't thrilled by the idea of being stuck with Rob, and even though it was a setup, she couldn't muster the will to be upset with Alice. She'd been cooped up in the house for three weeks. It would do her good to get out and socialize. She needed this. And maybe she and Tony would hit it off. Alice could certainly benefit from meeting a nice guy for a change. Not that Carrie knew Tony all that well. But if he was anything like the rest of his family, she had nothing to worry about.

She had the sudden vision of her and Alice both settling down in Chicago, and a double wedding with Carrie and Rob and Alice and Tony tying the knot.

A double wedding? Seriously? Where the heck had that come from?

She shook away the ridiculous notion.

"I'm sure they won't be too long," she said. At least she hoped they wouldn't.

"Where do you want the cradle?" Rob said, and she realized he was still holding it.

"The living room, I guess, until I figure out what I'm going to do with it. It just didn't seem right to keep it in the basement."

"I know what you mean," he said, carrying it into the living room for her.

"You do?"

He set it down by the couch, then sat down. "Weirdly enough, yes."

The fact that she'd felt that way was weird, but his feeling it, too? That was downright creepy. Maybe, instead of cleaning it up, she should hire an exorcist.

She sat in the chair. "Do you like old furniture?"

"Not particularly."

Neither did she. She didn't dislike it, but her preference was a more modern look. But the cradle, there was just something about it....

"Maybe that's why the door kept opening," Rob said. "Maybe whatever is down there wanted you to find it and bring it up. Maybe that's why it touched you that first night."

She narrowed her eyes at him. "Are you serious or just making fun of me?"

"I heard it, too," he said.

"The baby crying?"

"Just before you closed the basement door. But it didn't sound like a baby. It was a woman."

The hair on the back of her neck rose. "Wow, that's really creepy."

"I have to admit that it is."

"Speaking of creepy," Carrie said, "something happened at work last night that I thought I should mention."

"Don't tell me doors are opening by themselves there, too," he said, with a grin so adorable she wanted to eat him up.

"This is about a door that wouldn't open, actually."

She told him how she had caught Rose trying to break into his father's office, and how his secretary conveniently called at the last second.

"You think she was lying?" Rob asked her.

"I'm usually pretty good at reading people, and I definitely had that feeling. But that doesn't mean I'm right. I just thought I should tell you."

"I'm glad you did. Just between us, there's something about her that bothers me."

"Me, too! She's so quiet—not that quiet people are bad—but it always seems as if she's up to no good or hiding something. Do you know what I mean?"

"I do. She and my sister have become pretty good friends. Megan bought an apartment and Rose is going to be moving in the end of this month."

"You're worried?"

"Yeah. Her mom worked at Caroselli Chocolate for years as *Nonno's* secretary, so when she showed up looking for a job, my uncle Leo felt obligated to hire her."

"In what position?"

"At first, just general office stuff, but then she offered to digitize all our old records, and that's been her job description ever since."

"So she has access to a lot of company information."

"You think she's a spy?"

She shrugged. "It does happen."

"I think I'll do some digging. See what I can come up with." He looked at his watch. "If Tony ever comes back."

It was obvious that he didn't feel like hanging around. She didn't know if she should feel relieved or disappointed. "I can drive you home."

"You wouldn't mind?"

"Consider it my thanks for moving the furniture." It beat having him stuck there until God knew when, driving her crazy. "I'll get my coat."

It was snowing lightly as she backed out of the garage. She still wasn't crazy about driving in the snow, but it wasn't half as bad as she'd expected, and the compact SUV she'd leased totally kicked ass.

"Are we supposed to get much snow?" she asked Rob.

"They said something about six inches tonight."

"So," she said, glancing over at him, "average?"

He laughed and shook his head. "That's what I hear."

She could really go for six inches tonight. Or in Rob's case, seven or eight.

What? No! Did she really just think that? She had to get her mind out of the gutter and stop flirting with him. This is why she didn't like to see him outside of work. She forgot how to behave. And being in such a confined space with him, the scent of his aftershave was doing funny things to her head.

It was making her fantasize about things. Bad things, like what he would do if she took her hand off the steering wheel and laid it on his knee, maybe slid it up his inner thigh...

Don't even think about it.

This is why it was such a bad idea to see each other socially. She had no self-control.

"Make a left here," Rob said. "My building is two blocks down."

They couldn't have gone more than half a mile from

her place. "I knew you were close, but I didn't realize it was this close."

"If it wasn't so cold, I would have just walked."

The area was an eclectic blend of old restored and new buildings. Rob's was a converted warehouse. "Beautiful building," she said. "What floor are you on?"

"I have the penthouse."

"Sounds nice."

"It's open concept. Very modern. Want to come up and see it?"

Hell no. "Um…sure."

What? No, you don't!

If she got him alone in his place, she wasn't sure if she could be responsible for her actions. In fact, she knew she couldn't.

"Do you have a roommate?" she asked.

"No, why?"

She shrugged. "Just curious."

She needed to come up with an excuse as to why she couldn't go inside. But as he pointed out a parking space just a little ways down the street, the car seemed to drive itself there.

This was a *really* bad idea. But that didn't stop her from getting out of the car and walking with him to the building. It was as if she was having an out-of-body experience, watching the scene from above but not really participating.

The lobby was clean and modern and even better, toasty warm.

"How long have you lived here?" she asked while they waited for the elevator, hoping that idle conversation would keep her from doing something crazy like throwing herself at him. She'd actually had sex in an elevator before. It wasn't all it was cracked up to be. But with Rob, there was no such thing as bad sex. Or even mediocre sex.

They stepped off the elevator into a hallway with just two doors. He pointed to the one on the right. "This is me."

He unlocked the door and gestured her through, and as she stepped inside, what she saw took her breath away.

When he said open concept he hadn't been kidding. The apartment was one big open space with a gourmet kitchen, a dining space and a cozy living area. A mix of steel and wood beams crisscrossed above their heads, and a winding iron staircase led to a loft-style bedroom. Tall windows that looked original to the building lined one entire side of the unit.

"This is beautiful!" she said.

"Take off your coat."

"Oh…I can't stay."

He shrugged out of his coat and hung it on a hook beside the door. "You in a hurry to be somewhere?"

"Well…no, but—"

"So stay a few minutes." He held his hand out for her coat. "You don't have to worry, I'm not going to put the moves on you."

As if she needed encouragement from him. If anyone was going to be putting moves on, it probably would be her. Knowing that, she slipped off her coat anyway and he hung it beside his own.

"I'll give you the grand tour."

He showed her around, pointing out all the unique, special touches, but she was having trouble concentrating. Her eyes kept wandering to his ass, which looked exceptionally nice in jeans. He had his usual afternoon stubble and she longed to feel the roughness of it against her palms and her lips…maybe her thighs. She kept her hands wedged in the pockets of her jeans so she wouldn't be tempted to use them, and as they climbed the winding stairs to his bedroom, she couldn't help thinking that she was making a huge mistake.

"The bedroom is my favorite room."

She didn't ask why. She didn't want to know, but as they walked to the window, it was obvious.

The view from downstairs was nice, but from up here, it was breathtaking. She could see the entire neighborhood, and in the distance, the skyline of downtown.

"It's amazing," she said, aware that he was standing just a few inches behind her. So close she could feel his body heat and smell his aftershave—or maybe that was just how the room naturally smelled. On an oversize chair beside her lay the clothes that Rob had worn to work yesterday—yes, she paid attention—and she had to fight the urge to pick up his shirt and hold it to her nose, breathe in the scent of his skin on the fabric.

Maybe when he wasn't looking...

"I can lie in bed and watch the fireworks at Navy Pier."

"Nice," she said. She could think of other things they could do in bed, too. They could make their own fireworks.

"Is everything okay?" he said. "You're awfully quiet."

She shrugged. "Not much to say, I guess."

"You always have something to say."

He was right. She didn't like quiet. She was always filling the empty space with conversation. Today was different. Today she was terrified that she would say something she shouldn't, which might encourage him to do something *he* shouldn't. Something she would find it impossible to say no to.

She turned to him, looked up into his dark, bottomless eyes. The longing that she saw there, the unmasked *need,* made her knees go weak.

She never should have turned around.

"I want you," she said, regretting the words the instant they left her lips.

He nodded. "I know."

"But I can't. I can't want you."

"I know that, too."

Did he have to be so damn agreeable?

"The thing is, you're a lot bigger than me," she said. "If you were to grab me and throw me down on the bed, there wouldn't be much I could do to stop you."

"So you have someone else to blame later?" He took a step back. "Not a chance."

She blinked in surprise. He was turning her down?

"This isn't a game," he said. "Not to me, anyway. Not anymore."

"I know that."

"Then you need to make up your mind. Either you want me or you don't."

"I do, but—"

"No buts," he said. "Either we're together or we aren't."

"What about work?"

"Work is work. We keep it professional. It's no one's business what we do outside the office."

No, but they sure liked to make it their business.

"You can't tell anyone. Not even Nick and Tony." She paused and said, "Well, I guess it would be okay to tell them. If they ask. I would never expect you to lie to them. But no one else."

"So I should forget about that announcement I was going to run in the Sunday paper?"

She smiled. He *always* made her smile. He made her... happy. Why would she deprive herself of that? What reason did she have to say no?

Because you like him, dummy. Too much. In her entire life she had never met anyone she would have even considered seeing long term, yet here she was doing crazy things like imagining double weddings. This was a totally new experience for her. It was exciting and terrifying. What if she got too attached? What would she do when it was over? Did she really want to put herself through that?

But what if this time was different? What if there wasn't a letdown? What if there really was someone for everyone, and Rob was her someone? Wouldn't it be worth it to at least find out? To at least give him a chance?

She thought about what Alice said, about what Carrie had to go back to in Los Angeles, and she was right. When Carrie wasn't working, her life was barren and lonely. Here she at least had people who genuinely seemed to care about her.

"I want you," she said.

He looked skeptical. "But?"

She shook her head. "No buts. Not this time."

"You're sure?"

"Very sure." She slid her arms around his neck, rose up on her toes and kissed him.

Fourteen

"Is he in there?" Carrie asked, poking her head into Mrs. White's office.

"He already went down to the conference room," she said, her tone considerably less chilly than it had been eight weeks ago.

No matter how impersonal or cold the older woman was, from day one Carrie had greeted her with a smile and treated her with respect. It had taken a while to realize that she wasn't really a bitch, just very focused and private. And one hell of a good secretary. She liked to come in and do her job and she didn't like to be interrupted, which Carrie could certainly relate to. And she was fiercely loyal to Rob. He told Carrie that when he was a kid she worked in one of the stores and was a totally different person. He said she would always slip him an extra piece of his favorite candy when he came in with his mother to visit. Even if his mother said no more—which was usually the case.

Then Mrs. White's only son was killed in an accident, and she hadn't been the same since.

So Carrie and she would never be pals, or even friends, but their working relationship was now amicable.

"Did he get my report?" she asked Mrs. White.

"He did. He took it with him."

She shouldn't be nervous, but she was. After compiling all the data, Carrie had worked up a rough plan of what she thought was a viable solution to Caroselli Chocolate's sales drop. Now she would present it to the rest of the team and hoped they agreed she was on the right track and were willing to implement a plan. She was especially nervous about what Rob would think. For the past five weeks, since they began officially secretly "dating," they had managed to keep their private and professional relationships separate. But if he thought her idea was total crap, her pride was going to take a hit. And her feelings would probably be hurt.

"You'll do fine," Mrs. White said.

"Huh?" Carrie blinked, sure she'd heard her wrong.

"You're smart and the entire team respects you. You'll do fine."

Mrs. White was giving her a pep talk?

Coming from her, that actually made Carrie feel much better. "I have a lot riding on this."

"Well, no matter what happens in there, it won't change the way Rob feels about you."

Carrie opened her mouth to deny that they had anything but a professional relationship, then realized, by Mrs. White's wry smile, it would be a waste of time. Instead she sighed and said, "I hope not."

"I've known Rob almost his entire life. I've never seen him like this before."

"Like what?"

"Happy. Focused on something other than work."

"Mrs. White," she started, wanting to say something nice to the woman, but she shooed Carrie away.

"Go. He's waiting."

Carrie walked down the hall to the conference room. Mrs. White wasn't the only one who noticed a change in Rob. Tony, whom Carrie saw quite often now that he was dating Alice, had said basically the same thing.

"He's a different person when he's with you," he'd told Carrie, and she could only assume he meant that it was a good thing. It seemed to Carrie that Rob was happy, but with no frame of reference it was hard to know exactly how happy he really was now compared to before her arrival. She couldn't really ask anyone else, because no one else knew about them, so she was constantly second-guessing herself. Believing that things with her and Rob were so good, they were *too* good, and even if they ever did start to talk long term—which they hadn't—the relationship was bound to fail.

Maybe Alice was right. Maybe she *was* afraid to be happy. The question was, how did she stop being afraid? How did she learn to trust her own feelings, when deep down they were telling her that he was the one?

She stopped in front of the conference room door, took a deep breath, squared her shoulders and walked in. She'd expected the entire team to be there, but it was just Rob.

"Hey," she said. "Where is everyone?"

Her report was on the desk in front of him. "I wanted to talk, just the two of us first."

Uh-oh. That couldn't be good.

He gestured to the chair across the table from him. "Have a seat."

"You think it's crap, don't you?" she said, sliding into

a chair, feeling a bit like she was facing a one-man firing squad.

"On the contrary," he said. "I think it's brilliant."

She blinked. "Really?"

"And I'll show you why." From under her report he
pulled a second report and slid it across the table to her. It
was dated almost six months ago.

"What is this?" she asked.

"The report we put together before they made the decision to hire you. Take a look."

She flipped it open, noticing immediately how similar it
was to hers—which wasn't too unexpected—but when she
got to the proposed solution, her jaw dropped. "Oh, crap."

Rob laughed. "Yeah."

"Why didn't you show me this before?"

"Because you're the marketing genius."

She wasn't the only one. Rob and his team had drawn
the same conclusions that she had, and with a few slight
variations, the outline of his proposed plan was identical
to hers. "Did you show them this?"

"They shot it down," he said. "Told me it was too radical. That we should stick to tradition."

It was radical because that was what the company
needed to divert a potential disaster. Tradition was nice
in theory, but to survive in the current economy, one had
to change with the times.

No wonder Rob had been so resistant to hiring her. He'd
come up with a plan himself that he knew was exactly what
the company needed, but they hadn't trusted his judgment.

"They were wrong," she said.

"I know."

So they had just paid a tremendous fee to have her tell
them what they had already been told. She could just imag-

ine how well that was going to go over. What it would do to her reputation.

She dropped her head in her hands. "Oh, my God, I am so screwed."

"Why? You did exactly what they asked you to do. It's not your fault if they're too stubborn to listen to their own people."

"What are we going to do?"

"Work up a very detailed plan to present to them. Maybe this time they will listen."

"And if they don't? If they reject it again?"

He shrugged. "I'll resign."

She blinked. "You would really do that?"

"They're my family, and I love them, but that only goes so far. This is business. Family or not, how long would you stay on a sinking ship before you decided to jump?"

He was right. "So we'll give them the report and hope for the best."

The conference room door opened and Carrie expected to see Al, Will and Grant, but it was Nick who walked in.

"Sorry to interrupt. Have you got a minute?"

"Sure," Rob said. "What's up?"

"The news is going to spread fast, so I wanted to be the one to tell you."

"Tell me what?" Rob asked.

"Terri is pregnant."

At first Rob looked surprised, then he laughed and said, "Congratulations!"

He got up and walked around the table to shake Nick's hand, then gave him one of those man-hug things.

"I know how badly you guys wanted this," Rob said.

"We've actually known for about a month, but Terri wanted to wait to make sure everything was okay. You can't even imagine how tough that was."

"And is it?" Rob asked. "All okay, I mean."

"She feels great. The baby is growing exactly how it's supposed to. She's due September twenty-first."

"She's excited?"

"You would think she was the first woman in history to conceive a child."

Rob shook his head and laughed. "You and Terri. Who would have imagined?"

Nick grinned. "I know, right? Best move I ever made. I guess it was just our time."

Nick looked so happy, and Terri was lucky to have someone who loved her so unconditionally, Carrie actually felt a tug of jealousy. She'd always just assumed that some day she would settle down, get married and have a family, but only because that's what people were supposed to do. Now she realized it was something she wanted. *Really* wanted.

Al, Will and Grant walked in, and Nick told them the good news. There were more handshakes, hugs and congratulations, and she couldn't help feeling a little left out. Caroselli Chocolate really was like a big family. One she wished she could be a part of.

Rob looked over at her and grinned. She tried to imagine what it would be like, her staying in Chicago and moving in with Rob. Her and Rob getting married. Making their own excited announcement that she was pregnant...

Speaking of, she thought, trying to recall the date of her last period. Shouldn't she be starting soon? She'd been so busy lately that she hadn't even thought about it.

She picked up her phone and opened her calendar. Her last period had been not too long before she and Rob began officially dating, which was...

Her heart gave a quick squeeze. *Six weeks ago.*

No, that couldn't be right. It couldn't have been that

long. Because that would mean she was two weeks late. And she was *never* late.

She looked over at Rob. He must have sensed something was wrong. He was watching her with a furrowed brow.

She closed her eyes. This was not happening. It couldn't be. She could not be pregnant. She had been working her butt off and the stress was getting to her, that was all. Didn't Terri mention that stress could throw off a woman's cycle? Even though as long as Carrie had lived it had *never* happened before.

"Carrie?"

She looked up to find Rob standing beside her chair.

He leaned down beside her and lowered his voice, so no one else would hear him. "Are you okay? You're white as a sheet."

She couldn't draw enough air into her lungs to answer him, so she shook her head instead.

"What's wrong?"

Should she find out for sure first or tell him now? She hated to freak him out until he had something to be genuinely freaked out about. But was that really fair? And did she really want to do this alone?

"We need to talk," she managed to squeak out.

"Now?"

"Yes, now."

"Let's go to my office."

She rose from her chair, her knees squishy and her head spinning, hoping she would actually make it to his office. She had never passed out in her life, but it sure felt like she might now. He must have been thinking the same thing because he took her elbow to steady her.

"Where are you two going?" Al asked.

"Carrie isn't feeling well," Rob said. "Let's postpone the meeting until later this afternoon."

"Is there anything I can do?" Al asked, and hearing the concern in her voice, everyone else turned to them.

"It's not a big deal," Carrie lied. "I skipped breakfast. My blood sugar is just a little low."

"I'll take care of her," Rob told them, walking her to the door.

She wavered a little on the way to his office, but they made it there. She must have looked way worse than she realized because when Mrs. White saw her, she rose from her chair and said, "What's wrong?"

"She's not feeling well," Rob said as they walked past her desk. "Could you hold all my calls? And get us a cold bottled water from the break room?"

"Right away," she said, scurrying out.

Rob got her seated in his chair and sat on the edge of his desk. "Are you all right?"

She nodded. The initial shock seemed to be wearing off and she didn't feel nearly so woozy. "Sorry about that."

"How late are you?" he asked.

She was so stunned by the question that for a full thirty seconds she could barely breathe much less speak. "How did you…"

"I pay attention."

"To my menstrual cycle?"

"Not specifically. But when Nick announced that Terri was pregnant, it got me to thinking—"

"Thinking what?"

"That maybe, someday, that could be us. And then for some reason it dawned on me that since we've been dating I don't recall your having had a period. Then I looked over at you and you were pale as a ghost and checking your phone. Like I said, I pay attention."

"I can't be," she said. "There's no way I'm pregnant."

"Why not?"

"Because I just…*can't be*, that's why. I'm a little late, that's all. A measly two weeks. Stress can do that."

"It can?"

"That's what Terri said. Besides, we've been super-careful, right?"

"Well…" he said, trailing off.

"Rob?"

"We did have a small breach."

Her heart slammed the wall of her chest. "A *small* breach?"

"Very small, just a little tear."

"When?"

"A month ago, give or take."

"And you didn't *tell* me?"

"It didn't seem like that big of a deal. And I was worried you might freak out. Which I should point out, you are. I figured, there was nothing we could do at that point anyway, so there was no use worrying about it until we needed to. I was so not worried that until today, I forgot all about it."

"I can't have a baby."

She heard a throat clear and they both looked up to see Mrs. White standing in the doorway with Carrie's bottled water.

"Thank you," Rob said, taking it from her.

"Is there anything else I can do?" she asked, wearing what could almost pass for a look of sympathy.

"No. But please, just…keep this to yourself."

"Carrie?" Mrs. White said. "Do you need anything?"

Feeling shell-shocked, she shook her head. "No, but thank you."

She left, closing the door behind her.

"Actually, there is something you need," Rob said. "A pregnancy test."

Fifteen

"I don't need a pregnancy test," Carrie said, opening her water and taking a swig. Some of the color had returned to her skin.

"Would you rather see a doctor instead?" Rob asked her.

"I don't need either, because I'm not pregnant."

"And you know that because?"

"Because I *can't* be. That's why. I'm not ready."

"I don't think it works that way," he said.

"Besides a missed period, what other symptoms do I have? I don't have morning sickness and I haven't been especially tired. I feel completely fine. Totally normal."

"Maybe it's too early in the pregnancy for that."

"I am *not* pregnant."

"Wouldn't you like to know for sure?"

"I do know."

Her sudden descent into total denial was a little disturbing. "Carrie…"

"Just humor me, okay? Let's give it another couple of days. If I haven't started by then, I'll take a test. I just... I'm not ready to know yet. I need a few days to process this. And if I am, well, then I am. A few more days isn't going to make any difference."

He wanted to argue, because although she may not have wanted to know, he did. But shy of forcing her to take it, there wasn't a whole lot he could do. She was obviously scared and confused and pushing her would only make it worse. And she was right. If she really was pregnant, waiting a few days wasn't going to make a big difference. And there was no reason why he couldn't start making plans now, just in case.

"We'll give it until Monday," he said. "If you haven't started by then, we'll get the test."

"Sounds fair," she said. "If you don't mind, I think I'm going to go home early today."

"Go ahead. I'll stop by after work."

"Actually, I promised Alice we would do something together tonight. Maybe you and I can do something tomorrow?"

"Sure," he said. There was hardly a night they didn't spend together. Was it just coincidence that she chose today to spend the night away from him?

She probably just needed time to think.

She pushed herself up from his chair and seemed much steadier on her feet this time.

"Would you like me to walk you to your car?"

"No, I'll be fine."

"You'll call me if anything happens?"

"You'll be the first to know."

He leaned in to kiss her, aiming for her mouth, but she turned her head at the last minute and he got her cheek instead.

"I'll see you tomorrow," she said, offering him a weak smile as she walked out the door.

When she was gone, Rob sat down at his desk, feeling uneasy. Carrie's total lack of enthusiasm at the idea of being pregnant worried him. What if she really didn't want the baby?

There was a soft knock, then Mrs. White poked her head in. "Are you okay?"

"Yeah, I think so. A little…stunned, I guess." Or something like it.

"Are you sure there isn't anything I can do for you?"

"Any words of wisdom you care to impart?"

She considered that for a minute, then said, "A baby is a blessing."

"That's it?"

She smiled. "You don't need me to tell you what to do."

No, he didn't. With her time here running short, he'd already been seriously considering asking Carrie to relocate to Chicago. No, not just considering it, but he wanted to wait until the right time. When he felt she was ready to hear it. He knew that rushing things could potentially backfire. And he was more than willing to take things slow. The way he'd figured it, she could keep renting Terri's place, and in the appropriate amount of time, when they were both ready, move into his place.

It surprised him to realize that he was in no way disturbed by the idea of moving up his timetable. His feelings for her weren't going to change. And if he was going to collect his fifteen million, marriage would have to be part of the deal, anyway. He hadn't expected it to happen quite so soon, but he was ready. But how did Carrie feel? What if she wasn't ready?

She just needed time to process it, to get used to the idea of being a mother. Right now she was just scared. They hadn't actually discussed how he felt about their having a baby. Maybe she was worried that he wouldn't step up. Although he would hope she knew him better than that by now. But wasn't she used to people letting her down? He needed to assure her that he was behind this one hundred percent. That they would make it work. And in the process, he would earn himself a hefty chunk of change. Though he couldn't deny that the idea of profiting from the situation was a little…sleazy.

There was another knock on his door, but this time it was Nick who stuck his head in. "Hey, can I come in?"

"Sure."

He stepped inside and closed the door. "Is everything okay? I saw Carrie leave. You guys have a fight or something?"

"Not exactly."

"In other words, you don't want to talk about it."

Well, if anyone could understand what he was feeling, it would be Nick.

"Why did you turn down the money?" he asked.

"The baby money?"

"Yeah. You were married and planning to have a kid, anyway. Why not wait it out in case you did have a boy? I mean, where's the harm in that?"

"Because the money didn't matter anymore."

"Didn't matter how?"

"When it happens to you, you'll know." He paused as the light bulb suddenly clicked on. "Is Carrie…?"

"Maybe. Probably. But keep that to yourself."

"You know I will."

Rob shook his head. "This is surreal."

"Are you going to marry her?"

"Of course."

"If it's a boy, will you take the money?"

He shrugged. "That's what I don't know."

"Do you love her?"

"I've sure never met anyone like her."

"But is that a good enough reason to marry her?"

"You know that *Nonno* said we have to be married."

"Oh, so you want the baby, but you're marrying her for the money?"

No, but it sort of sounded that way, didn't it? And it wasn't like that at all.

"I'm going to marry her, because I *want* to marry her."

"You think she'll ever believe that when she finds out you took the fifteen million dollars?"

"How will she find out? No one but us knows about it."

"A lie by omission is still a lie, Robby. Is that something you could live with for the rest of your life?"

"Probably." Maybe.

"Until the answer to that question is hell no, you have no business marrying her. And you sure as hell don't love her."

The words stung, but even worse, Nick was right. As many times as he'd heard her say that he deserved better than her, she sure as hell deserved better than that.

Carrie called in sick the next day—leaving a message with Mrs. White—and wouldn't answer his phone calls all morning. When he got ahold of her after lunch, she claimed that she'd shut her phone off and had been sleeping. "I must have that bug that's going around."

"Can I bring you anything?" he'd asked.

"I don't want you to catch this. Anything I need Alice can get me."

"I take it we don't know for sure yet."

"If you're asking did I start my period, no, I didn't."

"Maybe under the circumstances you should go to the doctor, if you're sick and pregnant—"

"It's a bug, Rob. I'll be fine. I just need rest."

"I'll call and check in on you later, and if you need anything, call."

"I will."

She didn't call him, and when he tried to call her later that evening to check on her, it went straight to voice mail.

The next morning she called in sick again—Mrs. White took the call—and when he tried to call her back, she didn't answer. She texted him a little while later to say that she would be fine and to text if he needed her. It didn't take a genius to figure out that she was hiding from him, and he knew the best thing to do was to give her space. Give her time to deal with the idea of being pregnant. But by Monday, when he hadn't heard a word from her, voice or text, he reached the end of his patience. He left the office at noon and drove to her condo, with a quick stop at the pharmacy in between.

She opened her front door—and thank God she did open it—wearing orange sweat pants, a stained white sweatshirt and green slippers. Her hair, which looked as if it had gone days without seeing a brush, was pulled back in a limp ponytail.

He couldn't tell if she was sick, depressed or a combination of the two.

"Come on in," she said, looking equal parts guilty and apologetic. "I'm sorry I haven't called. I know that if there actually is a baby, that it's your baby, too, and I didn't mean to shut you out. I just didn't want to be that insipid, clingy woman who couldn't deal with things on her own."

"Carrie, you are the least clingy woman I've ever met."

"I'm the opposite. When things get too hard, I bail. You might want to keep that in mind, seeing as how I'm the potential mother of your child. What if I am pregnant, and we have the baby, and I bail on you both?"

"You won't."

"How do you know that?"

"Because I do."

"How?"

"Because you're a hell of a lot stronger than you give yourself credit for." He held up the bag. "We said Monday. So let's find out."

"And if I am?"

"We'll figure it out. Together."

She took a deep breath and held out her hand. "Let's have it."

He handed her the bag.

She gestured down the hall. "You want to watch me pee on a stick?"

"Do you want me there?"

"Why not? If we're going to do this together, we should do all of it together. Even this part."

For the past five days he'd been pretty confident that Carrie was pregnant, and the test was just a formality. But as he followed her to her bathroom, a ball of nerves coiled in his gut. If she was pregnant, his entire life was going to change. It stunned him to realize that as scary as that was, he was okay with it. Maybe he really was ready. Maybe, more than being nervous, he was just…excited.

He sat on the edge of the tub while she went through the process, which was pretty simple. Pee, then wait five minutes.

It was the longest five minutes of his life.

"Ever done this before?" Carrie asked.

"Once, in college. How about you?"

"Never." She rubbed her palms together. "So I'm pretty freaked out right now."

"In this case, practice does not make perfect." He looked

at his watch and his heart started to beat faster. "It's been five minutes."

"Here we go." After a slight pause Carrie very cautiously turned the stick over and peeked at the tiny display. She put it back down and exhaled, turning to him. "Negative."

He was so prepared to hear positive that when she turned and said negative instead, he was sure he misheard her.

"Negative?" he repeated, just to be sure.

She nodded, looking relieved. "I'm not pregnant."

"Oh." He wasn't sure what to say. "I really thought you were."

"But this is good news, right? I mean, you must be just as relieved as I am."

"You would think so." So why didn't he feel relieved?

"Rob, you are relieved, right? I mean, think about it. Sleepless nights, diaper rash, spit-up. College funds."

"I thought about it. And no, I'm actually not relieved. I mean, I know the timing wasn't great, but I'm still a little disappointed."

"Oh, thank God," Carrie said, holding up the test so he could see it. "Because I lied. It's positive."

"You *lied?*" Rob said, looking at Carrie as if he wasn't sure what to believe. "Why would you do that?"

"Sorry, but I had to know."

He took the test from her and checked it, then he shook his head, like he thought she was nuts.

He was probably right.

"You needed to know what?"

"How you really felt."

"You could have just asked me?"

"No. It's that nice guy syndrome."

"Nice guy syndrome?"

"You're a nice guy…a stand-up guy. So if I told you the test was positive you would have said you were happy, even if you weren't. Right?"

He hesitated.

"The honest truth."

"Probably," he admitted.

"But if you were disappointed that it was negative, even a tiny bit, then I would know that you were okay with it."

"That was risky."

She shrugged. "It worked on *Friends*."

"Friends?" He laughed. "You stole the idea from a *sitcom?*"

"Yup."

"Out of curiosity, what if I had been relieved? What would you do then?"

Good question. "I hadn't actually thought that far ahead. But at least I would know how you *really* felt."

"Tell me what you need from me," he said.

"How about a hug?"

Rob reached for her. She walked into his arms and he held her close, and she had the feeling that everything would be okay. She wasn't nearly as freaked out as she thought she would be. Maybe she was less freaked about the actual pregnancy, and more afraid of Rob's reaction. Not that she wasn't still terrified.

"What if I'm a terrible mother?"

"Think about it. If you learned nothing else from your mom and stepdad, it was how *not* to be a bad parent."

He had a point. Whatever they had done, she could just do the opposite. "What if I get scared and I bail?"

"I won't let you get very far."

"Really? Because I can be a very difficult person."

"Really. And you won't ever have to bail if you remember to communicate. If you just talk to me, I promise I'll listen. And whatever it is, we'll fix it."

It sounded wonderful, like a dream relationship. He also made it sound awfully easy.

But what did she know? Maybe for normal people it *was* that easy. Maybe if she was lucky, some of Rob's normal would rub off on her. Or maybe it was time she grew up and found her own normal. And stopped blaming all of her shortcomings on her crappy past. At some point she had to just let it go.

She could be anything she wanted to be. "It may take some time but I'll learn. Just try to be patient with me."

"I will."

She closed her eyes, nestling up against his chest. "Five days away from you is way too long."

He squeezed her. "I was thinking the same thing."

She breathed in his aftershave. It was so familiar now. *He* was so familiar. Suddenly *wanting* him was starting to feel a lot more like *needing* him.

"So what do we do now?"

Grinning down at her, he said, "I guess we have a baby."

Sixteen

Five seconds after he learned that Carrie really was pregnant, before he'd even had time to process it, Rob finally understood what Nick had meant the other day. It was one thing to think you might have a child, but to know it? There were no words. He and Carrie had a real shot at being a family. She could be the love of his life. Would he really jeopardize that for money?

Maybe *Nonno* was trying to do more than bribe them into having families. Maybe he was trying to teach them a lesson, too. Of what was and wasn't important in life.

He and Carrie agreed not to say anything to anyone until she'd seen a doctor. And there were still all these unanswered questions. Like where would they live? And would they get married? Carrie wondered how she would work and take care of a baby. Would she have to quit, or was it socially acceptable to put kids in day care?

And shouldn't they have at least a vague idea of what

they planned to do before they started telling everyone? Before people started asking questions they didn't have the answers to? And of course after the questions would come all the unsolicited advice.

So, the day the doctor gave them final confirmation, Rob knew they had to have a plan. And first things first. As soon as they got back to his place, he dropped to one knee and asked her to marry him. It wasn't as romantic as he'd hoped, but effective, because after asking him three times if he was really sure, she said yes. They decided that until they were married they would stay in their own places, but they would start looking for a bigger place that was a bit more kid-friendly than his loft, and unlike the condo, something with a fenced backyard. There was no mention of the L-word from either of them, but that was something he was sure they would both get to later. He didn't see any hurry, as long as they were on the same page.

After all of that planning, they decided to announce their marketing plan first. So no one could accuse her of being biased.

With everyone from the first meeting there, plus the entire marketing department, the conference room table was filled to capacity. "Well, let's have it," Rob's dad said, and Al passed out the folders.

It didn't take too long for the grumbling to begin.

"I'm getting old, son, but my memory is still pretty good," his dad told him. "Which is how I know that besides a few variations, this is the same plan you proposed last year."

"It's not." He gestured to Al to pass out the second set of binders. Personally, he didn't see the need to be so dramatic, but Carrie insisted that everyone see the difference between the two proposals. "This is mine."

"The first was mine," Carrie said. "And I did it with no knowledge of the first plan."

"Which means what?" Uncle Tony asked her.

"It means that I'm not the only marketing genius in the room. And I'm sorry, gentlemen, but you've wasted your money on me. Rob doesn't need me or anyone else to tell him what's good for this business. And you would all be fools not to listen to him. I know some of the ideas are a bit radical, and it's always nice when you can stick to tradition, but to survive in business, you also have to learn to change with the times."

His dad steepled his hands, looking to his brothers, then finally to Rob. "Well, son, it would seem we owe you an apology. We should have trusted you, listened to what you had to say. But we didn't and we paid the price."

"And now?" Rob said.

"I want to see a combined report on my desk by Wednesday."

"We anticipated that as a possibility," he said. "Al, number three."

Al passed out the third round of binders.

"Here's your combined report."

"Give us a day to look these over, and we'll meet again Thursday."

As everyone was piling out of the room, Rob pulled his dad aside.

"While you're feeling so forgiving, there's something I need to tell you." Carrie cringed a little as he gestured her over. Rob slid his arm around her shoulders and pulled her close to his side. "I'm not sure if you know, but Carrie and I have been seeing each other. Socially."

"Should I act surprised?"

Meaning he—and Rob would bet a lot of other people in the family—already knew they were a couple.

"Well, Carrie is pregnant."

"Okay," his dad said. "*Now* I'm surprised." He looked back and forth between the two of them. "I don't like that I have to ask this, but can you both assure me this had nothing to do with the proposal you just presented us?"

"He didn't show me his until I showed him mine," Carrie said, then cringed when it sank in what she had just said. "That did not come out right."

"I understand what you meant," his dad said. "And don't worry, you'll fit into the family just fine. Assuming that's the plan."

"She's staying in Chicago, we're getting married, we're going to buy a kid-friendly house or condo and we are going to put the kids in day care because even though we love them to death, we both love our jobs and neither of us wants to give them up."

"When is the baby due?"

"Around Halloween," Carrie said. Which they both found a little creepy considering the basement door and cradle incidents.

Since the day they'd brought the cradle up to the living room, the door stopped opening by itself. The cradle hadn't rocked again either. At least, not as far as he, Carrie or Alice had seen. It was almost as if someone or something knew they were going to be needing it.

It was creepy, yet comforting in a strange way to know that whatever it was, it had their back.

Within twenty-four hours, everyone in the family *knew* Rob's dad was going to be a *nonno,* and then his mother made sure everyone knew it was actually Rob's baby that would give him the title, because no one was clear on that point.

Everything was falling into place, almost too smoothly,

but there was one more thing that he had to do. He called *Nonno* and told him he didn't want the money.

"I'm proud of you" was all *Nonno* said, as if that was the reaction he'd been expecting all along. And while giving up fifteen million wasn't too tough, Rob wondered if Tony would be able to resist the draw of the entire thirty million for himself.

After Mrs. White left for lunch, Nick poked his head into Rob's office. "So you're really going to do it?"

"Do what?"

Nick leaned in the doorway. "Tie the knot, have a baby. It's worth the fifteen million?"

"You're forgetting I don't get a penny if it's not a boy."

Easygoing as Nick was, it took a lot to rile him. Now he was riled. "You're seriously going to take the money?"

"What reason do I have not to?"

"Dude, *seriously?* Where should I start?"

"How about, I love her. That would be a good reason."

Nick narrowed his eyes at him. "Are you screwing with me?"

Yeah, and it was awfully fun. "I called *Nonno* and told him no deal. I'm not taking the money."

"When?"

"A little while ago. You were right. No amount of money is worth screwing this up. I can live without the money, but I can't live without her."

"What did *Nonno* say to you?"

"That he was proud of me."

"He said the same thing to me. I got the distinct feeling that he counted on us not taking the money. Like that was part of the plan."

"That might not work with Tony." While Nick and Rob both loved the satisfaction of doing their job well, Tony lived by the philosophy that he who dies with the most toys wins.

"I guess we'll just have to wait and see," Nick said. "He seems pretty smitten with Alice, and it looks as though the feeling is mutual."

Rob shrugged. "Maybe *Nonno* will actually manage to get us all married off before this year is over."

"And there's a fifty-fifty chance that one of our kids will be a boy."

So there was hope that the Caroselli name would live on for at least one more generation. Rob also didn't doubt for a second that even if there had been no baby, no accidental pregnancy, they would have eventually wound up in the same place.

A half hour or so after Nick left, Rob got a call from Alice of all people. And for some reason she was whispering.

"What the hell happened? Did you and Carrie have a fight?"

A fight? "No, why would you think that?"

"Because she's packing."

"Packing what?"

"Her *stuff*. She's shoving it all into suitcases. She's *furious*. If she knew I was talking to you right now she would kill me."

"I haven't talked to her since this morning and everything was fine then." Could it just be cold feet? "Did she say anything?"

"I tried to talk to her, but she wouldn't say what was wrong. All she said was that she was going back to L.A. *Alone*. She said I could stay at the condo until the lease ran out."

This sounded like something a bit more serious than cold feet. "Don't let her go anywhere," he told Alice. "I'll be there as fast as I can."

Seventeen

Rob made it to Carrie's condo just as she was shoving her bags into the back of her SUV. He parked in the driveway behind her, so she couldn't make a run for it.

He climbed out of his car and said, "Going somewhere?"

"Home," she said, shoving the last bag in, not even looking at him.

"You are home."

"Home to L.A."

"Can I ask why?"

"If you can't figure that out for yourself, you're an even bigger ass than I thought."

"What the hell happened?" She started to walk away and he reached for her arm.

She spun to face him, yanking it free. "Don't touch me. You don't ever get to touch me again."

She wasn't just a little upset or even scared. She was

seething mad. She stomped into the house and he followed her.

"Carrie, I honestly have no idea what's going on."

She spun around to face him. "Fifteen million dollars, Rob. Fifteen million to get married and have a male heir. Is this ringing a bell?"

Oh, crap. "You heard me and Nick talking."

"Did you knock me up on purpose, or was it just a happy coincidence? And is this the real reason why you were disappointed when I said it was negative? Why you didn't ask me to marry you until after I saw the doctor?"

"It wasn't like that. If you had heard our entire conversation you would know that."

"Did your grandfather offer you fifteen million dollars to get married and have a male heir?"

"No one is supposed to know about that, but yes, he did. What you heard was me screwing with Nick. I wasn't planning to take the money. I had already called *Nonno* and said I didn't want it. If you had stayed and listened you would have heard me say that I can live without the money, but I couldn't live without you."

"Sure you did."

"You don't trust me."

"After what you did? How could I possibly?"

"I don't mean now. You never did. If you trusted me you would have come to me first. You would have stuck to the plan. We would have talked about this, figured it out together. Like you promised. But it's so much easier to bail, isn't it?"

"That's not what I'm doing," she said, but she didn't sound quite as confident anymore.

"No, that's exactly what you're doing. It's all you know how to do. I thought that because I really love you, it would be different for us. But it's not, is it? It never will be. No matter what I do to prove how much I love you, it will never be enough. I'm going to spend the rest of my life chasing you, because running is all you know how to do."

"Haven't I told you a million times that you deserve better than me?" she said.

"You did. And shame on me for not listening. Have your lawyer call my lawyer and we'll work out some sort of custody arrangement," Rob said, then turned and walked out the door.

Carrie wasn't surprised, and still, she felt sick. Sick all the way through to her soul. He'd given her all sorts of chances, put up with more crap from her than the average guy ever would, and once again she'd gone and screwed it up. She had driven him away, when what she should have done was tell him that she loved him, too, and that she was just scared. The sad part was that she really did believe that he wasn't going to take the money, but it had been the perfect excuse to drive him away. Because he was right. That was all she knew how to do. If she had stuck to the plan and had just talked to him, they could have worked it out. Everything would be fine now. They would be making wedding plans, and looking for a place to live.

And as much as she wanted to race after him and beg him for another chance, tell him she would do anything to make this right, she didn't deserve another chance.

She'd hurt him enough.

She closed her eyes and took a deep breath, but it did nothing to quell the feeling of panic swirling inside her. The realization that she loved him. Really truly loved him. And maybe she didn't deserve another chance, but she wanted one. If she could just convince him that this time it would be different, that she would never doubt him again. If she could catch him before he drove away...

She opened her eyes and nearly jumped out of her skin when she realized that he was standing right in front of her. For a second she thought that she had conjured him up out of her imagination. Until he shook a finger at her and said, "You almost had me."

"I did?"

"I made it all the way to my car before realizing what an idiot I am. I accused you of not sticking to the plan, but I did the same damn thing."

"You did?"

"I told you that if you tried to bail on me, I wouldn't let you get far. You needed me to prove that I'll be there, that I'll fight for us. Instead, I bailed on you. So this is where I draw the line. This is as far as I let you go."

"Okay."

He blinked. "Okay?"

"Yes, because you're absolutely right. I was looking for a reason to push you away, but only because I am absolutely terrified by the idea that you might actually love me. But you know what? I love you, and being afraid and in love sure beats being all alone."

"From this day forward, for better or worse, like it or not, you are stuck with me."

Even after all that, as he held his arms out to her, it took every bit of courage she possessed to walk into them. To take that final step, that last leap of faith. But she did it, and she knew without a doubt, as they wrapped their arms around one another, neither would ever let go again.

* * * * *